If you liked *The Proposition* and *Her Every Fantasy* why not try

Her Intern by Anne Marsh
Double Dare You by Cara Lockwood

The Proposition is the third instalment of
The Billionaires Club series,
which began with

The Debt by Jackie Ashenden
The Risk by Caitlin Crews
and concludes with

The Deal by Clare Connelly

Join an exclusive, elite, exciting world and meet the globe's sexiest billionaires!

Discover more at millsandboon.co.uk

THE PROPOSITION

JC HARROWAY

HER EVERY FANTASY

ZARA COX

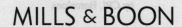

MIX
Paper from
responsible sources
FSC
www.fsc.org
FSC C007454

This book is produced from independently certified FSC™ paper
to ensure responsible forest management.
For more information visit www.harpercollins.co.uk/green.

Printed and bound in Spain

MILLS & BOON

First Published in Great Britain 2019
by Mills & Boon, an imprint of HarperCollins*Publishers*
1 London Bridge Street, London, SE1 9GF

The Proposition © 2019 JC Harroway

Her Every Fantasy © 2019 Zara Cox

ISBN-13: 978-0-263-27391-5

This book is produced from independently certified FSC™ paper

For more information visit: www.harpercollins.co.uk/green

THE PROPOSITION

JC HARROWAY

MILLS & BOON

To the DARE team for their vision, guidance and support—I have the best job, writing these stories!

CHAPTER ONE

Orla

I TAKE THE first delicious and well-earned sip of my drink with a sigh, my lip curling with satisfaction as the decadent flavour of the Macallan Scotch glides over my tongue. Not because I drink a lot of the spirit, or alcohol in general, but because it's a Scottish single malt, and therefore considered inferior by my Irish-born father. Even at the age of thirty-six, I feel the need to break free from his expectations.

The oppressive feeling that's followed me since I arrived in Monaco to pursue my latest client, Jensen's, weighs down on me once more, as if the air itself is too heavy. My intel that Jensen's are shopping around, sniffing at my father's door, adds to the pressure. Perhaps I'm burning out, pushing myself too hard to be the best, to outmanoeuvre the man who considered me unworthy to take the helm of our family business. But this deal has too much riding on it for me to blow it now; better to back off, to let the prospective client feel as if they've been wooed, but not cornered.

My fingers toy with my glass, slowly spinning it on the sleek and shiny bar. I look around the dimly lit intimacy of the casino, trying to shake off any thought of work, more determined than ever to embrace a change of pace for the evening. That's why I'm here, dressed to the nines, pretending to enjoy myself at Monaco's most glamorous club; why I left my sumptuous suite in the hotel upstairs despite its stunning views of Port Hercule in the dusk, a million lights dancing on the gently bobbing Mediterranean Sea. To let off a little long-overdue steam after a day of meetings, of waiting for the email that will tell me I've won Jensen's' business from under my father's nose.

I clink the ice in my glass, smirking at my pathetic efforts to cut loose from working, which is pretty much my entire life—a single-drink party for one.

Wow, Orla. You really know how to let your hair down...

Ignoring my snarkier side, and to distract me from ruminating on the high stakes of the Jensen's deal, I slide my stare around the casino, scanning the tables beyond the bar while I contemplate a tame gamble to liven up my rare night off. A small bet won't hurt, even if it goes against every cell of my venture capitalist's brain to risk money on a whim of chance. But it's exactly what I need—a release valve, a way to break free from my own head, my own high expectations, my endless desire to succeed.

A distraction.

I sigh, disgusted with myself. It's been ten years

since I was passed over for my younger and less qualified brother. Ten years of hard work, one successful global investment firm and one marriage casualty later and I'm still trying to prove him wrong. My father, that is.

My roaming attention is drawn to the group of excited onlookers around one of the roulette tables. Someone must be about to either lose or double a significant chunk of his net worth on a single spin of the wheel for the game to attract such interest. We're all members of the M Club here, all wealthy enough for an invitation-only membership and therefore used to top-shelf hedonistic pursuits, so this big roller must be something else.

I click my tongue against my teeth at such reckless behaviour. To me money is sacrosanct—a means to live on my own terms and a marker of success beyond being from one of Sydney's most affluent families. My entire livelihood is based on how much wealth I can generate for my clients, who trust me with their investments.

I crane my neck despite myself, curiosity winning over the distaste of witnessing someone about to gamble with daredevil abandon, if the crowd of onlookers is any indication, catching only a glimpse of the back of a blond head. His hair is a little long for the usual immaculate clientele of the M Club, but whoever it is who's providing this evening's entertainment, at least he's enjoying himself and thrilling the crowd. At least he's not moping at the bar with a barely touched drink, thinking about work. At least he knows how to have fun outside of endlessly striving to prove something to a father who happily overlooked his daughter in favour of having a son at the helm.

I finger the two-carat diamond stud in my ear, my mind dragged from the audacious stranger. The earrings were a twenty-fifth birthday gift from my father—a gift I consider a consolation prize. A gift I wear every day as a talisman, a reminder that what I've achieved in the ten years since, I've done alone and in spite of my archaic, misogynist father. A fresh layer of impotence settles over my skin, a familiar layer of prickly heat, one that drives me to be better, to aim higher, to prove him wrong…

The second sip of my Scotch fails to deliver the escape I crave. Now all I need to complete my misery is to ruminate on my failed marriage to Mark…

I release a sigh. For fuck's sake, can't I spend one evening having fun?

I glance back at the roulette table, more in need of a distraction than ever now that my thoughts have turned maudlin and focused on my greatest failure in life. The crowd around the man who seems to be causing the casino security team to sweat inside their pristine white collars parts, gifting me a full, uninterrupted view of the high-stakes gambler.

In the same heartbeat he looks up from the table, the chip he's twirling between his fingers stalling as our eyes collide for a split second.

My breath catches. I slide my parched tongue over my lips, seeking the remnants of the sip of Scotch to steady my pulse at the violent jolt of attraction. This place is crammed to the gills with wealthy, beautiful and successful people, but this guy...

Harshly masculine, from the cut of his square, stubble-covered jaw to his body's uninterested lounge in the chair, he's hotter than Hades, explaining at least half—the female half—of the attention he's assembled. But he's younger than I assumed—mid-to-late twenties—young, in fact, to be a member of the M Club, which is exclusively for billionaires.

Too young for me. But I *did* ask for a distraction, and they don't come more eye-catching than a gorgeous man in his prime.

My finger traces the rim of my glass as I watch. He's focused once more on the spin of the wheel, and yet I can't drag my greedy eyes away, even though I've seen this kind of display before, met *his type* before. Playing hard and fast, they never last long as M Club members, no doubt blowing money they have no idea how to master, allowing it to own them until they lose every cent and their membership is delicately, but adamantly, rescinded.

But despite his flagrant display, my body warms, the delicious stirring of interest kicking up my pulse as I watch the latest easy-on-the-eye hotshot from my vantage point at the bar. From his appearance, the way he's flouting the strict dress code of tuxedos for men and evening wear for women with his absence of a bow tie and his unbuttoned shirt collar, I'm surprised he was even admitted to the casino. Somehow, and for reasons I can't fathom, his devil-may-care attitude adds to his appeal. My existence must be particularly dull at the moment for me to be impressed by someone who, on the surface, seems to be intent on making himself considerably poorer. After all, I, and most of the people in this casino, are in the money-making, not money-losing, business.

The rebel lifts a glass of amber liquid to his mouth and I'm caught off guard anew by his hands: the manly size of them—serious, capable hands that look more accustomed to manual labour than they do to running an empire from a smartphone as do most of the M Club's members.

Teasing fingers of intrigue dance down my spine. What would those hands feel like holding my face as we kissed? Rough or smooth? Hesitant or demanding?

In unison the crowd around him sighs, snapping me from lusty fantasies about a younger stranger and informing me that his winning streak has dried up. But not a flicker of emotion crosses his handsome face. With less interest than if he'd tossed away a soiled napkin, he slides a stack of chips forward, placing another bet seemingly at random.

Then our eyes collide again.

I freeze, too startled to look away, although I should in case my intrigue is written all over my face, but I'm too fascinated by his expression of both boredom and challenge to do anything other than gape.

His eyes—I can't tell from this distance whether they're blue or grey—travel my face, dip lower and then bounce back up. In that second I know he's appraising me as I am him, and by appraising I mean assessing availability clues, scanning for a wedding ring and generally lusting.

And why shouldn't I lust? My sexy side is long overdue an outing; in fact, she's probably desperate to break free, she's been so neglected recently. This guy certainly looks as if he could bring a nun out of her shell...

I smooth a hand over my sleek chignon, adjusting a hairpin that's slipped a fraction in a largely unconscious gesture.

The stranger's expression shifts again, his lip curling with mild derision, telling me that *he,* with his overly long hair and his disregard for the club dress code, very much sees that I'm exactly the type of member the M Club was created for—wealthy, demanding, with an appreciation for the finer things in life. But rather than my membership earning his respect, I can tell he's somehow judging, as if he thinks he has me all figured out.

I stare a little harder, sit a little straighter, spurred on by defiance and used to fighting my own corner against the men in my life. His mouth stretches into a sinfully sexy and lazy grin that seems to burn through my designer silk dress as if it's made of cobwebs.

Perhaps professional exhaustion and sexual frustration is messing with me, because he's definitely interested, despite his judgement, our age gap and our apparent differences.

For a split second, danger and excitement zaps through my bloodstream as if he's delivered a potent shot of the Macallan directly to my system from across the room with that seductive smile. But before I can suck in a calming breath, he looks away.

My pulse plummets. What was I thinking?

I spin back to the bar on my stool, trying to shake off the uncharacteristic bout of sexual curiosity for a younger man. Curiosity for *any* man since my divorce is a rarity. If I'm not working or travelling I'm thinking about work. Yes, I wanted to blow off some steam, but not with *his* kind of distraction. I need something more forgettable, less consuming and more…fleeting.

The idea of a horizontal distraction takes root as I tap one fingernail against my glass. Why not? It would be more fun than drinking alone at the bar. I dressed and came downstairs in search of a change from the norm, a break from the long hours I habitually put in, a way to stop myself pushing my latest deal into the hands of my main competitor—my father's company.

With the reminder that, in my father's eyes, and despite my having built my own international firm, I'll never be quite good enough. I'm back to square one. Instead of celebrating the successes which have brought me this far, I'm mired in the two great failures of my life. I take another sip of Scotch, fighting the bitterness I usually harness for motivation. Hell, my entire marriage was squeezed into an unforgiving schedule of meetings, world travel and time zones, my workaholic nature almost certainly the reason it failed. Another thing to credit my father with. If he'd been a little more emotionally present, a little less professionally demanding, maybe I wouldn't be so distant, so goal orientated, so driven. Perhaps then I might have given my marriage the attention it deserved.

Come on, pull it together.

I'm not looking for another doomed relationship. I'm not looking for a relationship, full stop. Just an anonymous night of pleasure…

I look up from my drink again, scanning the patrons around me for someone more forgettable than the roulette rebel. Someone my age. Someone safe.

Then everything happens in a frenzied blur.

A commotion breaks out at a nearby blackjack table. A woman cries for help and before I've even swivelled in my seat, my sexy stranger dives from his laid-back slouch and strides towards the woman's husband, who is pale and sweaty and an alarming shade of grey.

While roulette guy commands what is clearly some sort of medical emergency—tossing off his jacket, crouching down and loosening the older man's collar— an air of panic settles over the entire room. The man clutching his chest accepts some sort of tablet from his wife, popping it under his tongue, his colour improving almost immediately. Security rallies and within seconds the blackjack table has been cleared of players to afford some space and privacy, the club's in-house nurse is in attendance and an ambulance has been summoned.

I turn away, but from the corner of my eye I see roulette guy and the nurse help the man into a wheelchair and he's wheeled from the casino, even managing a weak smile and handshake for his rescuer, who waves off the smattering of relieved applause around him as he scoops up his jacket. He returns to his table to collect his chips, passes an impressive stack to the croupier and saunters towards the bar.

A kind of forced normality returns to the room. The croupiers smile thin smiles as they resume games, the waitstaff clear already immaculate tables and members, myself included, breathe a sigh of relief that the drama was quickly and efficiently dealt with.

But then, this is the M Club.

I settle my own adrenaline surge with a shaky sip of Scotch. Then a male figure enters my peripheral vision, the space between us flooding with a spicy masculine scent and an almost palpable wall of testosterone.

I look up. Way up—sexy roulette guy is tall.

Grey—the eyes are grey. And, up close, searing and intense.

'You look pale,' he says, his confident voice distractingly deep and resonant and exactly how I imagined it would sound. 'Let me buy you a brandy—it's better for the nerves than whatever it is you're drinking there.'

I detect an Aussie twang to the accent. Although my private education rubbed the corners from my own lilt, I still have an ear for a fellow Australian.

I take a deep breath, fighting the urge to rush to the ladies' room and check if, in fact, I am pale. 'I'm good with my Scotch, thanks.'

As if deaf to my assertion, roulette guy signals the barman. 'Brandy for everyone, please—the good stuff.' He adds, although he should know the *good stuff* is all they sell at the M Club. Of course he would shout the entire casino a drink. The stack of chips I saw him tip the croupier with moments ago is more than most people will bet in an entire evening of entertainment.

But now I'm curious, although I try to affect boredom, which is out of sync with the raging of my pulse. 'Are you a doctor?' I want to blank him, to ignore the tantalising aura he seems to have around him, and return to my preconceived ideas of a privileged playboy intent on flashing his cash.

But if roulette guy wants to impress women with his affluence, he's in the wrong joint. No one crosses the threshold of an M Club establishment without a string of zeroes at the end of their bank balance.

He drapes his suit jacket over the back of the stool next to mine and unbuttons his cuffs, rolling up his sleeves to expose strong, tanned forearms in a move that hints he's dying to get out of his suit.

'No, I'm not a doctor.' The look he delivers seems to bathe me in the beam of a thousand floodlights. 'But I'm no good at sitting back and watching things unfold either. I'm used to…getting my hands dirty, shall we say?'

He looks at my mouth while he says the word *dirty*. I press my lips together, already imagining the taste of his kiss. Bold, firm, all-consuming.

What is wrong with me?

He thanks the barman for his glass of brandy with a jerk of his angular chin and tosses back the liquor in a single swallow. 'And I have some first-aid training—he'll be fine, I'm sure. He just panicked because the angina attack was worse than usual. I'm sure most people here would have helped—I just got there first.'

'I guess, although, as M Club members, we're used to everything, medical emergencies included, being dealt with efficiently and discreetly.'

His eyes swoop over the length of my body from head to toe, and I feel his scrutiny again, as if he too has made a snap judgement on our differences.

We're interrupted at that moment by a petite brunette in her twenties with a winning smile.

'Excuse me, sir, I'm Ellie Little.' At his nod, she holds up an M Club key fob. 'The key to your new supercar, sir.'

I smile at Ellie and then look back to my smug companion, my eyebrows raised in question. I passed the display of sleek sports cars in the ballroom on my way to the casino, but I paid them little attention, short of wondering who would succumb despite their hefty price tags. I guess now I know.

'Thanks.' He takes the key and pockets it, his smile for Ellie wide and engaging.

Ellie leaves us, and I spy her joining Ash Evans, the club owner, at the casino entrance. When I turn back to face my companion my expression must speak for me.

'What?' he asks, all innocence.

I shrug. 'You're having a great night, if you exclude your losses at the roulette table. Which car did you buy?' I may not know anything about cars, but I do know you can't walk into a regular showroom and drive away with a supercar. They're made-to-order, top of the range, one of a kind.

He looks away, appearing bored. 'I'm not sure…the yellow one, I think.'

'You're not sure,' I deadpan. Is he for real? Despite my growing attraction to him, I can't decide if I feel appalled or delighted.

'I bought the winning car—were you in town for the race earlier?' he asks, and I shake my head.

'No—I'm here on business.' I don't elaborate. The last thing I want to talk about is the deal that brought me to Monaco. The deal I'm trying to forget for one night.

He scoffs. 'That figures.'

I narrow my eyes. 'What does that mean?'

'You have that look about you—impatiently tapping your glass, frequently checking your phone. You look like a woman waiting for either a date or a business deal. Since no one in their right mind would stand you up, I'm guessing it's work that has you distracted.'

'Oh, nice recovery,' I say.

He flashes another disarming smile. 'So—' he glances down at my still half-full drink '—is this a party for one, or would you like some company?'

I flush that he's noticed my lacklustre attempts to let loose. Then I bristle that he's judging me. 'Are you suggesting I don't know how to have a good time simply because I'm not blowing a small fortune on a single spin of roulette or buying the latest thing on four wheels?'

I mash my mouth closed, irritated with myself for

admitting I hadn't been able to stop myself watching his little show.

He lifts one eyebrow in a look that says *if the shoe fits*, but then his eyes darken, the heat behind them kissing my skin wherever his stare trails. 'Do you know how to have a good time?'

Why does it feel as if we're talking about something more intimate than gambling or drinking? 'I... Of course I do.'

He rests one elbow on the bar. 'I assume you're here to let your hair down in a safe, luxurious space—isn't that why you're an M Club member?' He leans in. 'Or is it all about the networking? All work and no play?'

His spot-on assumption leaves me squaring my shoulders with indignation, a move that in no way combats my attraction to his particular brand of insolent swagger. 'Why are *you* a member? And why Monaco? Why so far from home?'

He shrugs, feigning boredom with my question, but I see a flash of hesitation in his eyes, a hint of vulnerability, rapidly blinked away and replaced with that roguish smile. 'Can't you tell?' He tilts his head in the direction of the roulette table. 'I'm on a bender, a pleasure spree, free and easy and hoping to broaden my horizons with luxury travel, fast cars and—'

'Let me guess,' I interrupt, 'beautiful women?' I try to laugh but I'm too attracted to him for the sound to emerge.

But *he* laughs, a deep rumble in his broad chest, and I flush hot at the power he seems to hold over my out-of-practice libido. His tongue swipes his bottom lip as he watches me more intently. 'Well, what's not to love about that combination? You're a stunning woman, intriguing, alone—what are you doing here if not seeking your own kind of hedonistic escape?'

'Arrogant much?' I try to look away, but it's as if we're pinballs, bouncing and sparking off each other. I search his eyes, if only to show I'm not intimidated. But now he's brought up pleasure it's all I can think about... How can he tell I'd been sitting here contemplating exactly the kind of distraction he's talking about? Would he be open to sex with an older woman looking to blow off some steam for the night? Isn't that what the look of intrigue in those smoky eyes is saying?

He shrugs, a mocking twist to his generous mouth. 'I saw you looking at me—you want something, and it's not to drink or gamble like everyone else in this room.'

'No, I don't make a habit of risking my hard-earned money.' I shrug. 'Perhaps the occasional tame flutter.'

He inches closer, drops his voice to a conspiratorial level. 'I'd bet the stack of chips I have in my pocket—' he shakes his jacket, the telltale rattle indicating his point '—that *you* don't even know what it is you want.' His teeth scrape his bottom lip and, despite myself, my body leans a fraction closer to his imposing masculinity.

'But I'm guessing *I* do,' he stage-whispers, his breath gusting over my exposed shoulder and sending delicious tingles down to my fingertips, which itch to reach out, to tangle in that slightly too-long hair and tug him down to my kiss...

'Is that so?' I hold my breath, trying to avoid his delicious scent, but my body has other ideas, my thighs clenching and my underwear growing damp at the mere thought of what he'd be like as a lover. Can he really see me so clearly? See what I want when I've spent the past thirty minutes sitting here trying to figure it out for myself? And do I care who's right? Wasn't I, only moments ago, contemplating what his deep voice might promise?

An anonymous night. A delicious distraction?

My heart leaps against my ribs. I wanted to unleash my sexy, playful side for the night. My ex gloried in telling me how uptight I was, that I didn't know how to be a wife, how to switch off from work. Well, I came to this casino to do just that. But with a man like him? Arrogant. Reckless. Some sort of fly-by-night success intent on brashly disposing of large chunks of his wealth...

He nods, his fingers drumming out a beat on the bar only he can hear. 'You want to let down that gorgeous but tightly leashed hair. You want to slip out of yourself for a while, loosen up a little.'

I do, not that I can admit it to the perceptive man who thinks he has me all pegged. My throat tightens, hot and achy. It's as if he can see straight through me, as if he can see that, for just one night, I want to break free of it all. But why shouldn't I have my sexy diversion with a stranger I'll never meet again?

'Why don't you sit down before you fall down?' I say, defensive. No matter how hot, how confident, how intuitive he is, I'm not rushing into something I'll only regret in the morning, for all his persuasive skills.

He grins, but his eyes harden a fraction, telling me he's fully in command of all his faculties and won't be slighted. 'I'm not drunk, if that's what you're implying. And I prefer to stand.'

'So women have to look up to you?' I might be currently captive to the unexpected revival of my hormones, but I'm not in the market for a cocky young buck, all talk but lacking in substance.

He smiles as though he knows the effect he's having on my erogenous zones, as though he can read how I'm drawn to his brand of lazy confidence simply by looking into my eyes.

'Who am I to spoil anyone's fun when I could be the source of it?' he says.

I swallow. Hard.

I'm so tempted. I promised myself a little fun. Who better to let loose with than a man who looks built for sin and seems to see what I need tonight as some sort of personal challenge? I'd bet my anticipated deal with Jensen's that his confidence is justified and he could deliver a night of hedonistic sex designed to make me forget everything but my own name.

Don't I deserve an unforgettable, anonymous night? A way to recharge the batteries? A reminder that all work and no play does not a happy Orla make?

But first I need to suss out his intentions. Make him work a little harder. 'So you have a cougar fantasy, is that it?'

I expected an arrogant shrug at best, but he leans closer, stares more intently, as if seeing deep inside me to my darkest desires. 'I'm twenty-eight, but don't get hung up on the numbers when we could already be heading upstairs.'

I scoff at his arrogance, even as my nipples turn to hard peaks beneath the silk of my dress. Do I really care that he's eight years younger than me? 'I've met your type before—'

He interrupts. 'I very much doubt that. And if by *type* you mean the kind of man who can give you the anonymous night of your life, then you're right. Admit it—you knew we'd be good together the minute you looked at me and you're even more certain now, which perhaps tells me the reason you're fighting it so hard—fear.'

'Fear?' I laugh, although the sound lacks conviction, just like my shaky resolve. He's spot-on, but really, what do I have to lose? I wanted a distraction and he's irresistible. The urge to step off the hamster wheel for a moment and become lost in the pleasure I'm certain would follow is tantalising. His challenge is irresistible, because it aligns so perfectly with the one I set myself tonight: to let go.

'There's not much I'm afraid of,' I say. My heart, banging against my ribs, proves me wrong and him right.

He nods—slow, confident, almost luring me to kiss the smooth smile from his lips. 'It's fear all right. Fear of letting go of your tightly leashed control. Fear that you might actually have a good time. Fear I'll ruin you.'

His eyes slide to one of my earrings. 'You and your four-carat-diamond, one-glass-of-single-malt life.'

Instead of the outrage I should feel at being so neatly dissected and accurately pigeonholed, even insulted, every nerve in my body fires alive with electricity.

Fight, flight or fuck? I should definitely take option one or two…

I roll back my shoulders and stare into his cool grey eyes, seeing the hint of challenge. 'Are you suggesting I'm uptight? I'm amazed you, with your devil-may-care attitude, even know what the concept means.' I should walk away, go back upstairs and check on Jensen's—but oh, the temptation to prove him wrong is overwhelming…

'Hey, princess, if the shoe fits…'

We face off, sparks flying and heat building.

I can let go. I can have fun. He's right, I do want him. I *want* to be ruined for one night.

And I always get what I want.

'The earrings are two-carat,' I say. 'And, okay. I have a suite upstairs—let's go.'

CHAPTER TWO

Cam

HER WORDS—WORDS that shatter my certainty that she'd toss her Scotch in my face—bounce around inside my head to the beat of my pounding heart as she slides her drink away, unfinished. Yes, she's my type looks-wise—tall and willowy, naturally rich red hair, and a body whose every inch I want to acquaint with my tongue. But, by the earrings, the immaculate hairdo and the general air of class around her, I assumed she was way too buttoned-up to take our flirtation to the next level.

She reaches for her clutch and prepares to slide from her stool.

Eager, now she's stopped fighting herself. Another fucking awesome surprise.

'Wait.' I stall, my dick throbbing in revenge. 'I think we should at least introduce ourselves so you know whose name to scream later.' I hold out my hand. 'I'm Cam.'

She purses her delicious-looking full lips and strokes her hand over her sleek chignon as if mildly annoyed by the interruption of formal introduction. She takes my hand in hers, her greeting as firm as I'd expected.

'Orla.'

'Irish Australian?' I say, prolonging the handshake, deliberately sliding my roughened thumb over the back of her hand to gauge her reaction to my touch, because I'm certain that under normal circumstances, in our everyday lives, she wouldn't give a man like me the time of day. She's too polished, too precise and undoubtedly super-high maintenance. There's not a hair out of place or a wrinkle in sight, but I have the driving urge to see her all dishevelled and undone. She'd look twice as sexy rumpled and satisfied, those sea-green eyes pleasure-drunk…

'Yes. I'm from Sydney.' She looks down to where my thumb swipes across the delicate skin of her inner wrist, her small smile masking a look bordering on aversion while her free hand toys with the diamond stud in her ear.

In spite of my work-roughened skin, there's excitement drawn all over her ethereal face, but her eyes say she's all too aware I'm not her usual type. No doubt she's used to the type of man who belongs in this club. The type who's certain of everything in his life, especially where he comes from and where he's going.

'I grew up in Sydney, too.' If only she knew that we came from opposite sides of the tracks before I inherited enough money to be thrust into her sphere. I look down at our joined hands, the sick slug of satisfaction at my rough and calloused hand swallowing hers, which is by comparison as delicate as a bird's wing and impeccably manicured, adding to the thick desire humming through my veins.

Prior to my current fucked-up predicament—the very reason I'm here in this club for the elite and obscenely wealthy, having earlier this evening bought a supercar I'll likely never drive and gambling as if I'm spending Monopoly money—I worked in construction.

And now?

Now I'm frittering through as much of the unwanted inheritance my no-good asshole of a father left me as I can. Oh, how he'd hate to see me now, wasting the money he sacrificed his family for, travelling the world in a private jet, gambling, bedding beautiful women in the most exclusive club in Monaco.

The familiar nausea I get whenever I think about my father takes hold, a part of me repulsed at becoming his puppet. I focus on the exquisite woman in front of me, a strong urge flaring up to push her out of her buttoned-up comfort zone until I know exactly how far she'll go for her night with a stranger.

She glides from the stool, her hand still in mine. Instead of pulling away, she sidles up close until I see the golden streaks in her green irises, streaks that perfectly match those in her silky auburn hair, and I'm overwhelmed by how fantastic she smells. Classy and expensive.

She presses a fingertip to my mouth. 'Don't tell me any more. Anonymous, remember.'

I nod, dislodging her soft fingertip from my mouth

while I wrangle the thick thud of my desire under control. She may as well have kissed me for the effect that simple touch from a solitary fingertip has on my body.

Yes, she's way too rich, too straitlaced for my blood, but damn is she sexy. I want to haul her slender frame up in my arms, press every inch of her against my body until those eyes glow with the desire I see lurking in the shadows.

But could she let go enough to embrace this fierce chemistry?

'Give me your phone.' My voice is low but firm enough to encourage a frown of defiance from her stunning face. She likes being challenged, but wants to be in control. She's clearly used to giving the orders.

I can handle that.

'Why?' She purses perfect lips. Lips I'm dying to taste.

'Because I'm a stranger you're about to invite into your hotel room. I'll take a photo of myself, and you can send it to someone you trust, giving them your suite number and mine, too, if you like—two-seven-six-six.'

She nods, hands me her phone and I snap a quick selfie before handing the device back. I watch as she fires off a text, fascinated with the way her lips press together when she's concentrating and how, despite the safety-conscious turn of the conversation, her nipples are hard peaks beneath the tight-fitting, backless black dress that hugs her toned frame and caresses the gentle flare of her hips.

'So, shall we?' She looks up, her chin tilted and face

relaxed, but there's vulnerability in her eyes, and I wonder what her *real* story is. Not the sanitised version she probably tells herself every day as she peruses her markers of success. But the version deep inside, hidden vulnerabilities which, if probed, wobble the confidence she wears like a tiara balanced on her regal head and perhaps the reason she's alone in a bar in Monaco, far from home, toying with a drink she barely touches in the first place.

But then, who am I to judge? I swallow a bitter lump in my throat. Fuck knows what I'm doing here apart from running, hiding, while dispensing of the blood money I can't stomach even thinking about.

I want to form a fist as the anger that chased me from Sydney swells inside. But I've tried and failed to keep things normal for six months, tried to ignore the inheritance sitting in my bank account accruing more interest daily than I formerly made in a year of building houses with my bare hands, but somehow my life, who I am and what's important to me have still changed beyond recognition.

I swallow down the acidic taste and focus on beautiful Orla and her mesmerising eyes. Perhaps we're both hiding from something bigger than us, and that's perfect. Perhaps we'll succeed in fucking it from our systems, a perfectly timed distraction, and tomorrow go our separate ways, usual service resumed…

Damn, if only it were that simple for me. My stomach rolls at the reminder that normal is a distant memory. I ignore the gnawing pain, the yearning for my old

life, and nod. I grab my jacket and follow her towards
the bank of lifts. When we're inside the empty car and
she's selected the correct floor I move closer, my restless body demanding action and the need to touch more
of her than her wrist driving me hard.

I expect her to back up as I invade her personal
space, but she holds her ground and simply levels bold
eyes at me while her chest rises and falls with the excitement I want to see.

I keep my hands by my sides. My reward is waiting for me and I want to string out the anticipation for
as long as I can, knowing the moment will be twice as
sweet when we both, finally, surrender.

But neither can I stay away.

I look down, loving how small she is in comparison
to me and the way it defies her bold and confident manner. Damn, I bet no one ever says no to her. I bet she's
always had things exactly on her terms.

That part of me, the part that wants to test her, rears
up.

'How do you want this to play out, beautiful?' I suck
in an Orla-scented breath, my blood pumping harder.
Despite our chalk-and-cheese differences, I wanted her
the minute I saw her walk into the casino—a beautiful
woman, composed, alluring and sexy as fuck. But the
fact she tried to fight her obvious interest…well, that
simply added another level of challenge. I'm a scrap-
per who's spent every day of his life until six months
ago earning his honest, comfortable place in life, earn-

ing every cent of what he deserves—beautiful women no exception.

She takes a shuddering breath and licks her lips, the first hint of hesitation. 'You know, just the usual…'

She clearly doesn't do this often—sleep with a stranger—and for some reason she's decided tonight's the night and I'm the lucky guy. But there'll be nothing usual about our night together.

I nod, noting the slow ascent of the lift and deciding we have time to start this right here, because I'm done waiting. She knows what she wants and I plan on giving it to her. That and more.

'Ask me to touch you.' Her full, kissable mouth draws all my attention. I've wanted to taste those lips since she spotted me at the roulette table, her mouth twitching with intrigue. And why shouldn't I taste? Now, when I can have anything I want in life, is not the time to begin denying myself a damned thing, beautiful Orla included.

She too glances at the digital display and back, and before I can ready myself for the impact she grabs the back of my neck and drags my mouth down to her kiss.

The first taste is rich and decadent, just like Orla, the hint of Scotch lingering on her soft but demanding lips. While she seems too prim and proper for a simple, spit-and-sawdust kind of guy like me, my body clamours for more, because I can already tell there's another level to this woman, a tightly leashed wanton ready to be coaxed to reveal her uninhibited side. And I'll take as much wildness as she's willing to give, in my current mood—anything to stop the endless feeling I'm trying to outrun something while wearing lead shoes.

Her lips part and she slides her tongue to meet mine with a throaty little moan that screams *woman*. My pulse roars with triumph, centring me with the assurance sex brings. In this moment, I'm me and in control.

I walk us back to the wall, and she drops her clutch and hikes up her dress so she can spread her thighs to accommodate my hips, which pin her in place. She tugs my hair and moans as if she wants to be fucked right here in the elevator, and bloody hell, I'm tempted.

We part for breath and she reaches for my fly, her teeth trapping her bottom lip as she rubs my cock through my trousers. Then her eyes roll closed and her head hits the wall behind her. 'Oh, I knew you'd be good, exactly what I need.'

I clench my jaw, fighting the rush of pleasure her palming my cock brings. I can be what she needs for one night—easy. Our backgrounds don't matter for what we have planned.

I lift her thigh and press closer until my dick and her hand are crushed between our bodies. She looks at me then, and I grin.

'I'm happy to be your man toy for the night, gorgeous.' I scrape my mouth up the soft, silky column of her neck, sucking in her scent as I reach her earlobe and the massive rock sitting there, a beacon to our stark differences. My hand on her thigh slides north as I tongue the stone, tugging her earlobe, complete with earring, into my mouth. I finger the lace of her underwear, which is stretched across the gorgeous handful of ass cheek I have in my hand, while I press my erection between her legs, where she's hot and damp and grinding against me.

'Your hot little clit is hungry for what I can give you.' I slide my hand forward, finding her underwear drenched. 'Question is, can you take it?'

'Yes…oh, yes.' She doesn't flinch at my candour or deny my assertions, simply tugs my mouth back to hers with a frustrated yelp.

Her *yes* thrills me. We might be from different worlds, but tonight our goals are aligned and all about pleasure.

The lift pings and we quickly straighten our clothing to perform the hurried walk to her top-floor suite. Inside, a quick glance confirms it's a carbon copy of mine—the best money can buy—but then, I'm too focused on the woman in front of me to care about décor or square footage.

While I shrug out of my jacket, she tosses her bag, turns to face me and begins to undo the clasp of her dress at the back of her neck, but before she gets anywhere, I grip her waist and back her up against the wall once more—I have plans for Miss Buttoned-Up and they don't involve staid missionary position with the lights off.

Let's see how much she wants to let go.

I kiss her, coaxing more of those greedy little whimpers from her throat as my hand travels under the dress once more to find her drenched and scorching hot.

I break free from the kiss as I slide my fingers past the crotch of her underwear to the silkiness beneath. I rub one fingertip over her clit, watching her eyes grow unfocused.

My other hand grapples with the tiny, frustrating clasp at the back of her neck. It feels like a bra clasp but the hooks may as well be welded together for all the luck I'm having. I reluctantly remove my hand from the delicious, soft slickness between her legs and try with two hands, my frustration to see what the dress conceals building and making my fingers clumsy. On my third attempt, while she's given up waiting and is clearly intent on driving me insane with the kisses she's pressing over my neck, jaw and mouth, I say, 'Are you particularly attached to this outfit?'

Confusion registers, chasing away the lust, but she shakes her head. 'No, why?'

I press my mouth back to her arched neck—I can't seem to get enough of her taste and scent. 'I said I'd ruin you.' I look up. 'I wasn't joking and I'm afraid this dress is going to be the first casualty.'

'I don't care. Hurry!'

I grip the low neckline of her dress, tearing the fabric clean in two from neck to waist so her fantastic, bra-less breasts spill free.

She gasps, but the sound turns to a low moan because I cover one bare breast with my mouth, sucking hard on the firm, pink nipple. While she twists handfuls of my hair between her fingers as she cradles my head and watches my mouth devour her breast, I hoist up her skirt and perform the same trick with the crotch of her underwear, tearing it in two so I can access my reward unhindered.

I pull back, surveying my handiwork while my knees grow weak. She's perfect. Mouth red and swollen from our kisses and the three-day scruff I couldn't be bothered to shave earlier; her clothing bunched around her waist so all that creamy skin dotted with golden freckles is on display; my hand wedged between her pale thighs, the strip of reddish hair on her mound a beacon guiding me to paradise.

Fuck, I'm not sure who will ruin whom. Her willingness to ride this storm with me spurs me on to keep pushing... Perhaps I'm wrong about her being strait-laced.

'Put your legs around me,' I say, my strangled voice gruff. But she doesn't seem to care that I'm giving orders, any more than she cares that I've torn what must be an obscenely expensive outfit. I fully intend to replace it, of course. In fact, tomorrow I'll buy her a whole new wardrobe in compensation.

I carry her the short distance to the suite's living area to a wide armchair, where I deposit her delectable ass. She tries to tug me down on top of her but I resist. I want to look. To gorge my fill of this incredibly sexy woman, who's smashing all my assumptions to bits.

She's still debauched, her hair mussed as I wanted it and spilling free of the uptight chignon she wore, her eyes glassy with desire.

'Fuck me,' she says, still in control.

I quickly strip off my shirt while she watches, her tongue wetting those lush lips as her eyes trace the ink on my shoulder and across one side of my chest. But she can't have everything her own way.

'All in good time.' I drop to my knees and spread her thighs wide open so she's completely exposed to me and my own greedy stare. 'First I want a little taste.'

She nods, then her head drops back. 'Oh, my God, yes.'

I chuckle at her enthusiasm. 'Cam will do.' But then I'm done talking because her pink, wet pussy calls to me and I dive in.

The erotic scent and taste of her drags a growl from deep within my chest, but it's her thighs clamped around my shoulders and her hands tugging at my neck and head as if trying to urge me closer that thrill me. If I wasn't already there, she'd bring me to my knees with her passion and honest desire.

My dick is dying to be buried in the tight, warm haven greedily sucking at my fingers, but she's fully embracing this, watching me eat her out, her mouth slack with pleasure as she rides my face. Orgasm number one is going to have to happen right here for Orla, and I'm going to enjoy every second of watching this woman detonate. She may not remember my name, but I'll make it my mission to ensure she'll remember every orgasm of our night together.

I add another finger and suck down on her clit, grinning when her thighs begin to judder and eyes widen with ecstasy.

'Cam, yes…oh.'

So my put-together princess is not above begging or riding my face to get what she wants. She comes, her sex squeezing my fingers and my name a protracted cry on her lips. I milk every spasm from her and then withdraw, leaving her sprawled and spent on the chair while I loosen my belt, unzip my fly and take a condom from my pocket before lowering my trousers and briefs. All I want now is to be buried inside her, to forget my woes for a few mindless minutes, and just be the old Cam.

She sits up and takes my cock in her hand, tugging my length and then helping me with the condom. When I'm sheathed, I take her hands and yank her to her feet, spin her around and bend her over the wide arm of the chair.

'Hurry,' she says as she braces her arms on the cushion and spreads her feet wide, staring back at me over one shoulder. My knees weaken at the exquisite sight, her red hair splayed down her pale back, her post-orgasmic flush staining her cheeks and her ruined clothing bunched around her waist—a sign that neither of us had the patience to do this primly or properly.

Who knew the poised woman delicately sipping her drink hid such a sensual being? Such an unexpected siren?

I position myself at her entrance and grip her hips, every cell urging me to rush while my brain clamours to go slow and enjoy every second.

But we have all night.

Patience spent, I surge forward, my cock swallowed

by her tight pussy. I fist the fabric of her dress and thrust in the last inch until our joint moans tell me I'm as deeply seated as possible. For a few glorious seconds I suck in calming breaths and simply enjoy the view. Her skin is like porcelain, her pale ass cheeks round and her hair a wild, tousled mess across her bare shoulders. The dress ruched around her waist gives the impression of bonds, a reminder that, despite being the most put-together woman I've ever met, Orla was as impatient to let go as I was to help her.

I grip the dress and her hip tighter and begin to thrust, every slap of our flesh together and every gasp of her pleasure riding me harder until sweat stings my eyes.

'Touch yourself,' I say, because I'm not going to last much longer and I want her coming with me. I want to make her come all night. I want to prove to her that we're the same on one level. That, like this, we fit together perfectly.

She whimpers but complies, her hand disappearing between her thighs, where I feel her stroke my balls before she sees to herself. I grit my teeth, the drugging pleasure sucking me down. 'Are you close?' I grit out.

She cries out but doesn't answer, and I'm running out of time.

I widen my feet, still thrusting at a punishing pace, abandon my grip on her dress and slide my finger along her crack to tickle her asshole. That does the trick, and as she screams a hoarse cry, her muscles clamping around me, I let go, fiery heat rushing down the length of my cock as I fill the condom.

We slump forward over the chair, although I'm careful to take my own weight and not crush the fantastic woman under me as I catch my breath.

She recovers first, wriggling free and turning to cup my face and smatter hot kisses over my lips.

'Wow.'

My chest burns but I grin.

'Glad you had a good time.' I just didn't know she'd embrace it so thoroughly, so honestly and so fucking sexily.

'I hope you didn't plan on getting any sleep, because we'll be doing that again.' She tugs me towards what I know is the bathroom, and as I watch the sway of that gorgeous ass, I concur.

Yes; yes, we will.

CHAPTER THREE

Orla

I RISE FROM the desk chair in my hotel suite, a triumphant smile making my cheeks ache while a surge of adrenaline leaves me searching the bed for Cam. I want to share my news with someone. With him. Jensen's made up their mind and signed on the dotted line this morning.

Then I remember that he's gone. After the sex marathon, I spent half the night working while he slept. He woke around six, crept up behind me where I worked and kissed me goodbye. Such a gallant, old-fashioned gesture, I practically swooned…

As I look at the debauched but empty bed, my sense of achievement dwindles a fraction. It shouldn't matter—I don't need to share my success in order to feel its validation, but a celebratory orgasm might have been nice…

I stretch out my back muscles, frowning when I realise how long I've been sitting in one place. I've hustled this deal for the past three months, a deal snatched from under the nose of my main competitors—the firm now run, rather sloppily, in my opinion, by my younger brother under the critical tutelage of my father. A firm that should have been mine to run by rights after my years of hard work and the long hours that cost me my marriage. Another casualty of my father's expectations…

Thinking of my ex, and how he bailed after seven short months because he couldn't handle a wife who worked harder than him, sours my mood further.

I ignore the well-worn path of anger and rejection that courses through my body every time I think about how I was overlooked, passed over on the basis of my sex, as if my years of commitment and my qualifications counted for nothing in the eyes of my old-school father. What century does he even inhabit? I'm the eldest. I put in the most work. I'm the best qualified—the company was mine by rights.

When the sting in my lip tells me I'm taking out my frustration with my own teeth, I relax my jaw and sigh. Even this success with Jensen's feels somehow tainted by the past. No matter how hard I work, I can never quite reach the finishing line.

Casting a look of longing at the empty bed, I head for the shower, recalling the pleasure I shared with a stranger to sweeten this morning's professional victory.

Cam—my reward.

Yearning builds in the pit of my stomach. He claimed my body, used it and his to drive us both mindless with desire. His obscene stamina. His wicked, inventive challenges and almost impossible positions… I've never experienced anything like it. He effortlessly brought out the sexy side I wanted to embrace the minute we stepped into the lift.

Who even was I with him?

I ache, aware of every step I take, every muscular twinge—all Cam's fault…

But he was gentle too. Thorough and attentive and considerate. My breath catches as a feeling of invincibility courses through me. After a night like that, I can accomplish anything. Alone and without validation.

The hot water spray buffets my skin, reminding me of Cam's rough, calloused hands gripping and possessing. The water on my breasts and between my legs mimics the glide of his demanding tongue, the caress of his dirty mouth, and when I press my fingers to my clit, trying to banish the renewed flutter of hunger, I relive every single orgasm of our decadent night together.

This is what well-fucked truly feels like.

I sigh a happy, sated sigh, the emotional impulse as unexpected as the man himself. Perhaps he's a good-luck charm, if I believed in luck. Perhaps letting loose, embracing my wild side, is good for me, allowing me to achieve some much-needed work-life perspective. Either way, I can't deny I feel more alive, more enthused for the months ahead than I have in years.

I shampoo my hair, hair that Cam wrapped around his fist as he pounded us both to oblivion that last time, sometime in the dark early hours. He fell asleep soon after, splayed on his stomach, his muscular back and tight buttocks a visual feast I struggled to tear my eyes from. I was so energised, my mind so focused, I worked through the rest of the night. Even now I'm in no way tired, although pulling all-nighters isn't that unusual for me. When you run an international firm, sleep is an expensive luxury.

But could I afford another luxury, one in the form of a sexy Australian with grey eyes who reminds me I have needs? I slide my soapy hands over my skin, an idea forming. He said he was free and easy. No work commitments, money clearly no issue. The way he threw it around last night, almost as if trying to offload as much as possible, perhaps he'd be up for a whirlwind tour of the globe with stopovers at all the international M Club establishments? We could continue this arrangement for a few weeks… A way to explore the sexy side he's unleashed in me. A way for me to keep this feeling, this newfound perspective, alive.

My proposition takes form in my mind as I towel dry and comb through my hair. A month, six weeks ought to be enough time to work my *man toy*, as he put it, from my system. I'd have to make the sex-only proviso crystal-clear. My one trip down the aisle confirmed that relationships and I definitely don't mix. I have no desire to repeat *that* mistake. I don't need a relationship, which in my experience is just another way to fall short of someone's expectations.

If Cam agrees, if he too wanted more than just one fantastic night, he could accompany me while I toured my international offices to ensure everything is as I like it—ticking along like clockwork and expanding on our year-by-year profits.

A sex-only arrangement.

'Amazing sex,' I say aloud, catching my laughing reflection in the fogged-up mirror—eyes bright with excitement, hair tousled and damp the way it was last night after our first shower, when Cam fucked me from behind in this very spot, ordering me to tweak my nipples hard until I saw stars right before I came.

The man was some sort of sex god, a G-spot genius, and I his willing, eager-to-excel pupil. But I didn't simply want to excel. I wanted to be top of the class.

I smile at my reflection—a feline smile.

I'd show him I could let go.

I'd ruin *him*.

Dressed in my favourite floaty Capri pants and a silk spaghetti-strap top in deference to another stunning Monaco day, I make discreet enquiries at Reception for Cam's whereabouts. There was no answer when I knocked on the door to his suite, just down the hall from mine. Even if he hadn't made a splash in the gaming room last night, he's pretty unforgettable—his height, his commanding presence, not to mention his *fuck you* air of flouting convention and living the good life.

I find him in the club's gym, the sole occupant. He's ignoring the *Shirts must be worn at all times* sign, performing chin-ups on a bar facing a wall of mirrors. And I don't blame him. If I had his body, every inch cut slabs of muscle draped in golden skin, a gorgeous, intricate tattoo covering one shoulder, I'd watch myself move too. I'm instantly damp between my legs just from one glance at his sweaty torso.

In fact, there's no reason I can't enjoy the show for a few hedonistic seconds. My pulse throbs through my sex while I watch, hypnotised. His back muscles flex in unison to drag his long, built frame up the foot or so required to place his chin above the bar. Sweat runs in rivulets down the bumps of those muscles. My tongue darts out to wet my lips, keen for another taste of the skin I sampled last night.

That happy sigh is back, thankfully silent and in my head, but again it strikes me I haven't felt this rejuvenated in years. Cam's the kind of man who makes a woman feel feminine. It's effortless for him—his sheer size, those calloused hands, the formidable sexual prowess I've now experienced, plus his nurturing, caring side and impeccable manners.

Enough looking.

I'm on a plane out of here shortly. Time is money. I want his answer.

I approach with confident steps, although my belly twists with uncharacteristic nerves. What if he turns me down, or has a life to get back to in Sydney, or thinks I'm too old for him beyond one anonymous night? The pinch of disappointment speaks of the calibre of Cam's brand of fucking. But I'm a big girl. A grown woman. I tell myself his refusal would be no big deal, that there are plenty of other Cams in the sea, although the shaky quality of my breathing confirms it's a lie.

But I'm not giving up yet. I'm used to getting what I want, and this will be no exception.

I meet his eyes in the mirror, and just like last night

the eye contact feels like a physical waveform buffeting me with his aura. With all the eye contact we've shared since, the physical intimacy, I should be over the starry-eyed phase by now. Bloody hell, I'm not sixteen.

Cam drops to the ground, not a hint of surprise on his face, as if he'd been aware of me staring from the doorway. He's probably used to women hounding him for more sex the morning after.

My brain scrambles to recall exactly why I'm here, other than to watch his ripped body work out while I drool.

'Has working all night refreshed your appetite?' he says, grabbing a towel. He wipes sweat from his face and chest and then slings the lucky piece of towelling around his neck. 'Women don't usually hunt me down before breakfast.'

I drag my eyes away from the bulge of his cock, visible through the thin fabric of his workout shorts, all but panting at the memories of that spectacular part of his anatomy. 'I only worked *half* the night. The other half—'

'I remember what you did the other half,' he interrupts, flashing that grin that reminds me he's in his twenties.

'And I didn't need to hunt you down,' I say, stepping closer. 'After your antics at the roulette table last night, purchasing a bright yellow supercar, you're something of a celebrity—all I did was ask for your whereabouts at Reception.'

He tilts his head in acknowledgement of my statement, his own stare taking a similar swoop of appraisal down the length of my body. 'Did you receive the re-placement dress and lingerie?' I can tell that, like me, he's remembering what he did while my ruined dress and torn panties shackled my waist.

I free a groan in my head, the remembered sound of fabric ripping sending delicious spikes of pleasure to my core. I fight the urge to kiss him in that way that seems to drive him crazy—my tongue surging against his, a scrape of my teeth along his decadent lower lip.

'I did. Thank you.' At the crack of dawn this morn-ing, shortly after he left, there was a knock at my door. I rushed to open it, secretly hoping to find Cam on the other side, but it was a hotel porter delivering a garment bag. 'The replacement wasn't necessary—how did you even do that? It's Sunday morning.'

He arches one brow in that noncommittal way of his. 'I have my methods. As you know, money opens doors.' His mouth flattens, a hint of cynicism in his expression.

'So, did we leave something unfinished? Did I leave my boxers in your room…?' He laughs and I join him, more certain than ever that spending time with him will be good for me and therefore good for business. It's been an age since a man made me laugh, since *I* laughed full stop. I deserve to celebrate such a land-mark victory over my father's firm, and I want to cel-ebrate with Cam.

'I have a proposition for you,' I say, letting him have it straight between the eyes. Now I've seen him again in the flesh, I'm even more set on my course of action. I need the next few weeks to run as smoothly as clockwork, professionally speaking, and, with Cam around as an after-hours distraction, my mind would be clear, my focus sharp and my energy restored.

Bloody hell, Orla, he's not a multivitamin!

'Oh? Sounds intriguing,' he says. 'Why don't we discuss it over breakfast? I'll just jump in the shower and meet you in the restaurant.'

My body clamours to join him in the shower, my mouth parched for another taste of his talented, thick cock. I swallow, suddenly ravenous. 'I don't eat breakfast, and I'm flying out to Zurich in—' I check my watch '—ninety minutes.'

He's not remotely disappointed with this news. My stomach plummets. No woman wants to be so easily forgotten.

'Okay—well, shoot, then.' He leans one hip against a nearby weights machine, the fabric of his shorts stretching across his crotch leaving nothing to the imagination, and grips the ends of the towel around his neck. A perfect pin-up pose for a raunchy, get-you-wet calendar. And I don't need my imagination—I have fresh and vivid memories to keep me warm.

Of course, I'd rather have the real thing…

'You said last night you were on a pleasure spree of luxury travel. Does that mean you're free of other commitments at the moment?' We haven't talked about what we do for a living. We haven't talked about anything.

'I'm free as a bird. What do you have in mind?'

'I wondered if you'd like to join me on a tour of some of the other M Clubs. I'll be travelling for work for the next five-to-six weeks… Perhaps we could have some fun along the way…?' I trail off from my perfect sales pitch, concealing most of the desperation from my voice, and I silently thank every single business proposition I've ever made for getting me through this sexy proposition without so much as a voice wobble.

'Well, that's intriguing.' His eyes glow. 'So you enjoyed your walk on the wild side, huh?'

I arch my brows. 'And you didn't?' He couldn't keep his hands off me. I have the soreness between my legs as a trophy of his insatiable stamina.

'Fair point.' He grins. 'But aside from the obvious pleasures,' he looks me up and down, 'what's in it for me?'

I splutter. Gape. I didn't expect him to play hardball. I'm used to telling people how high to jump.

'You said it yourself—you spent half the night working. Have you even slept? You don't have time for breakfast…' He shrugs, his point illustrated.

I roll my shoulders back, defensive—his censure reminds me a little too closely of my ex-husband's complaints. 'I don't need more than a couple of hours' sleep.' But he's right; my work habits do make me rather a dull travelling companion.

'As good as last night was,' his eyebrows flick up in that roguish way, 'I'm not interested in spending the next six weeks watching you working in between snatched naps only punctuated by the odd fuck. I prefer my dates—'

'We wouldn't be dating.' My temperature soars. How dare he see me so…clearly?

He ignores my interruption. 'I prefer my hook-ups to have a pulse, to have the energy to offer me a few scraps of attention and to be awake long enough for us to have a good time.' His lip curls in that playful way he's so good at. 'I'm old-fashioned like that.'

I bristle, lifting my chin. 'I know how to have a good time. You just said so yourself about last night.' It wouldn't sting quite so much if his assumption wasn't true, but I'd never admit such a thing.

He steps closer, his beautiful eyes holding me captive. 'You're right,' he looks me up and down in a way that makes me feel naked again, 'you look too put together to be as hot as you are, but once you let your hair down the sex part was great.'

'But…' I say, because I know it's coming, despite his compliments.

'But, when I woke up and reached for you because I wanted more, you weren't there.'

I fist my hand on my hip. 'I work odd hours because of international time zones.'

He nods, but continues. 'And when I found you working before dawn this morning, I assumed we were done, that the sexy woman I'd spent the night with was safely tucked away, normal service resumed.'

'Normal service? What does that mean?' Didn't I prove I could have a good time with the right incentive?

'It means this.' Cam waves a finger at me. 'You're back to being immaculate and untouchable. Perhaps last night was a one-off. Don't forget I saw your idea of fun yesterday—until we left the casino it was hardly thrilling. But perhaps I'm judging you harshly.' He folds his arms behind his head and stretches out his back. 'Why don't you help my decision-making process by coming to a party?'

My stomach drops with disappointment. This should be in the bag by now. 'I told you, I fly out soon, and what kind of party happens at ten in the morn—' I break off mid-flow, realising my mistake with a full-out blush.

No. I grind my teeth in frustration. He's wrong. I can have as much fun as the next person...

His twisted mouth tells me he finds me amusing, but then his face turns sincere, eyes alight with that flicker of challenge I recognise from when he was buried inside me, instructing me to fondle my nipples or touch my clit.

'The kind on a superyacht—the Monaco Yacht Show is in town. That's one of the reasons I'm here. And it's party time twenty-four-seven on board those things. How else can prospective buyers fall in love with the benefits of owning a floating luxury hotel?'

The depth of my irritation catches my breath even as I long to project a go-with-the-flow attitude. I can't go to some debauched gathering at ten in the morning—I have to work, vet a press release cementing my deal, catch a plane...

I grip my temples. Listen to me. He's seriously considering my proposal and I never concede this easily. I remind myself of what happened when I cut loose last night, of my elation this morning when I opened my emails to find Jensen's was on board. Relaxing the reins a little had paid off then; why not now? Plus, I can't have sexy, carefree Cam thinking I'm a decrepit old dullard.

'Tell you what,' he says, gripping the ends of the towel once more and buffing his astounding pecs, 'you come to the party so we can discuss this proposition of yours further, and I'll ensure you get to Zurich today— I have a plane.'

I almost roll my eyes—of course he has a plane— but stop myself in time. 'I have a perfectly adequate first-class ticket…' But isn't this what I hoped? That he'd consider my outlandish plan?

He shrugs. 'That's the offer on the table—take it or leave it. What's it going to be, princess? Party or goodbye?'

The desire to have things go exactly my way shunts my pulse higher as I stare, while he simply grins. But I *can* have things my way. All I have to do is go to his stupid superyacht party, drink some champagne and take his private plane to Zurich, with or without him—I can get some work done on board, have a decent sleep in a proper bed.

'Come on, you know you want to.' He winks.

My annoyance builds at his self-assured smile—he knows he has me over a barrel. Not a position I've previously enjoyed. But with Cam… My head spins with all the sexy ways I can make him pay. Ruinous ways…

'Okay,' I sigh, 'I'll come to the party.'

His eyes light up. 'I'll meet you out front in ten minutes, after I've showered,' he says, pushing away from the weights machine, all male swagger.

'Great.' My tone is sarcastic. I can't believe he's playing hardball.

But he didn't say no…

He keeps walking in my direction, slow and studied like a panther. I'm hit with a wave of his body heat, the scent of his fresh, manly sweat and undertones of pure, sexy Cam. Damn, he's worth waiting for and he knows it.

He grips my chin, his thumb swiping my bottom lip, and then he tilts my face up to his kiss, which is slow and thorough, as if he's relearning how our mouths slot together. I suck in a breath—unbelievably I'd forgotten how good he is at kissing, how it's almost a full-contact sport—all strong, demanding lips and probing tongue. How he dwarfs me, one hand practically swallowing my entire jaw and half my face, and how, when he pulls away, his eyes glassy with that now familiar desire, I want more. Want it never to end.

How can I crave him again? How do I have any more orgasms left in me? How can I convince him to say yes?

He pulls away, not unaffected by our chemistry—I see it in his eyes—and now I'm looking forward to this party, to proving him wrong, to showing him I'm worth his time.

'Give me ten.' His voice is husky, his breath warm on my wet lips.

I nod, too scared to trust my own voice because of the lust raging through my bloodstream.

* * *

I'm not surprised to see him driving the low-slung, sleek sports car he bought last night, even if it does look as if it belongs in some futuristic movie. The sight of him behind the wheel makes me wish I was someone who employed dirty tactics. I want to ride him right there in the front seat.

'So this is your new car?' I say as he lifts my suit-case into the back. My stomach sinks a little when I see his solitary brown leather messenger-style bag next to it. No suitcase.

'Yes. It's a supercar, remember, a Python—custom-made.'

'Is everything super-sized with you?'

He waggles his eyebrows and I laugh.

'I'm glad you appreciate the finer things in life,' he says. He's talking about himself, so I shake my head in mock disgust, although I'm smiling.

'So what are you going to do with it?' I ask about the car.

'We're going to take it for a little test drive.' He opens my door, and I slide in.

'Shouldn't you have done that before you made such a rash purchase? What if the wheels fall off?'

'I'll get it fixed,' he shrugs. 'You wouldn't worry if you'd seen the race yesterday. It hugs the road like a dream, and wait till you hear the soft purr of the engine.' He winks as if nothing fazes him and a pang of longing shoots through me at his easygoing outlook.

I watch him stride around the front of the car, wondering anew at how he amassed such wealth at such a young age. I had my trust fund to help me out when I first started my own company. But I take full credit for what I've built since. I may not be any good at relationships, I may not have the belief of my father, but money I can make.

He joins me in the car, and, as if he's read my mind, starts the conversation. 'So, what do you do that sees you travelling for work?' he asks as he guns the engine, pulls away from the M Club and heads towards the harbour, Port Hercule.

I love the way he drives, the way he handles the wheel with the same masculine self-assuredness with which he handled my pleasure last night, everything about him exciting new areas of my body and mind until I'm aching for him to agree to my proposition. 'I'm in finance. I'm CEO of an investment multinational.'

He shoots me an assessing look, something akin to disbelief in his eyes.

I lift my chin and try not to take it personally.

'So you make money for people?' he says.

'Yes, lots of money, otherwise I'd have no clients. I'm very good at what I do and it's true what they say—money makes the world go round.'

He shakes his head and I wonder what's upset him about my profession. Most people I meet ask me for investment tips, but Cam looks as though I've said I drown puppies for a living.

'What is it? Do you think women can't be at the top of their field?'

He shoots me an incredulous look. 'Of course not—that you would suggest such a ridiculous thing shows how little we know each other. I was merely wondering just how good you are at your job.'

'Come to Zurich with me and we can work on getting to know each other,' I push, ever the opportunist. 'I'll even give you some free pointers—the markets are in flux at the moment, but there are always opportunities if you know where to look.'

'Mmm...' he says, sounding bored. 'If you were good at *losing* money for clients, I might be tempted.'

I can't tell if he's joking—he looks a little annoyed, his jaw thrust forward, lips pressed together. But he can't be serious. His gambling last night, the large tips, shouting the entire casino a drink...that was one thing. But losing money?

'Why would anyone want to lose money they'd worked hard for?' I could understand my brother's casual attitude to the company's turnover, having stepped into our father's ready-to-wear shoes, but not even he would willingly risk his affluent lifestyle. I wince at my spiteful thoughts. It's not my brother's fault our father has old-fashioned values that make no sense and are completely disloyal.

'They wouldn't,' says Cam. 'Not real hard work—blood, sweat and tears.' He's still borderline hostile at this turn of the conversation.

I should steer clear of anything personal. Clearly my mention of money is some sort of issue for him, perhaps explaining why he didn't seem to care about his losses at the casino last night.

'What's the difference between *real hard work*, as you put it, and what *I* do?' His comments skate too close to my own touchy subject. No one works harder than me. 'Everyone wants to be successful, and putting in the hours is how it happens. Isn't that how you made *your* money?'

His beautiful mouth twists in earnest now, a sneer of disgust. 'Of course, there's nothing wrong with that— I apologise if I offended your work ethic earlier. I've always worked hard, too, until recently. I…' He swallows, seeming to battle with something momentous, but then he recovers just as quickly.

I hold my own breath, waiting.

'Six months ago I came into an obscene inheritance— more money than anyone needs, to be honest.' He pulls into a parking spot, flashes me his live-for-the-moment smile and kills the engine as if closing down the line of conversation.

Intrigue sharpens my vision. Easygoing Cam has hidden depths. Demons. He hides them well behind that carefree persona. For some reason, he seems to be doing his best to offload the money he inherited, even lose it. It seems preposterous to someone in my field.

But this new information certainly explains the chip he seems to have on his shoulder, explains his casual attitude to gambling and extreme acts of generosity— the drinks, the car, replacing my outfit with the best money can buy.

'I'm sensing you don't want to talk about this any more than I want to drink shots off someone's stomach aboard this yacht, but is it a problem for you…the inheritance?' Prying lies outside the terms of my proposition, but I can't help myself. Perhaps I can help him with some investment advice. Of course, he hasn't said yes, so the point may be moot. I might never see him again.

He ignores my question, jumps out of the car and swings open my door. Reaching for my hand, he guides me from the low seat.

I ignore the sinking feeling in my chest and press on. 'Most people would embrace such a life-changing gift.' But I'm quickly coming to understand Cam isn't like most people, in many respects—his two-fingered gestures at convention, the way he sprang from his seat last night to assist a stranger in need, the fact he's even entertaining my proposition; most—no, all the men I know are way too rigid and full of their own importance to contemplate what I'm proposing. But with Cam it's as if normal rules don't apply, or perhaps it's just the age difference, or perhaps he's just exactly what he seems, killing time and enjoying his *bender*.

'Let's just say it's more the origin of the gift that's a problem, that and the terms…' He locks the car and heads towards the marina, reaching back to take my hand.

I try to conceal my flinch, because despite our kiss back at the hotel, despite what we shared last night, my hand in his feels alien in its intimacy.

Alien, but thrilling every nerve in my body.

I swallow the surge of lust and longing. 'Well, I'd

be happy to advise you on how to manage your wealth beyond gambling it all away and buying impractical fast cars, if that's of any interest to you—I have been known to make a savvy investment or two over the years.' I'm over-talking to cover my reaction to the hand-holding.

His head snaps in my direction, his smile almost maliciously bright. 'You think I'm frivolous.'

'No... I didn't mean—'

He comes to a halt. 'Why would you want anything to do with a man who wastes money—is the sex that great?' He delivers this with a smile, but there's pain in the tension around his mouth.

I look down at my feet, stung but also ashamed that he's spot-on—I have judged him, thinking only of what he can do for me, how he makes *me* feel, rather than what he might be hiding from, because years of swimming in the corporate shark tank have honed my instincts, so I know it's something.

He didn't get those calloused hands tapping computer keys. He's hinted that we work in very different worlds. He has an inheritance he doesn't seem to want. But he's more than the clichéd playboy I pegged him for on first impressions, just as, despite my age and my hard-won success, there's a little girl inside me still seeking her daddy's approval.

Who is the real Cam? And who left him an obscene amount of money he doesn't seem to care about?

I look up, regret that I can't see into his beautiful eyes, which are hidden behind sunglasses, stealing my breath. 'I'm sorry—making money is what I do. Pretty much all I've done my entire adult life—first for my father's firm, and then for my own. It's a hard habit to break. I didn't mean to judge, but you're right. I don't know anything about you beyond the fact that, yes, the sex is pretty sensational. That doesn't mean I don't want to know more, so why don't we rectify that? What's your surname, Cam?'

He lifts his sunglasses. 'North. Cameron North.' He smiles then, a belter of a smile. I release a shudder, appalled at how absurdly we've behaved—sharing a night of incredible sex without even knowing each other's surnames.

I smile too.

'And you are?' he asks, his hand outstretched in my direction for the formality of a handshake.

'Orla Hendricks. Nice to meet you.' We grip each other's hand, the fresh start unspoken but welcome.

'So, Orla Hendricks,' he says, guiding me towards a waiting speedboat, which will take us out to the yacht. 'Let's go have ourselves some fun, and then we'll talk about this proposition of yours.' He jumps ahead of me into the speedboat and then swings me after him, his hands gripping my waist. I want to kiss him again, but now I'm unsure of where we stand, the easy pleasure-seeking vibe we shared last night long gone.

We're taken to the biggest yacht in the harbour, the *Abella*—sleek, at least seventy metres, her pristine hull gleaming in the sun. I hear the music before I see the throng of people on deck—most of the women bikini-

clad and many of the men wearing shorts. I grind my
teeth in frustration—I have a swimsuit in my case back
on the dock. Why didn't I think to put it on?

We disembark the tender and climb aboard the
Abella. Cam takes a glass of bubbles from a member
of the smartly dressed welcoming crew and hands it to
me with a smile. Every inch of the stunning vessel is
packed with beautiful people in a full-on party atmosphere. I grip Cam's hand as we head to the upper deck,
which features an infinity pool, a hot tub and the best
views of Monaco.

We wind through the partygoers and head towards
the rail. My phone vibrates in my bag, and I pull it out,
scanning the message from my assistant but checking
the time. Despite Cam's promise to deliver me to Zurich, I'm aware of every second he delays. Perhaps this
was a mistake. I certainly didn't get to where I am by
making many of those.

Cam spies my phone and I shove the device back into
my bag. 'So, are you thinking of buying this?' I want
to caution him against making such a rash investment,
but then, boats like this are more about hedonism and
status than sound returns and I don't want to sound
like a killjoy. But really, most people who own one of
these spend a few weeks a year actually enjoying the
lifestyle. Who has the time to take a year off work?

People like Cam, I guess, deciding to ask him about
his inheritance if he agrees to come to Zurich.

'She's beautiful,' he says. 'Who wouldn't want to
own her? You could permanently live on board. She's

fully equipped—a cinema, a gym, a spa. And you should see the stateroom.'

'But?' We might be here so I can prove I'm not a stick-in-the-mud workaholic, but I can sense that sailing around the Mediterranean in the *Abella* isn't his dream, despite her charms.

He smiles as if I cracked a code no one else has. 'But I prefer bricks and mortar, preferably something I've built myself.' He holds up his calloused hands in proof.

I nod, impressed. I want to get to know this side of him more but stop myself, remembering what happened when we steered too close to personal. 'Blood, sweat and tears?' I say.

'Bingo,' he says, his easy smile wider.

Then I spoil the moment by handing my untouched glass of champagne to a passing waiter.

'You don't like champagne?' he asks.

'I have work to do later—I need a clear head. And you're not drinking.'

'I'm driving you to the airport after this.' I sense his disappointment, feeling as if I've failed the first test.

At his reminder that I'm on probation, I seize the change of topic to push my agenda. 'So, will you come to Zurich?' I want his company. I want the way he makes me feel, what he brings out in me, to be that woman who remembers how to enjoy herself, remembers that it's allowed, even beneficial.

'You're very direct, aren't you, Orla Hendricks? Direct, not afraid to proposition a stranger, and very driven.'

'That's a fair assessment, given we don't know each other very well.'

He tilts his head in acknowledgement. 'No, we don't know each other. So, here's what you need to know about me beyond the fact I'm a sensational lay,' he says with a wicked grin that tells me he's teasing me again, so I can't help smiling along. 'I'm a decent bloke. I'm not harbouring any sexually transmitted infections, so you can shag me with complete peace of mind, and if you want my company for the next six weeks I have two conditions.'

My pulse leaps with excitement, warm, syrupy heat forging through my blood as my lips twitch at his forthright declaration. 'Thanks for the honesty and the practicality. What are these conditions?' I say, my blood roaring through my ears with anticipation.

His eyes darken in that sexy way that reminds me of last night's Cam. 'One, you name the destinations and leave the rest up to me—*I'll* foot the bill, the transport…' he waves a dismissive had around at our current luxurious location '…the off-the-clock itinerary.' One eyebrow lifts above the rim of his sunglasses in that self-assured way. 'Even the wardrobe—I have a feeling I might ruin a few more of your outfits now I know what's hidden underneath. All you have to do is come and come and come…'

My current underwear goes up in flames at the very idea of him being impatient enough to get to me that he goes all caveman. He's sufficiently evolved that he sought my consent first. I hold in a smile and offer a droll, 'I get the picture.'

I'm woman enough, secure enough, to concede a little control to this man. After all, I hold the advantage in terms of age and life experience, and it's not as if we're entering into a relationship—this is about pleasure, and he's proved he can deliver. And, while I'm not used to relinquishing control over my life—it's why I'm successful—do I really care if he wants to pick up the travel tab?

'Okay, but I want it known I'm happy with more… frugal methods of transportation than supercars and private jets.' It's not as if I need his money or run any risk of becoming a *kept woman*—I almost splutter a laugh at the absurdity of that thought. My days of trying to play wife ended in disaster.

He shakes his head. 'Noted, but it's my call. You can be frugal on your own time.' He winks and I capitulate. For his own reasons, reasons he's already hinted at, his generosity and extravagance are motivated by more than altruism, but is his request any more outlandish than my proposition?

'And two?'

'Two—you won't like this one.' He pauses.

My pulse hammers in my neck.

'You have to loosen up a bit more. If this is about us having a good time, I'm going to want to see a whole lot more of last night's Orla.'

My jaw drops. 'What do you mean? It's eleven a.m. I'm at a superyacht party. How loose do I have to be?'

His head drops back and he looks at the sky as if seeking inspiration. 'Ah, Orla, you have so much to learn…' He smiles, perfectly pleasant, his tone teasing. But then he turns serious. 'You're at a party, checking your phone and thinking about work, probably biding your time until you can get back to it.'

My shoulders tense in defence. I heard similar criticism a hundred times from my ex.

'Actually, I was checking the time. I have other places I need to be, so let's wrap this up. Are you joining me in Zurich or not?' My patience is stretched to the limit.

Instead of answering, he sidles up close to my side and stretches his arm along the rail at my back. He leans in close, his mouth inches from mine, and my irritation evaporates in anticipation of being kissed.

'No need to get defensive,' he says, his voice low, seductive. 'Last night was fun. Fun that could have continued into this morning.'

I watch his lips move, reminded that I had the best sex of my life.

His hand slides between my shoulder blades and he urges me closer. 'Instead I woke up in an empty bed to find you working in the dark.'

My head spins, confused by the contradiction in the way he's looking at me, the way he's touching me, and the censure of his words. 'I'm not going to apologise for working—'

'Of course not, but when you're not working hard, where's the harm in playing hard?' He looks over his shoulder to where the most enthusiastic partygoers are climbing from the pool or hot tub and diving into the sea from a diving platform. 'Now, they look like they're really letting loose, wouldn't you say?'

I hear his subtext loud and clear, even as my body sways closer to his. He thinks I'm too straitlaced to let down my hair to that degree. He thinks because I work long hours, I don't know how to enjoy myself. Adrenaline floods my blood, my pulse leaping with defiance.

He turns back to face me and I touch my lips to his in a barely-there caress as I say, 'You're right, that does look fun.' I'm not wearing a bikini, but what better way to show Cam that not only can I be as outgoing as the next person, but also that I'm up for any challenge—in or out of the bedroom?

I hold his stare for one beat, two, my belly tight with anticipation, but I don't kiss him as I want. Instead I step away and slip off my sandals.

His eyes grow wide and then wider still as I slide my Capri pants over my hips. I'm wearing a black cotton thong and a strapless bra—no more revealing than half the bikinis here.

'What are you doing?' Excitement and awe war in Cam's eyes and I roll my shoulders back, the fact that I can impress him spurring me on to exhibit my best assets.

I scoop up my pants and drape them over his arm and then add my camisole top.

'I'm letting loose.' I press a kiss to his startled mouth, ignore the stares I'm attracting, stride to the swimming deck slowly and confidently and dive into the cool Mediterranean.

The water is warm after the initial shock. I break the surface and look up, expecting to see Cam's impressed face looking down at me, but he too is on the deck, stripping off his T-shirt and shorts and then following my lead by executing a perfect dive.

I have a split second to register the jealousy that heats my blood at the way some of the women ogled his spectacular physique, but then he surfaces not far from me and swims my way with long, confident strokes.

We tread water face to face, both grinning.

'Is that loose enough for you?' I ask, splashing him in the face.

He grips my waist and presses a kiss to my mouth with a growl that promises retribution. 'You're fucking irresistible, Orla Hendricks. There are a couple of guys up there I thought I might have to resuscitate—this gorgeous body is much too hot for general consumption. I can see I'm going to have to be on hand to protect the male population from your hotness.'

The air leaves my lungs in an excited rush, the familiar taste of triumph. 'Does that mean you'll be joining me in Zurich?' I mentally tsk at the flare of euphoria—a stupid, girlish reaction for which my libido is totally to blame.

He grins wider and then drags my body against his so I feel his hard cock pressed against my stomach. 'As long as you accept my conditions and you're happy to travel in style.'

'My first-class ticket was style,' I say, rubbing my lips against his, tasting salt and Cam.

'You'll like my style better; now let's get going before I change my mind and buy the *Abella* just so I can watch you do that again.' We break apart, laughing, and swim to the yacht's stern, where a crew member is helpfully waiting with two fluffy white monogrammed towels and our neatly folded clothes.

I dress quickly, driven by the heat in Cam's eyes, as if he's already mentally undressing me, almost promising the minute we're on board his private plane I'll be crying out his name.

By the time we reach the marina, my pulse pounds with excitement. 'What about your luggage, and what will you do with your car?' I slip into the leather passenger seat, eager to get in the air before he can change his mind.

He dons his sunglasses, guns the engine and pulls out of the parking spot. 'I have everything I need.' He indicates the leather messenger bag on the back seat. 'And I'm shipping the car to Sydney—I bought it for my cousin.'

I gape, my mind reasoning that we have sports cars in Australia. But by the time we get to Monaco's private airfield and I see the cute little Cessna on the tarmac, I'm grinning—there is something to be said for Cam's travel-in-style sense of hedonism.

CHAPTER FOUR

Cam

MY EYES STING with the trickle of sweat, but I can do nothing about it while I'm braced on both hands over Orla, who is close to climaxing. The minute we boarded the plane she jumped me, and I only too happily obliged, stripping us both while I headed for the craft's king-sized bed.

I know she's close because she clutches my arms until her nails dig into my skin, her staccato breaths becoming trapped in her throat. I've watched her come so many times in the last twenty-four hours that I've lost count. And this time is just as addictive. She lets go, her release real and joyful and noisy as if she's not expecting, as if it creeps up on her, as if she's embracing this sex-only proposition with both hands.

I ignore the needs of my own body and dive once more for her nipple—she loves it when I give her just a scrape of my teeth. Orla likes a hint of rough with her pleasure. Who'd have guessed this passionate, sexually adventurous woman and the serious, put-together financier I met at the bar are the same woman? If it wasn't for our differences outside of sex, she could be made for me.

'Cam... Oh, my...'

She comes with her beautiful eyes on me and I follow her—bareback. She's too fucking tempting and my control was shot to pieces the minute she suggested we ditch condoms for the duration of this sexy little interlude she proposed.

I collapse on top of her, spent for now, and then roll to the side as I slip from her body, my dick still half-hard. How could I be anything else? She's incredible. She blew me away with that stunt on board the *Abella*. I'll never forget the sight of her clad only in the skimpiest of underwear, her lithe, toned body glowing in the sun as she dived into the sea. I wanted to run around scouring the image from the eyes of everyone there, male and female.

My breathing slows and I rest my head on my hand, wondering, who is the real Orla? The siren or the CEO? Perhaps neither.

She's certainly the most ambitious and driven woman I know. But what about life? Relationships and family and the future? What does the real Orla want beyond global domination of the financial sector? I'm not even going to pretend to understand what she does for a living outside of the fact I'm certain my father would have used her wealth-building services.

She turns to face me, one thigh slung over mine, sliding the wetness we've both left between her legs over my skin. I hold in a groan because I want her again, and I've barely caught my breath.

She wriggles until she's comfortable, using my shoulder as a pillow. I kiss the top of her head, the scent of whatever shampoo she uses filling my senses. I breathe her in, congratulating myself on the impulse to accompany her. I was tempted the minute she asked in the hotel gym, but I wanted to push her, to see how far she'd go for my company, and boy, has she surprised me.

My first impressions of her were all wrong. Yes, she carries the poise and polish of her wealth, but with a little encouragement, when she's not glued to her phone or her laptop, she's more than willing to let loose and embrace this thing between us—two people who couldn't be more different united in a pretty constant need to slake our fierce attraction.

Who knew a woman so tightly controlled could be so hot, insatiable and demanding? Thank fuck she suggested a continuation of the sex, otherwise I might have resorted to some unflattering trawling of the M Clubs in search of another chance encounter...

Her small hum of contentment vibrates through my chest. I grip her closer, holding her wet dream of a body closer.

'Glad you said yes?' she mumbles from under her cloud of dishevelled hair.

'Too right.' She's become my favourite distraction technique from my personal predicament, fucking her the only thing that switches off the constant feelings of fury and futility. Better than hiding, drinking, gambling and pounding my body to exhaustion at the gym combined.

I snort a short laugh. Perhaps that's the answer to my father's legacy—to immerse myself in a sex coma so profound I'm numb to the sheer audacity of the man. How dare he think he can control me from the grave with his last will and testament and make amends with money for a lifetime of indifference and absence?

Orla shifts, mashing her breasts to my side. If only dear old Pa could see me now—sprawled beneath a beautiful woman on board a private jet, blowing my unwanted legacy in the most debauched way I can.

I swallow bile and focus on the light glinting off Orla's beautiful hair. No, her proposition of pleasure couldn't have come at a better time.

'Are you okay?' She sounds sleepy and guilt pricks at my skin. I should let her sleep—she's been up most of the night.

I mutter something affirmative and try to keep my body still and relaxed in case she wants to nap.

'You're so good at that. Sex.' Her fingers stroke my abs and my dick perks up—greedy fucker. 'I'm so glad you decided to come.' Her voice vibrates where her head rests on my sweaty chest, strands of her hair tickling my chin.

'Thanks.' I laugh, my restless fingers drumming a rhythm on her back. She's so honest and forthright. She knows what she wants—damned sexy traits. 'But you wouldn't have brought me along otherwise, right?

Unless you make a habit of seducing younger men and luring them to be your sex-slaves.'

She sees the joke in my words, and laughs, then raises her head to press a kiss to my mouth. 'You're free to leave any time,' she says, even as she entwines her legs with mine, preventing my immediate escape.

'Mmm…' I press my thigh between her legs, loving her scorching wet heat. 'But then I'd miss your delicious cunt and your tempting mouth.' I trace her full lips with my fingertip, dipping my head for one more kiss while I evaluate the chances of me being ready for another round, versus heading for the on-board shower.

She pulls back, mock censure on her face. 'So you wouldn't miss my scintillating, fun-loving personality?'

I love this sassy, playful side of her; I can imagine her wearing cut-off shorts and a bikini top, hanging out and drinking beer on the balcony of my place in Sydney while we enjoy the spectacular sunset over the harbour.

'I'd miss every fuckable inch of you,' I say, slipping my hand over her hip to caress her ass, watching with mounting excitement as her slumberous stare widens, heat banked behind her eyes.

'And I don't know you well enough to miss your personality. Why don't we rectify that—we have a few hours to kill?' And, second only to fucking, verbal sparring with this sharp, witty woman is the best distraction technique. Left to its own devices, my brain would try to problem-solve, freaking me out with thoughts of forgiveness for a man I detest, acceptance of his final bequeathed gift and ways I can use his money—because it will never be *my* money—to make a difference, to do some good. But only danger lies ahead of those insane thoughts. The danger that I'm becoming just like him—a man who chose the pursuit of wealth over love, over his family.

Over *me*.

'Mmm, I really should work…' Orla's contented, half-hearted excuse draws me back to the present. Despite using this trip as the perfect antidote to my predicament, and despite my jokes about being her man toy, I really do want to get to know her better, the real her, to work out which of the two awesome versions of Orla Hendricks is the real deal.

I cup her ass cheeks in both hands and roll her on top of me, pressing my hardening dick between her legs so she gasps. 'Work *schmirk*—haven't you made enough money for today?'

'Is that a thing? Can you ever have too much?' She indicates our luxurious flying bedroom. But I can't concede that point without divulging my father issues, so I change the subject.

'Come on. I promise no deep, searching questions.' I tilt my hips, rubbing her clit with the head of my cock. 'Just a quick-fire quiz so I can get to know you before I fuck you again. Stop me feeling like a gigolo and you like a cougar.'

She laughs from her belly—deep and throaty—and it's such a beautiful sight and sound, one that makes me forget my troubles, that I'm determined to make it happen as much as I can while we're together.

'Tell me,' I coax, pushing her hair back from her face, 'favourite animal?'

She doesn't hesitate. 'Well, they're just so cute-looking, I'd have to say wombat,' she says, choosing an Australian icon, embracing the game even as she grinds her hips, sending fresh blood to my already hard dick.

'Do you have any pets?' My voice grows husky. The shower will have to wait—she knows what she's doing to me, her tongue darting out to wet her lips. Perhaps she hates talking about herself. Perhaps, despite her willingness to embrace a challenge, there's nothing in her life besides work, after all. Her degree of professional success requires sacrifices; I would know. I'm a prime example—I refuse to think of myself as a victim—of such single-minded focus.

'No, I travel too much to own one.' She sighs, her eyes turning wistful with longing. 'I used to have a Labradoodle called Talia when I was growing up.'

I nod. 'You could have one if you wanted. It could travel with you on its own passport. I had a golden retriever who used to come to work with me every day until she died about a year ago. Her faithful company made the days fly by, and I always had someone to talk to.'

'I'm sorry.' She presses her mouth to mine, and again I forget. Forget that I started this game, forget that we're getting to know silly things about each other. But, now I've seen a flicker of the woman behind the trappings,

I'm intrigued anew. I pull away. 'Okay, what's your dream job?'

'Mmm… That's tricky. I've only ever done what I do now, and I've never wanted to do anything else. I started working for my father on the weekends at sixteen, joined the family company after university and left ten years ago to start my own firm.'

So she'd always been career-focused, even from a young age. 'I spent most of my weekends surfing or drumming at sixteen,' I say. 'What happened to the family firm? Didn't they miss you when you left to strike out alone?'

She snorts, her face hardening. 'I doubt it. My brother can, apparently, do my old job as well as me, despite working half as hard.' She shakes her head and changes the subject. 'What about you, what's your dream job?'

But it's too late. That single sentence tells me exactly what motivates her: she's competitive and wants to be taken seriously. I sanitise my answer, reluctant to confess I need never work again, if only I could reconcile dear old Dad's dying wish. Because the truth is it's ruined everything. *He's* ruined everything. In my life before, working hard, striving and grafting and being proud of where a poor boy from Sydney had dragged himself gave me purpose, a sense of accomplishment. It made sense.

But now…? When I could buy the construction company I once worked for outright a hundred times over and barely notice the cost…

I swallow, hedging how much to reveal. 'I used to

work for a construction company back in Sydney before
the inheritance, but I'd say I have the perfect job right
now—enjoying myself and everything that money can
buy.' I hold her closer. 'Travelling in style anywhere in
the world. And, of course, meeting a beautiful woman
who only wants me for sex is an added bonus.' I wink,
bringing out her throaty chuckle.

But then she turns serious. 'Do you miss construction?'

I shrug. 'Sometimes. I love building things, always
have, even as a boy. I like to be active and use my
hands. There's nothing better than a day of graft and
sweat and getting splinters followed by relaxing with
an ice-cold beer.'

I catch the curl of her lip, the wrinkle of her nose
that reminds me we're still very different. 'Well, almost
nothing better,' I say, sliding my hand over her hip to
caress her backside, steering us back to the reason we're
here: the sex. She may not be the straitlaced princess
I first had her pegged for, but that doesn't mean she'd
be happy hanging out with the real me—the me without the money and the jets and the cars and the billions
in the bank.

'You miss getting splinters?' she asks, her voice
mildly incredulous. She comes from wealth, her family own a business; she's probably known it her whole
life, despite whatever sibling rivalry sent her striking
out alone.

I nod, breathing through the urge to defend how I
once made a modest but sufficient living with my own

two hands. How I didn't need more than savings in
the bank and the pride of being able to look after my
mother.

Not like *him*.

My sperm donor. Because he didn't stick around long
enough to earn the title of father. A man who thought
he could come back into my life from the grave and
dictate how I live.

I choose my words carefully. 'Before the money I
lived an average life.' I try but fail to shake off the
memories of going to school hungry, of having to fake
a stomach ache to get out of gym class because I was
ashamed of my trainers, of having to stay late at school
to do my homework on the computers in the library because, try as she may, my single-parent mother couldn't
afford luxuries.

I force my muscles to relax when they scream with
tension. I don't want Orla to know the turn in this conversation highlights how different our worlds are. But
she doesn't have to fit into my life, my *real* life, the
life I had six months ago. All she needs to do is to fit
in my bed, temporarily. She wanted sex. She's already
stated she's happy I can deliver what she's looking for
and she's willing to embrace a challenge.

'So, next question,' I say, moving on. 'What's the
most sexually adventurous thing you've done?' My
mind ruminates on the infinite possibilities we could
cram into six weeks of sexual exploration.

She laughs, but doesn't falter. 'I'd say proposition-
ing a stranger for sex is pretty adventurous.' She kisses

me, eyes open, her tongue pushing against mine until I forget the question I asked.

'It's up there,' I say when she allows me up for air. Yes, she owns her desires; she's almost as insatiable as she makes me, and I'm damned well determined to enjoy every second of testing her boundaries, extending her comfort zone, pushing her buttons. Something tells me not only will she do her best to rise to the challenge, but we'll both reap the rewards as she continues to surprise me, to allow her outer shell to crack, revealing the real, uninhibited Orla inside.

'What about you? Threesomes? Bondage? Sex with an older woman?' Her eyes twinkle.

'Ah, a gentleman never tells.' I roll onto my side, taking her along, curious as to what led her to proposition a stranger. 'So why am I here? What do *you* need from this that you don't already have?'

Her mouth flattens as if she wasn't expecting the question, but then she sighs. 'As you've already pointed out, I work hard for long hours. I travel a lot. I'm divorced and have no desire to enter into another relationship. Why shouldn't I have the kind of sex-only fling I want with a gorgeous man who wants the same thing?'

'No reason at all,' I concede, fascinated for details of her failed marriage. But because I want to steer us back from the supremely personal, I say, 'What kind of sex are we talking about here? Threesomes? Bondage? Sex with a virile younger man?'

She throws her head back on a delighted, throaty laugh. 'Fishing for compliments?'

'I'll always take compliments, but how can I give you what you want if I don't know what that is?'

Her fingers trail through my chest hair, her eyes growing lazy with mounting desire. 'Hot sex. Frequent hot sex with a man who pushes all my boundaries.' Her hips begin to gyrate as she rubs her pussy over the head of my cock once more.

'You like having your boundaries pushed?' A slug of heat scorches through me at the idea of testing her limits, although the experience might just kill me, she's that hot.

'I'm happy to keep up with you.' She tilts her hips, aligning her pelvis so just the tip of my cock slips inside her.

I stifle a groan, my hand dragging her hip closer, my fingers flexing into the deliciously round cheek of her ass until I sink in another inch. 'So, sexual adventures are on the cards?'

'Anything is on the cards.' Her pupils dilate, swallowing the emerald of her exquisite irises.

'Really? Anything?' It's hard to think straight when her pussy sucks at the head of my dick.

'If you're asking if I've ever done anal, the answer is no, but…' Her breasts rise on a breathy sigh.

Excitement builds in my chest at the idea of taking her somewhere previously forbidden, of guiding her to explore something new, of extending her comfort zone.

Ruining her.

'So that's something you'd be open to—excuse the pun—not that I'm in any way pushing?'

She bites her lip and straddles me, sinking back on her heels until her hot sex swallows my length to the hilt. She stares down, levels me with that look—the one that reminds me she's driven, successful, older and, outside of anal sex, perhaps more experienced. 'I wouldn't *let* you push me, but I'm not into pain.'

I clasp her rocking hips, trying to force words out past my tight throat as pleasure grips me. 'Me neither, but pleasure...?'

She leans forwards, kisses me, her tongue surging against mine until I've not only forgotten my own question, but I'm also close to losing my mind. 'Perhaps,' she whispers. 'But we'd have to start off small. There's no way I'm ready to take this bad boy.'

I slip my hand between us, my thumb finding her clit, because all this talk about pushing sexual boundaries, the way she's riding me, means I'm close and there's no way I'm coming until she is.

I don't miss the gush of moisture bathing my dick as she gasps her pleasure against my mouth. 'I'm happy to explore anything, but only if you're as accommodating...' She trails kisses across my chest as she scoots back. 'Let's start with the bondage.' She smiles, the expression wicked and self-satisfied.

I grip her hips, guiding her rhythm, but she untangles my hold and pushes my arms above my head. 'Nuh-uh. I want to be in charge this time.' She reaches for her discarded bra and binds my wrists with it before securing them loosely to the headboard.

'Yes, ma'am.' Before I can speak another word she

starts the rocking again, this time cupping her breasts and rolling her nipples between her thumbs and fingers as if she's determined to drive me insane, even more insane than the idea of testing her, taking her on an unexplored journey of pleasure, showing her that nice boys from nowhere can rock her tightly controlled world.

But I can't enjoy it for long. She gasps as she rides me harder, sinking so deep there's nowhere left to go. I hold still, splayed beneath her, watching her pleasure her breasts, my eyes drawn to the way she tugs her lip under her teeth. I want to move. To suck on that sensitive lip until she begs me to take her places no one else has. To see my dick rest there before she takes me to the back of her throat. To buck up into her and take us both over the edge into mindless oblivion, where I'm just a man and she's just a woman—no differences, no complications, no expectations beyond finding the ultimate pleasure.

Her rounded hips undulate, finding the rhythm and angle she wants, that make her moan and start to chant my name. She looks down at me, her face rapt with pleasure and the hint of a feline smile on her lips. 'I'm intrigued now. You have my mind thinking dirty thoughts, Cam North. You're bad for me.' She rocks back and forth, her head thrown back and her cries telling me I'm nothing but good for where she wants to go.

I'm speechless at her astounding willingness to embrace this, although my mind fills with all the filthy words I could use to describe such an amazing sight as this woman riding me while she fantasises about other pleasures to which I'm going to introduce her.

And then she fumbles with my restraints, her hands jerky in their desperation. 'Do it. Do it now.' She guides one of my hands to her ass, her fingers over mine slipping between her cheeks to lead the way. 'Touch me like you did last night.'

She resumes her rocking, her hands returning to her breasts, and I grip both cheeks, thrusting up into her with her every down-stroke while my fingers explore her rear.

'Oh, Cam, yes…'

Fuck, she's incredible. How did I ever think she'd be too straitlaced for the kind of sex I enjoy? The kind with a woman who isn't afraid to own her pleasure, to claim it, to heighten it any way she chooses? She's glorious, a woman in her prime, taking her pleasure and then demanding a little more.

Her glazed eyes open, looking down at me through heavy lids. 'I'm going to come.'

I grit my teeth, bucking harder underneath her and pushing the tip of my finger, which is wet from the arousal slicked between her legs, inside her rear.

Her orgasm tears a scream from her arched throat and I come seconds later, the thought that, sexually at least, Orla Hendricks could have been made for me filling my mind.

CHAPTER FIVE

Orla

I DON'T RECOGNISE the hotel suite, although I've only been away for a morning, on the second day of meetings at my Zurich office. The bed is covered with shopping bags and parcels, the floor littered with stacks of shoeboxes, and there's a clothing rack filled with garment bags. I shake off the fatigue I felt when I found Cam absent and open one, my curiosity burning out of control; I find a beaded ballgown the colour of peacock feathers, the iridescent hues catching the light and changing colour before my eyes.

My first instinct, to roll my eyes at Cam's extravagance, fades, replaced by awe. My fingers trail along the exquisite fabric. It's exactly what I would pick out for myself, and I can't believe his thoughtfulness. He hasn't just mindlessly bought a year's worth of clothes. He's personally selected these, and I know because yesterday he told me how pretty I looked in my favourite green silk blouse.

With jittery fingers I open one of the parcels on the

bed, the delicate tissue paper parting to reveal a filmy wisp of lingerie—sexy but comfortable and the right size. With the shoes—my one weakness—I'm a little less restrained, flipping off the lids to reveal pair after pair of exquisite, barely practical heels from all the biggest fashion houses. Just how I like them.

I catch my wide smile in the mirror, Cam's gifts, no matter how excessive, forcing an ache to my cheeks. Cam never does anything by half measures, whether it's making me come or reserving the best suite money can buy—the suite we're currently occupying at the M Club, which has views of Lake Zurich with the Alps in the distance.

My phone pings, drawing my attention from Cam's gift, which is enough haute couture to make a supermodel weep. I scan the message and fire off a quick response to one of my assistants, my gaze returning to the outfits with longing. When will I even have the opportunity to wear most of these? We've been in town two days, and despite my assurances that I can play as hard as the next person I've had no time to explore.

I sit on the bed and kick off my shoes, my tired toes protesting. I've promised I'll take tomorrow off to go skiing—Cam has planned a day on the slopes. I try to recall the last time I had an entire day off. It's been at least a year.

I glance at the exquisite gowns with longing. Why have I allowed my life to become so…insular? And why has it taken meeting a sexy Aussie guy to bring me out of my self-imposed shell?

I text him my thanks and let him know I've arrived back at the hotel.

Thinking of Cam, I feel my pulse pick up, delicious fingers of anticipation curling around me.

Where is he?

I slip off my jacket and flop back on the bed, part of me wishing I'd been with Cam on his shopping spree— I rarely have time for visiting actual stores these days, preferring to purchase from my favourite designers on-line, but it's not the same. I used to adore shopping, the thrill of finding something I loved, the reverence of bringing it home in a pristine bag.

The door clicks and in he walks, casually dressed, unlike me, in worn jeans and a black T-shirt. I sit up, hit with his delicious, freshly showered scent seconds before he leans over me on the bed, his mouth finding mine, and I'm lost in his now familiar, demanding kiss.

'Good morning,' he says, pulling away, his smile wide and warm and filling me with regret.

I laugh while I wrestle my heart-rate back under control. 'It's afternoon.' I stand and wrap my arms around his neck, wanting to be closer.

He shrugs, holding my hips to his. 'Well, you were gone when I woke, so I missed my good-morning kiss.'

I fight the urge to sweep the parcels from the bed and drag him back there so we can have a do-over— this morning was the only one since I met him that my day hasn't begun with my waking to find him raising an eyebrow of enquiry before wedging himself between my thighs, coaxing my clit equally awake with his tongue.

'Yes, I had a seven a.m. meeting.' The only way I would be able to squeeze in what I needed to work on and spend tomorrow skiing the Zermatt with him before we leave the day after. 'I see you've been shopping…'

He shrugs, one corner of his mouth kicking up at my gross understatement. 'Just a couple of things. An extension of my apology for tearing your dress.'

'A dress you already replaced. This is too much, Cam.'

His mouth twists in that sexy way of his, one usually preceding some sexy command or request. 'I noticed that you travel light, so I thought you might need a few things, especially for the opera tonight.'

'Cam, I'm a woman, a woman who loves shoes, but even I wouldn't go this far.' I look around the room, my financier's brain totting up a dizzying sum.

'That's because you're frugal. Indulge me,' he says before I can take umbrage. 'And remember the rules— you get to have your wicked way with me as often as you like, and I dictate the after-work itinerary and cover the costs.'

I nod, breathless because now I want to have my way with him once more. I could use a dose of Cam's special magic after the morning of meetings, of hustling, of living up to my reputation as one of the industry's global trailblazers.

A strange and unfamiliar restlessness infects me; it was there when I walked through the door. I probe the feeling so I can label it.

I'm jealous.

Jealous of the time he spends without me, even though *I'm* the one who's leaving *him* to work. I'm jealous that he's doing who knows what, while I have the same meeting over and over, only in different countries and different languages. And I'm jealous that living the high life seems to come naturally to him; wherever we are, he hunts out something fun to do. This is my sixth trip to Zurich, and I've never been to the opera.

I stroke Cam's strong arms. He's becoming an addiction—the more I have, the more I want. An edge of panic grips my throat. It wasn't supposed to feel this way…

'So what else have you been up to while I've been at work?' I hadn't thought about how he keeps himself busy when I'm not around—I guess I assumed he works out at the club gym or goes for a swim.

His expression turns shifty, pricking my curiosity. 'You won't approve.'

'Why? Did you elbow an elderly lady out of the way to get to that ballgown?'

He laughs but his eyes stay wary. Then he sighs. 'I visited a music store—I still play the drums.'

'So that's why you're always tapping something?'

He pulls me in for another kiss and I sink into it, grateful he made the first move because the urge to kiss him is pretty constant. I'd practically zoned out during one of my meetings this morning, fantasising about him, what he might be doing, whether he was naked, in our bed, perhaps jerking off because he couldn't wait for me to get back.

I'm drawn back to the present when he pulls away. 'I bought a drum kit.'

I look around in confusion. 'There's no room here for a drum kit.'

He shakes his head. 'More's the pity. No, these weren't for me.' He turns serious and I hold my breath, certain he'll show me a little piece of himself if only I'm patient.

'There was a kid at the music shop. The sales assistant told me he comes in every week to pay off some money towards the kit he wants.' He shrugs, his eyes taking on a faraway look. 'I remember what that was like, how hard I saved for my first set—I worked surf lifesaving all summer.'

I smile and slide my fingers through his glorious hair. I can picture a teenaged Cam, all tanned, his hair bleached by the sun.

'I couldn't resist—I paid off the kid's balance and had the kit delivered to his house.' Suddenly he scoops me around the waist, hoists my feet from the floor and swings me in a circle. 'You should have seen his face.'

I squeal and laugh, and then my feet touch down and I sober as I look hard into his eyes. 'Cam, that was such a kind thing to do.' I try to picture the man I know doing that, the one who tips everyone he meets and spends money with reckless abandon. It makes my stomach hurt.

He downplays his generosity with a shrug, but I can see that this means something to him, something more than purchasing exquisite gowns he thinks I'll like.

'Playing drums helped me through my teens. Music is a great hobby.'

He looks uncomfortable and I squeeze his biceps, because I'm still holding on to them as if I'm scared he'll disappear. Were his teens difficult? Did he go through a rebellious phase? Butt horns with his father? My chest aches with questions but I bite my tongue, not only because it's clearly a soft spot for him, but also because it's personal. I know from the haunted look in his eyes that he once struggled and strived to buy things I would have taken for granted. I want to ask, to know this side of him, but it's not what we're about.

I take a shuddering breath as the restlessness returns, twice as fierce. I think about the meeting I have this afternoon with my Zurich chief financial officer and head of investments. I'd much rather spend time with Cam, break my own rules and get to know the drum-playing, sexy Santa side of him better.

'Anyway,' he says, releasing me and walking to the bed. 'I see you haven't had time to unwrap everything,' he picks up a black box I hadn't noticed and holds it out in my direction, 'but I want to watch you open this one.'

I accept the change of subject, shelve my curiosity and take the box, which is heavier than it looks, black velvet, monogrammed with the M Club logo and slightly smaller than a shoebox.

'What is it?' I ask, the look of heated challenge in his eyes leaving me nervous and so turned on I'm hyperaware of every breath I take.

'It's for you—I couldn't resist.' His voice is deep,

dark, and his eyes gleam, that sexy secret smile of his firing every pleasure centre in my brain so I want to abandon my own curiosity as to the box's contents and jump him, to drag us both back to the safe place where we lose ourselves in each other, in pleasure.

'Open it.' It's a husky demand, just like the ones he issues in bed.

I prise open the lid and gasp, and then laugh, locking eyes with his in time to see the excitement dancing there. Inside the box, nestled in deep maroon satin, is a matt-black vibrator, the base bearing an M Club logo encrusted with tiny diamonds.' I finger the two rows of sparkling stones on top of the *M*.

'Are these real?' Pressure builds in my chest, as if I'm oxygen-deprived. Only Cam would buy such an extravagant and intimate gift.

He nods, slow, confident, sexy, and then he watches my tracing finger.

With a breathy shudder I can't hold inside, I slide my fingertip up the length of the sex toy as slowly and sensually as I can, tracing the realistic ridges to the very tip, and then meet his stare with a challenging one of my own. 'It's not as big as you.'

His eyes darken with sexy promise and that hint of challenge he seems to love where I'm concerned, one I'm only too happy to meet head on. Can't have him thinking he's besting me in our little arrangement.

'No, but it's big enough. I thought you needed a sex toy for when I'm no longer around.'

Lust is a tangible aura around us, impossible after

the amount of sex we've had this week, but there all the same. Lust and something else. Perhaps trust. A deeper awareness. I focus on the lust because that's the only feeling I'll allow myself, although Cam's reminder that this is temporary dampens some of my excitement.

Because you want it to be temporary.

I latch on to Cam's eyes to stop my head spinning with what-ifs. I see my own desire reflected. He too is turned on.

We're both fully clothed, no longer touching, but his need is there in the husk of his deep voice and the avid way he's watching my every move, like a predator about to strike.

And now I'm desperate to reschedule my afternoon and break in my new toy with Cam. Mmm… Perhaps I could make time for that.

I know exactly what I'm doing to us both when I abandon the vibrator and lift the second item from the box, holding it up between us with a questioning brow, because all I want to do is laugh, kiss the self-satisfied delight from Cam's handsome face, and then drag him to bed and force him to introduce me to these gifts.

'What's this?' I say, my voice low. 'A butt plug?'

He nods again. 'You wanted to experiment.' He steps closer, grasping my hips and grinding his erection between our bodies as he kisses me with his trademark thoroughness.

My hands are occupied with his over-the-top provocative gifts—who even knew diamond-encrusted sex toys were a thing?—but I embrace the kiss as always, my pulse galloping to keep up with my filthy mind. When I'm panting, the tops of my thighs slick with arousal, I pull away, now determined to reschedule my meeting and forget. Forget that my life is so work-focused and that it no longer feels like enough. Forget that I'm sleeping with a man I hardly know but I'm too scared to change the status quo. Forget everything apart from the way he makes me feel invincible.

'Show me,' I whisper against his mouth. Everything else fades, as if nothing is as important as losing myself in my addiction to Cam.

I hear the sharp intake of his breath.

His pupils are so big I can no longer see the grey of his eyes. His hands fist in the fabric of my skirt over my hips, and he hisses between his teeth, leaning down to rest his forehead against mine and scrunch his eyes closed with obvious regret.

'I will—hell, I will.' He breathes hard, his sincerity pouring from him in waves of intensity I've only seen when he's turned on, battling his control to push me into that final, exhausted orgasm before he allows himself to follow. Cam takes my pleasure incredibly seriously, perhaps as if he sees *me* as some sort of challenge beyond the challenges he sets for me, the ones my competitive nature demands I embrace.

He grips my hips tighter before pushing me away and groans, clearly getting himself under control. 'But, for now, we have a delivery to make. Are you done for the day?'

My high plummets, the expectations of being immediately gratified and chasing off this edgy feeling hitting a brick wall.

'No.' I pout, my disappointment as effective as a cold shower, to be replaced with a flush of shame at the deflated look on his face. Whatever he had planned means something to him, perhaps as much as purchasing a drum kit for a stranger, and it's clearly more important than getting naked and trying out his newest extravagant purchase.

I fight the heat rising in my face; I was willing to cancel my meeting for sex, but not for whatever Cam has planned? My priorities confirm we're still very much on different wavelengths where the pursuit of pleasure is concerned. But I can give him time after everything he's given me.

I mentally reshuffle my schedule so I can spend the afternoon with him, in or out of bed, because I want to see more of the look he wore when he told me about the drums. I want to see more of the real Cam.

'But I can be free—I'll just need to make a few phone calls. What did you have in mind?'

Cam smiles and my decision feels right. 'I'll make it up to you, I promise.' He takes the butt plug from my hand and places it back in the box, snapping the lid closed with a frustrating finality. 'Want to go on an adventure?'

His excitement infects me with a feeling of lightness, of possibility, of freedom. It's heady and terrifying all at once. 'What kind of adventure? I thought you'd planned skiing for tomorrow?' I breathe through the feeling that I'm escaping my comfort zone emotionally, because I just don't do this—cancel work commitments, play hooky for the afternoon, do something just because I'm overcome with the heady urge.

'I have. Heli-skiing—it's the best way to ski.'

'Of course it is. And the most expensive, no doubt.' I smile, because I know by now that Cam lives to the max. And how do I live? I love to ski. Despite all my visits to Zurich, I've never taken the time out for one of my favourite pastimes.

My earlier shame intensifies. I don't have time for pastimes. All I do is work. Mark was right. Not only was I emotionally distant, but I was also absent most of the time.

What is Cam doing to me, and why does it feel both naughty and liberating? 'So where *are* we going?'

He must sense my residual petulance, that I'm not entirely happy about postponing my orgasm, because he kisses me, his lips firm and coaxing and his smile both hot and indulgent, as if he's already thinking about what we'll do when we return from our fully clothed adventure. 'It's another surprise.'

'I hate surprises.' I exaggerate the pout that earned me one of his delicious kisses.

'Because you're a control freak.' He softens his reprimand, giving me the kiss I wanted. 'Trust me, you'll love this surprise.'

Still, I wheedle. 'As much as I love the sex toys?' I lick my lips and watch the flare of heat in his eyes with satisfaction.

Such a low blow…

He laughs and looks down at my outfit: a sharp business skirt and a silk blouse. 'I can't promise that. But you might want to change into something more casual.'

Defeated for now, I change, choosing my favourite pair of soft denim jeans and a simple white T-shirt for any eventuality, trying to embrace the surprise Cam has arranged.

With my phone calls made, my meeting rescheduled for seven the following morning, we leave the hotel hand in hand. I'm eager to get whatever this is over with so I can persuade Cam out of his clothes, and Cam is just plain eager, because he knows where we're going and, to him, life seems to be one big adventure.

When we approach a covered truck instead of the sleek sports car I'd been expecting, I skid to a halt. 'We're going in this?'

He said we had a delivery to make, but I was expecting…well, I don't know what I expected. Nothing Cam does is expected.

Cam nods, climbing up on the footrests to open the passenger door for me.

'Can you drive this?' I hide the scepticism from my face, certain he'll surprise me with his answer.

'Of course. I'm a jack-of-all-trades.' He winks. 'Come on, up you go.' He guides me up into the cab, his hands helpfully shoving me in by the backside so my core clenches and I can't wait to get whatever diversion Cam has planned out of the way and head back to the hotel so he can make it up to me, as he promised.

When he's sitting beside me, his big hands expertly wielding the power-assisted steering to direct us on our way, I ask, 'So where are we going?' It's certainly not lunch on the shores of Lake Zurich or a boat cruise, otherwise why would we need the delivery truck?

'I want to make a donation. A personal delivery to some very deserving recipients. I thought you might enjoy helping.' He looks over to gauge my reaction. 'Don't worry, I promise I'll make it up to you later—those toys won't be staying in the box.' He chuckles at my obvious exasperation, so I shove him in the shoulder and then slide my hand over his thigh, grinning. His excitement is palpable, infectious, so I almost don't mind that we're not back in the hotel room trying out his gifts, and now I get my wish to play Santa with him. I can be his naughty elf…

I'm still none the wiser as to our destination, but I've learned that Cam can be bull-headed, so I let it drop—I'll find out soon enough.

'You know the M Club organises many charitable events throughout the year, right?' I say. 'There are plenty of opportunities to make sizeable donations. That's one of the beauties of membership, and it's what I do.' His extravagance shows no signs of letting up; in fact, he seems to go out of his way to best himself day by day. He said his inheritance was *obscene*, and, short of giving it all away, he seems at a loss to know what to do with his newfound wealth.

He nods, his mouth tight, which tells me it's something of a touchy subject. 'I know. I already give as much as I can, but this donation is a little more personal—you'll see.'

We pass the rest of the journey in companionable silence, which is laced with curiosity on my part and what looks like knowing glee on Cam's. My mind wanders back to my cancelled meeting with my Zurich team. I have hordes of people I delegate the small things to, but I've never fully let go of the reins and simply watched the profits come rolling in. I'm not built that way. I'm too much of a control freak, as Cam pointed out.

I check my phone, pulling up my itinerary for my time in Dubai, which is where Cam and I are heading after Zurich. It's a packed week—after London, Dubai is my second largest office, my clients among some of the wealthiest people on the planet, but even so, Cam's filled all the gaps with 'must do' activities—dinner in the tallest building in the world, an Arabian Desert safari, our own private yacht tour of Dubai Creek.

My head spins, already exhausted. But I promised him. Perhaps this is his first world trip.

'Have you ever been to Zurich before?' I brush a speck of lint off my jeans, keeping my tone light and conversational rather than nosy and intrusive.

He shakes his head. 'Until I left Sydney for Monaco, the furthest I'd been was New Zealand.'

'So you've never been to Dubai either?' No wonder he wants to cram in as many tourist attractions as he can, although surely he can return any time he wants.

'No. Construction isn't the best paid work in the world, but I had a comfortable life.'

'Why not go back to your job, if you love it so much?' My scalp crawls—if someone told me I couldn't do my job, I'd be lost. Perhaps that's why he's struggling with his inheritance. But just because he never needs to work again, it doesn't mean he can't do what he loves. I do.

'My boss looked relieved when I told him I wanted to take some unpaid leave. I think the company is struggling. And in theory, I no longer need the work.'

'In theory?' My probing is hesitant because I'm in the same position. I choose to work, because I love it. It's my life. It's what I'm good at.

'It's complicated.' He keeps his eyes on the road, but his jaw is bunched, telling me he doesn't want to elaborate. I've already suggested financial advice, so I don't repeat the offer. But I want to help him.

The questions I want to ask clog my throat, because he's hinted that he hasn't always known modest or even comfortable wealth. That perhaps he has more in common with the boy at the music store than he does with me or any other M Club member; that none of this, the luxury, the charitable donations, the escapist hedonism comes naturally to him.

After ten minutes, he pulls the truck to a halt. I look out but all I can see is what appears to be an animal-welfare facility—not that my German is very good, but the logo of a cat and dog give it away. I'm even more confused, but Cam's already hopped out of the vehicle to open my door. I slide from my seat in the cab and he helps me down, his lips still tight. At least the haunted look has disappeared from his eyes.

I follow him to the back of the truck. 'Where are we?'

He opens the rear doors and I get my first glimpse of our cargo—sack after sack of dog biscuits. 'Dog food?'

Cam nods with a smile, tossing one giant bag up onto his shoulder. 'Yep—enough to last them at least a year.' With his free hand he grasps mine and tugs me towards the entrance as if he can't wait to get inside.

I want to tell him he's the only billionaire I know to be this hands-on, that if he loves dogs this much he could buy the pound or become a lifetime sponsor, but since that first day in Monaco I've learned that the quickest way to shut Cam down is to mention his wealth.

'What about the rest? We're not emptying the entire truck ourselves, are we?'

He shoots me that indulgent smile, the one that tells me he thinks I'm a bit of a princess. 'No need—I'm donating the truck too. Come on.'

'Wait.' I can't have him thinking I'm too precious to get my hands dirty or break a nail. I hoist a bag of dog food from the back of the truck and lift it onto one shoulder, as he did.

He stares, his eyes full of something that looks like respect and the smouldering heat I'm used to seeing. 'Let's go.' I walk ahead of him towards the shelter, my back burning with the knowledge of how easy it is to impress Cam North.

We're greeted by the manager, a man named Klaus, who speaks perfect English as he thanks us for the generous donation. Cam places his sack of dog food down on the counter in the small foyer and I follow suit.

'Is it okay if we look around?' asks Cam, addressing Klaus.

'Of course,' says the manager, all smiles for his generous new benefactor. 'This way.'

We're led to the rear of the facility, following the sound of barking.

'All of the dogs here are up for adoption,' Klaus tells us. 'We usually rehome around ninety-five per cent of our dogs, but sadly, there are always one or two we find it impossible to place.'

Unease grips me, drying my mouth. Does Cam expect me to walk away from here with a new pet? Is that why he brought me here? I know I told him I had a soft spot for dogs, but that doesn't mean I want to own one. Panic settles in the pit of my stomach like a rock, even as my pulse flutters at the extreme sweetness of Cam's gesture. Once the door is open and I see those expectant canine eyes, it will be harder to stay strong.

I tug Cam to a standstill and speak to him in a hushed whisper. 'What are you doing? I can't adopt a dog. I told you my life is completely unsuitable for pet ownership.' My phone buzzes in my pocket but I ignore it. It's important Cam understands me, that my resolve is rock solid before Klaus opens that door and we're greeted with a hundred pairs of puppy eyes, including Cam's. This is why he's so irresistible, why I can never say no to him. He's full of contradictions— big and sexy and manly on the outside with a heart of gold and a massive soft spot for the underdog, human or four-legged.

He takes both my hands and squeezes my fingers. 'I know. I don't expect you to adopt one, although how awesome would that be?'

At my stunned silence he continues. 'You just said you liked dogs, so I thought it might be nice to hang out with a few for the afternoon. Pets are the perfect stress reliever.' He looks down at my pocket, where my phone is happily buzzing again.

My fingers, nestled in his, twitch to answer the phone, even as I acknowledge the thoughtfulness of his surprise and that it means for him we're not just having sex. He's listened to me. He remembers my favourite colour and the fact I miss owning a dog.

My throat grows tight at his show of consideration. When was the last time someone, anyone, did something like this for me? Something simple. Just because.

'I'm not stressed.' I flush hot with guilt. I sound ungrateful, but I'm too busy to be stressed. I think of the stack of work requiring my attention back at the hotel, my crack-of-dawn meeting tomorrow and the next month of travel, all to ensure my firm is the biggest, the best, and ticking along like clockwork.

Because *I* need to be the best? Because work is all I have?

I sigh—how can I be such a mess? A week ago I had everything sorted, my life engineered exactly the way I want it. What has changed?

Cam.

I know an afternoon off won't do me any harm. In fact, I know I'll feel refreshed and energised by his infectious energy. But at what cost? I shake my head, trying to assess why I'm overthinking this so endlessly, another new trait I seem to have acquired.

Cam clearly feels I need a little more persuading. 'Look, you work hard, and you said you can play hard, too. Isn't that why I'm here? Why you invited me along? So we could have a good time along the way? Will one afternoon off really make that much difference? I find it hard to believe your empire will crumble that easily— you're too good to allow that to happen.' His argument is a recurring one and he doesn't really need to coax me. He's right. This is what I wanted when I propositioned him. A distraction, a way to unleash my playful side. To find some balance. I'm worrying needlessly.

'We'll just stay an hour, and then I'll take you back to the hotel and run you a bath before the opera. What do you say? Will you come meet some Swiss dogs?'

My mouth twists as I attempt to hide my smile, my lips drawn back to his for another kiss I can't deny myself. He's so open, so generous, not just with money, but also with his time, his enthusiasm and the easy way he sucks every scrap of enjoyment from any activity, simple or grandiose. How can I refuse him?

'Okay.'

He blasts me with his dazzling smile, and we follow a patient Klaus to the kennels. The inhabitants of the shelter are so excited to see us, I'm immediately overcome with feel-good emotions, all thoughts of work forgotten.

We're taken to a large garden behind the shelter where we can throw balls for the dogs, who without exception seem to want nothing more than to be close to us. I know how they feel; I'm developing quite an attachment to Cam myself. I watch him use his superior athleticism and strength to toss the ball to the far corners of the garden, his T-shirt riding up as he throws to reveal a tantalising strip of skin that snares my attention.

There's a beagle cross that seems to feel a particular affinity for me, returning time after time to my side and obediently dropping the ball and sitting, patiently waiting for me to throw it again. I stroke the dog's silky head, an uninhibited giggle bubbling up. Funny how you don't realise the toll something takes until you're forced to stop and pay attention. Perhaps I am stressed. Perhaps the burn-out feeling I had in Monaco wasn't temporary. Perhaps that's why the triumph over my father doesn't taste quite as sweet as I'd expected.

I glance over at Cam, who is with Klaus examining some partially constructed storage sheds along the far wall. He gestures to the other man, pointing at the roofline and indicating for a hammer left on the ground by the builders.

Before I know what's happening, he's knocked out some sort of upright and is repositioning the wood with the absolute authority of a man who knows what he's talking about. I take a seat at a rickety table and chairs and relax back to watch the Cam show. He wields the tools with proficiency, but what did I expect? He tackles everything that way. Confident, taking control, but with enough humility he's in no way arrogant. I watch the way his back, shoulder and arm muscles move and bulge while he works, my eyes glued to his spectacular physique.

In some ways he's a conundrum, in others an uncomplicated man—no agenda, what you see is what you get.

What am I doing with him and why do I feel as if I'm in over my head when this was my idea?

My phone pings for the umpteenth time and I pull it from my pocket with a sigh of regret that I have to look away from Cam's sexy show-and-tell.

It's from my number two back in Sydney. I quickly scan the message, my equilibrium returning at the good news. The lawyers have finished with the paperwork, and the Jensen's deal snatched from under the nose of my father has hit the international financial headlines, the ripple effect so predictable, I can almost see the zeroes at the end of my net worth multiplying. The kick of satisfaction I always feel at a job well done is there, but today it's muted, its potency somehow diminished, as if making money, being the best, proving I, a mere woman, can do anything my brother and father can, no longer holds the same all-consuming appeal.

Perhaps the news would taste sweeter if shared. Perhaps the shine of my success would return if I had some of Cam's balance. Perhaps he's right about me, after all—I don't know how to have fun…

My head jerks up from the screen of my phone in search of him, my good-luck charm. He's striding my way with a Jack Russell in tow. The dog has abandoned the ball and seems content to simply follow him to the ends of the earth.

I swallow hard. I know that feeling. It's the same feeling—dangerous and terrifying—that I get when I open my eyes and find him asleep next to me in the morning.

Cam sits opposite me at the rough wooden table and the dog settles at his feet. 'I'm sorry I'm neglecting you. I got carried away. Some cowboy builder has left the sheds half built and they're not sure if he's going to come back to finish them.' He spots my phone. 'Is it work? Do you need me to take you back into the city?'

I shove my phone away and try not to focus on the attention Cam lavishes on the delighted Jack Russell's ear rub.

Nice one, Orla. Jealous of a dog.

'No, I'm sorry—breaking news in the financial world—money never sleeps.' My attempt at humour, designed to cover my embarrassment that I can't even enjoy half an hour off to be in the moment, falls flat and a chasm opens up between us across the scarred and weathered tabletop.

His quiet scrutiny makes me wince, not that he's judging, but I see acute awareness in his intelligent eyes. He sees me all too thoroughly. And even before he asks, I know his question is coming.

'Can I ask you a personal question? I know we've avoided too many details up to now, but I'm…curious.'

As if sensing the tension radiating from us, my own new doggy friend curls up against my foot and promptly closes her eyes, as if all she's needed this whole time was a warm leg to lean up against while she sleeps.

'Sure, although I reserve the right to not answer.' I keep my voice light-hearted, although my tummy is tight with nerves for what he might ask and, worse, for what I might expose.

One of his big hands stretches across the table and covers my hand, his thumb rubbing back and forth over my knuckles, and I want to curl into him and admit that, just like these dogs, I'm a little lost and in need of a new direction.

But he's not my rock. I don't need a rock. He's not even my boyfriend. I'm just using him for sex.

I shudder inside—I can almost see the grins on the faces of my married girlfriends, hear the cackles of excitement over cocktails and the names they would bandy about if they could see me now—*toy boy, man toy, cougar.* A protective streak slices through me, even as the words *it's not like that* ring hollow in my head. Because it *is* like that—that's what I wanted. Sex on tap. No feelings. No personal details. No consequences.

Was I naive, or just deluding myself, because sex, even sex as hot and liberating as the sex I share with Cam, is bound to come with consequences? And they've already begun. I feel it. He's changing me. Just by knowing him I'm different, more open to new experiences, wanting to challenge myself and emulate the person I'm beginning to admire.

'I just wondered why.' Cam's voice is low, gentle,

as if he doesn't want to spook the slumbering dogs. Or perhaps he's worried about spooking me.

'Why what?'

'Why you work so hard. Why you put in the hours you do. The travel, the lack of sleep. I…' He looks down at the table as if embarrassed. 'I looked you up on the internet. I wanted to know more about you without prying into personal stuff.'

'And what did you discover?' I've been tempted to do the same myself and research him, only every time I open my laptop, work snatches my attention.

'That you're worth a fortune. That you probably don't need to work ever again,' he says.

'Just like you, then.' I wince, scrunch my eyes closed for a second to block out the wounded look on his face, because I already know that was a low blow. He told me it was complicated. He told me his inheritance came with conditions and I know he's come from a very different background.

'Sorry. I didn't mean that.' I try to lift the atmosphere I've created with levity. 'I was kind of hoping you hadn't noticed that I get up in the early hours to work.' I stroke the dog's silky head as I formulate my answer, because for once it doesn't come easily. Cam wants the real answer, not the throwaway flippant version that rolls off the tongue.

No, it's not a crime to be driven. But that's not what he's asking. He wants to know the motivation behind my success beyond wealth and status and security, and that's harder to define or admit, especially when examining too closely what pushes me to be where I am brings up painful emotions.

'I've always worked hard, just like you.' I turn his hand over and rub at the calluses across his palm. He looks up from our hands, answering my smile with a watery one of his own.

He wants more. And, while it's not what we're about, I can't help but give him a piece of myself I don't normally share. With anyone. He's given me so much— his time, his generosity, his joie de vivre. It's as if his energy is contagious.

'When I joined my father's firm after university I felt like I'd found my niche. The work was exciting and everything I wanted in a career, but it was never about the money. I was lucky. I've always had a privileged life. But my father is old school. When he talked about succession planning I felt confident I'd be the next CEO. I'm the eldest. I worked hard for him for five years.'

I look away, watch the dogs roam and sniff, the remembered betrayal tightening my throat. 'When he overlooked me in favour of my younger brother I realised I had no choice but to leave and start my own firm from scratch. Ever since then, I've put in the hours, but the difference is I'm doing it for myself.'

It sounds so shallow, so single-minded, that a new wave of defensiveness courses though me, although he's in no way attacking, just asking in his gentle, insightful way. But I rear back from the vulnerable place I've exposed with my confession, bringing my motivations back to general rather than personal drivers. 'And it's a competitive field—I didn't get to the top without work-ing harder and longer than anyone else.' I shrug. 'Some sacrifices are inevitable.'

He nods, his mouth a flat line, and even though he's still I sense the tension coiling in him. His thumb re-sumes its hypnotic swiping. 'You mentioned you're di-vorced. Was your marriage one of those sacrifices?' There's no censure in his expression, but his eyes are hard and the reminder of my failure forces heat to my face.

'For my part, I rushed into that marriage without loving Mark. For his part, Mark thought he was fully evolved, but at the end of the day he didn't want a wife who worked as much as he did, and I can't say I blame him. I guess he expected I'd change after the honey-moon. Perhaps he wanted his shirts laundered and a prop on his arm to make him look good.'

'Don't you know? Didn't you ask?'

I swallow hard, admitting, not for the first time, that my emotional distance, a trait I learned from a lifetime of trying to meet my father's standards, likely contrib-uted to the breakdown of my marriage. 'No, I guess I wasn't any good at being the kind of wife he needed.'

Cam's fingers flex into mine in silent support. 'Couldn't he launder his own shirts?'

I shrug and laugh at the image of my ex working a washing machine or an iron. 'He's happily remarried now.' I swallow hard, old bitterness foul-tasting. Per-haps if I hadn't been so caught up in proving my worth to my father, in trying to project an image of having it all, I might have evaluated my relationship with Mark more thoroughly. 'I'm happy with my decision. He's happier married to someone else. And I learned a valuable lesson—I'm good at what I do. That's nothing to be apologetic for.'

'Absolutely not. Mark sounds like an asshole who didn't know what he had, if you don't mind my saying.' He smiles that secret smile he uses in the bedroom, the one that makes me forget I'm older than him.

'Thanks, but I played my part. I'm sure I wasn't easy to be married to. You said yourself, I'm always working.'

He shakes his head. 'You're not working now, and it sounds like he had expectations you had no desire to fulfil—good on you. You're a person, not a puppet. No one likes to feel they're being controlled.' He's more animated now, his eyes ablaze with defiance, as if my confession has pricked some wound inside him. Easygoing, carefree Cam has his own demons.

Who doesn't?

'You were probably that way when he met you, right?'

I nod.

'So he was arrogant enough to want to change you, to squeeze you into some mould, to try to make you perform to his expectations.'

'I guess, although I have to take my share of the responsibility—I'm pretty stubborn. As you've witnessed, I push myself hard, without compromise, something I learned from my upbringing. And at the end of the day, marriages—the ones that last—are about compromise. I guess Mark and I both failed. If you know anything about me already, it's that failure doesn't sit well with me, which is why I'm single. That's why what we're doing suits me perfectly—we get all the good bits of a relationship like spending time together, having fun, amazing sex, without all the heavy stuff.'

'Lucky me,' he says with a wink, and I know he's letting me off the hook. That my confession is enough to satisfy his curiosity about the woman he's sharing a bed with, for now.

'Lucky me, too.' I look down at our hands, moved by his solid, refreshing presence in my life, albeit temporarily. I want him to know that I appreciate him and everything he does to enrich our time together, even if I'm not always present in the moment.

'Thanks for this. The dogs. For taking the time to organise everything—the clothes, the opera, the skiing.'

'Wait until you see what I have planned for Dubai.' He winks.

'I'm serious, Cam—thanks for bringing me here. You were right. It was just what I needed.' I bend down to stroke the coat of the sleeping beagle cross, wishing I could take her home, to a home I'm hardly ever at myself.

'Want to go back to the hotel and remind ourselves how clever we are to have come up with such a perfect situation?' I ask, shying away from pressing him for his own secrets, telling myself that, despite my confession, this is still about sex.

'Absolutely. Sounds like the next best plan short of adopting all these dogs and transporting them home to Sydney in the jet.' He grins and tugs me to my feet, slipping his hand into the pocket over my ass as we head inside, a trail of dogs in pursuit.

I laugh nervously. Knowing Cam, he just might do something that awesome.

CHAPTER SIX

Cam

I LOOSEN THE bow tie around my throat and roll up my shirtsleeves. I went all out tonight with the full tux. For Orla. I reserved the M Club box at the Zurich Opera House, and just as I predicted she looked sensational in the green beaded gown, so I felt compelled to play my part, even if it meant dressing like a trussed-up penguin.

I pour a glass of chilled white wine and loosen the top few buttons of my shirt, tempted to strip off completely and join her in the bath. But she looks beat. Perhaps I'm pushing the after-work agenda too hard. Now I understand why she's as driven as she is, everything makes sense. She pushes herself, almost as if she still has something to prove to her traditional father and perhaps even her ex-husband. Neither of whom seem to have any concept of her true worth.

She made light of it but she's proud. I understand the emotion. Her failed marriage bothers her, not for the man himself, but in the sense that she sees it as a black mark on her track record, perhaps even uses it as a reason to avoid getting involved in another relationship.

Not that I should care outside of the fact some asshole might have hurt her, although it seems I need look no further than her own father to find the source of *that* damage. Who behaves that way in this day and age? Fuck, I thought my father was bad, but at least he simply took off. At least he didn't stick around to inflict daily damage on my self-esteem. At least I don't have to prove a damn thing to the man.

Of course she's driven by success, of course she needs the success. Somehow it's all tied up in her self-validation. But to what degree? Could she loosen the reins, live a more balanced life and still be herself?

I scrub a hand through my hair, gutted that my instincts about her, about our differences, were spot-on the money. I proved myself correct at the dog sanctuary. I'd expected her to be more delighted. Of course, she embraced the visit, even hefting in a sack of dog food like it weighed no more than the designer handbags she loves. But I spied the sneaky looks at her phone, the way she checked her watch as if she had somewhere else to be. She couldn't relax, couldn't take off her CEO hat for even a couple of hours.

Not that it should matter. I should focus on the end game, focus on the trip we're taking together, focus on having a good time at my father's expense. Isn't that why I agreed to come along for the ride?

But my aimless bender no longer holds the same appeal, not now I've met Orla.

I snag a beer for myself and return to the bathroom with her glass of wine, my own personal dilemmas tucked neatly away behind my smile. Orla looks more relaxed than I've ever seen her, and I suffer a sharp pang of regret at how hard I pushed her to divulge personal details earlier, especially when I'm such a closed book, literally changing the subject every time she probes a bit too close.

I place the glass on the side of the bath and pull up a chair, taking a long draw of my ice-cold beer.

'Cam, stop spoiling me. I might get used to it and chain you to my bedpost.'

I grin—I wouldn't put it past her. At least we work sexually. No problems on that score.

'I wouldn't complain, as long as I get to see this sensational body naked every day.'

Without moving from her relaxed wallow, she holds out her hand for my beer. I hand it over, my eyebrows raised in mock censure. She's taken to stealing a sip every time I open a bottle.

'What?' she asks, tilting the bottle to her pursed lips for a swallow. 'I'm just trying them out until I find one I love. Don't be stingy.' She takes a second swallow and hands the beer back with a contented sigh.

I grin, my insides on fire for her and the way she makes me feel, like the best version of myself. 'I don't care. You can drink all my beer. It's just...funny.' Funny, sexy, comfortable. 'Who'd have thought when we met in that casino that the stunning, classy woman drinking single malt alone would like a regular old beer in the bath?'

'You should never judge a book by its cover, Cam. Haven't I proved there's more to me than the uptight princess I know you had me pegged for the first time we met?'

I laugh, heat for her burning out of control. She gets me as much as I get her. I want to be a better man when I'm around her. I want us to fit outside the bedroom. But could we? Seriously?

I place the beer bottle on the floor. 'Drink your wine, princess.' I wink, trailing one hand along her soapy thigh, down her slender calf. At her soft sigh, I lift her foot from below the surface of the water so I can press my thumbs into the sole of her foot, one after another in a slow, rhythmic massage, because I want to touch her. All the time.

Her head lolls back on the edge of the bath, and her toes curl. 'Mmm…you are so good at that—another skill to add to the list. Is there nothing you can't do?' she says without opening her eyes.

'I feel the same way about you.' Having her by my side, persuading her to travel in style and play hard, and the way she's embracing the sexual adventure too—we understand each other. Just her presence makes me feel like I'll figure out my own dilemma over the money. Like it's not as big a deal as I'd fanned it up to be. Like anything is possible.

The pretty constant resentment and bitterness I've

had since the summons to the solicitor's office back in Sydney wanes. If only I could bottle the Orla feeling.

'A good foot massage will help you sleep,' I say, my mouth twitching because I know as soon as she leaves this bath I'm getting lucky, despite her long day. When we returned from the dog shelter she was visibly deflated to find all the purchases I'd made, including the intimate M Club gift, cleared away, out of sight. She mentioned twice at the opera that I'd promised her a reward for her patience. She's so fully embracing her sexually adventurous side; I wanted to strip her there and then. But I promised her a night at the opera and a relaxing bath, and I'm a man of my word.

She looks up, her eyelids heavy but in that turned-on way that tells me she has other plans before sleep. 'What if I'm not tired? What if I feel like squeezing a little more enjoyment out of the day?'

I hide my smile. I've created a monster.

'I thought you'd rescheduled your meeting for seven a.m. I don't want you to be too exhausted to enjoy the slopes tomorrow.'

'Cam…' Her eyes stray closed as if she's enjoying my foot massage, but there's a hint of warning in her voice. 'You'll be using that vibrator on me before we sleep. No getting out of it. Or I'll use it myself and force you to watch.'

'Yes, ma'am,' I say. 'Such hardships I have to endure as your plaything…' I release her foot and lift the other one from the water, subjecting it to the same treatment.

After a few seconds she reopens her eyes, which had fluttered closed on a contented moan the minute I pressed my thumbs to her instep.

'Cam?'

'Yes, Orla.'

'Have *you* ever been in a serious relationship?' She takes a sip of wine and watches my face from over the rim of her glass. This is payback for my bout of curiosity earlier. But I couldn't stay silent any longer. She works practically twenty-four-seven. Her travel schedule is punishing—I know she's allowed me to add a few days here and there for extras, but what's the point of visiting all these countries if you're too busy to enjoy what they have to offer? What's the point of earning the kind of money she makes when she's never in one place long enough to spend any of it?

I allow her foot to sink back below the surface of the water and reach for a sponge and a bottle of body wash. 'Not really. I've had girlfriends off and on. But I'm in no hurry to settle down.'

'So you've never been in love, then? Never met your perfect woman?' With any other woman I'd assume she was fishing. But not Orla. She's made it clear she's done the marriage thing. Done it and failed. Effectively crossed it off her list.

'Not sure I believe in love—I watched it all but destroy my mother, so, like you, I'm pretty sceptical.'

Her smile is small, her eyes searching. 'See—I told you we're perfect for each other.'

Yeah, perfect but temporary. The clock is ticking

on our arrangement. By the time we reach Sydney I need to have some sort of definitive plan outside of using our sexual relationship to help me forget, because going back to pretending the inheritance doesn't exist isn't an option and spending it will take three lifetimes…

Orla sobers, her eyes searching. 'What happened with your parents?' Her voice is low, whispered, as if I'm already giving off an injured-animal vibe.

I suck in a deep breath and stand, moving behind her to slide the soapy sponge over her shoulders and the back of her neck, which is exposed, her hair piled up in a messy topknot.

I'm literally hiding, but I need cover. Talking about my mother, the grief and anger when I think about how she pined for my father, still tightens my throat so I feel like I can't breathe.

'My father left her for greener pastures. I was three.'

I hear her gasp, but I ignore it and slide the sponge around first to her clavicle and the top of her breast, and then I sweep it down one arm.

When I reach the back of her hand with the sponge she grips my fingers, squeezing. She's silent for a beat or two and I think I'm out of the woods. No such luck.

'That must have been really hard on her. And you.'

'Not really. I don't remember him ever being there.'

She releases my hand, as if she can sense my discomfort. It's hard to feel her touch, something I associate only with pleasure, and think about the worst parts of my past in the same heartbeat.

'Was it another woman?' she asks.

I really want to distract her, to drag her from the bath and make her forget her inquisitiveness, pleasure her into silence. But she's relaxed, and she deserves some answers after my days of vagueness, hedging and changing the subject.

'No—he remarried eventually, but money was his mistress. He bought a tech company at the right time, invested heavily and got lucky, making lots of what he loved—money. And, as you know, money makes money.' I sigh, my anguish over his last will and testament undoing what an evening with Orla had accomplished. 'At the end of the day he loved money more than he loved his wife and kid.'

'Did your mother remarry? Did you have a stepfather? You talked about how the drumming helping you through your teens.'

'No. It was just the two of us.' My answer sounds harsh, echoing around the tiled room. But further explanation sticks in my throat. Does she really want details? Is she truly longing to hear that my mother worked two jobs to make sure I was fed? That she pawned her wedding ring to buy me my first bike? That she never stopped loving a man who chose the pursuit of wealth over her, so much so that she never once chased him for a single cent towards raising me?

As if sensing the rage building inside me, coiling my muscles to snapping point, she doesn't press for more details. 'Well, she raised a fine man in you. Are you still close to her?'

'She died a year ago. Cancer.' I deflate. What is the point of harbouring hatred for a man when they're both gone? What's the point of my regret? It won't bring either of them back—him so I can toss his damned money back in his face and her so I can try to convince her he wasn't worth her love.

'I'm sorry,' whispers Orla.

I've stopped washing her, too caught up in useless emotions. I move around to the other side of the bath, performing the same moves with the sponge down the opposite arm. But now she's probed, the words come a little easier. 'To that day I think she still loved him. That's why I can never forgive him.'

'I don't blame you—it must have been very hard for you to watch. Hard for you to grow up without a father. I'm so sorry to hear about your mother, Cam.' This time when she grips my hand she tugs me forward and sits up in the bath, so I have to slap on a mask to hide the resurgence of resentment from my face.

'You know, it's not the same, but my father was pretty absent too. He worked long hours, and even when he was home he never seemed interested in me, what I'd done at school or that I'd passed a piano exam or joined the school choir.' She laughs, a humourless snort. 'He always made time for my brother's sporting events though. Funny, that.'

We stare, fragile threads of memories and the emotions they bring connecting us.

'Have you told your father that you feel that he wasn't

there for you growing up?' she says, her voice barely above a whisper.

Every muscle in my body tightens. Even if I could reach out, there's no room in me for forgiveness. Not for what he did to my mother, or for how he tried to control me from the grave with his beloved money.

'Have you told yours?' I say, the venom in my voice shocking us both.

She looks down and I swear under my breath, tilting her chin back up so she can see the sincerity of my apology. 'I'm sorry. Look... I...I never really cared that he wasn't around for myself. If my mother had been happy, I doubt I'd have given him a second thought.'

Ah, the lies we tell ourselves...

I focus my anger. 'He treated my mother worse. And anyway, it's all in the past. He's dead too. Six months after her—ironic, right?' I take a deep breath, too close to every feeling I've battled to contain these past six months—my entire adult life, if I'm being honest. And, despite her relationship with her own emotionally distant father, we're different enough without my tales of woe, my sad little poor-boy-turned-billionaire sob-story.

Her intelligent eyes latch on to mine. 'Is the inheritance from—'

I cover her mouth with my fingers. 'Enough.' Of course she would make the leap. She's smart. But I don't want to talk about my father's legacy. The legacy I'm working day and night to forget because of what it represents.

'I thought we were keeping the details out of this—just sex…?' The words taste jagged because I'm a hypocrite. I care about her—why else would I take her to see rescue dogs, worry about her burning herself out with work and lavish her with gifts? Because I like the way she looks in green? Because I enjoy seeing her sensational figure clothed in everything from a simple T-shirt to the sexiest lingerie?

But caring isn't allowed. More than sex is a fool's game. She knows that and so do I.

My own reminder of our boundaries helps me back to safety. This is sex. No matter how she makes me feel, or how much I enjoy her company outside of the bedroom. No matter how her stare seems to penetrate, her intelligent eyes stripping me bare. I'm here for one reason only—enjoyment. Well, two if you count my own personal goal to spend as much money as I can, a goal on which I should refocus my attention and forget about crazy ideas like testing Orla's suitability as a potential partner. Because she's not mine. She's not interested in anything beyond the good time we have together.

It's a dream scenario for any guy…

'Ready to get out?' I ask, because she wants this to be about sex—on-tap sex—and right now that's the only thing that will chase away my demons.

At her nod, I tug her hand and she rises from the water, rivulets of foam sliding over her perfect skin. She meets my eyes and I see empathy in the depths of her stare. She knows I'm hiding something bigger than me. She knows I'm a coward, but she sticks to our nothing-personal rule and offers me an out clause.

My hand still holds the sponge. She guides me to wash her breasts and her stomach, only releasing my hand when she's pressed it between her legs so she can grip both my shoulders while she rides my hand and the sponge with undulations of her hips.

'Cam,' she whispers, her eyes on mine. 'Let's get lost together.'

I don't need a second invitation. I toss the sponge and lift her from the bath, snagging a towel on my way out of the bathroom. In the bedroom I deposit her on her feet and slide the towel over every inch of her skin until she's dry, by which time my erection is painfully hard and straining behind my fly. But I don't touch her, nor do I give her my mouth, which is what she wants, her head lifting to mine every time I move close, her lips seeking the kisses that make her moan.

I hold my own body taut to prevent me from swaying her way. I've got this. I'm here for the sex. I can control the sex. She likes being nudged to explore her sexual boundaries, but beyond that…

There is no beyond.

'Go to the wardrobe and get the M Club box,' I say, my voice tight with longing. Yes, the urge to be close to her, to be buried inside, to kiss her into silence, is as strong as ever, but there's a new driving force in me tonight. A dangerous force—to be more to her than her sex toy. To gain her trust, to hear her acknowledgement that I'm not like the men of her past, men who've betrayed her, underestimated her, overlooked her. That I'm different.

I swallow hard. It's just sex. That's all she wants from me.

Her eyes flare with excitement and she sashays to the wardrobe, loosening her hair from its messy bun as she goes. I'm momentarily lost in the sight of the sway of her heart-shaped ass, but then she's back before me, a sexy smile of challenge on her face. 'Now what?'

I take the box. 'Lie on the bed.'

She obeys, her movements slow and sensual as if she wants to put on a show for my eyes only. As if she knows she's driving me mad, pushing me every inch as far as I push her. Because she's right. Maybe we do both need to get lost, and this is the best way.

With hands that could tremble from the adrenaline surging in me, if I wasn't wound so tightly, I deposit the box beside her feet and strip my shirt overhead, tossing it onto a nearby chair. Her teeth scrape over her bottom lip and her eyes follow my every move. I retrieve a bottle of lube, watching every subtle nuance of her reaction when she sees what it is.

She's excited, her chest rising and falling rapidly, and like the impatient, self-sufficient woman she is, not content to wait, she slips her hand between her thighs to touch herself.

I place the lube next to the box and take off my dress trousers and boxers, my eyes glued to her hand working her clit. 'Don't come. Not yet.' I stand over her, scooping her head up from the bed by the back of her neck so

I can angle her mouth up to mine. I kiss her until we're both panting and then I break free.

'Fuck, you're so sexy. I want to take you to a place no one else has. I want you to remember me, just like, when this is over, I'll never forget you.'

I have no idea where that comes from, but I accept its truth. It's too late to take it back anyway.

'Yes. Cam, yes.'

So she feels it too, that we're skirting dangerous territory. That, if we're not careful, our feelings could become all snared up in this thing we've started. But neither of us has room in our lives for that complication.

I flip the box open and reach inside for the vibrator. 'Tell me to stop if this gets too intense, okay?' I flick the hidden switch so the device emits a barely audible hum. 'Lie back.'

She listens, abandoning pleasuring herself to sprawl back on the satin bedspread with her arms slung casually over her head.

Perfect.

Splayed out for our pleasure.

I lean over and kiss her, my tongue duelling with the push and slide of hers until she's panting and writhing once more. Then I touch the tip of the vibrator to one of her nipples. She arches off the bed, a ragged moan torn from her throat. I break free from the kiss to watch my handiwork, sliding the toy to the other nipple in order to drag out another whimper.

'Open your mouth.' I trail the black phallus over the

curve of her breast and along her breastbone. Her lips part and I slide the tip past to her waiting tongue, which she laves seductively over the toy before wrapping her mouth around the shaft.

The sight is so erotic, I take my cock in my free hand, offering it a few lazy tugs in appeasement for the torture I'm putting us through. Orla watches me, her eyes widening, but then she abandons the toy and reaches for my hips, tugging me forward and over her so she can take the head of my cock into her mouth in place of the vibrator.

I grit my teeth, grunt a few unintelligible curses and then slide the now wet toy back to her nipple. But I'm done teasing us. With a groan of protest I pull back and position myself between her thighs. I lap at her clit, sliding the vibrating toy up and down her inner thigh as I do to stimulate as many nerves as I can.

Orla grips my head, her fingers twisting and tugging. I keep the suction on her clit slow and subtle while I work the head of the sex toy inside her tight pussy, plunging and mimicking what my own body is desperate to do. But not yet. I have plans. Plans I hope will lead us one step closer to our end goal.

While I keep up the tonguing of her clit, I discard the vibrator and reach for the lube and butt plug.

Sensing my movements, Orla lifts her head from the bed and looks down.

I pull back, needing to hear her confirmation. 'Do you still want this?'

'Yes.' No hesitation, just a blaze of challenge burning through the desire in her beautiful green eyes.

'Do you trust me?' I'm a fool, I know, but her answer matters more than just physical oblivion.

'Yes, oh, Cam, yes.'

I slide my tongue over her opening back to the tight bud while I slather the plug with lube. But Orla's not content to lie back and simply feel. She settles on her elbows and watches me, her mewls and moans of encouragement a guide to her pleasure.

When her hips begin to buck and her hands grow greedy, tugging on my hair as she rides my face, I press the tip of the plug to her rear. It's small and she's so close, it slides in with minimal resistance, but her moans grow to cries of pleasure and my beautiful, sexy Orla starts to chant my name like a prayer, filling my head and my chest and the parts of me that want more than her body with euphoria.

I keep up the suction on her clit, adding slow twists of the plug, while I watch her face with rapt attention, seeing every streak of pleasure. That she trusts me with her body, with her act of sexual exploration, resets my priorities. I can be myself with her; like this we're just a man and a woman enjoying our near violent chemistry.

No amount of money, extravagant spending or working can re-create this feeling. This is real.

She may have had her fingers burnt in the past, she may not want a relationship, but now she's embracing her sexy side. Hell, I've lost count of who's challenging whom here, because she's almost more woman than I can handle.

With one last twist, one last flick of her clit, she comes, her neck arched back on a long cry that I'm worried will cause complaints. But then I'm past caring because she collapses back onto the bed, tugging me down on top of her and spreading her legs wide to accommodate my hips. She holds my face between both palms, pressing kisses to my mouth as I hold my weight on my arms, braced over her.

'Thank you.'

I smile. 'What for?'

'You know what for. That was…oh…incredible.'

My ego inflates. I press a gentle kiss on her lips, overcome by tenderness for this dauntless, exceptional woman. She lifts her legs and crosses her ankles in the small of my back, her eyes widening with renewed sensations as she moves with the plug in situ.

The tip of my cock slides between her lips and I wince at the sharp burst of pleasure. 'Want me to take it out?'

She shakes her head and tilts her hips so I'm engulfed in her heat. 'No. I want you, Cam, now.'

I roll my hips forward, working my way inside, the tightness enough to make my eyes roll back, but I find her slick, swollen clit with my thumb and rub out any discomfort she might feel at the dual penetration.

'You okay?' I bite out, taking it as slowly as humanly possible. And I am only human, never more so than when I'm with this woman, who makes me feel exposed, and vulnerable, and ten feet tall all in the same heartbeat.

'Yes, better than okay. You?'

I groan against the side of her neck, placing a tender kiss there where her skin smells fantastic—pure Orla. 'You have no idea.'

She presses her mouth to mine, a strange intensity on her face, and she doesn't stop kissing me until we come, me seconds after her, wondering how in the world I'm ever going to get enough of Orla Hendricks.

CHAPTER SEVEN

Orla

I LOOK AWAY from the view of the Persian Gulf from my office window in Dubai's International Financial Centre and try to refocus on the business proposal on the computer screen when all I can see is Cam's face, his sexy, playful grin and his sparkly eyes, which always seem alight with animation.

Somewhere between leaving Zurich after our thrilling heli-skiing trip and arriving in Dubai, I've experienced a seismic shift—I can't seem to get Cam off my mind, as my current daydream proves. It's almost as if my mind is sick of numbers and craves the intrusion. As if he's there because he belongs. Because I want his presence in more than my bed. But that's crazy...

Is it because he finally opened up to me, telling me about his loss and his childhood, which must have been far removed from my own? Is it because seeing his pain, filling in the gaps, makes me desperate to help him overcome the issues holding him back? I'm certain it was his father who left him the inheritance. The timeline fits, and the fact that he doesn't seem to care if he loses every cent. That money represents more than a life-changing windfall. For him, it's tainted, tangled up in rejection and pain and resentment. Even when he seems to be enjoying it, living a lifestyle most people would jump at in a heartbeat, deep down I'm certain Cam would be equally happy to return to his life before.

Cam's in pain. He's hurting. The big-spending gambler I first met is far removed from the real Cam North. The real Cam gives a wicked foot massage. The real Cam takes the time to talk and, more importantly, to really listen. The real Cam is a roll-up-your-sleeves kind of man: a man who loves the simple things in life— an ice-cold beer on a sunny day, a view of the sunset, throwing a ball for a delighted dog.

As fascinating and addictive as he is complex.

I push away from my desk in self-disgust, admitting my productivity is done for the day, and head to the hotel for a shower. As I turn on the water, tie up my hair and strip off, I berate myself further. It's one thing to care about the wonderful, thoughtful and capable man I'm sleeping with—after all, I'm not a robot, despite what my ex-husband thinks—but to allow it to interfere with my work?

I've never once struggled with focus before, so why now? And why to this degree? There could be any number of explanations: jet lag, too much of what Cam likes to call *playing hard*, the pesky burn-out, which seems to be getting stronger, not lessening as I'd hoped.

But I suspect it's just Cam. Clearly I underestimated

how much of a distraction a man like him could be—stupid, stupid Orla.

Thinking about him has an inevitable effect on my body and I turn the water to cool to douse the reaction. Perhaps there's such a thing as too much sex? If we're not screwing, which is at least a twice-a-day occurrence, we're teasing each other, whispering, sharing stolen secret glances, a torturous form of foreplay.

I step under the spray and lather my body with divine-smelling body wash. If only I could wash my confused and intrusive feelings away with the suds. Because they have no place here. This was never for keeps. Thanks to my father, my ex and my own high expectations, I'm just not emotionally built for relationships.

Why is this so hard, when I've never before struggled to compartmentalise sex? I can blame physical exhaustion. Between my own punishing schedule, the inability to keep our hands off each other and always exploring somewhere Cam deems essential, it's no wonder I can't think straight.

The last few days have been a whirlwind. An ice bar on our last night in Zurich, dinner last night on the one hundred and twentieth floor of the Burj Khalifa, the world's tallest tower, and, as today is opening day at the Meydan racecourse, we're due to spend an evening at the races.

Despite my cold-shower distraction technique, waves of anticipation move over my skin—he'll be here any minute. It's as if my body has a sixth sense: Cam detection. Perhaps he'll look for me and join me in the shower. But even as I feel the flutter of excitement low in my belly, I probe my feelings deeper. Yes, the sex is amazing. Yes, he brings out some sort of lust-craved wanton in me—who could resist such virile and enthusiastic attention? But he's more than that; he puts my life into perspective. When I'm with him I almost forget that I'm Orla Hendricks, CEO. The bitterness I feel towards my father seems irrelevant and trivial. I don't care about proving myself worthy. I don't care about being the best. I can simply exist. No need to strive to be anything other than myself.

A woman to his man.

My sigh is shaky, tinged with fear.

Oh, no… No, I can't do this. I can't feel the things I'm feeling. Not for him, not for anyone. I swallow, forcing myself to be brutally honest. Despite the age gap and my determination to avoid relationships, Cam is exactly the sort of man I could fall for, and that's bad.

B.A.D.

I freeze, the realisation of how dangerous Cam is to my resolve a shock, as if the water had turned instantly icy. Then I laugh aloud, although the sound is hollow and unconvincing. We're too different. Cam would no more think of me as a relationship candidate than I would think of him, in our normal, everyday lives. He's twenty-eight years old. I'll be thirty-seven in a few months.

It's ridiculous.

Even if I *wanted* a relationship, we'd never work. Deep down he's a solid, steady, dependable man who says it like it is. I'm a hustler. I always need to be moving, striving, ticking off the next goal.

I try to visualise introducing Cam to my Sydney girlfriends over brunch, or picture him being content to see his woman once in a blue moon, if the stars align. My washing movements become slow, automatic, as I'm lost to the pictures my imaginings paint, as if they're tantalising in their reality. I've never asked him, but surely Cam wants a wife and a family one day. I've long since sworn off such trappings, finding contentment in the one thing I'm good at: my career, making money for my clients and for myself along the way.

But is that enough any more? Can I go back to my sad, workaholic existence after Cam?

I slam off the shower spray, my irritation directed at my flights of fancy.

Of course I can. I'm set in my ways. This is my life, a great life I've built—self-sufficient, independent, successful. I'll move on from my fling with Cam, just as I moved on from my marriage to Mark.

With my equilibrium restored by my harsh mental pep talk, I dry off and put on the modest green silk dress with buttons down the front that I've chosen for the races. I apply light make-up and slip on nude strappy sandals with a low heel.

When I emerge from the en suite bathroom, Cam is sprawled over the leather sofa near the window. I come to an abrupt halt, my eyes sucking in the sight of him, as if they know time is running out and one day he'll only be visible in my memory.

He too is dressed in smart-casual attire for the races—chinos, a shirt and tie, and a blazer. His hair is tamed, slicked back from his handsome face with product, and he's focused on the screen of his phone, his brows dipped in an act of concentration that should make him look adorable, if he wasn't too much man for that particular adjective.

My stomach clenches at the sight of him, sexy, suave and in his prime, the epitome of masculinity. I tug my bottom lip under my teeth and close my eyes for a decadent second, remembering the way he woke me this morning before my alarm. Sleepy, warm and demanding, he'd dragged me close with one strong arm, spooning me from behind. As I nodded and smiled in agreement, his hot mouth had found my nipple and I'd arched against him until he'd seated himself inside me from behind—a perfect position for Cam to toy with my clit until I climaxed and he'd achieved the unforgettable wake-up call he'd wanted.

For some reason I kept my eyes closed throughout, and we didn't speak, because it somehow felt different—slow, sensual, reverent—almost as if we were making love.

I shake the alarming thought from my head and clear my throat to alert Cam to my presence.

He looks up. A grin stretches over his face, but his eyes are hot, just like every other time he looks at me: full of promise, provocative, and deeply piercing, as if he sees me to my soul.

I approach, my legs shakier than they should be,

given the stern lecture I'd only moments ago adminis-
tered to myself. Cam stands, the perfect gentleman. I
accept his hungry kiss, returning it with my own. It's
as if we've been separated for years, not hours, but with
his mouth on mine it's hard to overthink, so I simply
surrender to the moment.

When we part, the exposed, unfocused feeling I've
experienced for the past few days intensifies, so I reach
for his phone to distract myself.

'What has you so absorbed that you didn't hear me
come in?' I expect to find a list of statistics for today's
thoroughbreds, but instead I see pictures of a shabby-
looking cottage, the paint peeling, the steel roof warped
and the veranda partially collapsed where the boards
have rotted.

'What's this?' I flick through the pictures. The views
are enviable, but the house is a mess.

Cam shrugs, his expression wary. 'A cottage. I
bought it a while ago. Before the money. To renovate.'

It can't be larger than a hundred square metres. And
the ceilings are low. 'Do you plan to live here? You'll
be constantly bumping your head.' He's already told me
he owns a Point Piper penthouse with harbour views
back in Sydney.

At my confused expression, he takes the phone from
me and scrolls through the pictures, as if showing off
a prized possession. 'I'm not sure. Perhaps. It's in an
amazing location. Look at the views.'

I nod. He's right—this cottage commands an enviable spot on Sydney's North Shore.

'My mother grew up close by. After she moved away, we'd go back to her favourite spots for picnics or to the beach. She always admired this cottage, and when the elderly owner passed away I purchased it. For her.' His face falls and he tucks the phone into his breast pocket. 'She died before I could make a dent in the work it needs.'

My heart clenches, the urge to hold him and chase away the defeat in his eyes intense. 'But you're going to finish it anyway? Earn yourself a few splinters and build up a sweat?'

He grins because I understand him. It's almost a tribute. My chest burns with empathy. I touch his arm, wanting to do more, but too afraid of the feelings I've battled all day.

'Yeah, once I'm back in Sydney. Mum was right—it could be perfect.'

I take his hand and lead us back to the sofa, where I tug him down at my side. 'How much work have you done?'

His enthusiasm falters. 'Not that much. I bought it before the inheritance with my savings. It made Mum's last weeks happier to think of me one day living in the cottage she admired from afar.'

My throat aches for his loss, the desire to be there for him building until I confess something I rarely allow myself to think, let alone say aloud. 'You know, I often wonder what it would be like to live somewhere like that.'

Surprise flitters across his face. 'You do…?' A small, almost delighted smile kicks up his mouth.

'Yeah. How peaceful it would be to wake up to the sound of the sea every morning. To step outside before the sun is fully up and drink coffee on a quaint old veranda like that, taste the salt in the air. Simple. Everything I need. To be…content, I guess.'

His silence and the frown that steals his smile and draws his thick eyebrows down over his eyes make me feel self-conscious. He stares, as if seeing me for the first time.

My face grows hot. I've revealed something from deep inside, a place I hardly ever delve. I want to stuff the telling words back inside my mouth. Instead I stand, collect my bag and the wide-brimmed hat that matches my outfit, and breathe my emotions back under control. What is he doing to me? Where did that insane and impractical confession come from? I have a perfectly adequate penthouse in Sydney with its own enviable views. Not that I spend much time there.

I wait for him to join me near the door, my shoulders tense as if I'm anticipating his next words.

'You know, you could live like that, Orla. There's nothing to stop you.' His words are predictable, his tone mild, but the subtext is loaded with the unspoken. If I were that content woman, then perhaps there'd be a chance for us, or perhaps that's just what I want to hear because maybe the appeal of that cottage, that life, is that it would include Cam.

But I can't want that, to be his woman. It's a dead-end fantasy.

'I know.' My clipped tone closes down this alarming conversation, but I soften it to say, 'You should finish the cottage, Cam. I can tell it's going to be beautiful. Shall we go?'

He accepts my change of subject, although there's an undercurrent of unease between us on the journey to the racecourse in another of the sleek sports cars Cam loves. It's as if we're both wearing armour on top of our clothes. As if we need protection from each other, when prior to today everything was easy and open.

We park in the VIP car park and enter the grand-stand, which is over a mile long and houses not only the immaculate racetrack, but also a trackside hotel and entertainment venue. I'm relatively well-known among Dubai's business community, so I introduce Cam to some clients and local dignitaries. I'm deep in conversation with a former client who wants to talk shop when I sense Cam's edginess. The unfamiliar taste of guilt makes me wince as I try to fight my first reaction to become defensive. I'm not used to having to explain my actions to anyone. But I'm supposed to be off the clock. This is supposed to be a social event.

He's right; I never stop. I'm never off the clock. My stomach twists, a strange mix of resentment for the life I chose and longing for something more. I shoot him an apologetic look and wrap up my consultation as politely as I can, reassuring the sheikh I'll see him before I leave Dubai.

'I'm sorry,' I say when I've escaped. 'He's a very good customer and he prefers to work with the top dog, not the very competent minions.'

Cam's expression is free of judgement, but I hear the censure from inside my own head. *Don't you want more than work?*

'I'm not surprised. She's beautiful and talented—it's almost a shame there's only one of her...' He smiles, and I slip into the comfort of his arms, because I'm less sure of my life plan than I was yesterday.

We head to our private suite with a terrace overlooking the racetrack. It's a perfect day for the races, although I'm glad for the air-conditioning of our suite. As it's the first race of the season, the grandstand is packed with spectators. We can't bet, but our waiter informs us there are several competitions running for correctly guessing the place-getters. I choose the three horses with names that appeal the most—Desert Haze, Buyer Beware and Human Condition—knowing nothing about their pedigrees, owners or trainers, but Cam seems more interested in the pre-race action at the edge of the track.

'There he is.' He hands me a pair of binoculars and points in the general direction of the milling jockeys and horses.

'Who?'

'My horse—number seven.' He slips his arm around my waist and tugs me close, his enthusiasm a distraction I need.

I focus in on the thoroughbred—a magnificent chestnut stallion—the jockey bedecked in red and gold. 'Did you place an offshore bet?' Of course Cam would find a way to offload some cash in a country where gambling is illegal.

'No.' He sounds so pleased with himself, I take a good hard look at his face, which is wreathed in smug excitement. 'I bought him. He's mine. Contempt of Court—isn't he perfect?'

Unease dries my mouth as I take another look at Cam's latest purchase. It doesn't matter. I should let it go. I don't want to spoil our evening, but really? A racehorse?

'How long have you owned him?' I hedge, hoping to discover it's a lifelong dream of his or a regular hobby. But the hair rising at the back of my neck tells me I'm unlikely to be comforted by his answer.

'A week. When I knew Dubai was on your itinerary, I put out some feelers. He was already registered for the race, the name is perfect, so I offered the owner a number he couldn't refuse.' He takes two glasses of champagne from our waiter and hands me one, clinking his glass to mine with a grin.

I stare, a shudder passing through me at how much a thoroughbred already registered for one of the world's richest races must have cost. It's none of my business, he's hardly bankrupting himself, and I'll damage the fragile mood between us, but I can't stay silent. On the surface he's enjoying his inheritance, yes, but deep down it's because he doesn't care about the money, which makes sense if it's from his father.

'So you bought an expensive racehorse just for his name?'

He sees the disapproval I'm trying, and clearly failing, to hide. 'I bought him because I could—the name was an added bonus. And I knew you wouldn't approve.'

'You're right, I'm…cautious with my money, but it's not that I don't approve.'

'What, then? We're here to enjoy the races. Having a horse in the race will add to my enjoyment. I'm just making the most of this moment in a way I can afford.'

The unspoken is there again, hanging in the air between us like a swarm of irritable wasps. A dig, a rejoinder, aimed my way. *What's the point of having it all if you don't take the time to enjoy it?*

'So what will you do with him? He's not a homeless dog. Do you plan on shipping him back to Australia too, like the car?' I can imagine why he's struggling with his father's legacy, since the money came from a man who abandoned him, but can't he see that the excesses won't help him deal with his anger and resentment? I can no longer ignore the two sides of Cam's personality and the inconsistencies that tell me he's hurting, despite his live-for-the-moment attitude and his hedonistic pursuits.

'I told you, the car was a gift for my cousin. And I haven't thought what I'll do with him beyond today.' Another shrug, but his body is tense, defensive. 'He'll pay his way, I guess, or I'll sell him.'

'So why buy a racehorse for a single race if it's not a particular hobby of yours or a dream to fulfil?' I can't let this go. The dog food was cute, the drum kit for the boy heartbreaking but understandable, given what he's hinted at about his own spartan upbringing with his single-parent mother. But this? It's deeper than lavishly throwing around money.

'Why does this bother you so much? I can afford to buy ten racehorses if I want them. I'm living the high life.'

I ignore the jibe I could interpret as some sort of comparison. 'Are you? Or are you running from something?' I sigh and touch his arm to show him that, although I'm crossing a line here, I'm doing so because I care. 'I'm sorry, I don't want to upset you, I just… I can't stand by and watch you struggle with your inheritance. There are ways I can help.'

I see the look on his face, an expression I've never seen before on easygoing, laid-back Cam—cold, hard anger. 'Well, thank you for the unsolicited financial advice but I know exactly what I'm doing. I'm not some schoolboy with a winning lottery ticket.'

'No, but you don't care about the money either, do you? It's because it's his, isn't it? Your father's?' I'm walking a fine line here, but I ache for him. 'That's why you're blowing it with private planes and racehorses and fast cars. You're not at peace with it.'

He's still angry, malice glittering in his beautiful, expressive eyes. A desecration. 'What makes you think I'm struggling? I'm having the time of my life, aren't I? World-class luxury, every hedonistic pursuit known to man, and a beautiful woman on tap, for whenever I want a good fuck.'

My hand curls into a fist and I'm tempted to slap him, but he's clearly hurting, lashing out. I've backed him into a corner and he's fighting for his life. I step closer, when I'm certain he expected his harsh words to drive me away. 'One minute you're passionate about the underdog, tipping the hotel staff, making some kid's drumming dream come true, even taking time to play with abandoned dogs, and the next you're blowing millions of dollars with a cavalier attitude. We're all complex beings, but this,' I wave a hand at the racehorses, 'isn't you.'

His eyes dart, some of the anger leaving him, as if he's warring with some internal demons.

The race is about to start, so I'm aware my timing sucks. But is there ever a good time to feel exposed? Don't I feel the same way every time he pushes me to talk about my father or brings me to account over my workaholic tendencies? Every time we've been intimate this past week, as if with each searing look he peels away another layer of my armour? Every time I peer into the future and see a terrifying glimpse of a life I thought I was long past craving?

I lean up against the rail, pretending to watch the race I'm no longer interested in. I feel his struggle in the tense air between us, and regret makes my posture deflate. I want to close the gap. To touch him again. To offer physical comfort if he won't accept my emotional support. He's there, right beside me, but may as well be miles away.

'You're right.' His sigh carries in the dry air, my

hearing highly attuned to the strain and defeat in his voice. 'The inheritance was from my—' he makes a fist and then relaxes it as quickly '—my father.'

I hold my breath, desperate to hear what he's finally decided to tell me, but feeling every blade of his pain. It's my penance for pushing him, for caring this much, for breaking my own rules.

'I didn't want it. Why would I? From a man I never knew? A man who considered my existence irrelevant, who held little score in the values of integrity and family commitment.'

A man so unlike him.

He turns to face me then, both of us deaf to the starter gun and the roar of the excited crowds as we hold each other's eye contact with brittle and fragile force.

'I'm sorry, Cam. I understand. I can see how you might harbour resentment for your childhood, but your anger won't make a difference to what's done. There are other ways to compensate.'

He presses his lips together, but I see in his eyes that he's heard. He's a smart man; he's probably told himself the same thing a thousand times.

I plough on. 'Perhaps he was sorry. Ashamed. Perhaps leaving you that money was his way of apologising. The only way he knew how to reach out to you after having left like he did.'

I'm shocked speechless by the venomous expression souring his face. 'Well, neither of us knew him, did we? Maybe he just wants to control me from the grave. To disrupt my life, which by the way was pretty near perfect before all of this, and dictate how I live. Just because money was the most important thing in his life. I'm not him.'

'Of course you're not him. You're wonderful. I'm just trying to point out that there are other things you can do with your money.'

'*His* money. You know, Orla, you more than anyone should understand what it's like to have a manipulative parent.'

I ignore his reference. I've laid him bare and he's lashing out again. And, of course, he's right. My father has done his fair share of damage. My shoulders slump. Am I still jumping through my father's hoops? Is that what drives me still? Yes, maybe in the beginning…but now, when I'm more successful than ever, more even than he is?

But this isn't about me.

'Why are you so convinced your father wanted to control you? Why isn't it just a gift? A way to make amends?'

'Gifts are yours to do with as you please. They're not conditional. They don't chain you.'

I think about my earrings, the gift designed to send me away, quietly and without a fuss, from a role that was mine by rights. A gift I wear to remind myself that we don't always receive what we deserve, and that not everyone, even those who should do, sees the real us.

'I know that.' My voice is small, because Cam's touched a nerve.

'Without conditions I could do what I like with it,

but he put a clause in the will which prevents me from giving more than twenty-five per cent away. I couldn't even donate the entire sum to the hospice that nursed my mother through her last days. Even from the grave, he still cares more about that money than he does about me or his ex-wife and mother to his only son.'

His smile is so vengeful, my stomach turns. 'I'd stake my life on the fact that he would detest what I'm doing with his billions,' he says. 'Frittering it away with a cavalier attitude, as you called it.'

A brittle silence settles between us. He's right. Neither of us knows his father's intent.

I grow hot under Cam's focus. I want to rewind, to start over, to hold him until I've chased away the distress I've put in his eyes. But how do I repair the damage? We're not a real couple. We only have a few weeks of shared history to fall back on, most of that superficial and impersonal, at my insistence. Why would he seek comfort from me of all people? And I shouldn't offer it, not after admitting that my feelings are dangerously ensnared.

But…

I glance down at the racetrack. The race is over. 'I'm sorry, it looks like Contempt of Court lost.' I turn back to face him, seeing him, understanding him in a whole new light. 'You're right though—it's a perfect name.' A two-fingered gesture to a man he can't confront any other way.

All the energy drains from my body. I've messed up. I should have known Cam would never do anything frivolous or erratic. He's the most thoughtful and considerate human being I know. This is what happens when I forget my rules. This is what I hoped to avoid by keeping things purely physical. This feeling of failure. That I can't do this. That relationships just aren't my strength.

I should stick to what I know.

'Do you want to get out of here?' I want to touch him, to show him my regret for both his situation and for drawing out his secret pain. I want to get back to where we were this morning. Restore my own equilibrium and his in the only way I can allow: physically.

But not here.

His struggle to let go of the things I've dragged up passes over his face, but he finally nods and I gather my bag and hat.

The journey is tense, quiet, stomach-churning. Back at the M Club in Dubai's downtown, I assume we're heading for our room, but without comment Cam takes my hand and leads me to the basement club, which is alive with the insistent beat of some dance track. The last thing I want to do is dance, to pretend that everything between us is okay. But perhaps that's exactly what I need to do. Pretend. Pretend this is still about no-strings pleasure.

I follow him, weaving through the crowds of clubbers.

'Let's get a drink,' says Cam, his voice hard, all that lovely deep and sexy resonance rubbed away. 'I've reserved one of the private rooms.'

I nod, my heart heavy, but I follow him to the club's perimeter, where discreet private booths are located.

The interior is decorated in signature M Club black—a womblike space, a fully stocked bar, a wide and sumptuous sofa, an adjustable PA system so the volume of the thumping music can be altered to personal taste or allow conversation, and a wall of one-way glass, to ensure absolute privacy, even as the occupants feel part of the club's vibrant atmosphere with a view of the dance floor.

Cam hands me a Scotch, knocking back his own in a single swallow. He doesn't adjust the volume of the music, but I don't think we're here for conversation.

I take a mouthful of my drink, my mind scrambling for something to say. I want to make things right between us. I shouldn't have pushed so hard. I shouldn't have lowered my guard enough to care. But I do.

'Cam, I'm sorry.'

His fingers settle against my mouth. He hushes me as he glides the pad of his fingers across my sensitive lips.

He takes my glass and drains what's left and then replaces his fingers with his mouth, parting his lips to allow a trickle of the liquor to pass from his mouth to mine in a decadent, provocative kiss.

I swallow, my lips clinging to his in silent apology. His kiss turns demanding, his tongue probing while his eyes burn into mine as if begging for something. Silence? Understanding? Escape?

He pulls back. 'I don't want to talk any more.' His hands settle on my hips and his body starts to move to the pounding beat of the dance track. I move with him, lost in the intensity in his eyes, deep, dark desire concealing the earlier pain. I clutch the lifeline. The desire. It's easier to chase because I want him, despite my other, harder-to-name feelings. Our need for each other is the only stability left now everything else feels as if it's shifting underfoot.

He wants to hide. To retreat behind what we do, what we know—how to make each other feel good. I do too. Haven't I done the same myself, more than once? Used him in the same way? Isn't a part of me doing exactly that now? Avoiding the treacherous thoughts of us being more than this?

This whole proposition began because I wanted a distraction, and now so does Cam.

I loop my arms around his neck and kick off my sandals, my hips matching his rhythm, which is confident and inherently sexy—like everything else about him. He bends so low, our lips brush as we move, not quite a kiss, but somehow more, a presence, a reminder that the other person is there, breathing the same air.

His hands curve over my backside, his fingers curling and bunching up the silk fabric of my dress as he grinds me against his hard length. 'Turn around,' he murmurs against my mouth, his hard stare glittering with now familiar challenge.

I obey, pulse leaping. When I'm faced away from him, his big hands on my hips and my hands looped around his neck behind my head, I push my ass back to torture him some more. Him and myself. Because he's hard and ready for me and I want him, as always.

We dance on, my back to his front, one of his arms

around my waist and the other hand on my hip as we sway together in a way that's more foreplay than choreography and would be completely prohibited in any other establishment in this country other than here in the privacy and decadence of the M Club.

The track changes, seamlessly blending into one that's more sensuous. No longer content to merely tease, I drag Cam's hands north to cup my breasts through my dress. He gives me a hint of friction, his thumbs and fingers rolling my nipples, but it's not enough. I want more. I always want more of the way he makes me feel.

But can this, just this, ever be enough?

To switch off my mind, I tangle my fingers in the hair at his nape as I rest my head on his shoulder and turn my face to his, begging for his mouth.

'Cam.' His name sounds like a plea and it is. A plea to drag me with him into oblivion, to guide us both until we're lost in sensation. Because otherwise I'll think, and thinking about this man, and the way I am with him, is as addictive as it is foolish.

Cam presses his mouth to my neck, below my ear, and judders wrack my body—he knows how sensitive I am in that spot, knows it turns me on to feel his scruff against my skin and hear his breath panting because he feels the same need.

'Let's go upstairs,' I say, twisting so I can capture his mouth, touch my tongue to his, swallow the sound of the low groan he lets free. I want to ensure everything is right with us after our fight. I want to know he's still with me, still happy to travel to Singapore and then on to Sydney, our hometown, where this heady whirlwind will come to a natural end.

As if it's still part of our dance, Cam nudges me forward, following close behind until I'm only inches in front of the wall of one-way glass that gifts us a panoramic view of the club. Before I can repeat my desire to take this upstairs to our suite, his hands slip to the button between my breasts and he slowly undoes one after another.

I gasp, the rational part of my brain tricked into believing the people dancing only a few metres on the other side of the glass can see us.

Can I do this? Here?

The answer is as clear as the window in front of me. The same answer as every other time Cam's challenged me, or I've challenged myself.

Yes.

'Tell me to stop.' Cam speaks against my throat, his lips a sensual glide and his chin prickling my nerves alive.

Stop is what we should do. Not just this display of exhibitionism, but also the arrangement we made. Before I slip any deeper into the building feelings and before we push each other to expose more than we can recover from.

'Tell me to stop.' He presses his erection between my buttocks and I brace my hands flat on the glass, pressing my lips together to hold in the words. Because I want him. In any way. All the ways it's possible to want someone.

I ignore the racing of my heart and the spike of adrenaline warning me to pull back. His hands continue with the buttons, his hips still swaying to the beat behind me, where I'm too turned on to do more than hold my body upright and glory in the decadence of his touch. While he scrapes kisses up and down my neck, he scoops the cups of my bra down, exposing my breasts.

The cool air hits me and I gasp at being naked here, in front of strangers.

With a grunt, Cam presses up even closer so I'm shunted forwards the last inch and my bare nipples touch the frigid glass. I groan at the foreign sensation. But I have no time to absorb the pleasure, because Cam slips one hand between my legs and delves inside my lacy thong to stroke my swollen clit, which is aching and ready.

'Tell me to stop,' he says, gruff, his face buried against the side of my neck. I hear him inhale deeply, sucking in my scent, and I almost smile, because I've done the same thing a hundred times, sniffing his sweater left on a chair or his tousled hair while he's asleep.

At my answering moan, he taps my foot with his and bunches my dress around my waist from behind, his intentions clear. He's going to do this, right here. And I want him with equal desperation.

I spread my feet wide, excitement rising when I hear the clink of his belt buckle and the rasp of his zip. I can't believe we're doing this, but it's as if we both need the reminder of why we're here and only this—hot, demanding sex—will reset the boundaries.

His hand shifts from between my legs, and I cry out at its loss, only to press my mouth up against the glass to stave off the pleasure of his fingers, which he plunges inside me from behind, as if testing my readiness.

'Cam, yes. I'm ready. Do it.'

His fingers disappear and I feel the fat head of his cock nudge my entrance. I tilt my hips back to allow him access, my palms pressing against the glass for leverage. He's going too slowly. I want to control the pace. To chase away our fight and my own confusion.

I feel him enter me, just an inch or so, and it's not enough.

'What are you doing to me, Orla?' he grits out, his fingers digging into my hips. 'Tell me to stop.'

'I don't want you to stop,' I cry. As to what we're doing, I have no answers, because whatever I'm doing to him, he's doing to me tenfold. I'm more alive when I'm with him, more myself than I've been in years, so long I've almost forgotten how it feels.

He surges inside with a protracted groan. I brace my palms against the glass as he drags my hips back to meet the thrust of his hips. His possession fills me and in that moment I want to be more to him, although I can't define in what way. I just know that if he walked away tonight, after our fight, I'd grieve more than his company and the regular, earth-shifting orgasms. I'd grieve his loss.

As if he's already decided to leave and I'm determined to give him something to remember, I lock my arms and push back from the glass, the illicit scandal of what we're doing in such close proximity to the other club members and the thump of his hips against my backside making me cry out with acute waves of pleasure.

Cam grips my hips with punishing fingers, clearly battling control himself. 'Touch yourself, Orla. Touch that greedy little clit that wants to be mine.'

His words thrill me, because all my body is his. I rush to obey, slipping one hand between my legs to rub myself while he pounds into me from behind.

It's carnal, uninhibited and glorious. But it's also communication. We've strayed from the path this evening, and this is a reminder that we can't do that again, not without sacrificing something more. Something bigger than both of us. Something so good, we'd be fools not to enjoy it for whatever time we have left.

Just when I think he's close to finishing, he grunts, pulls out and spins me around. He backs my ass up against the window as he kisses me and hoists me around the waist so my feet leave the floor.

'I want to watch you come. Hold tight.'

I nod, his puppet, willing to have my strings pulled, because I know this man. I know his values and his desires and he sees what I need.

He grips my waist in one arm, his other hand pressing our entwined fingers against the window, and I wrap my legs around his hips. With my free hand I guide him back inside, and we groan together, as if it were the first time all over again.

Cam's thrusts turn fast and shallow, his fingers pressed hard into the back of my hand as if he never wants to let me go. I grip his shoulder and tunnel my hand into his hair and hold on tight with everything I have. 'Cam…'

His eyes lance mine and his thrusts knock the breath from me, but I need to say this. To make things right between us. 'I'm sorry for what you've been through. Sorry for bringing up painful memories.'

His face twists with emotion. He drops his forehead to mine as he says, 'Hush…'

His kiss tells me I'm forgiven, and then I can't speak another word because he stops holding himself back, his hips powering into mine as he sinks as deep as he can go and we're finally lost together.

CHAPTER EIGHT

Cam

As I PULL up outside Orla's Raffles Place office in Singapore's financial district a few days later, my phone rings. I slide the car into park and answer on the Bluetooth. It's Orla.

'Hi. I'm just outside,' I say, already grinning with anticipation.

'I figured you wouldn't be far away. I'm on my way down. I just wanted to say I'm ready and I've cleared everything on my desk—no interruptions tonight. I promise.' She's mildly breathless, as if she's talking on the move. 'Perhaps I should even wear one of those glasses and moustache disguises so I don't get cornered by someone who recognises me.'

I throw my head back and laugh. 'There's no need to go that far. But I appreciate the gesture.' Since the evening at the races, where we had our first fight—although I'm not sure you can have a fight if you're not a couple—Orla and I haven't spoken about my inheritance. In fact, we haven't spoken about anything that could be considered real, only travel arrangements or her work schedule, or where we'd like to eat that evening. But every time I pay for a meal, tip a waiter or add drinks to my M Club tab, I feel her eyes on me, as if she wants to say more but is holding back.

I understand the impulse. For days now I've been fighting the urge to ask where this is going. Where we're going, because time is running out. Our trip will soon be over and we'll be back in Sydney before we know it.

What then?

Do we shake hands and walk away without a backward glance? Will we hook up every time she's home long enough to give me a call? Cam's dial-an-orgasm? Will we date other people in between? Fuck, of course we will, because we won't be dating each other—she made that clear from day one. I check my feelings, the roll of my stomach confirming without a doubt that I want more from Orla than a goodbye the minute we touch down in Sydney or an occasional booty call.

I want everything.

But what does she want? Probably nothing more than she's wanted from the start. A good time. But surely we've moved past just physical pleasure? Surely she feels the same stirrings to explore this further, back in the real world?

But whose real world?

I wince, remembering the woman tying my insides into knots is still on the line. 'Okay…well, hurry down. I've got a surprise.' Two if you count the box in my pocket.

I'm taking her to the Singapore Grand Prix, which just happens to be in town this week. She's spent a gruelling four days working, leaving the hotel suite before I'm awake and returning late in the evening, pale and about to drop. The humidity here is draining and she's been visiting a technology satellite manufacturing company on one of the islands. It's all I can do to encourage a few mouthfuls of the delicious room-service menu into her before turning on the shower and tucking her into bed.

At first I thought her drive, work ethic, and independence made us incompatible, but it's true what they say—opposites do attract and we slot together well.

But could we take this chemistry, this astounding connection, and translate it into something real once the travelling and the hedonism stop? On my turf, my *real* turf, would her enthusiasm dwindle? Would she decide that we just don't have enough in common after all?

As to her feelings…

I swallow bile—I have no clue. I'm only just waking up to my own…

I grip the steering wheel, hoping to dislodge the lump in my throat threatening to cut off my oxygen. Time is running out. The real test will come back in Sydney, on home ground. I already have plans to throw myself into finishing the cottage renovations, but I still have no definitive solution for my financial woes. Do I return to work at my old construction firm and ignore the money in my account? Will they even have me back? When I said I needed some unpaid leave to get my head around things, they didn't put up much of a fight. I knew the company was struggling; as with most Sydney-based construction companies, the building slump had taken its toll. But could I simply slot back into my old life as if none of this—the money, meeting Orla—had happened?

More importantly, could a woman like Orla—so driven, so intent on making her business the best—be happy to come back down to earth with me? Live that simple life in a cottage by the sea?

I try to picture her there, both in its current state of disrepair and once finished. I'm so used to seeing her in glamorous, decadent surroundings that the image doesn't quite gel.

There's a tap at the window. I look up to find her beautiful, lit-up face smiling down at me and I'm struck with the force of a baseball bat to the skull that I want that reality. Me, Orla, simple moments in a cottage by the sea.

Fuck, I'm falling for her. Actually falling.

I clamber from the car, my heart pounding.

I scoop one arm around her waist and pull her in for a kiss. Our first of the day and all the sweeter because I've had to wait and because each kiss we share is better and better.

'Hi,' I say after she releases me.

She laughs. 'Hi, yourself. So where are we going? I'm excited.'

My chest grows tight with nervous energy, the box

in my pocket burning a hole through the denim of my jeans. I wanted to wait, to give her the gift at a suitably romantic moment, but I can't help myself. In view of my lightning-bolt revelation, I'm impatient to start.

'I have something for you first—a gift.' I tug at the box, which is snagged on my pocket.

'Cam. No more gifts.' She covers my hand, the hand struggling to release the box. 'I know you don't want to hear it, but I can give you a list right now of a hundred sound investments to absorb your disposable income.'

'Investing is the last thing I want to do.' She's only trying to help, I see that, but perhaps because I've already had similar thoughts myself, my stance on the money I neither wanted nor asked for softening, I dig in my heels.

'Enjoying myself at my old man's expense is one thing, but touching that money in any meaningful way feels too close to forgiveness, and I'm not sure I'm ready for that.'

'I understand what you mean about forgiveness. I've struggled with that myself. But I'm not talking about making money,' she says, and my ribs pinch because she sees me, understands my struggles and, as much as I don't want to hear it, she's right. I need to find a way to come to terms with my new life. To build a new future for myself, because even if I want to return to the old life, it can never be the same.

'There are lots of ways to invest thoughtfully and with a social conscience. You're already doing it in a small way. But I can help you get around the restrictions in the will, too. Why don't you let me put together some proposals?'

I want to say so much in that second that I can't speak at all. Would she want to help if she didn't care about me? About us? And I'll take any future contact with her I can get, even if I have to sit through a million financial proposals.

'I do have something I'd like your advice on.' Since thinking about my old construction company, an idea has taken shape. She may not know anything about the building industry, but I'm certain she can advise me, let me know if my plan is feasible. But I don't want to have this conversation now.

'But right now I want to give you my gift.' I kiss away her pout and tug the box free. 'This gift is different.' I hold her stare so she understands my meaning. I know technically all my money is my money, but some of it I earned. 'I bought it with my *own* money. My savings before the inheritance.' Part of my cottage renovation fund, but she doesn't need to know that.

Her eyes widen. 'Oh, well…thank you.' She presses a kiss to my mouth, and I know she gets me. She understands the distinction and what it means to me.

I hold the box up at eye level, flat on my palm.

I know she wants to berate me for my extravagance, but she takes the box without further comment. Inside is an intricate pair of traditional Singapore gold earrings, their beauty and delicacy reminding me of her.

'I notice you always wear these,' I touch one diamond stud, 'and I thought you might like a change, so…'

Why am I so tongue-tied? It's a gift. I've given her hundreds of gifts over the past few weeks. Perhaps it's because I want to say more, to tell her that I want to see her beyond the six weeks we agreed, but I clamp my jaw shut, because I'm not sure she's ready to hear that yet.

'They're beautiful, Cam, exactly what I would choose myself.' Her mouth is back on mine, and her arms scoop around my neck so I hear when she snaps the box closed.

I guess she's not going to wear them tonight. I swallow down my disappointment. It's no big deal. 'Let's go. It's not far, so I thought we could walk.'

She tucks the earrings inside her bag and loops her arm through mine. It's a short walk to the premier grandstand, which has the best views of the street circuit's more challenging turns and spectacular views of Marina Bay, the focus of the post-race fireworks.

I take Orla's hand. 'Do you like Grand Prix?'

'Yes. It's so exciting. Is that where we're going?' She smiles her dazzling smile, and I nod, no longer interested in the motor racing. I want to take her back to the hotel and strip her naked, save for the earrings I bought. I want to drag a confession from her of how she truly feels about me. If she wants to see me once we're back in Sydney.

'Not long until we're home. It's going to be a struggle after all this adventure,' I hedge, testing the water.

'Yes. I'm sort of dreading it, to be honest. I'll have

to see my father and he's going to be pissed about Jensen's.'

I squeeze her hand in solidarity. 'Tell him to stick it. You did nothing wrong apart from being the best.'

She nods, but her eyes appear far away. 'You know, he bought me these earrings for my twenty-fifth birthday.' She touches one of the diamond studs she always wears. 'At first I was incredibly touched. We weren't that close while I was growing up—I always felt second best because I didn't have a Y chromosome. But after he'd given me a second to open his gift and thank him, he chose that moment to tell me I wouldn't be the next CEO, but Liam would.'

I stare, because I don't know what to say. I don't even know how to feel. 'I'm sorry he treated you that way.' What does it mean that she wears them every day without fail? I try to recall if I've ever seen her without them, instinctively knowing the answer is no.

'It's silly, I guess, but I wear them every day to remind myself that I don't need him or his company. That I'm perfectly capable of running my own firm. That I can be just as successful as him and Liam.'

'Probably more successful, if you think about Jensen's,' I say, and she nods. The idea she still wants to prove something to the man after all these years depresses me. I hide the heavy feeling dragging at my feet with an unconvincing smile. 'A two-fingered gesture, eh? I get it.'

Her nod is hesitant, as if she's remembering our fight over Contempt of Court, but four-carat diamond earrings…a racehorse… They may as well be the same. She squeezes my hand, because now she knows I've made enough of my own two-fingered gestures while we've known each other. 'My father never gave me anything—not a birthday card, or a pat on the back, or even a phone call. Trust me, you know I understand the impulse.'

She looks down and then tucks herself closer to my side as we walk. 'I'm not bringing that up again. I just wanted you to understand why I wear these.' She touches a stud, which may as well be a padlock to the cage she's constructed around herself.

A daily reminder. There every time she looks in the mirror. A reminder she has something to prove.

I've never met her father, but I already know the guy is an asshole. She's worth ten of him, except somehow, despite all her success, all the billions, she still feels she needs to prove to him that she's worthy.

I tug her to a standstill, the exotic scents of Singapore around us reminding me we are far from home. But we're together, and I want to be there for her. 'You know you don't need to prove anything to me, right?'

Her eyes dart. 'Of course.' She lifts her chin, the way she does when she's cornered and comes out fighting. 'What do you mean?'

'I don't care if you don't wear *my* earrings, but isn't it time you took these off?' I touch the stud with one cautious fingertip. 'You're the most driven and successful woman I've ever met. You've already bested him, made it on your own, won a major client from him. You have nothing to prove.' I hadn't planned the serious turn in the conversation, but as I see it, we both need to face our fears, to conquer our demons and move on. How else can we focus on what's really important in life? How can we focus on any sort of a relationship?

'I know that.'

'Do you? Really? Because from what I've seen you'll never stop. Ten billion, twenty, thirty. When is enough enough, Orla?'

'That's different—I...don't do it for the money. You know how frugal I am. I love my job. I'm good at it. I'm happy.'

Her statements feel like blows. I want to dismiss them, to call her a liar. But part of me is scared that if she's right, if she has everything she needs, life all figured out, completely self-sufficient, is there any room for an ordinary guy like me?

'Would you ask that question if I were a successful man?' she says, her guard now fully up.

I grip the back of my neck in frustration. 'I'm not some sexist idiot. It's got nothing to do with your gender.'

'So despite saying I have nothing to prove, you're trying to change me. Is that it?'

'No.' I cup her face. 'I wouldn't change a thing. I just... I care about you. I see how hard you work, how hard you push yourself, and I'm just worried that you feel you have something to prove, which you absolutely do not.'

Some of the anger in her deflates. She places her

hand over mine, pressing it closer to her cheek. 'I care about you too, Cam. That's what I tried to say in Dubai. That's why I'm offering to help you invest, to help you see that perhaps your father had no other choice, no other way of apologising than to leave you that money, the money he abandoned you and your mum for.'

The tables turning knocks the wind from me. 'You're talking about forgiveness again.' I tug my hand away and shove both in my pockets.

'Perhaps it might help.' She crosses her arms over her chest.

How did we get here? And why can't she see that she's enough, just the way she is? Enough for me, at least.

'I'm not sure I'm ready for that. What about you?'

My question, my challenge, falls on deaf ears. We complete the walk in silence, but it turns out that race cars and fireworks aren't as thrilling when you've glimpsed the finishing line but find yourself somehow right back at the start.

CHAPTER NINE

Orla

CAM'S PENTHOUSE IS the crowning jewel of Sydney Harbour's Darling Point. Even I'm impressed with the spectacular bridge views. I park at the top of a long, steep driveway and let myself inside with Cam's security code.

Tonight is the club's Masquerade Gala and, as we're going together, I prefer to arrive together, so I've had my outfit delivered here. Not that the tension between us is completely resolved, but since our exchange in Singapore we've called a truce, as if we're both aware time is ticking and there's no point wasting the days and hours we have left fighting.

It doesn't matter who's right.

Cam and I had our fun, and soon it will be time to say goodbye.

With that certainty weighing me down, my heels click as I make my way upstairs from the ground floor. I glance around his home, looking for clues of the real Cam. While luxurious, the whole space seems cold and cavernous, every sound echoing off the bare walls. Hardly any colour, no personality, and no sign of the warm, compassionate, vibrant man I'm lucky enough to know.

When I reach the second floor and the main living areas, my adrenaline pumping as it always does in anticipation of seeing Cam, there's still no sign of him. Neither in person nor in any evidence that he even lives here, although he told me he only bought the place four months ago. A single solitary leather armchair and a telescope face the wraparound windows, which open onto a spacious veranda and give almost three-hundred-and-sixty-degree harbour views. But there's no character, no life anywhere to be found, certainly no sign of the fun-loving, energetic Cam, a man who's entirely occupied my head since we landed in Sydney twenty-four hours ago.

My throat grows tight. This isn't Cam. This flashy, modern residence that screams status. Then it hits me. It's another of his revenge purchases against his father. I'm no more likely to find the real Cam here than I am searching the moon. Not that I should want to find the real Cam, because I have to give him up. And soon.

I pace over to the window and grip the back of the armchair, my nails digging and my heart clenching as I imagine him sitting here. Alone, trying to work out a way forward. Trying to be himself in a world that's shifted on its axis.

But then, what do I know about having everything all worked out?

I thought once we arrived back in Australia, things would fall into place. We'd share a parting kiss, perhaps laugh as we recalled the highs of our adventure, and part with only a modicum of regret. Instead, I found myself inviting Cam to the gala even before his private plane touched down.

I can't want him, but I can't do without him.

I sigh, my nerves and my need demanding I find him when I'm fully aware that all I've done is prolong the agony, drawn out the final farewell, which must come. Because my stance on relationships hasn't changed. The past week of disagreements proves my theories are correct: I'm no good at emotional entanglements. I'm better off with my single life and my shocking work-life imbalance.

My breath catches, my insistence no longer carrying the same certainty. In practice, within the limitations of my proposition, Cam and I work. But outside of that? Despite his struggles to come to terms with the inheritance left to him by a man who let him down, I know he'd be content to return to his simple, hard-working life. And I know he's going to be just fine.

We spent most of the flight from Singapore brainstorming his ideas for a construction school that teaches vulnerable and underprivileged young men and women valuable skills they can take into the workforce. Young people who need a break in life because of the path they've found themselves on. Young people like Cam might have been without his hard-working mother and his own determination to make something of himself.

With some financial guidance from me, and with Cam's passion, their lives could be rich and fulfilling in all the ways that matter.

And me?

I fight the hot tears threatening, swallowing them down. Cam needs a woman who can share that life. A woman who shares his goals. A woman free to walk and sleep and love by his side. It's what he deserves.

But I'm not that woman.

He was right about me. I need to work. It's who I am.

With a gnawing feeling in the pit of my stomach, I go in search of him. As I walk towards a corridor lined with what I assume are bedrooms, I hear a series of low, rhythmic thuds. Some sort of bass-heavy music.

My pulse leaps. He told me the penthouse has a gym; perhaps I'll get another show of Cam working out—half naked, sweaty, a visual feast. My mouth dries in anticipation, and a surge of acid burns behind my breastbone, jealousy I'm going to have to get used to if Cam gets the happy-ever-after he deserves with some other woman.

The beat builds. I open the room the noise seems to be coming from and freeze in the doorway.

The sound is deafening. Cam sits at a massive drum kit facing a floor-to-ceiling window with ocean views. He's stripped to the waist, his back slicked with perspiration and his muscular arms almost a blur as he creates the rapid drum loop that goes on and on, as if he's pounding out the rhythm of my regret.

I'm frozen. I want to watch. I want to go to him. I want to run away and sob myself into oblivion. Without making a sound I cast a quick glance around the room. Like the rest of the house, the furnishings in this room are sparse—a large bed, a sofa and some sleek Bluetooth speakers, but there's more of Cam's personality in this room than the rest of the house combined, as if he's carved out a sanctuary inside this cavernous shell. A place he can be himself.

I watch and listen from my spot by the door, indulging myself for what will likely be one of the last times. The last grains of sand are sliding through the hourglass, and any day now I'm going to have to give him up.

The thought traps my breath and sends shards of pain between my ribs. How can I walk away from someone who makes me smile without effort? Who brightens my mornings and competes with the constant draw to stay at the office? How can I go back to boring, burnt-out Orla when all I want to do is stay in our bubble with Cam?

He must see my reflection in the glass because he stops, the sudden silence ripping me from the insanity of formulating ways I can continue to see him now the proposition has run its course.

He's panting, his chest heaving as he drags in air and looks at me from beneath his brows. I'm instantly damp—hell, I was damp before I entered the house, because I know him. I know how good we are together. I've always known that, from the moment our eyes met across the roulette wheel in Monaco.

I don't speak a word.

As if he too knows this is close to finishing and he's as desperate as me to keep the illusion alive, he simply stares.

Waiting.

I saunter over, slowly shedding my blouse, skirt and heels as I approach. My need for him hasn't lessened since our first time together. If anything it's stronger, because I'm alive when I'm with Cam, but never more so than when I'm in his arms, his heart thudding against mine, our breath mingling.

I reach him and I almost chicken out, flee. I extend a shaky hand to skim his shoulders and back as I round him. His skin is warm, his muscles tense under my touch. I stand between his spread legs and he pushes back his stool to accommodate me in the small space between his body and the drums.

I twirl my fingers in his hair, holding his handsome face, tilting his mouth up to my kiss. He groans, dropping the drumsticks so he can slide his hands up my thighs and around to cup my buttocks with possessive fingers.

'Orla, what are you trying to do? Kill me?' he mumbles against my lips.

I smile, but nothing inside me feels light enough for humour. It's as if I'm weighed down by my feelings, as if there are too many of them for me to even contemplate lifting my feet from the sumptuous carpet.

'I want you. I've missed the way you make me feel.' I almost gasp at the stark honesty of my words.

He grips my hips tighter, his hands so big they span

half my lower back. He drops his head to my chest, where he nuzzles my cleavage, his breath hot. 'And how do I make you feel?' His hands slide up my back and he unhooks my bra without looking up, while he presses kisses to the tops of my breasts and my breastbone.

My head drops back as I absorb the heady sensation of Cam's touch. The words spring from nowhere, or perhaps from that tightly guarded part deep inside. 'Alive. Free. Invincible.'

It's as close to a declaration of my feelings as I dare.

I sense his smile, but when I look down his expression is bittersweet. 'You were all those things before you met me.'

The burn is back in my throat. My beautiful, broken Cam. But I know he'll be all right. He's young, he's resilient and he has so much to give.

'Well, perhaps you make me appreciate them more, then. Perhaps playing hard has put working hard into perspective.' I press my finger to his beautiful mouth, shushing him. 'I want to play hard now.'

I slide off my bra and lean over to kiss him. I want to forget that this is almost over. Forget that life after my adventure with Cam will go back to pre-Cam predictability. But I'll never forget how he unleashed this sexual being I neglected for so long. How he challenged me and then cherished me.

Slipping my thong off, I straddle his thighs where he sits. My hands push down his shorts just enough so his erection is freed. I take him in my hand between us and pump him while we kiss, and then I angle him back and sink slowly onto him, inch by glorious inch.

He holds me so tight to his chest that I fear I won't be able to draw breath, but then I stretch up on the balls of my feet and lower myself into his lap and we groan-gasp together at the depth of the penetration. This feels so right I never want to give it up, but despite the journey we've travelled, I'm still me.

We rock together, clinging tight while we kiss and move just enough to stay balanced on the stool but also to give and take what we need from each other. But it's not enough. I want him to know how much he's meant to me, to understand that, while I can't give him commitment, or the kind of future I see for him, the kind he deserves, I can give him all of me, physically.

I pull back, my lips swollen. 'Cam. It's time.'

He knows what I mean. Ever since Zurich we've skirted this issue. I want him every way I can. He'll know that I was his, briefly, but completely.

He grips my waist and stands without slipping from my body. In two strides we're on the bed, me on my back and him taking charge of our pleasure by thrusting above me. He clasps my hands, his fingers locking with mine, his beautiful face tight with pleasure, and then he dives for my nipple, sucking hard so I cry out and arch my neck.

I get lost, so lost I think he's missed my meaning or has changed his mind, but when I'm close to climaxing, my body drunk on the pleasure Cam delivers without fail, he finally withdraws and guides me onto all fours.

He takes my hand and directs my fingers to my drenched and swollen clit. 'Rub yourself.'

I hear him tear into a condom and then I feel the thrilling chill of lube between my buttocks.

'Don't stop.' He handles me like I'm made of glass, his rough hands sliding over the skin of my back and shoulders and hips, even as I feel him push against my opening for the first time.

I want this. I want what only he can give me. And I want it on my timescale, not Cam's, which I'd bet my entire wealth is in deference to my comfort. But there is no more time. There's only now. Us. This moment of trust and forbidden intimacy.

I push back, the feeling foreign and thrilling but not uncomfortable after all his care and preparation. And just as I know I can trust him with my body, that he'd never hurt me, I also know he needs convincing. 'Cam, I want this. I want you this way. Every way.'

I hear his groan, feel his fingers digging into my hips as the pressure of his possession increases. I rub my clit faster to counter the slight twinge of discomfort but then I'm full and he leans over me with a long moan, his sweaty chest plastered to my back.

'Fuck, Orla. I'll never get enough of you.'

It's as close to any sort of declaration as we've come, dangerously close. And it electrifies me even as I try to block it out by rocking my hips to distract us both towards pleasure. My ploy works because Cam's hand joins mine between my legs, our fingers working in unison on my clit until I start to see stars and need both my hands to brace for the impact of my inevitable orgasm.

Cam arches over me, taking his weight, but I want it, I want it all. To be smothered in him, to forget where I end and he begins, to be his completely, just in this moment. Not Cam and Orla. Just a man and a woman, lost together.

'Cam, I'm close.' I struggle to get the words out, but I want him to know what he does to me, how he's changed me, enriched my life, made me feel impossible things I thought were long past. But I can't confess anything remotely as vulnerable, so I focus on the sensations that wash my body.

'Come for me, then, squeeze me, show me the real you, and what you like.'

His words liberate me and I fly, every convulsion a tribute to him, every cry his name until I'm certain that I know I've made the biggest mistake of my life inviting Cam North into my world.

When I'm fully spent, he surprises me by easing out of my body, allowing me to collapse onto my back to catch my breath. He tears off the condom and repositions himself between my thighs, his fingers spreading me open so he can guide himself back inside me. He looks up, a million emotions written in the depths of his grey eyes, before they roll closed with pleasure and he whispers one word.

'Orla.'

I know then that I've ruined him, that he's developed feelings for me, because it's there in the tenderness of his touch as he uses both hands to push my hair back from my face. It's there in the possessive and agonising eye contact he pins me with and the reverent way he kisses me time after time. He's making love to me. He's given me everything I wanted and now he's showing me what *he* wants.

I struggle to breathe, although I crave his weight on me pressing me into the mattress as he seeks his own climax. He groans, pushes his face against the side of my neck and I breathe in his familiar scent, as if committing it to memory.

His hips start to buck, his rhythm stalling as he reaches his orgasm, and I grip him tight, holding him even though I know the pain will come as soon as I have to let him go.

The Masquerade Gala is held in the lavish ballroom of Sydney's M Club, a dazzling waterfront location with harbour views featuring the iconic Opera House and Harbour Bridge.

As dinner is over, most members have removed their masks, Cam and I no exception. Not that he needed the simple black mask to look dangerously handsome—he was that the day I met him. I just didn't anticipate the end would be quite so hard.

On the dance floor, I look up at Cam, determined to enjoy tonight as it's likely to be our last date. He's been uncharacteristically quiet since our arrival, although he was attentive and charming at dinner, and as soon at the music began he asked me to dance, dragging me away from some long-time business associate and saving me from talking shop. And he's kept me here, for song after song. It's as if he doesn't want to let me go, as if he too wants to live in denial for as long as possible.

Like me, apparently, because I ask, 'How is work on the cottage coming along?' I steer the conversation away from the inevitable train wreck I can sense approaching from the haunted look in Cam's eyes.

He takes the bait with a small indulgent smile. 'Good. I ripped out the old kitchen today and knocked down a wall.' His arms grip me a little tighter and I feel cherished, as I always do in his arms. 'I'd like to show it to you sometime, if you're free.' His hand presses between my shoulder blades and I rest my head on his chest, sniffing him, inhaling deeply and hiding from his searching stare.

'I'd love to see it.' It's not a lie. He's so passionate about his beloved cottage, so committed to undertaking all the renovations with his own two hands...

'Tomorrow?' I feel the enthusiastic thudding of his heart under my cheek and my stomach tightens with a reminder that I'm going to have to end this sooner rather than later, before Cam develops crazy ideas of attachment or worse...

I look up, real regret pinching my eyebrows in a frown. 'I'd love to, but I can't tomorrow. I'm required at that family barbecue I told you about. I'm dreading it, to be honest.'

'Still?' he asks.

I sigh. I thought I wouldn't have to think about this

until tomorrow, but it's a perfect distraction from wondering how and when to end the incredible journey with this man. 'Well, things between my father and me are strained at the best of times. I'll have to tolerate his snide remarks that I stole Jensen's' business out from under his nose, for the sake of family harmony and for my mum.'

He glances down before he says, 'Why go at all if that's how he's going to behave?'

'What do you mean?'

His jaw clenches in the way I've learned means business. 'I mean, if your father is going to make things awkward because he's a sore loser, why put yourself through that?'

'Cam…' I say, a hint of warning in my voice. I know he means well, but someone telling me what to do is almost as bad as someone telling me what I can't do, and guaranteed to make me dig in my heels.

'What? I'm serious. You owe him nothing. You said yourself he was distant while you were growing up, and then he overlooked you for CEO. He's had enough chances. If you're good enough to steal a client from him, perhaps he should have valued you more when he had you on his team—it's too late for sour grapes.' His face grows sombre and I wonder if he's making comparisons, thinking about his own father. And he's right. My father has always made me feel as if I'm not good enough, probably the reason relationships and I don't work, but I told Cam those things in moments of shared intimacy, not to have them thrown back in my face.

The storm that's been brewing all day strikes, my hackles rising. 'Perhaps he has had enough chances, but just because you're carrying resentment about your father doesn't mean I have to do the same.'

He frowns, his eyes sharp with anger. 'I wasn't suggesting you should. This isn't a competition, Orla. We're not talking about me. I'm simply suggesting he doesn't deserve you if he's going to disrespect you.' He grapples his frustration under control and I hold him closer, each of us stepping back from the edge.

I ignore the warning bells sounding inside my head. I want to rewind. I want to go back to the start, diving from that yacht in Monaco, seeing the delight and awe on Cam's face. But there's no going back. I've had my six-week proposition, and although our differences didn't seem to matter at the start they're still there, bigger and uglier than before.

Cam drops his mouth to the top of my head, presses an apologetic kiss there and says, 'Just let me know when you have time to visit the cottage.'

A wise woman would offer a non-committal smile. I shrivel, thinking about my week ahead and the week after that… I can't commit, even to a brief visit to the cottage I so long to see in person because it's important to him.

This is what I've told him from the start.

My throat burns, but I swallow, resolved to be honest, not to drag out the inevitable pain of us ending. 'I will, but it won't be for a while—I'm flying to London the day after tomorrow.'

Cam says nothing. His feet stop shuffling around the dance floor. The air around us hisses with awkward tension.

He leans back so I'm forced to lift my head from his chest and look up. 'But you've only just returned to Sydney.' He presses his lips together, disappointed. 'Do you absolutely have to go again? Don't you have people all over the world, people who can do everything for you?'

I feel weighed down by sadness. I wanted to do this in a thoughtful way, perhaps over coffee. But Cam's invested. Hell, *I'm* invested, and the time for thoughtful is long gone. 'I do have people, but this is my life, my job—you know that. Nothing's changed.'

Liar. Everything's changed...except me.

His expression hardens, his jaw tense.

I feel trapped, his arms, which only seconds ago were comforting, now feel like chains. 'Why am I defending myself, Cam? It's not a feeling I like.'

He rubs one palm down his face, hurt and defeat lurking in his expression, and my stomach lurches with nausea. 'I'm not trying to make you defensive. I just... Look, you don't need to explain your actions or defend them, never with me.' His hands find my waist and he tugs me close again, as if trying to re-create the intimacy of earlier. 'I'll just miss you, that's all.' His voice is low, heartfelt, torture to my ears, because I believe him. I want to be able to return the sentiment but it's as if my tongue is stuck in my throat.

He presses a kiss to my forehead and whispers, 'I'll wait. Come and visit the cottage any time you can.'

I don't want to hurt him so I say nothing, simply nod, foreboding churning in my head. Wonderful, considerate Cam… I can't make any promises. Nor can I admit that it's business as usual for me. Or exactly where this relationship is on my priority list. But I must. This is the moment I've been dreading. This conversation proves I've allowed this to go on too long, that I've been selfish.

I look up, my heart pounding. I see hope and passion and understanding in his expressive eyes. And he must see the opposite in mine.

His body stiffens.

I lock my knees, my legs fully absorbed with keeping me upright. I know what he wants. He showed me earlier when he made love to me. He wants some fairytale, happy-ever-after future for us. But I'm a realist. I know my limitations. I know my strengths. And I know Cam and what he deserves.

'I don't want this to end,' he says, his mouth a grim line, as if he's already anticipated my refusal.

Perceptive.

I look away. I never wanted to hurt him, but it's pointless taking this any further. 'Cam, we agreed this was temporary.'

My throat is so crushed, I can't breathe.

'I…I have feelings for you and I think you have them for me too.'

I do, I do, my beautiful, caring Cam. How could I not?

I shake my head as if I can shake out his words from my memory. 'I can't… I told you. I'm no good at relationships.'

'Why, because you had one bad experience?'

Another shake.

'Why do you have to be good at it? Why can't you just give me a chance and see how this goes?'

The lure of his words, so simple in theory, makes my head spin. 'Because I'll fail and we'll both get hurt. Why put ourselves through that?'

'Just because your marriage failed doesn't mean we will. He tried to change you and I'd never do that. Why should I suffer because of his actions?'

I step out of his arms, his touch now claustrophobic. 'Aren't you doing that right now? Trying to change me? Suggesting I ditch my family barbecue so I don't have to face my father, encouraging me to delegate more work so I can be around more to play…girlfriend?' I snort. 'Even the word is ridiculous. I'm thirty-six. I'm not cut out for the commitment of a relationship.' I lower my voice. There are people all around us. Happy, relaxed, smiling people.

I move away and he reaches for my hand. 'Where are you going? We need to talk about this.'

'We do,' I say with a sigh I feel to the tips of my toes. But this is more about me than it is about him, and if I have to tell him that, I'm going to need Dutch courage.

'I'm going to get a drink. We can talk more privately.' I head for the bar, which is relatively quiet now that the after-dinner dancing is in full swing.

I'm almost there, my mind racing with suitable let-downs that sound trite and hurtful and make me feel sick to my stomach, when I spy a woman I've met before, the M Club founder and entrepreneur Imogen Carmichael. The usually composed blonde seems flustered. I'm stalling, sidestepping my own impending disaster, but it will only take a few minutes to say hello and check she's okay.

'Imogen.' I snag her attention and she smiles, a flash of relief on her face. I'm aware that Cam will be right behind me, that we need to finish this, but something has the normally unflappable Imogen nervous. And it will give me a few precious minutes to gather my wits and compose myself for what I need to say to Cam. Otherwise I'm at risk of caving, of throwing myself into his arms and agreeing to try…

'Are you okay?'

'Oh, I'm fine,' she says, her eyes darting around the ballroom. 'I'm sorry, I can't stop and chat. I have an appointment. It was good to see you again, Orla. I hope we can catch up properly in New York next month at the Christmas Gala.'

'Yes, I'd like that.' I watch her leave, and then I continue to the bar, where Cam is waiting with two glasses of the Macallan.

'Was that Imogen Carmichael?' he asks, his body language wary and distant, as if he's sorry he lifted the lid on any discussion of a future for us. But it's too late now. We've come this far.

I swallow, my head pounding and my chest hollow and aching. 'Yes. Have you met her?'

'No.'

One-syllable answers…

I didn't want it to be like this—awkward and full of recrimination. But then, what did I expect, just because my heart is made of stone?

'You'd like her—she runs several charities,' I say. 'I'll introduce you sometime.'

He hands me my drink, his eyes glittering, all friend-liness gone. 'When? Next time you're in Sydney long enough? Next time we bump into each other at an M Club function? And will we just pretend none of this ever happened?'

I have no answer, but I say, 'I don't know when. Look, Cam, I didn't want things to go this way. I…I heard what you said about trying, and I want you to know I'm flattered that you think we could be…more. But you knew from the start—'

'I get it, you don't do relationships.'

I ignore him, the reasons almost crushing my chest as I verbalise them, forcing them out. 'You know my hours. My commitments. I clock up tens of thousands of air miles. I'm hardly ever home in Sydney. I'm just not relationship material. And you'd soon grow to re-sent me for it. It's already started.'

'I don't resent you,' he bites out, and I shrink, shame at how cowardly I'm behaving blotting out the other feelings like panic and grief that have no place, because this is what I wanted all along.

'You're the most amazing woman I've ever met— smart, inspiring, accomplished. I celebrate you.' He sighs, runs his hand through his hair. 'As long as you work the way you do because it makes you happy and not because you're still trying to prove you don't need your father's, or anyone else's, approval—including mine.'

'I know you think that's what motivates me, and maybe once…in the beginning… But this isn't about my father. It's about me not being right for a relationship, not being right for you. Look, you'll find someone you have more things in common with, someone with time for a relationship, someone your own age.' I wince because I can hear what's just emerged from my mouth and I couldn't sound more patronising if I tried.

Fury flits across Cam's face. He swallows the Macallan in a single, knocked-back swallow and then places his empty glass on the bar. 'I've never cared about our age gap and the fact you're bringing it up now, when you've nowhere else to run, tells me what a bullshit excuse it is, and you know it.'

He steps closer, one hand finding my hip, his fingers flexing in a way that reminds me of when he's turned on and about to undress me. But I can't succumb to the touch my body craves so badly; even now I feel my resolve wobbling. It would be so easy to forget this fight, like the ones that have gone before, to mend what's broken the best way we know how. With sex. But it's not just sex any more and I can't risk another dose of the searing intimacy we share.

My eyes burn and I blink hard. The longer we draw out the goodbye, the worse it will feel. For both of us. Because we've both been stupid. Both allowed feelings to creep into what should have been a simple trans- action of pleasure. I can't toy with him, now I know what he wants, know that his feelings are involved. I should never have toyed with him in the first place.

'Look, my job is my priority. I thought you under- stood that.' The words scratch at my throat like tears, but I hold myself in check, wound too tightly to sur- render to the emotion that will make me weak enough to confess that yes, a part of me wants to believe in a future for Cam and me.

'Oh, that's crystal clear, believe me.'

'That's a low blow. Just because you were handed your fortune instead of earning it, like I've had to, it's not fair to make me feel bad for making a living while you fritter away an inheritance you don't even appreci- ate.' As soon as the words are out I want to suck them back in.

He's so angry, his eyes glow, his beautiful mouth flat. 'Well, it's good to know how you really feel.'

My chest collapses, squashed by the weight of my regret. I make a move to touch him, but before I make contact he says, 'I can see you're not prepared to give us, to give me, a chance after everything we've shared.'

I gape, because I'm stunned at his insight, his matu- rity, his quiet delivery after I've verbally slapped him in the face. I've been blind or simply hiding because I'm too scared to be emotionally vulnerable.

'You know, Orla, your father isn't worthy of the amazing woman you are. You're ten times the human being he is. You're probably smarter than him, a daughter to be proud of, whose successes should be celebrated.'

'I know that.'

'Do you? Because you seem to need a daily reminder.' He touches my diamond stud with one gentle fingertip, and I want to curl into a ball.

'Every day you push and strive and work to the point of near collapse, to prove yourself to a man who'll probably never see you, the real you. I might not be worthy of you either, but at least I see you. And I want you, I want us to have something real like I thought we've had these past weeks, but you can't even give me one single chance.'

I want to tell him he's wrong, that I want to give him everything, that I already have, but until five minutes ago it would have been a lie. 'Cam, I—'

He stands tall, slides his empty glass away on the bar. 'Perhaps I was right about you all along. We *are* too different. Because I refuse to dance to my father's tune, to be his puppet. You showed me I don't have to see the money as a bond, that I can use it for good, to make a difference. You said it yourself, Orla. It's how we live our lives that defines us. How do you want to live? If you're happy making money every second of every day, then that's fine by me, but do it for yourself. Not for him. I wanted you in my life because you're enough for me just as you are, but now I see that's never going to happen because you need to work out what is enough for you. And I see now that that isn't me.'

I sway towards him, my stomach in my throat and his whispered name ringing in my ears. But I'm frozen by the choices I've made. Trapped, when all along I believed the illusion I was free to live on my terms.

Cam hands me his phone, his face now devoid of emotions. 'Text my driver when you're ready to leave.'

He turns on his heel and heads for the exit.

I stop him. 'Wait—where are you going?'

He pauses. 'I'll walk home.'

I watch him leave, my eyes burning into him, but he never once looks back.

CHAPTER TEN

Orla

I PARK MY Mini Cooper in the garage of my parents' Point Piper mansion and head into the house, my stomach hollow and my muscles clenched, ready for a fight. It's been weeks since I've seen my family, but as I step out onto the terrace, donning my sunglasses against the glare of another fantastic Sydney day, I want to switch off the sun and hide. Not from my family, although gatherings these days are usually fraught with competitive undercurrents and entrenched dysfunctional dynamics I could do without, but from myself. From the decisions I've made. The mess. The knowledge that the mistakes I made before are minuscule in comparison to this one—losing Cam.

Holding on to the torrent of emotions inside, I wave to my mother, who's in the infinity pool with my nephew, and head for the barbecue, where, typically, the males of my family congregate, as if grilling a steak requires testosterone. Before I even arrive

I can sense an argument brewing between my brother, Liam, and my father.

I sigh, every bone in my body aching with self-inflicted grief. What am I doing here? I could have made any number of excuses—I have tons of emails to catch up on, six weeks' worth of laundry to organise…damn, even airing my own long-neglected penthouse would be preferable to this, although I'm mostly here for my mother's sake. But what I really want to do is lick my wounds while I try to work out if I've just sabotaged the best thing that ever happened to me.

My hollow stomach gripes again—ever since I arrived home last night after the gala I've wanted to throw up and it gives me a sick sense of satisfaction. I got what I wanted and it hurts like hell. It's over, the end not neat as I'd hoped, but then when is anything ever neat when matters of the heart are involved?

Something inside my chest lurches.

It's grief, just grief.

It will pass.

I force my face to conceal everything I'm feeling and greet my brother, accepting his kiss on the cheek. I pour myself a drink and take a tiny sip of the iced water, but even that gets stuck in my throat. I put it down and tune in to the argument to take my mind off Cam and the gaping hole he's left in my life, although this is the very drama I was dreading.

Cam was right. Why am I putting myself through this? I'm a grown-ass woman, not a dutiful child. And today there's only room inside my battle-sore body for one fight: staving off tears.

If I weren't afraid of bursting into those unheard-of tears, I'd join my mother in the pool, because I'm too heartsick to deal with family drama, but perhaps Liam needs my support.

'Have I interrupted a fight?' I say, watching my father stab at a steak on the grill with barbecue tongs.

My brother is uncharacteristically annoyed. 'More of an ongoing discussion of how badly I'm running the ship,' says Liam. 'You know, sis, you did well to bail when you did.' He stares at the back of my father's head as if daring him to contradict this in front of me.

I'm shocked speechless. This is the first time I've heard of any discontent between my father and his golden boy, not that the fault lies with Liam.

I try to keep the bitterness from erupting, from saying something I'll regret, but then it hits me.

I really don't care.

I'm thirty-six. I've just lost a man with whom I suspect I've fallen in love. I have bigger problems than causing a scene at a family barbecue. Massive problems. Insurmountable problems…

What have I done?

I focus on my brother. 'Well, I wasn't given a choice. As I recall, my services were no longer required.' Sympathy for Liam wells up inside me—so he's not good enough either, in our father's eyes. 'Is this about Jensen's?'

I have no desire to be the source of tension between

these two men, but really, where does my father get off with his expectations and constant criticism? I shouldn't need to impress this man, and shame, hotter than the November sun, licks at me that I even tried. I'm his daughter. His pride should be automatic. His love un-conditional. Like Cam's...

Cam—the only person whose opinion matters.

The pangs of longing twisting my stomach into knots grow stronger.

Liam's clearly more pissed than I've ever seen him, because he ignores my question and puts down his beer at the nearby table.

'You know, Dad, Orla bested us because she's just better. Perhaps you should have thought of that when you were succession planning.'

Liam turns away from our father in disgust and squeezes my shoulder. 'You look great, sis. It's been years since I've seen you look this relaxed. Whatever you've been doing these past few weeks suits you. If you want my advice, you should keep it up.'

He moves away to the other side of the terrace to join his wife, presumably to calm down so he too can get through a simple family gathering. I watch him kiss my sister-in-law and wave to his son in the pool, pangs of jealousy slicing through me, not for his position as CEO that I once coveted above all else. But because he has a life. A rich and balanced life. A life like the one I could have tried to create with Cam, if I wasn't so caught up in my fear of failure.

I close my eyes, clarity arriving like a smack in the

face. What is failure but evidence that you've tried your best?

Cam's already said I'm enough for him, just the way I am. No changes, no expectations, no conditions. I touch an earring, the earrings Cam gave me in Singapore, hoping somehow to connect with the man who's taught me how to love. Properly, unconditionally, and without fear. I located the box last night when I returned home to my dark and empty home. I fell asleep clutching it, the only part of him I had access to. The first thing I did this morning was change my earrings.

Even if I've lost Cam for ever through my own stupidity, I need a fresh reminder every time I look in the mirror. A reminder of everything he gave me. A reminder I'm more than Orla Hendricks, successful CEO. I'm also Orla Hendricks, woman, and I can have a fulfilling, complete relationship as long as I'm prepared to work just as hard at it.

Not that loving Cam would be hard.

I gasp. I love him…

For once my head is as clear as the cloudless blue framing Sydney's famous skyline in the distance.

He sees me. The real me. Despite our differences, he wants me. Or perhaps, in all areas that matter, we're not that different after all. I was just too scared to believe in those qualities. But Cam's shown me balance. He's shown me that I can have it all—a job I'm good at and a relationship I want to work equally hard at. For the first time in my life, I want the commitment. I want to devote my time and energy and everything that I am to making us work.

I want him. In every way.

My father's voice interrupts my thoughts. 'I hope Jensen's isn't more than you can handle.'

I open my eyes with new resolve that has nothing to do with justifying myself to this man. 'Really? Talking business? This is family time.'

I look down at the steaks. There's no way a single mouthful of the delicious-smelling lunch is going to make it past my throat, now I've acknowledged my feelings for Cam. But have I left it too late? Have I ruined the only thing in my life that I love more than my work?

Him.

'I've spent the past ten years building my firm,' I tell my startled father. 'It's a well-oiled machine, and even if it wasn't, it's only a job, so don't you worry about whether I can handle Jensen's. But while we're on the subject, I'm going to be taking some time off—my personal life is a mess and I'm hoping to rectify that.' The barest surge of hope wells inside me, in no way diminished by my father's dismissive grunt.

'I'm not hungry and I have somewhere else to be. Tell Mum I'll call her later.' I kiss my father's cheek and for the first time in years truly see him, see the stress lines, the grey hair and the near perpetual scowl he wears as the toll of his ambition. I want better than that for myself. And, like always, I can have what I want; I just pray I'm not too late to have it with Cam.

'You know, Dad, you should try to find greater work-life balance and support Liam in doing the same.'

I expect some scathing retort or splutter of anger, but his jaw actually drops and I wish Cam were here to witness the look on his face.

'Oh, and by the way,' I add, 'your steaks are burning.'

I pull up outside Cam's cottage as the sun kisses the horizon. When I climb from my car and hear the faint, rhythmic sound of hammering, I know I've found him at last, my body flooding with chills of relief.

It has taken the rest of the afternoon for me to track him down. He wasn't at his cold and sterile penthouse—no surprise. I checked the local beach, knowing he likes to surf. I even reached out to the construction company he used to work for, my mounting frustration turning to panic. I finally called a contact in the real-estate industry, someone I made obscenely wealthy last year, begging him to flout the law and provide me with the address of the cottage Cam purchased a year ago.

I collect the cool-bag full of Cam's favourite beer from the passenger seat of my car and head down the driveway towards the sound of banging, every nerve in my body firing like the cascade of fireworks we watched over the bay in Singapore only a week ago. As I round the property, ducking under an overhanging eucalyptus tree in desperate need of a hearty prune, I'm temporarily blinded by the last rays of the setting sun.

Then my vision clears and I'm blinded anew, only

this time it's the sight of the man I love, shirtless, with a tool belt hugging his hips, that scorches my retinas.

The rear of the property boasts the enviable sea views he showed me on his phone that day in Dubai. A newly constructed deck extends the width of the cottage, and Cam is busy framing up what appears to be a perfect sunroom off the existing living area. I can smell the sawdust before I approach, my head spinning with hopes and fears and what-ifs.

He'd have every right to turf me off his property. He's spent the past six weeks building me up, pushing me to be the best version of myself. A whole version. Not afraid to let go, to loosen the reins that have trapped me inside my own beliefs and expectations for so long.

But can I be whole without him now that I know I love him?

I must have stepped on a stick or piece of sun-scorched bark from the eucalyptus, because he hears the crack and spins. Sees me.

His arms fall to his sides, the hammer hanging in his hand. A million emotions pass over his face in the few seconds of silence that we spend staring. If I could stop the wheel spinning on the love I saw yesterday at his penthouse I would, but there's no sign of it.

Did I kill it for good? Am I too late?

I hold out the cool-bag, my arm trembling. 'I thought you might like a cold beer. It's your favourite.'

Still he stares.

I swallow, my throat parched.

He sniffs, tucks the hammer into his work belt and looks back my way. 'Why are you here, Orla?'

I try to un-hear the accusation and hostility in his question. It's not unreasonable after the way I treated him. As if he didn't matter. As if he wasn't important. As if he isn't the very reason my heart beats.

'You invited me.' My voice is small. Where is my smiling, devil-may-care Cam?

He smirks, shakes his head, but it's an expression of disbelief. 'That was before.'

Before I hurt him. Before he tried to tell me how he felt and I shut him down.

'You threw my invitation back in my face, along with my dreams for us.'

His words are like shots from the nail gun I see on the new deck. 'I know, and I want to apologise. You were right about me. My life isn't enough.'

I take a shuddering step forward and then halt when the expression on his face stays blank and cold. I put the cool-bag down on the grass.

'I want those dreams, Cam. I want you.'

He looks away to the horizon and I crumple a little more. I'm blowing this, allowing my one chance to slip through my fingers. I lift my chin, willing him silently to look back at me with every cell in my body.

Our eyes meet, just like that first time in Monaco, only now I love this man about whom my first impressions were so wrong. 'I want this dream, Cam. The cottage, waking up to the sunrise, sitting by your side on that deck to watch the sunset. I know I said I didn't want a relationship, but that was because I was scared that I had some vital emotional piece of me lacking. Scared to try. Scared to fail. Scared that I'd be nothing without my career because that's all I've had, all I've been able to control for so long.'

'So what's changed? I'm still the same me I was yesterday. The same me you didn't value enough to give a chance.' He hooks his thumbs into his worn leather tool belt in a way I'm certain he's done a thousand times, and my body jolts, because I want to be there to see him do it a thousand times more. To watch him build this cottage, his dream, and to help him build many more dreams of our shared future.

'Nothing's changed, or everything.' I twist my hands together. This isn't going well. 'I know I'm not making sense. But I spoke to my father earlier, and I realised something. Well, I realised lots of things, actually. But the most important ones were that I don't care what he thinks. I only care about proving something to you.'

'I told you last night. You never have to prove anything to me—'

'I do.' I step closer, urgency driving me, although his sphere of personal space vibrates around him like a force-field, keeping me at a distance. 'I need to prove that I love you, because I know I've hurt you and it's my biggest regret—that and letting you go in the first place. Thinking I could live without you.'

He still looks wary, even as his eyes latch on to mine, penetrating and searching.

'I know you won't believe that I love you for a while,

but I'll keep trying, keep showing you until you're convinced.' I pop one hand on my hip and push my sunglasses up onto my head so he can see I mean business.

'I mean it, Cam—you know how driven I am when I want something. You, multi-billion-dollar deals…it's all the same to me. I won't give up.' My weight shifts from one foot to the other, despite the confident spiel. I wish he'd say something, even if it's *Get off my property.* Anything to break the tension.

I'm about to turn away in defeat when he says, 'You're wearing the earrings.'

I'm so focused on breathing so I don't collapse that it takes me a moment to understand. 'What? Oh, yes.' I touch the earring again, the intricate gold filigree reassuring under my fingertip. 'I wanted a new reminder. Every time I touch these, every time I look in the mirror, I want to remember you, remember all the moments, incredible moments we shared. Because that's the life I want, Cam. A life filled with incredible, joyous, sexy, fun-packed, simple moments. With you.'

My pulse roars in my ears.

He stares, unmoving, his beautiful eyes expressionless.

And then, with his strangled grunt in my ears, I'm dragged into his arms, his big, strong, comforting arms. I'm pressed against his bare, sweaty chest, which is all dusty with sawdust, and I've never felt more at home. His mouth covers mine, and I curl my fingers into his hair, never wanting to let him go ever again.

I pull away from the kiss, keeping a hold of his face.

'I'm sorry. Thank you for challenging me, showing me I can be whoever I want to be. I can re-invent myself and break free of my own cage.'

He grips my shoulders. 'You're wonderful, just the way you are. I love you.'

I kiss him again and he pushes me back by the shoulders. 'Thank you for putting everything into perspective. You showed me I'm not defined by my inheritance, that I can rule it, rather than it ruling me.'

'You're not your father, Cam. It's just money. It's this,' I wave an arm in the direction of the cottage, his labour of love, 'and this,' I press my palm flat on his chest, over his heart, 'how you live your life, how you use your inheritance to make a difference—that's who you are.'

We kiss again and this time when we pull apart we're both laughing, joyous, thrilling laughter I want to hear and feel every day for the rest of my life.

'So are you going to show me the cottage or not?' I put my arms around his waist and rest my head against his chest, feel the steady thump of his heart.

My heart.

His voice rumbles from deep within his chest. 'Sure, but there's nowhere else to sit apart from here.' He points to two dusty, paint-splattered deckchairs on the lawn, perfectly positioned to watch the sun rise and set.

I look up, lift my eyebrows, new pangs of envy making me pout. 'Two? Had company, have you?' The thought of anyone looking at my man while he's shirtless makes me form fists. I might have to erect a privacy fence until he's finished the cottage.

He tucks me under his arm, kisses the top of my head and leads me towards the house with a chuckle. 'My cousin's been helping me.'

'The one you sent the car to?'

He nods.

'Good, because from here on in, that second deck-chair has got my name on it—I'm going to enjoy spending the summer watching you sweat shirtless and get splinters I can kiss better.' I lift his hand to my mouth and press a kiss over his fingertips.

'Is that right?' he says, his mouth twisted in that way that makes my blood sing and my insides clench in anticipation. He leads me through the demolished kitchen and down the hall to the cooler rear part of the house. He kicks open the last door. It's a bedroom, a single camp bed is pushed up against one wall, and Cam's tuxedo from last night hangs from a rusty nail on the back of the door.

I turn, already mentally undressing him as I undo the buttons of my blouse, making it clear what I propose we do with the rest of the night.

'What about my beer?' He pops open his fly and heels off his work boots, his heated stare tightening my nipples to hard peaks.

I smile at my man. 'It'll keep. Let's take a moment.' And I kiss him, flopping backwards onto the narrow mattress and tugging him down on top of me.

EPILOGUE

Cam

THE NEW YORK M Club's ballroom is packed with party-goers, every member dressed to the nines and in festive spirit. It's the biggest gathering of immense wealth and beautiful, glamorous people I've ever seen—twice the size of the Masquerade Gala in Sydney— but I only have eyes for one woman.

My woman.

I watch her talking to Imogen Carmichael, her exquisite face animated and her eyes dancing with the reflection of a million fairy lights scattered throughout the ballroom. She carries herself with the same grace and poise as the first time I saw her, perched on a stool at the casino in Monaco, only now she's relaxed. She smiles more, laughs more, and waking up with her every morning is a privilege I'll never take for granted.

She's taken her first holiday in five years. As promised, she's spent the summer sitting on that tatty deck-chair watching me work on the cottage while she drinks my beer. She even comes surfing with me sometimes.

The only time she complains is when I put my shirt back on. She told me yesterday that my working semi-naked helps her to think.

She catches my eye, winds up her conversation with Imogen and slinks my way, so by the time she reaches my side the only thoughts in my head are how quickly I can get her out of here so I can love her the way I want to.

'What are you thinking about?' She slips her arm around my waist and tucks her body into my side. 'Tell me now, because I think I know that look on your face.' She presses her lips to my neck with a sexy little hum.

I smile down at her and bend low to press an all too brief kiss on her lips. 'I was wondering what *you* think about when I'm shirtless.'

Her eyes dance. 'Well, duh, the same thing half of Sydney thinks about—ways to get you out of the other half of your clothes, of course.' She laughs, rises up onto her tiptoes and kisses me back. 'You know you're becoming quite the celebrity, right?'

She's talking about the changes I made to the construction company I once worked for after I bought it and the training school I set up to give apprenticeships to youngsters who need a break in life.

'Well, you showed me how to let go of my resentment. I think he'd approve of how I'm using it,' I say of my father, the remorse in my voice causing Orla's eyes to shine with love and support.

'Of course he would. Opening new hospital wings you've sponsored, delivering brand-new equipment to the local surf lifesavers, planting trees. You're always splashed on the front of some newspaper or magazine these days, usually shirtless. I think he'd prefer it if you wore a shirt though.' She pouts, mock censure on her beautiful mouth.

I roll my eyes but I can't help smiling at her teasing. 'I was shirtless one time, Orla. One time. And that was only because I was trying out the surfboards.'

She laughs, a lovely tinkling sound I never grow tired of hearing. 'Oh, don't worry. If I had this body,' she runs her hand over my abs and up to my chest, 'I'd want to show it off all the time too.'

I put my arms around her waist and hold her close. 'You're doing just fine with the body you've got. Trust me.'

Our exchange turns heated, X-rated, non-verbal communication passing between us in that way couples do when they know exactly what the other is thinking.

'Want to get out of here?' she asks, her voice smoky with lust. 'I have a surprise for you.'

'Yes.' It's a no-brainer. The chemistry, the bond we share, shows no signs of letting up; if anything it gets stronger every day. And I have a surprise for her too.

My Christmas present.

The cottage is almost finished and it's hers. I signed over the deeds today and the key feels heavy in my pocket. Excitement joins the slug of potent, almost incapacitating desire I always feel in Orla's company, desire made stronger by whatever is putting that gleam in her eyes, because I know she'll always keep me on my toes.

We make our way out of the ballroom, stopping briefly to say goodnight to one or two friends. Instead of heading for the exit, she leads me towards the club's private rooms.

'Where are we going?'

She unlocks one of the doors, her small smile knowing. 'I thought we could spend the night here.'

Inside, the room is intimate and romantic and exactly what she deserves after weeks of sleeping at the cottage with me because she knows I'm more comfortable there than at the penthouse. Of course, we upgraded to a double camp bed, but she deserves a little luxury after weeks of sawdust, dodgy plumbing and unreliable electrics.

She reaches for me, her hands coming around my neck, and I kiss her once, twice…but before I get carried away I pull the key from my pocket. 'I have a surprise for you too. Merry Christmas.'

Her hand covers her mouth and she gasps, because she knows what it is I'm giving her. She understands me. She shares my dreams as I share hers.

'Cam… Oh, I don't know what to say. Thank you.'

Her reaction, her obvious delight, makes me feel ten feet tall. My heart pounds, but I plough on with the second part of my surprise. 'Say you'll wake up by my side every morning to the sound of the sea. Say you'll sit next to me on the veranda, drinking my beer. Say you'll marry me?'

I present the ring I bought earlier today, my insides twisting with nerves. 'I know it's quick, but I want to live dreams and make moments with you for the rest of our lives.'

'Yes.' She jumps up and I catch her around the waist, staggering towards the bed so I can deposit her under me and kiss her the way I want to.

Her smile, when we part for air, fills my chest with joy and love and too many euphoric emotions to name.

'Of course, you know what this means, don't you?' I say between her kisses.

'What?' She lies back on the bed and looks at me with such love in her eyes that I struggle to breathe. Struggle to believe that she's mine.

'Well, not only will I be able to offload half my fortune onto my new spouse…' I wink because only she understands how far I've come that I can joke about something as serious as my inheritance.

She cups my face, her eyes swimming.

'But I also get to keep you for ever.'

She nods.

'And I get to keep you.'

* * * * *

HER EVERY FANTASY

ZARA COX

MILLS & BOON

This book is dedicated to friends
and lovers everywhere.

CHAPTER ONE

Bryce

Two days, three hours and…seven minutes.

That was how long the email had been sitting in my inbox unopened. I detested that I was reduced to even knowing how long it'd parked itself in my consciousness, taunting me with its presence. Taunting me with that gut-twisting mix of hope and bitterness I thought I was finally rid of.

How I wished it were one of those mundane work emails I'd become so adept at passing to my assistant to deal with. Then, from a safe distance, it would've been so easy to tell her to handle it. Or, better yet, delete it.

But here it was. Not handled. Not deleted. And about as far from mundane as it could get.

Not when her name was blaring from the 'sender' line: Savannah Knight.

Not when the subject matter stated three simple words: I Need You.

I tossed my pen onto the desk in disgust and shoved my chair backwards, swivelling away from the offensive email for good measure.

Fuck this.

Who the hell did she think she was? Not a single word in three and a half years. Then this?

I'd held out for over two days. Long enough for her to know I wasn't going to jump.

A fragile but welcome burst of satisfaction settled my ire a little. She needed to know I wasn't the same person who'd stumbled away from that quaint little chapel in sunny Sittingbourne, Kent, three summers ago a pathetic, emotional wreck.

That man was long gone, after years of living on the edge of *'Will we? Won't we?'* was definitively answered once and for all: *We won't. We never will.*

In his place was someone I respected better but didn't always like. A man whose future and focus were as steadfast as a striking sledgehammer.

I might have deluded myself into thinking I was different once upon a time, that I could be softer, less… Mortimer, more…something else, but that time had long passed. For better and, I suspected, worse I was a bloody Mortimer down to my last cell. It'd just taken a little longer, and ironically her help, to make me accept my true self.

Ruthless. Competitive. Take no prisoners. Crazy ambitious. And yes, sometimes, utterly selfish in my quest to achieve all the above.

So why wasn't that ruthless selfishness directing my finger to the delete button? One quick tap on the mouse and she would be erased as definitely as she'd erased me.

Teeth gritted, I fought and irritatingly lost the fight,

compulsion swivelling me back around to face my laptop. To the neat little blue rectangle of temptation taunting me with its secrets.

Open me. Read me.

With a tight curse, I clicked on it, my greedy eyes devouring the words.

Bryce,
I know this is out of the blue so...surprise! It's a been a while, huh? Guess we've both been crazy busy. ☺

Anyway, a little bird told me you're opening a brand spanking new building in Singapore. Congrats on all your awesome accomplishments, btw.

But I'll get to the point. I need you.

I cursed that traitorous little flip in my gut when I lingered on those three words. Then forced myself to read on.

More specifically, I need a space in your building for the launch of my flagship store.

My team have researched several locations and they all agree your building will be perfect for my needs.

Another little bird told me you haven't yet accepted a bid for the ground and first floors. If that's true—and I really hope it is!—I'd love to be considered for an initial five-year lease of the space.

If my info is wildly inaccurate, then let me know.

Look forward to hearing from you.
Best,
Savannah

Anger blazed in my chest. Singeing. Devastating. So this was how she was going to play it? Act as if nothing had happened? As if we'd simply…fallen out of touch and she was initiating a reconnection while she had a few minutes to spare in her busy day?

Well, I could do cool and impersonal. Hell, I was a master at it.

I yanked my laptop closer and stabbed the keyboard with more force than was necessary.

Savvie,

No, scratch that. Best keep things formal.

Savannah,
It is a surprise. You'll have to remind me how long it's been if we meet in the future.

Sadly, my schedule is atrociously tight, so these days I delegate requests like yours to my commercial leasing team. I've passed your request on to them—see cc above. They'll be in touch at some point, I expect.

Good luck with your launch, wherever that may be.
Bryce Mortimer

I hit 'send' with one last smug little stab at the button and lounged back in my seat.

An hour later my glee had turned to ash. The button I'd clicked to let me know she'd read my reply had been activated almost immediately.

She'd seen my email. Most likely read it.

Anticipation had risen like an unstoppable tide in-side me, only to crash back as the seconds ticked by without a further response. What did I expect? Con-trition? Hell, an apology? A plea for me to grant her wish for old times' sake despite my rightful disap-pointment in her?

Delusion soured my mouth.

We were both equally successful in our chosen fields. Why would she need a helping hand from me when she could reduce grown men into drooling schoolboys with a flick of her long, seductive eye-lashes?

Another sensation stabbed, this time the acrid jeal-ousy I thought was long in my past.

Fuck it. I rose from my desk, determined to put greater distance between me and my laptop before I did something foolish—like fruitlessly click 'refresh' on my email. The ping of an incoming message arrested my movement.

Bryce,
Sorry for taking up your precious time. But thank you for the good wishes and for passing me on to your team. I've emailed them directly.

Excuse me for saying this, and perhaps it's just in my imagination, but you sound...cold and distant.

But...whatever. I'm around from tomorrow until the launch date in a little over a month's time.

I would like to see you again, Bryce, but I under-stand if your super-tight schedule doesn't allow it. On the off-chance you haven't turned into a robot and still like a good steak I'd love to buy you lunch.

Let me know.

Best wishes,

Savvie

PS Since you seem to need reminding, it's been three years and four months since we last saw each other. Your memory used to be sharper than this. Guess some things do change!

I was torn between grinning at her sheer nerve and cussing at her unsubtle hints that my response was in any way defective. But even as I vacillated between anger and amusement, my gaze remained riveted on the eighth line:

I would like to see you again...

A pulse of resentment sizzled beneath my skin, laced with abrasive disappointment I hadn't been able to let go in over three long years. That inability to let go, to consign her to my past where she belonged, where I'd successfully archived a lot of emotional crap, was what pissed me off the most.

Case in point: my parents.

Another case in point: my crappy relationship with my siblings, in particular. My extended family, in general.

But somehow, Savannah Knight remained a burr under my skin that wouldn't be evicted.

Somehow, years ago she'd made it past the barricades I'd erected; somehow even set herself up in her own little bunker, immune from all the shit going on in my life. And every now and then...when I'd felt as if I were drowning, that bunker had been a godsend.

My safe place...until it and *she* wasn't.

Maybe I hadn't dug deep enough to evict her.

Maybe it was time to confront it...her...head-on. Thrash it out once and for all and put it behind me. It'd been festering for long enough and I knew that corrosive wound, coupled with my feelings towards my own family, had contributed to keeping people at arm's length.

On the family front, I was more than okay with maintaining the status quo. Years of rebuffed advances and the eventual realisation that the Mortimers would never be a close-knit, happy unit like the ones I'd dreamed of had finally put paid to childish imaginings.

Even my brother Gideon's out-of-the-blue phone call that he'd met *the one* a few months ago hadn't dented my cynicism. As for my parents, they'd never wanted me, hadn't hung around even long enough to see my first day of school before cutting me out of their lives.

But Savannah...

She'd let me believe that, despite hard-learnt lessons, there was a possibility for *more*...for *joy*...long after I'd sworn never to let anyone close. Long after a confused eight-year-old had been summoned into a cold study of one relative accompanied by a nanny and informed that the mother who didn't want him was never coming back, having died when her car went off some cliff in Switzerland. That his hopes of a Disney-style reconciliation were turned to dust for ever.

That child had grown into a cynical teenager, fully steeped in the dysfunction that ruled his super-wealthy, super-emotionally-bankrupt family.

Somewhere along that journey as a fully-fledged teenage malcontent, one Savannah Knight had illuminated my dark soul with grace, humour and a mega-watt smile.

And then taken it all away like a magician's cruel trick.

If nothing else, she deserved a piece of my mind before I relegated her to the past for good. I'd done it with my siblings. I'd achieved it with my parents. With Savannah, all it needed was some good old-fashioned face-to-face.

My answer was shorter than the last. Straight to the point.

Lunch tomorrow. One p.m. My office.
Get your little birds to tell you where if you don't know.
Bryce

She replied within seconds.

I'll be there.
Savvie

I wanted to resent the shortened nickname that reminded me so much of our past. Of laughter and secret angst. Of beauty and betrayal. Of daring to stretch the limits of friendship and ending with nothing but broken promises. And yes, for reminding me of giving in to uncontrollable urges in the privacy of my bedroom.

I wanted to remain steadfast on formal ground. What did it matter, though? Savannah or Savvie, she remained the same person.

The girl who'd been my best friend. My port in the storm. Who'd coaxed me with smiles and laughter to step onto the edge with her. Then left me there.

The woman she'd turned into had betrayed me, shown me in no uncertain terms that our friendship meant nothing.

The phone on my desk buzzed. I ignored it, my fingers creeping once more towards my mouse. The website I called up was one I was unwillingly familiar with, driven to all those years ago by that same crazy compulsion that fuelled everything to do with Savannah. That stuck onto my skin like an unwanted tattoo.

The page had been created before she'd become famous. Before she'd exploded onto the world stage and into the fantasy of every red-blooded male who set eyes upon her.

The Personal Fan Page of Savannah Knight: World's Number One Plus-Size Lingerie Model.

Her pictures were plastered all over the page, each one more breathtaking than the last. Each shot showing a profusion of her signature dark gold corkscrew curls. Every single picture drove a hot spike of lust through my groin, and even before I was halfway down the page I was as hard as fuck, torn between frustration that she still had this effect on me, a hunger I couldn't contain and a compulsion to keep going. Keep devouring. Keep salivating. Perhaps even unzip my fly, take out my cock and masturbate like a randy teenager right here in my damn office.

I resisted that last urge by pushing myself closer to my desk, as if shoving my lower half under my desk would kill the insane urge.

Mentally rolling my eyes at myself, I scrolled faster. An addict seeking his sweet spot.

Since launching her own lingerie brand, every runway show Savannah had staged had been a huge success. Every season had brought her more accolades until she now needed a couple of bodyguards for protection from sometimes overeager fans.

At one picture, I just stopped…stared.

Bloody hell, she was gorgeous.

Skin a dark sunset gold, so smooth and soft and warm, it'd been a challenge to keep from touching her when we were platonic teenage friends, when what we'd had between us had been too unique, too sacred to mess with. Adulthood had brought further challenges but, with more restraint, I'd had a better handle on it.

Or so I'd thought…

I shifted in my chair, forcefully reminding myself why Savvie Knight, the only person who'd made it onto a list of one labelled Friendship, no longer resided there. The memories kept tumbling through my mind as relentlessly as the pictures flowing up the screen.

She'd disparagingly called herself a mongrel. I'd thought her stunning beyond words.

Lucky enough to have the noble blood of African chiefs and the integrity of not one but two accomplished professors flowing through her veins. I'd listened with unbridled jealousy, sprawled at the foot of her teenage bed, as she'd offhandedly rattled off tales of her African heritage alongside vexed recounting of interminable Sunday family dinners where her parents had deigned to be present. Had had the audacity to ask her about her day, her month, her year.

So what if there'd seemed to be an underlying discontentment over her family's single-mindedness about her life? I'd never drilled her over the details because I'd been too busy wondering why she wasn't just...*thrilled* to have a caring family in the first place.

Experiencing that unique bond, even from the fringes, had been unparalleled. A reason to safeguard what we'd had.

It'd taken a full year of friendship to confess that Mortimers didn't do Sunday family dinner. That we could barely tolerate one another even at Christmas. That birthday presents were often organised by executive assistants and presented by delivery men and one was lucky if one received a card. That to my memory and before she'd died, I'd never received a birthday or Christmas present directly from my mother, nor from my father.

That I'd swap my life for hers in a heartbeat. Hand over the multimillion trust fund with my name on it for a slice of the life she took for granted.

But all of that was before she'd shown her true colours.

Before she'd turned her back on me and married Daniel Fucking Wallis.

The name was enough to dispel my useless reminiscing and restore righteous bitterness to its rightful place. Enough for me to hit the X that closed the page and for my hard-as-rock erection to subside.

I slammed my laptop shut and veered from my desk. Across the bay my gaze flitted past skyscrapers and Singapore's breathtaking Gardens by the Bay, with its hanging gardens and fifty-metre-tall supertrees, to the one building I'd placed my personal stamp on.

Originally named The Diamond Bay, but later changed to The Sylph, a better fitting name.

An iconic building already racking up international architectural awards.

My baby. My special once-in-a-lifetime project.

The one my ex-best friend wanted a piece of.

Savannah might not be my enemy in the true sense of the word but, after her singeing betrayal and dismissal of me from her life, we weren't friends any longer. After my parents and family, she'd been the third and final strike.

My days of accommodating foibles and betrayals were behind me. She needed to be set straight on that score once and for all.

By this time tomorrow she would know in no uncertain terms that it was a mistake to resurface, to attempt to touch a place in my life that belonged on a crap pile of history.

* * *

I should've arranged lunch in my office just as I'd planned.

I knew I'd made a mistake even before the buzzer sounded in my Marina Bay penthouse apartment. I'd talked myself into the argument that geography didn't matter.

Straight. Sharp. To the point before *zàijiàn. Sayonara.* Goodbye.

Easily accomplished in any language and as effective here as in my office half a mile away. So I'd arranged for my executive chef to prepare lunch here.

In my private space.

Where she could read into it. Where signs of my existence were everywhere. Where everything now seemed…way too personal.

Clever, clever *Bryce.*

I grimaced at the very vocal inner voice and pressed the button that activated my private lift. The ding sounded in seconds. My stomach muscles tightened as I pulled the door open and awaited my first glimpse of Savannah in three and a half years.

The lift doors parted.

My first reaction was a filthy curse at the internet for the shoddy portrayal of the woman who would turn heads wherever she went. Because the real-life version was so much better than the pitiful digital imitation.

Vibrant. Vivacious. So fucking beautiful.

Dressed in a blush-pink floaty top and skin-tight, chocolate-coloured leather trousers, she was a magnificent vision, powerful enough to slacken my jaw before

I caught myself and pressed my lips into appropriately neutral, downright *unfriendly* lines. Her curvy hips and endless legs were balanced on sky-high heels matching her trousers and, with that combined with her bouncy curls and flawless make-up, I felt my breathing fracture into useless silent hiccups as I stared.

Mine was the only apartment on this floor, a request I'd worked into the architect's plans when I'd built the luxury complex. It meant that, with over seventeen thousand square feet to play with, the distance from the lift to my front door was substantial. Long enough to broadcast any nerves from my visitor.

There were none.

She effortlessly projected an ingrained confidence and inner strength I'd secretly envied for a long time before finding my own rightful place in the world. She'd exuded that same vibe on her debut runway show, earned herself positive adoration and cemented herself on the fashion landscape in one fell swoop.

That had been my one and only attendance of her show, and I'd silently watched, smiled proudly and applauded her then.

I wasn't applauding now as I watched Savannah saunter towards me, that heart-stopping smile curving her luscious lips.

I stayed put, let her come closer, looked deeper into her stunning eyes to spot the first signs of wariness.

Three feet from me, she stopped. 'Hello, Bryce.'

I shoved my hands into my pockets and narrowed

my eyes, almost deluding myself that minimising my vision would lessen her physical impact. 'Hi, yourself.'

'It's good to see you,' she murmured and I gritted my jaw against the evocative effect of her voice. Warm honey. Sultry nights. Hot tangled sheets. The stuff of a thousand wet dreams.

All forbidden best-friend territory.

Except we weren't best friends any more. Hell, we weren't even friends.

So I raised an eyebrow, deliberately, but didn't answer. The faintest flush stained her cheeks.

A little appeased at that reaction, I waved towards the open door. 'Come in. Lunch is just about ready and I need to get back to work within the hour.'

She studied me for one second longer, either reacquainting herself with my face or assessing my mood before walking past me into my personal domain. My involuntary swallow at the rich, flowery scent that trailed her was annoying but I gave myself a pass, extracting a hand from my pocket long enough to shut the door before I jammed it back into safety.

I arrived in the living room to find her examining every square inch of it. Yeah, definitely the wrong move, bringing her here. When she was done, she faced me with another tentative smile.

'Your place is amazing. Very stylish. Very…suave.'

I nodded briskly, totally dismissing the pulse of warmth that attempted to steal through me. 'Thanks. Would you like a drink? I have white wine chilling. Or

I can offer you something else?' No reason not to be civil before the takedown began.

She shook her head. 'White wine is fine, thank you.'

My living room was a wide, open space with the dining table tucked beneath a slanted floor-to-ceiling glass wall. Currently at a setting that dulled the blinding sun's rays by a fraction, the glass threw back a dozen perfect reflections. Through one, I saw her staring after me as I went to the silver ice bucket set up on its pedestal next to the dining table. Saw her avert her gaze as I plucked the Chateauneuf from the ice and turned around. I uncorked the bottle, poured two glasses and returned to the living room.

'Sit down, Savannah.'

Watchful honey-gold eyes ringed with lush eyelashes met mine as she accepted the wine. 'Are you sure you want me to?'

I froze. 'Excuse me?'

'I wasn't imagining it. You're cold. And distant. And seriously pissed off with me for some reason. So why invite me to lunch, Bryce?' she demanded.

One thing I'd forgotten about her. Savvie always shot from the hip, no holds barred. But I was determined to do this on my terms. I shrugged. 'It seemed as good a time as any to set a few things straight.'

She tensed. 'Things like what?'

I shook my head. 'Not until we've eaten.'

'I'm not sure I want to break bread with someone who's going to spend the whole meal glaring at me.'

'You're a grown woman, Savannah. I'm sure you can take it.'

'I can. But do I want to? There's such a thing as free will, you know?' she challenged without losing an ounce of warm seduction from her voice.

It really was the most maddening thing.

Irritated, I shrugged again. 'You're the one who reached out. You're the one who wanted to see me. And unless I'm mistaken you want something from me, correct?'

She opened her mouth, most probably to deny my crisp assessment. Something stopped her response, something apprehensive that raised my hackles. 'Fine. Let's eat,' she replied abruptly, heading across the room before I could respond, but she paused when she reached the table.

The table was set at perpendicular angles, one place at the head and the other at ninety degrees. I dragged my gaze from the tight, plump globes of her arse and the waist I knew I could span with my hands, and pulled her seat out. After casting another furtive glance at me, she set her suede clutch on the table and sat down.

I took the other seat, aware that neither of us had taken a sip of our wine. Again she latched on to my thoughts, reminding me of her uncanny ability to do so from our youth. 'Is it worth making a toast to a reunion or am I wasting my breath?'

I snapped out my pristine napkin with unnecessary force before draping it across my lap. 'Sure, I'll drink to something. Go ahead and make a toast.'

She stared at me a taut few seconds. 'To old friends and acquaintances?'

'Is that a toast or a question?'

My chef's arrival in that moment from the kitchen with the first course stalled her answer. My brief to the chef had been simple—my guest loved everything except string beans and had no allergies. The rest I'd left to his culinary expertise. He must have done his own homework because he'd pulled out the stops. The seafood starter smelled incredible even before he'd placed it on the table.

'Oh, lobster thermidor! My favourite,' Savvie gushed when the dish was uncovered, eliciting a wide, slavishly happy smile from my usually pompous Michelin-starred chef.

'*Bon appétit, mademoiselle.* And if you wish for anything else, don't hesitate to let me know.'

I swallowed an irritated snort. Jacques was only half French and grew up in Michigan but he loved to emphasise his accent in the presence of a beautiful woman. I uncovered my own dish as Savvie picked up her fork. 'I suppose we can drink to good wine and great food?'

'Why the hell not?'

She tensed, her eyes flashing at me. 'Bryce…'

I reached forward with my glass, clinked hers and took a large gulp. 'Let's not invite indigestion to a great meal, shall we? Jacques seems taken with you. You don't want to upset him, do you?'

'I don't want to upset you. You're more important to me.'

The unexpected response disarmed me for all of two seconds before I rallied. 'Am I? If I'm so important why have you done such a bang-up job of avoiding me for the last three years? Tell me, if it hadn't been for that prime piece of real estate you currently covet, would I have heard from you at all?' I asked with every scrap of bitterness broiling in my gut.

And watched all the warmth leave her face. 'You think I reconnected with you because of the lease?' she asked through stiff lips.

'Didn't you? Perhaps you should go back and read your email. See how many lines referred to me and how many stated what you need from me.'

Her fingers tightened around the stem of her glass. 'I was wrong. You haven't just become cold, Bryce. You've also turned nasty.'

The barbs bounced off me. 'I state things as they are. Sugar-coating is for little boys and girls. If that's too much for you to handle, we can end this right now.'

Eyes one shade darker with an emotion I didn't feel like examining stared back at me for several taut seconds. Then she picked up her fork. 'You're not getting rid of me that easily. I'm going to eat this starter, Bryce, because you're right, I don't want to upset your chef. And because for whatever reason he's known to prepare one of my favourite dishes even without having met me before. After I do it justice, we're going to settle whatever it is that's bugging you—'

'Are you really going to sit there and plead ignorance, Savannah?'

She flinched. 'I'm not going to accept blame for anything until the charges are spelt out. But if you think I
don't have a few bones to pick with you too, think again,
Bryce James Mortimer.'

For some absurd reason, hearing her say my full
name made my stomach flip. Followed swiftly by a
twitch in my trousers.

I took another sip of wine, watched as she tackled a
bite of succulent lobster before washing it down with
a mouthful of wine. Watched her swallow with a little
hum of pleasure, a habit she seemingly hadn't curbed.

'Is that so?'

'Hmm, very much so. Now, shut up for a minute and
let me enjoy my food.'

She forked another bite of juicy lobster, brought it
to her mouth and wrapped her plump lips around it.

Then closed her eyes and moaned with zero shame.

I cursed that thick heft of lust that dropped into my
groin and wrapped itself sinuously around my cock.
With a disgruntled shift in my seat, I set my glass down
and picked up my own cutlery. In silence we polished
off the starter, and I watched her charm the chef with
effusive thanks as he cleared away and hurried off to
fetch the main course.

The main course of creamy chicken risotto with
shaved truffles went down a treat with her too, while
my appetite dwindled in contrast, and I was staring
at Savvie's lips when she opened them after the last
bite and said the one word that knocked dread into my
stomach. 'Truth.'

CHAPTER TWO

Savvie

THE MAN I'D called my best friend until a dizzying series of events dissolved the title like sugar in hot water stared at me dispassionately. It was a good thing I'd finished my meal or I'd have lost my appetite. The look wasn't just in his eyes. It seeped through every shrug, every curl of lips I'd once thought were the most perfectly created set of lips on earth. Every indifferent sip of excellent wine.

I looked deeper, pathetically desperate to find something else. Something more. A reminder of those semi-carefree years when we'd talk on the phone for hours, sleep for an hour and resume conversations the moment we saw one another in person.

But the man I knew had been replaced by a harder, edgier version of a Bryce Mortimer who'd been hard and edgy and cynical to start off with. I'd only fooled myself into thinking our friendship had softened those hard edges, that being around me and my eclectic family he'd believed was perfect had smoothed a few jagged spikes embedded by his family and his emotionally stunted upbringing.

More fool me.

For the longest time, I'd hoped and prayed, hinted and whispered, while silently screaming, *See me. Me. Choose me.*

Bryce had seen. And concluded I wasn't enough.

Nothing and no one would ever be enough. It'd taken me far too long to accept that. Even longer to get over it. All he'd ever wanted was low-maintenance friendship, something to take the edge off his hectic social and dysfunctional family life. And stupidly, I'd forced myself to fit the mould, to be whatever I needed to be to stay in his life. Unfortunately by doing that, I'd almost lost myself. And yes, a part of me hated Bryce for it.

Well, he'd made it clear he was all about settling scores.

I had a few of my own to put to bed.

'Truth,' I repeated after I refused dessert and the chef had departed.

He sipped his drink, then gave a wry smile as he lowered it. 'You've always been terrible at this game. You're supposed to give me two options, remember?'

I remembered. Truth or Dare had always been our game. I'd loved it a little too much because it'd skated close to secret desires I'd tried to suppress for a long time. 'What's the point when you always choose dare?'

He shrugged. 'Dares are way more exciting.'

'Why? What's so wrong with choosing truth every now and then?'

He tensed ever so slightly. 'Sadly, the truth means different things to different people.'

'Not to me, and you know that.' He didn't answer. Now it was my turn to tense. 'Don't you?'

'Leave it.'

'Leave what? I haven't even asked you anything yet.'

'Exactly,' he replied tightly. 'And already you're getting bent out of shape. So let's drop whatever it is you think you want to know before things get more fucked, shall we?'

'More fucked? So you know things are fucked?'

He grimaced and for some reason stared at my mouth for an eternity before his gaze swept away. 'You know the one thing I haven't missed about you? This dog-with-a-bone inability to let things be.'

Maybe he was right and I needed to let things go. But I'd let too many things go for far too long. First by being too afraid to ever dig beneath the surface with Bryce to what I'd really wanted. Then with Dan and all the signs I should've heeded when things had started to go bad and he'd turned from sarcastically cruel to deliberately verbally abusive. Then the one thing I'd never thought would slip through my fingers—my friendship with Bryce.

I watched my best friend now. Correction, my ex-best friend. Outwardly, he appeared unaffected but years-long experience had taught me that his still waters ran deep and dangerous. He was also uncomfortable about something.

Something my instinct pushed me not to let go.

'Truth,' I demanded for a third time.

'Fine,' he griped, with less heat than a minute before.

'How long have you held this…grudge?'

He didn't hesitate. 'Three a half years, give or take.'

My heart dropped to my heels.

A large part of me had hoped he'd do the quintessential English thing and reply that of course he didn't hold a grudge. That I was being silly. That his cold email and general attitude were my overactive imagination.

But they weren't. His stark words landed and burrowed deep, robbing me of breath until I tightened my gut against the acute loss. Until I reminded myself that he'd absented himself, deliberately, for much longer than those three-plus years.

'Then why am I here?' I asked. 'Why not tell me to piss off if you don't care any more?'

'Because you've always been as stubborn as a mule when you get an idea into your head. Anyone else who believed I was *cold and distant* would've taken their business elsewhere. Instead here you are, thinking you can turn this around. Or it because you want to lend credence to the assertion that I'm *important* to you?'

His tone chafed. 'It wasn't a lie.'

'Yeah. Right.'

Irritation snapped my spine straight. 'Watch it, Bryce, or you'll seriously piss me off with that tone that suggests I'm lying. You don't want to believe it, that's up to you and that cynicism you wear like a second skin. I know my truth. As for the implication that I have ulterior motives for not taking my business elsewhere, you're right. And why should I? I checked out your place before coming here. It's perfect for my needs. So pardon me for not wanting to cut off my nose to spite my face.'

He appeared nonplussed for a moment. 'Fine. Calm down. Are you quite done?'

'No.' I took a large gulp of my wine, and totally denied it was for Dutch courage, even though it was. 'I want another truth, Bryce.'

His lips tightened but he didn't forestall me. Just fixed those signature piercing hazel Mortimer eyes that had the uncanny ability to sink hooks into me, and waited me out.

'Why did you come to my wedding?'

His glass clicked sharply onto the table and his tension grew. 'You *know* why I came. Because you sent me a bloody gold-embossed invitation. Because I was your friend.'

'My *best* friend. A best friend who never bothered to RSVP. A friend who turned up almost an hour late without so much as a phone call and then left thirty minutes after the ceremony.'

'Right, so I'm a mannerless bastard. I'm sure you'll find it within that over-generous heart of yours to forgive me at some point.'

'Oh, please. You don't give a rat's arse whether I forgive you or not. And what's that supposed to mean, *over-generous*?'

He shrugged again. 'You were always giving to a fault. And very early on in our friendship I remember you pointing out to me that we balanced each other out because *I* was selfish to a fault. It stands to reason that you'll forgive me for any atrocities, no?'

'People change, Bryce. I'm not that gullible person you think me to be any more.'

He frowned, then pointed an index finger at me. 'I never said you were gullible.'

I sighed. 'You don't have to spell it out—'

'No, rosebud, don't do that. Don't put words in my mouth. You know I'd have no problem calling you gullible if I thought you were.'

Something inside me clenched tight at the endearment. God, how long had I waited to hear it again? How often had I heard it in my dreams? 'Well, I don't forgive you, then. My generosity doesn't stretch to making allowances for you barely showing up for me on that day.'

'That day? You mean the most important, most magical day of your life, don't you? The day when all your dreams came true?'

His sneer cut me sharp and deep.

And yet I couldn't scream the *yes* that should've come readily to me. Because the day hadn't been magical. Not by a long shot. And it wasn't just because of Bryce's barely-there attendance, although that too had contributed to the curious hollow in my stomach. I'd woken that morning, like all the days before, with doubts. Doubts which I'd let a smooth-talking Dan sweep away with promises of the one thing he knew I yearned for. *Acceptance.* I'd believed every yarn he'd spun. Every promise broken with a glib, sugar-coated excuse. Right until the scales had been cruelly ripped from my eyes.

The reminder both hurt and angered me now. And justified or not, some part of me held Bryce responsible for it. He'd been my crutch until I'd needed him most. Then he'd simply…walked away.

'Just tell me, Bryce. Don't pick now to be a damned gentleman and spare me from whatever it is you're too afraid to spit out!' I knew taunting him was dangerous. He'd changed. We both had. He no longer even tried to mask his feelings behind dry, acerbic wit.

When his eyes met mine, I knew whatever was coming would be unvarnished. But still I held his gaze, daring him with mine. 'Truth,' I insisted, girding my loins nevertheless.

His face turned hard and bleak but no less breathtaking for its austerity. 'You really want to know? I came to find out whether you were really going through with it. Whether, after what you knew about Dan, you would still go anywhere near that bastard, never mind letting him put a ring on your finger.'

My gut turned to ice, which was curious because several inches below that the reminder of what had happened three nights before my wedding between Bryce and me was sending white-hot heat shooting into my pussy.

'And that was the only reason you came? To see whether I would compound the mistake you thought I was making by marrying him?' The whispered words left my lips with muted hope shrouding them. A hope that maybe he'd prove me wrong this time. Indicate that I'd been foolish to fear that deep down the reason

I'd clung to friendship while secretly wishing for more *wasn't* because he wouldn't want more. That friendship wasn't all we'd ever have.

And that I was desperate enough to cling tight to that rather than have nothing…because there was *more*.

'Why else, rosebud?' he asked softly. A little too softly. As if he knew the chaos running wild and unfettered through me. As if taunting me over it. He'd always been so good at that. Now, though, there was a dangerous edge to it that…God, turned me on.

Jesus.

I shook my head. A moment later, he stilled my movement by leaning forward to capture my chin in his hand.

'You seem to be on some sort of journey of self-discovery for both of us, so let's have it. Why else do you think I put a business deal I'd been working on for months on hold to fly five thousand miles to your wedding?' he asked.

My tongue slid out almost of its own accord. Licked my lower lip. His gaze followed the slow, languorous movement with eyes that grew steadily heated.

After a moment when words still failed to form in my throat, his eyes rose to capture mine. 'Would it be because the same night I warned you not to go back to Dan the Dickhead because he wanted you just for your money, you nodded that beautiful head and used that indecently sexy voice to reassure me that it was over? Did you not give me your *word* that you would end it?'

'Bryce…'

'There it is,' he breathed. 'That was the same tone

you used that night. The one that curls around my cock and strokes me until I'm hard as a fucking rock every single time.'

My jaw dropped. 'Bryce!' My heart kicked at the fact that we were talking, *really* talking about the stuff we'd always seemed to skirt around. Even if it was just about the physical. *For now.*

'You wanted honesty, rosebud. You assured me it was over, that you no longer belonged to another man, so I spread you out on my living-room floor and I finally got a taste of that incredible pussy, finally had the privilege of feeling your tightness around my fingers, of you gripping my hair as you screamed my name and came on my tongue. Only to have you go back on your promise to call off the wedding and marry the bastard three days later.'

The growled, hot words filled with deep censure robbed me of speech, shamed me and turned me on in equal measures.

His thumb rose from my chin, drifted at leisure over my lower lip as he continued to watch me with dark, hooded eyes. 'You want to know if that changed things between us?'

I licked my lip again, my heart pounding with apprehension and a whole load of sizzling lust. 'Did it?'

His hand dropped like a stone and he surged to his feet. 'What the hell does it matter?' he asked.

'How can you ask me that? You know why it matters. You never answered my phone calls after that and

I haven't seen you for years! It's not like you not to call me out if you think I've done something wrong.'

His eyebrows shot up. *'If?'*

'Fine, *when.* Whatever.'

He spiked his fingers through his hair. Then he threw me another of those indifferent shrugs that seemed to find the centre of my hurt with bullseye accuracy. 'I was busy. So were you. We were both busy empire-building, if I'm not mistaken.'

I scrambled to my feet too. 'Don't give me that. We were never too busy for each other before…before…'

'Stop clinging to this idealistic version of what you thought we were or would be. You want the truth? I stopped trusting you after you stopped trusting yourself. After you went against your every instinct and married that bastard.'

Hurt lanced deeper through me. 'How dare you?'

'Oh, come off it. I know you. Sometimes maybe more than you know yourself. You think I didn't see the doubt on your face when I walked into that church as you promised to *honour and cherish*? Not so deep down, you knew he was wrong for you, that you were making a mistake. And you married him anyway.'

'So you chose to punish me for it?'

He exhaled harshly. 'Damn it, I don't have time for this.'

'Really, then I ask you again, why did you invite me here? I may be stubborn but I don't trespass where I'm not wanted. If you don't have time for me or our friendship, then why did you agree to see me? You could've done what you did before and ignored my email, continued your grand empire-building. So why didn't you?'

He stilled as if my words had turned him to stone. For the longest moment, we stared at each other across the living room. Then, driven by that same instinct that had started this reckless path of discovery, I slowly made my way towards him, aware of every cell in my body, every stretch of heated skin as I'd never been before. Also aware of his intense scrutiny as his gaze raked me from head to toe and back again.

I was treading dangerous, *familiar* waters. The same undertow that'd sucked me in that night, three days before my wedding, when I'd thrown caution to the wind and ended up almost drowning. This thing could blow wide open, be irreparably damaged.

But then…wasn't Bryce already claiming we were beyond repair? That in not heeding his warning and marrying Dan I'd broken our friendship? For all I knew if I walked out of this apartment I wouldn't see him again for another three years. Or ever.

So what the hell did I have to lose? A friendship I'd treasured while wanting more, only for it to fall apart anyway?

I stopped a mere foot from him. The intensity of the emotions vibrating from him wrapped around me but I didn't let it deter me. I'd come through a very bitter divorce with a stronger spine and steely resolve never to doubt myself again. And now he was in front of me, six feet three inches of raw masculinity and long-denied secret craving.

A craving I'd received a quick, highly addictive but maddeningly brief taste of.

'Why did you change the venue for this meeting? Didn't you originally ask me to come to your office?' I modulated my voice to that tenor he'd confessed minutes ago turned him on.

As if on cue, his eyes darkened, his jaw clenching as he struggled to remain unaffected. When he swayed just that tiniest fraction towards me, I knew I had him.

For how long remained a mystery, but right now, in this moment, he was mine. And I wasn't about to lose my chance.

'Is it because you wanted something else besides telling me everything you think I've done wrong?' I didn't give him a chance to reply.

A simple step and I closed the gap between us. A slow tilt onto the balls of my feet and I was sliding my palms over his rock-hard abs and up his chest. I registered the fierce pounding of his heart echoing mine. Felt and revelled in it.

'Was it because you wanted another taste of me, perhaps?' I whispered on a soft breath right before I let my lips brush the skin beneath his earlobe.

A deep shudder powered through him. 'What the hell are you doing, rosebud?' he rasped.

'Dare,' I breathed.

'You're still playing the game wrong.' His voice was a night-dark rumble, his hands clenching and unclenching at his sides as if he was stopping himself from reaching for me. That glimpse of power over him spurred me on.

'Am I? Then I guess you don't want to hear my dare?'

I dropped my head a fraction to lick at the frantic pulse beating at his throat. His next breath hissed out. 'Just fucking say it already.'

'I dare you to do it again. I dare you to drag me to that sofa and use your tongue and your mouth and your hands on me. Just like you did last time. See if you can work some of this…angst out of your system.'

A pure, animalistic groan rumbled from his chest. 'And what makes you think I'll stop at just tasting you? That I won't demand a hell of a lot more?'

My answer emerged with more than a vein of anguish. 'You say you don't trust me. Well, I don't trust you not to abandon me after this lunch either. But I know you enough to know you'll stop when I say. And I'm telling you I'll let you…process your charged state if that's what you want too.'

His hands found my hips then, roughly tugging me back from my whisper-light exploration of his throat, to stare deep into my eyes. 'You think you still know me that well?' he asked darkly.

Maybe not, but some things never changed and Bryce had more integrity in his little finger than most men did in their whole life. 'Guess we'll find out. Unless you're too scared to take the dare?'

The words were barely out of my mouth before he was plucking me off my feet, the rugby-honed body he'd achieved in his time at Cambridge making light of my considerable weight. Bryce was the first and last man who'd been able to carry me without making me self-conscious about the extra pounds I carried. And while I'd shed a good few pounds during and after my divorce, I'd never quite achieved that golden figure of perfection in my head. And lately, I'd tried to be okay with that. It was, after all, what had earned me a dream career and sustained my growing empire.

But I still had moments of anxiety, moments when the mocking taunts and cruelty broke through my often solid barriers.

They tried to do so now.

But the moment Bryce tossed me onto the sofa and speared me with his dark hazel eyes, I let thoughts of the perfect BMI and cellulite melt from my brain. Instead I gave over to the tingling filling me from the inside out, registering in my peaked nipples, the dry anticipation in my mouth and the wet desperation between my legs.

He was still super pissed from our heated conversation and my final taunt, but already the anger was receding from his eyes, replaced by something earthier, something carnal that made my pulse stutter wildly before thundering even faster.

'You've always been bold. But you seem to have developed a penchant for the downright reckless.'

I toyed with the long ties of my favourite wraparound top and slowly inched the hem up until a sliver of my belly was revealed. 'I don't see you throwing me out the door, so I'm guessing you still love a good challenge.'

A blaze flared in his eyes as he followed the path

of my fingers over my taut stomach. In honour of this visit and simply because great lingerie always boosted my confidence, I'd donned one of my latest creations: fire-engine-red French knickers with delicate lace and cheeky ribbon ties and a matching balconette bra. With my reclined position, the bodice of my top had gaped to reveal my deep cleavage.

Another breath hissed from him as his eyes darted between my face, my full breasts, and the thighs I was slowly spreading. He stumbled forward and gripped the back of the sofa the moment I loosened the top to reveal the full effect of the bra and bullet-hard nipples.

'Fuck.' The word shot from his throat.

My gaze went its own journey, over the ripped chest I knew was hidden beneath his dark burgundy shirt to the bold outline of his cock beneath the fly of his tailored trousers. My mouth watered at the heat he was packing. Heat I'd secretly craved for as long as I could remember. But as much as I wanted to touch and explore, the need to experience what he'd given me that night in our distant past burned even hotter.

And Bryce felt the same if the rough hands that hooked behind my knees and spread me wide were an indication. My already rough breathing turned choppier.

'Stop playing with that tie and open your top for me,' he said gruffly as his hands trailed over soft leather to wrap around my ankles.

With a shrug and tug, I opened it, then arched my back to give him a full and unfettered view of my ample breasts.

He swallowed, then began to tackle my trousers with a wild little light in his eyes that triggered my own arousal. I should've been pleased that at least in this, we seemed to be in accord, but a tight little ball of anxiety wouldn't shift from my belly. What if we never found common ground again? What if the friendship that had been my whole world was never salvaged?

The questions evaporated when Bryce discarded my trousers and leaned forward to brace himself over me. For several seconds, he didn't move, simply stared into my eyes. Was he thinking the same? I never found out because his eyes swept over me, singeing every inch of me until his gaze was once again riveted between my thighs.

'Did you wear this underwear for me, rosebud?'

'Nope. They were for me.'

He dragged his gaze from my silk-covered sex to meet mine. 'You needed to shred my control that much?' he muttered.

'Maybe.' It was a little unnerving how well he knew me. To throw him off, I trailed a manicured fingernail over one heavy breast to my lace-covered nipple and slowly circled it. He caught and mangled one corner of his lower lip between his teeth as his gaze latched onto the tightened peak. After watching for a tense few seconds, he brushed my hand away and replaced it with his. Sensation screamed through me as he fondled me, his gaze darting between my face and my boobs, avidly absorbing my reactions, before he dropped his head to suck lace and flesh into his mouth.

My hot little gasp eroded my intention to tell him that, technically, my boobs weren't part of the deal. That his task was situated much farther south. But the havoc he was wreaking was too thrilling to deny, his fingers plucking at the nipple he wasn't sucking, a sweet torture that dragged a keening moan from my throat, and I lost the battle to curl my hands over his broad shoulders, to take a bite out of his gorgeousness.

God, he was far too good at this. My panties were already damp and he wasn't anywhere near my pussy.

My fingers tunnelled into his hair, holding him prisoner as his teeth grazed over one aching bud. Like a willing magnet, my back arched into his ministrations, desperate for more.

He raised his head a fraction. 'Tell me this thing has a front fastening. I don't want to ruin it.'

Breath in my throat, I shook my head.

'Bloody hell,' he growled, then dipped his hands into the lace and scooped out my boobs.

The erotic sensation of my double Ds spilling out made us both groan.

'Christ, you're so fucking lush,' he muttered, slashes of colour staining his chiselled cheekbones. 'There isn't an inch of you I don't want to taste.'

With needy hands I dragged him back, crying out when he latched onto my peak again. The suction was even more intense, tongue and teeth coming into deeper play.

'God, yes,' I gasped as he mercilessly tormented me.

Maybe the crazy depth of sensation careening through me was because I hadn't had good sex for so long.

By our first wedding anniversary, Dan had been hard-pressed to perform the bare minimum. By our second, we'd been down to the cursory once-a-month three-minute humping in the shower to convince ourselves we had something remotely resembling a marriage. The transition from there to divorce had been a measly miserable nine months.

Or maybe I was feeling like this because *this* was Bryce. An older, edgier version of the boy who'd blazed a memorable trail in the public school I'd despised until his arrival had made my existence bearable, the rugby-loving hunk I'd hung out with in Cambridge, and the man who'd been my best friend for years before he'd removed himself from my life.

Whatever the reason for my heightened emotions, a particularly clever twist of his fingers dragged me back to the present, to the heated blaze of his eyes fixed on me as he tormented me.

I gasped again as he lowered his head, flicked his tongue brazenly over my wet flesh and then blew on it.

'Bryce...'

He kept hold of one globe as he trailed kisses down my midriff and belly to the edge of my panties. Crouched over me like some dark overlord, he scoured his nails lightly over the skin above the panty line, leaving a trail of goosebumps in his wake. He repeated the action a few times, his other hand still tormenting my nipple, and each time I felt myself getting shamefully wetter.

By the time his fingers dipped beneath the scrap of silk, I'd forgotten to breathe.

One bold finger glided between my folds and he groaned. 'You're so fucking wet. You're close, aren't you?'

'Yes,' I panted, my hips lifting off the sofa to meet his next glide.

He circled slow and sure, then dragged wetness to my clit. At the first touch, I let out another cry. He removed his hands from my body, repositioned himself with one knee on the floor while dragging my panties down my legs. Tossing the knickers aside, he spread me wide, his gaze zeroed in on my pink, glistening flesh. A rough breath shuddered from him.

'Ah, rosebud. You're still as beautiful as I remember.' The quiet, almost reverent murmur made my heart lurch and, with his gaze fixed on my face, he slowly slid his middle finger inside me. 'And just as bloody tight.' He buried his digit to the hilt, then flicked it upward.

'Oh, God.' My thighs shook as pleasure rained through me.

Slowly, he finger-fucked me, his breaths harsher the louder I moaned. 'Is that the spot?' His voice was thick and hoarse.

'Yes!'

He gave a low, masculine laugh, then proceeded to pile up the torturous pleasure. One finger became two, but, although the pressure was deeply satisfying, it wasn't enough.

'More,' I demanded. 'Put your mouth on me.'

He shifted again, dropping his head between my legs. My fingers immediately buried themselves in his hair, a part of me terrified he would stop.

He didn't. And at the first glide of Bryce's tongue over my clit, I screamed. By the third glide I was pleasure blind. But not deaf to the decadent sounds of his fingers inside me or his pained groans as I grew wetter, screamed my way to the edge and flung myself over it as he sucked my clit into his mouth.

Reality returned in a cascade of harsh breathing. When I opened my eyes, Bryce was standing at the window, his back to me, his shoulders rising and falling in a rapid movement that attested to his scramble for control.

Tension screamed in the distance between us as I hastily fixed my clothes.

When I was reasonably decent, I exhaled. Now what? I'd dared him and he'd gone for it. But from his rigid stance, nothing much had changed, except maybe for the worse.

I went for the direct approach. 'Bryce?'

He turned without answering, his gaze heated but hooded.

'Is our friendship worth salvaging or am I wasting my time trying?'

His shoulders stiffened harder. 'You just exploded back into my life, rosebud. I'll need a minute to consider that.'

My shoulders slumped. 'I guess that's that, then. I sent you a save-the-date for the launch. It's going ahead whether I get a lease in your building or not. So I guess I'll either see you there or I won't?'

He shoved his fingers through hair I'd gloriously dishevelled, his eyes still a touch wild as they roved over me. 'You've got what you wanted. You can sleep soundly tonight knowing you've proved whatever point you wanted to prove. Let that be enough for now.'

'And if it's not? What if I want my friend back?'

He stared at me in that unique way that always made my skin feel tight and raw and exposed. That way that said he saw and knew much more than he should. But while in the past I would've dropped my gaze, mumbled something along the lines of *never mind* or *whatever*, this time I met his gaze full on.

Dared him to say the words I knew in my heart would flay and wound. He didn't disappoint me.

'The guy you knew is gone. You're doing us both a disservice by clinging to the past. It's time to move on.'

I didn't speak as he slowly strolled back to where I stood, praying my eyes wouldn't mist with the tears prickling wildly.

'My executive assistant will let you know if I can make it. If I can't, have a great opening. I'm sure you'll blow their socks off.'

'Bryce—'

'I have a meeting to get to. I'm sure you can find your own way out.'

And then, just as he'd done on my wedding day, he calmly walked out of the living room, the deafening silence left by his departure confirming what I already knew.

We'd crossed a line that night three years ago when I was forced to face the fact that the dream I was secretly chasing would never come true. That Bryce would never belong to me the way I fully and desperately wanted him to. That walking away instead of clinging to false hope had been the right thing to do then, and probably was now.

That really, when it came down to it, he didn't want or need me. I was the girl who'd made him laugh when he was bored, who'd challenged his intellect and dug him out of his funk when the family drama he'd always been so tight-lipped about drove him into deep, scary silences.

Basically, I'd been useful as a crutch until he hadn't needed me any more. Then when I'd needed him the most, he'd simply...walked away.

I'd seen the signs long before Bryce had left for good. The anguish of that distance, of being thrust farther and farther into the fringes of his life was what had made me give in that night, then made me deliver a promise I hadn't been able to keep in the long run, my need to belong sending me down the wrong path.

And as much as I wanted to blame him, the one thing Bryce had never misled me on was that he would never become something more to me than a friend. No, that layer of torment was all down to me and my foolish yearning.

With a thick swallow, I crossed his stunning living

room to retrieve my clutch. I paused for a beat, toying with the idea to confront him wherever he'd disappeared to, then dismissed it.

The best way to tackle an intransigent Bryce was to let him cool off. But if nothing else, this particular dare had proved one thing.

Bryce was still hot for me. I could either test the boundaries of this strange new world we found ourselves in, or heed his warning and back off.

In the lift, I leaned back and let a small smile slip free while the after-effects of the incredible orgasm trailed through my bloodstream as I contemplated my next move.

Twenty minutes later, I was back in the apartment I'd rented for the duration of my stay in Singapore. Padding on bare feet to the kitchen, I poured myself a glass of wine and sipped, my mind whirling with possibilities.

He was right. We weren't the same people we were three years ago.

But he was very much a man. And I was a woman with needs who was done relying on the cosmos to dictate my destiny.

Friendship or sex?

Friendship *and* sex. I'd settled for one over the other once upon a time.

This time…

My heart lurched wildly as it accepted my truth.

This time I wanted both.

CHAPTER THREE

Bryce

'MR MORTIMER, I have Miss Knight on the line for you again?'

I smothered a groan and raked a hand across my face. A small, non-disgruntled part of me was thankful she hadn't kept that bastard's name. I wasn't sure how I would've handled hearing her addressed as Mrs Wallis.

Nevertheless, her persistence had grown beyond just a pain in my arse. If I weren't frustrated and in danger of dying from blue balls, I'd admire her tenacity. She'd called every hour during business hours for the last couple of days. I was running out of excuses and my EA was using that put-upon voice that said come Christmas she would be expecting a hefty bonus.

I didn't want to lose Tandy. As an executive assistant she was second to none. And normally, she was good at dispatching unwanted calls. So why not now? What the hell was stopping me from instructing her to bar all calls from Savannah?

Because she was under strict instructions to pay special attention to all clients with a stake in The Sylph. And since my commercial team, without any involvement from me whatsoever, had all but fallen over themselves to fast-track her lease, she now fell firmly under that purview. And, as my commercial director had also informed me, having Savannah Knight open her flagship store in my building would garner the kind of publicity I'd be a fool to reject. So whether I liked it or not, she was now a top Mortimer Group client with access to me whenever she chose.

Access she was fully capitalising on.

'Sir?'

With a grimace, I hit the intercom button. 'Put her through.'

Soft breathing flowed from the phone a second later. 'Bryce, how wonderful of you to take my call,' she murmured in that sultry voice that came second in the instant-hard-on-achieving status only next to those sexy little whimpers she made when she was fully turned on.

Fucking hell.

I gritted my teeth and thumped my head against the leather headrest. I'd jacked off to the sound of that breathy voice fifteen minutes after I'd heard her leave my apartment after our doomed lunch ten days ago.

Since then, I'd masturbated a hell of a lot more times than I could recall in recent memory. Each time I reassured myself I had finally got her out of my system, I'd hear that voice in my head, demanding, 'Put your mouth on me.' And I'd be rock hard all over again.

'Seriously? You're giving me the silent treatment? When you said you'd changed, I thought you meant in the direction of evolution, not a regression to adolescence.'

'What do you want, rosebud?'

It was disconcerting how the nickname I'd coined for her rosebud lips fell so easily from mine. How calling her name while I jacked off in the shower felt so bloody right and hellishly wrong at the same time.

'Besides your overdue response to my invitation? We'll leave that for now. I have a more urgent problem.'

My back stiffened as a fierce urge to demand what it was so I could fix it scrambled up my spine. Had she missed me? Was she calling to demand a repeat of what happened on my sofa? The sofa I hadn't been able to sit on without recalling her stretched out on it in all her dark golden glory, her beautiful back arched and her juicy lips parted in delicious pants?

'Shoot,' I answered with more vim than I'd intended.

'I put in a request for a Venetian chandelier for the main showroom a week ago and I haven't heard back from your people yet as to whether it's arrived or when it'll be installed. It's the centrepiece of the store. Everything else revolves around it,' she stated crisply.

I struggled to change lanes from lurid to business, unwillingly admitting that Business Savvie turned me on just as much as Sexy Savvie. 'I employ an excellent team. It's on their radar. I'm sure they'll get around to it—'

'I'm afraid that's just not good enough. I'm paying

extra for an expedited service and I was assured things would be handled smoothly and in a timely manner. I don't feel efficiently or smoothly handled, Bryce,' she murmured, evoking another bout of racy images that made me bite back a groan. 'In fact I'm feeling the opposite. And not in a good way.'

I wanted to handle her in a great many ways, all guaranteed to leave her with that rosy afterglow and breathlessness I couldn't get out of my damned head.

'I'm not familiar with the ins and outs of your lease. I'll get Jerry to personally give you a call with an update. Will that suffice?'

'I called your site director this afternoon. His son is having his tonsils taken out today. The poor man was distraught. I didn't think it was fair to bother him.'

Damn it, I'd forgotten about Jerry's email telling me exactly that this morning. The man had done a stellar job managing a team of over three thousand workers getting my building ready and within a whisker of the projected schedule. It wasn't his fault his son had fallen ill. And none of the contractors would be around at this time on a Friday evening to confirm her request.

Even if they were, I couldn't very well pass her off to anyone but Jerry. The Mortimer Group was renowned for its top-notch reputation. I'd met every single one of my long- and short-term investors, taken a personal interest in their wants and desires.

Like my building, my singular attention to detail was what had made me a success. There were several rungs in the hierarchy before a client would normally request my personal input but, once they did, it went against my principles to pass them back down the chain or fob them off simply because the client at the end of the phone happened to make my cock react as if I were fifteen instead of thirty-one.

Yeah, time to stop hiding and man up, Bryce.

'I can be there in half an hour. Can you make it there by then?'

'I'm already here, Bryce. I'll be waiting.'

She rang off before I could reply. I dropped the phone back into its cradle, my bloodstream already humming as the pressure behind my fly grew.

Jesus.

Where the hell was my common sense? You'd think I'd learned my lesson after the one person I'd trusted had let me down so spectacularly. I might not have given her the unsavoury details about my family life and especially my parents—simply because I never discussed *that*…ever—but she'd known enough about dysfunctional Mortimers. Enough that I'd thought I could trust her with what our safe space meant. But the moment some idiot had clicked his fingers, she'd trotted off without so much as a *Goodbye, Bryce.*

When that same idiot had shown all the signs of being a complete and utter bastard much like my father, I'd tried to warn her. She'd lied to my face, demonstrating that the woman I'd thought I knew and trusted was just a figment of my imagination.

What the hell had Dan given her that I couldn't?

You know exactly what! She never made it a secret.

I smothered the voice in my head and rose from the desk. What the hell did it matter now? She'd broken a trust that had probably been only one-sided to begin with, all so she could chase some stupid dream of happily-ever-after. A dream I'd tried to tell her was a figment of her imagination.

And, like me, she'd been left with a pile of ashes. Only problem was, our friendship had been sacrificed in those flames too. Worse thing was, even after all that, a part of me had yearned to reach out, to ease the pain she must've been feeling during her acrimonious divorce.

Or perhaps I was projecting…

Whatever. I swallowed the bitter taste in my mouth, made my way to the door and dismissed Tandy for the evening.

Downstairs, I slid behind the wheel of my Ferrari and lost myself for a moment in the smooth throb of the engine.

All too soon I was pulling up to The Sylph.

Normally this was the moment I took a minute or three to look up at the building I'd poured my heart and soul into. The steel and blue-green smoked glass masterpiece that had taken two long years, singular focus and some deep, untapped desire to leave something beautiful, something memorable behind.

Without looking I knew the structure in the pleasing shape of a slender woman's torso, half turned, perhaps to view her lover over her shoulder, would be gleaming beautifully against the dying rays of the setting sun.

That soon lights from within and those reflected from surrounding buildings across the bay would bathe it in a stunning silhouette that drew awed gasps.

But tonight my pride and joy paled in comparison to my interest in the silver town car idling in the designated parking space beneath the wide double portico of my building.

Parked a dozen feet behind it, I watched Savvie step out, her long, shapely legs extending in that way that only models and trained dancers could execute without appearing pretentious or awkward. Her heels were a shiny rose-gold colour that drew attention to her delicate ankles. I'd gripped those same ankles ten days ago, as I'd spread her thighs and bared her wet, beautiful pussy to my hungry gaze.

Was she wearing another of those mind-blowing scraps of silk underwear? Did she have a garter belt on under that short, flared black skirt whispering against her thighs in the light breeze? My gaze climbed up her body to the black off-the-shoulder top baring her throat and the top of her cleavage, my hands gripping the wheel as the image of those full, heavy breasts emblazoned itself on my mind.

The girl and young woman I knew in school and university had been breathtaking when I'd eventually forced my head out of the sand and acknowledged her womanhood. But the woman I was looking at now had an extra layer of tenacity to her. I'd noticed it when she'd first walked into my apartment. She'd confirmed it when she'd issued that bold dare, then held her head high in the face of my less than stellar behaviour afterwards.

Now, she rested one hip against the boot, her head slightly cocked as she watched me, the corners of her incredible lips slightly tilted as if I amused her. Cowering behind the wheel, holding on for dear life, I guessed I was hilarious.

With a muted curse, I threw my door open and stepped out. Her light, alluring perfume reached out and curled around me as I approached. Her hair was up in a loose knot and the breeze caught at a few errant strands as she stared up at me.

'Thank you for accommodating me, Bryce,' she murmured, tucking a clutch the same colour as her shoes under one arm before reaching out to brush a runaway curl from her cheek.

I was jealous of that curl, jealous of the breeze whispering over her face, the rosy gloss clinging to her lips. *Bloody hell, get a grip.*

'No problem. Shall we?' I turned away from her, stared up at the building I poured my blood and sweat into. From all angles it was a masterpiece. One I was supremely proud of.

She followed my gaze and for several seconds neither of us spoke.

'It's a beautiful building, Bryce.'

Sincerity oozed from her and for a moment she was the woman I'd once called my best friend.

'Thanks.' The word emerged gruff.

She smiled and that illusion grew. What the hell was I doing wanting to smile back? She'd *ruined* us.

We entered the lobby that was empty save for the three security guards seated behind the newly installed monitoring desk. I waved the senior guard away when he offered to escort us, which probably wasn't the best idea considering being alone with her wouldn't help the situation percolating in my trousers. But damned if I was going to risk firing a valuable employee for ogling her the way the three guys were doing now.

'This way.' I strode across the atrium to the bank of lifts set against the east wall.

She kept up, her heels clicking in tandem with mine. 'When is the opening of the building?'

'Unofficially, it's open. Businesses are moving in but the official ceremony is two weeks after your opening.'

I stabbed the button for the lift, and waited for her to precede me when the doors slid open. She strolled to the back of the carriage, turned and rested her shoulders against the polished mirrored wall. She angled her body in a way that subtly thrust her chest and hips forward and it was all I could do not to drool at the lush display of her figure. Her clutch was still tucked under one arm and she was toying with the clasp of a diamond tennis bracelet. My gaze dropped to her wrist, and I wondered if her pulse was as erratic as mine. What it would taste like.

Christ, everything about her turned me on. It was becoming a huge fucking problem.

The doors opened directly into the store and, relieved, I stepped onto the polished floors. On either side of the entryway were already fitted glass and African oak cabinets that would display her world-famous lingerie come opening day. Against a back wall, boxes were piled high with fittings yet to be installed.

I headed over to them but a quick inspection showed none of them contained the special chandelier she'd ordered.

'It's not here,' I confirmed.

Her lips compressed, drawing my attention to the soft, glossy curves. 'Is there any way to track it down?'

I drew my gaze from her mouth. 'Of course, but let's check upstairs first. We're using one of the floors designated for office space as temporary storage. It may have been sent there.'

'And if it's not?'

'One problem at a time, rosebud.'

She inhaled sharply and her gaze darted to mine. 'Why do you still call me that?'

I grimaced inwardly. Didn't I ask that same question of myself a little while ago? I made a beeline for the door, more to escape my own question. 'Would you prefer I didn't?' I parried.

'I'd prefer you didn't treat me like some unwanted stranger you can't wait to be rid of.' There was a throb of irritation in her voice.

'You asked for my help. Here I am.'

'And you look like this is the last place you want to be. Am I really that vile?'

I gritted my teeth and pressed the button for the lift. 'Jesus. Since when did you get so melodramatic?'

She stalked into the lift, anger flashing across her face. 'Fine, since you've been avoiding my calls I'm guessing you still don't want anything to do with me, but can we keep things at least civil between us? I wouldn't have called you if your foreman was available so if you think I have some sort of agenda going on here, then think again. All I want is my chandelier and a date of when it'll be installed and I'll be out of your hair, okay?'

I couldn't look away from the pulse racing at her throat, the bright shine to her eyes. Hell, the sheer magnificence of her face. Every part of her that my gaze touched cemented what I'd suspected since her email had landed in my inbox.

I was well and truly screwed. In all the ways imaginable.

'All right, calm down. We'll get to the bottom of where your precious chandelier is.'

'And then?'

I sighed. 'And then I'll buy you dinner to make up for the delay and inconvenience. Does that work for you?'

That wicked little smile quirked the corners of her mouth again. 'How can I refuse such a gracious offer? I'll dismiss my driver.'

She drew her phone from her clutch. Slender fingers pressed a button before lifting the handset to her ear. In sultry tones, she dispatched her driver for the night. As she returned her phone to her clutch, the tip of her tongue flitted out to lick the corner of her lip, and it suddenly occurred to me that I'd never kissed her, despite having gone down on her twice.

I continued staring at her mouth as she zipped up the purse. A mouth I was having a hard time dragging my gaze from as the lift hurtled us into the sky before gliding to a stop on the fortieth floor.

The doors slid open. Waited.

'Are you planning on getting out?' she asked, those sleek eyebrows raised at me.

Stifling a curse, I waved her ahead of me. She sashayed her way out, the stunning hourglass figure that had made her millions as a plus-size model taunting every red-blooded cell in my body.

Yeah. Definitely screwed.

We found her chandelier tucked in amongst the previous day's delivery with a worksheet that said it was slated to be installed on Monday.

She inspected the crate thoroughly and then scrutinised the sheet before stepping back.

'Satisfied?' I asked.

She rested her hand on top of the crate, the other on her hip. 'Not until I get some food inside me. All this trekking around is making me hungry. Are you going to feed me now?'

Her appetite had been one of the many things I loved about her, even though she'd detested it. Most of the women in my family and the women I dated treated food as if it was the necessary evil to be endured and not enjoyed. Savvie had been self-conscious about her weight when we'd met, had still been hung up about it despite my not-too-obvious-because-we-were-only-friends reassurances that she was beautiful regardless of her dress size. Whether she was still hung up about it or not, she'd obviously turned her insecurities to her advantage.

The fact that I didn't even know for sure rattled. *Badly.*

Her other insecurities had been a little harder to overcome. My suspicion that it was one of those that had led her to hitch herself to Idiot Dan was one I'd never delved into. I wasn't sure I wanted to now.

'That was the deal,' I replied, shying away from admitting to myself that I was looking forward to dinner. That my irritation was taking a back seat to the need to stay…a little bit longer.

The return journey in the lift was much less strained, although I was still aware of every shift and slide of her body, every rise and fall of her chest.

Outside, she paused, resting her hands on my car's roof as she stared at me. 'Where are we going?'

'What are you in the mood for?' Fucking hell. Really? I adjusted myself as my body reacted to that suggestive line of questioning.

Her smile was wicked. 'I get to choose where we eat?'

I stopped my lips from twitching. 'Within reason.'

The tiniest pout plumped her lips. 'Well, I had sushi for lunch so anything but Japanese is fine with me.'

I nodded. 'Get in.'

Her smile widened as she slid into the passenger seat. 'Are you going to tell me or is it a surprise?'

She loved surprises. And I was getting carried away. 'We're going to Tetsuya's. I'm in the process of poaching their head chef for my restaurant at The Sylph when it opens. He cooks prime steak the way you like it. Unless your tastes have changed?' I added, reminding myself I was no longer privy to her likes and dislikes. Except maybe how she liked her nipples to be played with. How she liked her pussy licked.

Christ.

Oblivious to my struggles, she hummed happily, not reacting to the fact that I hadn't forgotten the way she liked her food, whereas I was kicking myself for letting it slip.

'Nope, I'm still a raging carnivore. Can we order ahead?' she said impatiently as she adjusted the seat belt between her breasts.

I tried not to stare at the perfection of her full breasts or recall how the dark pink tips had tasted in my mouth. 'Not without causing grievous offence, having my name scrubbed permanently off the guest list and possibly losing a potential head chef.'

She mock groaned and leaned back against the headrest. 'Of course, you'd have to pick one of *those* restaurants.'

I hid another smile. 'I can just as easily get you a pizza from a street vendor if you prefer?'

She made a cute moue. 'You've dangled Tetsuya's

and the wondrous talents of your soon-to-be chef in front of me. You can't take it back now.'

Traffic was relatively light and I glanced over when we stopped at a red light on Raffles Avenue. Her eyes were closed but the fingers drumming lightly on her thigh told me she wasn't asleep. A closer look showed faint signs of strain.

I curbed the concern nudging me. As I'd reminded her several times now, we were no longer the people we used to be. The people we imagined we knew. Best to treat this dinner as good client liaison and place distance between any possibility of rekindling false friendships.

And yet words tripped onto my tongue anyway. 'Tough day?'

Her long lashes swept up before dark gold eyes locked with mine. 'You could say that. Opening a new store is a hard work. Multiply that times ten for a flagship store and dealing with demands from investors...' She shrugged, but the trace of anxiety on her face remained.

A moment later, her gaze shifted and the look disappeared, wiped clean with a hard brush of studied composure.

I focused on the road, ignoring the part of me that hated the barrier she'd put up. 'It's not your first flagship opening though, is it?'

'No, but I have a new set of shareholders who like to poke their noses into how I run things. I miss the days of not answering to anyone but myself.'

The moment the words left her mouth, she tensed.

From the corner of my eye I saw her gaze dart to me and, try as I could, I couldn't stop my teeth from clenching in quiet fury.

She'd once been completely autonomous, the majority shareholder who called the shots in her own business until her money-grabbing ex had pushed her into rapid expansion that had almost cost her everything. Luckily, she'd seen the light in time to avoid major catastrophe. She'd divorced him, but not without parting with a large chunk of what she'd worked so hard for. According to a financial article I'd read a while ago, she was now in a fifty-fifty partnership with a Singaporean consortium.

'Are you ever not going to be pissed off with me about that?' she asked, her voice low and husky.

I saw an opening on the floodlit avenue in front of me and stepped on the gas, needing the extra horsepower to dissipate some of my anger. 'Not any time soon, rosebud.' I didn't see the need to add I was more furious with her ex than with her. That once or twice I'd wondered if *I* could've done things differently. The jury was still out...

She grimaced. 'Would it help at all if I said it was my life and I'm entitled to live it as I see fit?'

I exhaled. 'If it's your life then whether I'm pissed off or not doesn't matter, does it?' I pulled into the parking space in front of the restaurant and applied the brakes with more force than necessary.

Before I could exit she placed her hand on my arm. 'If the chef is as good as you say he is, then, like our lunch, I don't want to invite indigestion with this thing between us.'

I dragged the heel of my hand across my eyes. 'Let's make a deal to not talk about him or the past during dinner.'

A wave of emotion flitted across her face. 'The past is a huge chunk of our lives, Bryce. And for the most part, I liked what you and I had.'

For the most part. The light and frivolous parts that didn't matter.

Frustration bit me hard. 'Fine. Then we'll find something else.'

'Like what?'

I cast around for a subject that wasn't volatile. I came up with nothing besides an old…dangerous favourite. 'Truth or Dare. You got to play last time, albeit atrociously. I think it's my turn.'

Her hand dropped from my forearm, the look on her face a cross between anticipation and apprehension. If this ended anywhere like it had last time, we'd be straying into dangerous territory. But, fuck it if now I'd put it out there I was going to take it back.

I threw my door open and glanced at her. 'So, you coming?'

The reaction I wanted arrived in a millisecond in a form of a challenging toss of her head. 'Hold your horses. I'm coming.'

Our table was one of the best in the house. Semi private and ambient but with enough of the see-and-be-seen vibe that normally appealed to me. But tonight, too many male gazes veered to Savvie. And stayed on her once they recognised who it was they were staring at.

Even before the sommelier approached with menus, my mood was spiralling downward with an emotion I wincingly recognised as jealousy.

I yanked it back long enough to discuss wine choices, not surprised when Savvie went for her favourite Chilean Pinot Blanc. Our waiter arrived soon after that and I felt the tug of a smile when Savvie asked for the quickest starter on the menu.

Five minutes later, she was moaning in ecstasy as she tucked into a small plate of calamari dipped in creamy tartare sauce.

God, she was so predictable in many ways.

And shockingly unpredictable in the worst, most important way.

Enough. Let it go.

But no amount of admonishing myself would free that knot of arctic fury and disappointment in my chest.

'You're doing that thing with your mouth again, Bryce,' she murmured.

I frowned. 'What thing?'

'That thing you do when you're disgruntled.' She set her wine glass down firmly on the table, her eyes fixed on mine. 'If this was a bad idea—'

'You're hungry. We're having dinner. End of.'

After a moment, she nodded. 'Okay. But before we get to your games, I have a neutral subject to discuss.'

The back of my neck tingled. 'Yes?'

'I heard Gideon got married.'

I relaxed. My brother's engagement and subsequent wedding had taken everyone by surprise, not least the man himself. But so far, he and his new wife hadn't killed each other yet, which was great, I guessed. I liked Leonie a lot, but I wasn't holding my breath because, well…she'd married a Mortimer and we were notorious for being bad at matrimony despite our impressive clan numbers. If they proved me wrong and lasted a year, or more, so be it.

I nodded. 'Yep. He was supposed to lease a yacht to close a business deal. He ended up buying the vessel and marrying the owner.'

Her smile widened, her beautiful eyes glinting. 'That must have shocked Aunt Flo's hair white.'

'Especially when he was supposed to be on some sort of sex ban.'

She laughed, a warm sound that washed over me in ways I didn't want but couldn't help absorb. 'What?'

I mock shuddered. 'Don't ask me the details. I didn't want to know then, I'm even less interested now.'

She laughed again. 'I look forward to hearing it from the horse's mouth one day.' She took a sip of wine, then sent me a sober look. 'So how are things with you two?'

That tingling recommenced. Any and everything to do with my family had always been a touchy subject. In the past Savvie had heeded the *no trespassing* signs. I wasn't sure how I felt about this *interested* side of her. 'You want to know if we're bosom buddies now he's married?'

She toyed with the stem of her glass. 'Maybe not bosom buddies but…are you?'

'Answer is…we're better. He reached out when he was on the yacht and we've seen each once or twice since his wedding.'

'That's good.' Her face grew serious. 'And your sister?'

'Graciela passed through on her way to Australia for some PR assignment for TMG. I took her out to lunch. That was a few months ago. I haven't seen any members of my family since. Is the interrogation over?'

Her face closed. 'You said you weren't the same person you were three years ago but in some ways you haven't changed at all.'

'Because I haven't suddenly developed a huge fondness for my dysfunctional family?'

'Because from the sounds of it you're still pushing everyone away.'

'Thin ice, rosebud,' I warned.

She ignored me. 'They don't reach out to you so you don't reach out either?' She shook her head. 'Do you know how nuts that is? To have people you know are in the same situation as you and actively ignore them? To choose to remain alone?'

'Are we talking about me or you right now?'

I hadn't twigged onto the isolation she'd felt within her family until she'd flippantly informed me, after I'd asked what her parents thought of Dan, that she hadn't spoken to them in months. That they weren't coming to her wedding. When she'd insisted she didn't want to talk about it, I'd left it, the subject of family one I was deathly allergic to. But some part of me had experienced a sting of guilt for believing everything was fine all those years before.

For not seeing the real truth. But then, hadn't that been our way? Believing one thing only to discover it was an illusion?

She gave that same flippant hand gesture that didn't quite ring true. 'My situation is different.'

'Is it?'

'Yes. Stop deflecting.'

'Maybe we should've gone for a pizza after all,' I said, in no way welcoming the determined gleam in her eyes.

'Graciela called me when she was in New York last month,' she said abruptly. 'She told me about your lunch. She also told me you couldn't wait to be done. She even thinks you had your EA call with a fake business problem.'

'What the hell are you talking about?' I silently cursed the heat creeping up my neck, thankful our space was dark enough to disguise my guilt.

'Was it true?'

Only partially. The business call hadn't been fake, but I'd used it to shorten the lunch. Graciela liked to play the *why* game every time we met.

Why are we so screwed up?

Why did our parents leave us?

Why aren't we all in therapy about it?

Frankly, I resented her a little for not burying her

head in the sand like the rest of us. 'Would you believe me if I said no?'

Savvie hesitated a moment too long.

Bile teased the back of my throat. 'Why are we talking about this?'

'She was a little upset. When I told her I was coming here, she asked me to talk to you.'

The sensation congealed further. 'How long have you been waiting to drop this on me?'

'I'm not dropping anything on you, Bryce. I'm just passing on a message. Your sister misses you. Whether you ever had a connection or not, she's reaching out to you. Are you going to leave her hanging?'

I gritted my teeth until my jaw protested. 'How the hell can you ask me that? *You know.*'

She shook her head. 'No, I don't know. I *surmised* that your parents were worse than useless. But you never actually talked about them. Except that they were dead. And that the rest of your family was the worst of the worst. But don't you think you've hung onto that excuse for long enough?'

'You have no idea what you're talking about.'

Limpid golden brown eyes stared at me for several seconds, seeing goodness knew what. Making my stomach churn. Then she shrugged. 'Maybe not. All said and done, I guess I'm not an authority on family myself, right?'

I remained silent, fuming that she'd dragged up subjects I wanted to remain buried.

'I'm still starving. Can I order another starter?'

And just like that she'd moved on. Except that faint gleam of reproof lingered in her eyes, raking over my irritation. Who the hell was she to throw this in my face?

She's the girl who always made things make sense when your crazy family threatened your sanity. She saved you more times than you could count.

But then she lied and broke her promise.

I sat back, my gaze on her face. What the hell was her angle?

'Bryce?'

'You know you don't need my permission to order what you want.'

'True, I don't need your permission but I'm trying to make nice again. Obviously, I'm wasting my time.' She raised her hand, got the waiter's attention and ordered a small platter of oysters. When it came she devoured the first one, then, with a furtive glance at me, she drizzled chilli oil on the next one, just the way I liked it, picked it up and held it to my lips. 'Go on, take it. You know you want to,' she whispered, that hint of a dare back in her voice.

It reminded me of my Truth or Dare plan back in the car before the conversation had taken a left turn into crazy town.

I leaned forward and gripped her delicate wrist in one hand. Ignoring her sharp intake of breath, I opened my mouth and took the offered morsel, making sure to wrap my lips around her fingers too. She shifted in her seat, tried to pull back. I tightened my grip, rolling my tongue over the pads of her fingers.

'Bryce…'

Only when I was satisfied that the only thing on her mind was sex, did I release her.

'It's my turn to play the game, I believe?'

She blinked a few times but the haze didn't completely leave her eyes. 'Umm…'

'So, rosebud, truth or dare?'

Her elegant throat moved in a delicate swallow. 'Truth. Always.'

I wanted to disagree. She hadn't always been truthful. Hell, she'd downright lied when she'd made a promise she knew she wouldn't keep.

But I'd had enough heavy talk for one day. 'Very well. Tell me one thing you haven't done yet in the bedroom department.'

Her eyes flared wide and she blinked. 'What?'

I shrugged. 'You started us on this path in my apartment. I'm taking my cue from you. So…let's have it. Something you've been secretly dying to try. Something you never did with *him*.'

Her breath shuddered out. I wanted to lean in, rob her of the next one. 'I thought we weren't going to talk about him?'

'We're not. We're talking about you. Your wants. Your needs. Your dirty little *exclusive* secret.'

Her gaze dropped to the tablecloth and she fidgeted some more. After drawing meaningless patterns on the heavy damask, she glanced around, cleared her throat. Still she hesitated.

I drummed my fingers on the table, impatience devouring me.

'Fine. I've never tried the…back door.'

I stopped myself from barking out a laugh. 'The back door?'

She glared at me. 'You know…anal sex,' she whispered. 'I've…I've always wondered what it'd feel like.' She stopped. Blushed.

My already hard dick turned to stone and my vision blurred for a moment. I swallowed the lump of screaming lust in my throat.

'That's very good to know. So now we come to the dare part.'

'Do we have to do this right now?'

'Oh, yes. Twice now you've pushed me to the brink, rosebud. It's only fair that you let me play, don't you agree?'

'I guess…'

I leaned forward until our faces were inches apart. Until I saw the deep desire emblazoned on her face, knew that she was right there on that delicious, decadent precipice with me. Then I went for the kill.

'In that case, I dare you, petal, to let me fuck you in the arse, let me show you exactly what you've been missing.'

CHAPTER FOUR

Savvie

THE STARK HUNGER on his face was like a live wire attached to every erogenous zone on my body. I couldn't look away. Couldn't stop my feverish trembling. Couldn't do anything but snatch inadequate breaths as my imagination went into full 3D CGI mode.

Bryce wanted to give me that one fantasy I'd never been bold enough to voice to anyone, not even my now ex-husband. Maybe him especially, because deep down I knew he'd ruin the experience.

Three thoughts freewheeled through my mind as another raw shiver flashed through my body.

The first was that we'd jumped a few steps in this *friendship and sex* journey I'd prayed would get us back on, if not the friendship we once had, then at least an even keel. Which was somewhat already skewed considering we hadn't kissed and yet he'd given me two screaming orgasms with his mouth.

The second was that he was yanking my chain, paying me back for being the unfortunate messenger to deliver the message from his sister.

The third was all about screaming *yes* to his dirty proposition whether he even meant it or not. The subject of anal sex hadn't crossed my mind even once in that final year of marriage to Dan. But one half-hour of cunnilingus with Bryce and I was dreaming of the multiple ways he could pleasure me. And yes, at some point during the restless afternoon and night that had ensued after leaving his apartment ten days ago, my mind had swung to that part of my anatomy, my wicked curiosity awakened.

I sipped my wine, gauging his face for signs that he was messing with me. All I saw was a hard reflection of the arousal pounding through me.

This was what I wanted, wasn't it? What I'd hoped for when I'd called persistently all day today? Another chance to explore this thing between Bryce and me? To find a different kind of common ground since platonic friendship was no longer on the table?

Bryce understood sex.

Hell, he was a master of the carnal if all the girls I'd been forced to listen to during our time at school and then at uni were to be believed. Every single one of them had lauded his superior talents between the sheets. At first, I'd rolled my eyes, certain they were exaggerating. But then my own hormones had joined the party and I'd learned the hard way that even a mere brush of Bryce's fingers over my arm, or my cheek, or my hip, could make my nipples hard for hours. That one throwaway comment in his deep voice or a smouldering look from brooding hazel eyes could leave my panties damp.

Well, here was my chance. Still, I hesitated. Licked a drop of wine from my lips.

He lounged back a little, sleek muscles rippling under his shirt. 'Cat got your tongue, rosebud?'

Rosebud.

A flippant little term of endearment I'd desperately missed.

'You want to give me…anal sex? Just like that?'

He laughed, low and deep. 'Oh, no, rosebud, not just like that. There's a certain amount of careful build-up to it—'

'I don't mean the actual workings of it, and you know it. I mean, how can you toss aside the issues between us and just…?'

He raised an eyebrow. 'Just as easy as it was for you to skip past our issues and ask for oral sex. Regardless of how we feel about certain aspects of our past, you can't deny that there's a chemistry that just won't fucking quit. I thought the best way to deal with it was to stay away from you but that didn't work. So here we are.'

Because I'd pushed or because he'd been unable to resist? I chose to believe the latter.

'But if you don't want to play, just say so,' he added.

It wasn't a taunt like I'd thrown at him. A part of me even suspected he wanted me to chicken out so he would be done with me.

But I didn't want to be done with Bryce. The ache

in my chest wouldn't let me. No matter what had come after, some of my happiest memories were the ones I spent with him. When the criticism from my family had got too much to bear, he'd been the one I'd run to. A judgement-free space I could hide in, perhaps even count on since his own defunct upbringing meant he shied away from the subject of family. It had been enough...*then*.

But ultimately, those flaws gaped. For me or for him.

Sure, we were different people with different wants, needs and goals now. And there was more than one way to skin a cat.

Grimacing at the off-putting analogy, I trailed my finger over the swirls in the tablecloth. By not informing him I was going to marry Dan despite my promise otherwise, I was partly responsible for messing up our friendship.

'What happened in your apartment was my way of trying to get past all the...hostility. But it also got me thinking. I think you'll agree we're past the platonic relationship point?'

I'd probably need a shrink for this later, but right now, with my gorgeous hunk of an almost-ex-best friend sitting in front of me, I couldn't let it go.

When he gave a wary nod, I continued. 'I have a few weeks until the launch. And then I'm in town for another week after that to meet with my investors,' I said.

His finger skirted back and forth across the lip of his wine glass. 'And I have the official opening of the building taking up most of my time. But for this, rose-bud, I'll make the time. So?'

I wanted to ask if 'this' meant just the sex or our friendship but I chickened out. My heart had already taken a few bruises since he came back into my life. I didn't want to invite any more. In direct contradiction my body surged to stinging life, my core clenching in wild anticipation of having its needs seen to properly, perhaps for the first time ever.

My burning secret of never having had a penetrative orgasm was one I hadn't confessed to another soul. Would Bryce cure me of that affliction the same way he'd had me screaming within minutes of tonguing my clit and fingering my G spot?

'I'm waiting for an answer.'

The breath I took was shallow and useless. And when I looked into his eyes the sensation of being sucked under was dangerously strong. But not strong enough to deny the pounding urgency inside me. 'I want you in my life, Bryce.'

A peculiar, almost anticipatory expression flitted across his face. Before he could speak, I held up my hand.

'If *friends with benefits* isn't your bag, I suggest we go with *business acquaintances with temporary benefits*. Does that work for you?'

He tensed. 'What are you saying?'

'I'm saying I agree we can't go back. So let's find a...different path that works for us. Let's not pigeonhole or define our relationship.' And in that time, I'd try to win my friend back, I added silently.

'What about the dare?'

My belly somersaulted with a mix of disquiet and excitement. I was stepping into completely new, potentially risky territory. But…no risk, no reward. Right? 'I accept your dare.'

His smile was pure anticipation with dark, wicked speculation thrown in. It lingered for a while before he nodded. 'Okay, deal.' He glanced over my shoulder. 'Your steak is here. I hope it's been worth the wait.'

That sounded like a portent of things to come. For starters, the beef was melt-in-the-mouth glorious. Bryce stared drolly when I groaned on my second heavenly mouthful.

'What?' I demanded.

'The food is great, I know, but let's keep the *When Harry Met Sally* exaggeration to a minimum, yeah?' he griped.

'Wow, you're really in a foul mood, aren't you?'

'You're attracting attention with those sounds you're making. You sound like you're auditioning for a food porn hotline.' He punctuated that observation by re-directing his glare to the man on the next table whose head had snapped my way at my groan.

Another shiver raked through me as I carefully cut my steak. 'I'll bow to your superior expertise on what a food porn hotline worker sounds like. And I was wrong. You're not angry. You're jealous.' Why that realisation sent a thrill through my blood was a shameful joy I intended to hug to myself all night long.

His nostrils flared. 'You can attempt not to look so infinitely smug while saying that,' he said.

Clearly my poker face needed work. 'You got me, Bryce. I have my first concrete evidence that you still care about me. Forgive me for wanting to celebrate a little.'

He sighed. 'What are you talking about now?'

'You only go crazy over the things you care about. Remember Darcy Livingston? You threw a guy into a wall because he groped her in the lecture hall at uni. Three days later, you were dating her.'

His eyes widened a touch before his eyebrows clamped together. 'You're misremembering. It wasn't the lecture hall, it was the cinema, and it was the same guy she told me had been harassing her for the better part of a semester. Maybe if you hadn't been so busy enjoying Levi What's-His-Face shoving his tongue down your throat after just one date, instead of watching the film *you* picked, you'd remember correctly.'

'His name was Neville. And we'd been on three dates by then.'

A muscle rippled in his jaw. 'Remind me again why we're talking about our exes?' he griped.

'We're talking about the things you care about. The only handy examples are exes from the past.'

A dark shadow passed over his face. 'You think exes are the only ways I've shown you I cared?'

My heart lurched a little and I gripped my fork hard.

'I said they were *handy* examples. A way to make my point without dragging up other...deeper stuff.' Like when he'd broken his arm after tripping downstairs the month before I turned eighteen and spent three days in hospital without a visit from any member of his family, not even his own parents. His siblings had been in boarding school and the only one who'd turned up eventually had been his Aunt Flo, who'd cut short her trip to New Zealand to be at his side.

He stared at me for an age before he sat back farther, placing even more distance between us. 'I'm not sure this new...path works for me. Here's an idea. Let's simplify things.'

My heart dipped. 'How?'

'Truth or dare,' Bryce murmured, narrow-eyed.

Truth, always. Those two words were my usual stock answer. But seeing the myriad expressions shadowing his gorgeous features, knowing he thought he had me completely figured out, I did something I'd never done before. 'Dare.'

'Forget the one dare. I dare you to spend every minute of free time you have while you're in Singapore with me.'

My heart dropped into my stomach.

'Why?'

He shook his head. 'Did I say you were bad at this game, rosebud? You're beyond bad. Number one rule, you don't ask why a dare is a dare. It just is.'

'That's not going to work for me, Bryce.'

'Why do the details matter? You say I'm important

to you. That you want things to be different. I'm giving you a chance to prove it.'

I couldn't help it. I laughed. 'You want me to prove myself to you? Are you serious?'

He shrugged. 'It's my dare. I can frame it any which way I want. And I'm not done.'

'Aren't you?'

'Oh, no, rosebud. A significant amount of that free time will be spent in my bed, building up to that naughty little thing you want me to do to you.'

My fork clattered onto the table. It was a good thing I'd already consumed half of the impressive steak and was full, otherwise I'd have been seriously pissed off at my sudden loss of appetite and the wasted food on my plate. Although another appetite had swiftly taken its place. 'Sorry, you getting to call all the shots doesn't work for me either.'

'Fine. You get to call *some* shots along the way, but not all of them. I won't risk you running off the moment you get what you crave so first I get a taste of that tight pussy, then we'll work our way to the…what did you call it? The back door? Deal?'

I set my knife down next to the fork and picked up my wine glass. I took my time to savour the Chilean Pinot before I swallowed, revelling in the heated gaze that moved over my throat. If he was going to torture me, I intended payback in equal measures. 'No.'

His jaw went slack for a moment before he snapped it shut. 'No? To what exactly?'

'To you still treating me like I've committed some cardinal sin by leaving the morning after you…after we…'

'You gave me your word, and you went back on it. I don't take that lightly.'

'I know! But, damn it, are you going to hold it over my head for ever?'

'No. A month, give or take, should suffice.'

'And after that? We pat each other on the back and move on like our friendship never happened?' Sarcasm dripped from my lips onto the table.

'You broke it, Savvie. This new path is your idea. I'm just…making it interesting.'

A vice squeezed my insides tight despite this originally being my own plan. 'If you think I'm just going to roll over and accept your terms, think again.'

'I haven't stopped being reasonable since you sailed off into the sunset. I'm willing to hear you out.'

I laughed again, conscious I was attracting more attention. Again Bryce glared at the man on the next table, who was wilfully ignoring his dinner date and shamefully eavesdropping. 'You? Reasonable? When were you ever reasonable with me?'

'Savvie…'

'You didn't talk to me for a week after I got my first modelling assignment. And when you turned up at the show you spent the entire evening in a foul mood, and snapped at anyone who came within three feet of me. If I recall, you never attended another show of mine.'

'I sent flowers. Expensive ones.'

'Yes, and a note written by some random florist saying you were proud of me. But you really think they made up for your absences?'

His eyes narrowed. 'You expected me to drop everything and fly over to wherever you were just so you felt appreciated?'

Hurt lanced my diaphragm. 'Of course not, but we were in the same city for some of the time, Bryce. You always had something more important to do.'

'Gideon and I had decided to branch out on our own, away from the family business. Against the wishes of everyone but Aunt Flo. I needed to devote every minute to making it a success—'

'Okay, I accept that, but…'

'But?' he jerked out tersely.

The pain intensified. 'But I can't help think, even before the whole thing with Dan, that you were already pulling away from me.'

His nostrils flared at the mention of Dan's name and I wasn't surprised when his expression closed off completely. 'Don't put this all on me. One minute you were lining up interviews for a marketing internship in the City, the next you were packing your bags to fly to Paris for a modelling gig simply based on a random scout's offer of a job. I'd never known you to be flaky and even you have to admit graduating with a marketing degree, then abandoning it to pursue a modelling career, was a little surprising.'

'Not when you knew I'd minored in fashion design and had a sizable portfolio locked in my closet.'

'Doodles on art sheets you refused to show to anyone but me, and told me to ignore because you had no intention of doing anything with them even though I told you they were great.'

I tightened my grip around my wine glass, recalling another time he'd wholeheartedly believed in me even when I'd doubted myself. 'So I changed my mind. Was I not allowed to do that? Or was I just not allowed to do that without your permission?' I threw back.

His lips compressed and his gaze narrowed before it swept over my face, down my throat to my chest before rising again. The intensified gleam in his eyes escalated the heatwave sweeping through me. 'We're getting off-topic again, rosebud,' he rasped, his low voice containing a dangerous edge that lit up my nerves.

I took another sip of wine before answering. 'On the off-chance I accept this dare, here's my deal. If you get to choose the time and place for when I get my secret wish fulfilled, then I get to choose the when, where and how you get to fuck me before then. It can be as early as tonight or two weeks from now. I get to say whether you fuck me on top of your car in a dark alley or on three-thousand-thread-count sheets in my private apartment.'

He shifted in his seat and his fingers resumed drumming on table. 'It can't be two weeks, not if you're only around for another three weeks. Otherwise this is pointless.'

'A week with me in your bed is pointless?'

'If you choose to make me wait for two weeks, something has to happen in between. I'm not walking around with this fucking hard-on for fourteen straight days, that I can guarantee you.'

My breath strangled in my throat. 'What are you saying?'

His gaze dropped to my mouth and stayed fixed on it. 'I get to kiss you whenever I want.' His eyes skated several inches lower. 'I also touch you in a few…specific ways with or without your clothes on. Agreed?'

Delicious shivers raced up and down my spine. 'Agreed. My turn.'

He nodded immediately. 'Go for it.'

'Oral sex will be vigorously discussed and, when agreed upon, copiously engaged in,' I said, going all in.

The first genuine smile broke across his face, stopping my breath. 'Agreed. One hundred per cent.'

'You have yourself a deal,' I said, throwing in a porn-star huskiness to my voice just to intensify his torture. I expected a signal of his sweet discomfort.

What I got was a creepy grunt from the man on the next table.

Bryce's head snapped sideways and he glared at the hapless, eavesdropping fool. 'Seriously, mate, stop staring at my woman and pay attention to your own date,' he suggested tightly.

I couldn't help rolling my eyes. 'Why yes, Bryce, have a go at the man. Because that's so reasonable.'

He redirected his stare at me. 'I've lost my appetite, rosebud. Are you going to make me sit through dessert or can we go?'

I toyed with letting him endure dessert just for the

hell of it but I was happily stuffed to the gills and my instincts warned me I'd reached my threshold where riling Bryce for one evening was concerned. I mourned my lack of dessert for all of three seconds before I grabbed my handbag.

Creepy Eavesdropper saved his hide by keeping his gaze averted as we passed his table. It didn't stop Bryce from emitting intensely hostile vibes towards anyone who so much as glanced my way.

He was still pissed when we reached the car.

'Seriously, what was the point of buying me dinner if all you're going to do is give me indigestion afterwards?'

'You want me to give you something else, just say the word.'

The threat of indigestion flew out of the window to be replaced by the threat of something infinitely more carnal. More immediate. The screw-public-decency-and-fuck-me-right-here-on-top-of-your-Ferrari kind of immediate.

'Take me to your favourite place in the city,' I blurted.

His eyes gleamed, his bad mood receding. 'Why? You want to call one of those shots right now?'

'Maybe.'

He dragged his eyes from my face, breathed in and out for a handful of seconds. Then he nodded. 'I know just the place.'

He threw the car into gear and accelerated back into the street. The next few miles passed in thick, sultry silence. 'Are you going to tell me where we're going?'

'You'll see.'

Fifteen minutes later, I saw. 'Your building?'

He turned off the ignition. 'I never got to show you the best part of the building. Don't worry, here you'll be safe from my unreasonableness.'

I laughed. 'Safe? That's an…interesting outlook.'

He paused, his face shadowing. 'You don't feel safe around me?'

'There are several interpretations of safety, Bryce. You looking at me as if you want to eat me alive makes me wonder if going into your building with you is wise.'

'What if I guarantee that at least one of us is going to come out infinitely happier than they went in?'

'How are we going to determine which one it is? Flip a coin?'

A slow grin spread across his face. 'Why not?'

I shook my head. 'I never win your coin tosses. Never.'

He flicked open the centre console and caught up a silver coin between his fingers. 'Cheer up, rosebud. This might be your lucky night. Heads or tails?' he asked with a filthy smirk.

In the past I'd always gone for heads and lost. The law of averages suggested it couldn't always be the case. Could it? 'Heads.'

Eyes gleaming, he flipped the coin, caught it expertly and slapped it on the back of his hand. Then slowly lifted his hand. His smirk widened. 'Sorry, love.'

'No way.' I leaned forward to see for myself. It was tails. I reached for the coin.

He snatched it out of the way and slipped it into his pocket. Then he threw his door open, walked around to mine. 'Out you get,' he said, that gorgeous smile making my heart flip-flop.

Slowly, I slid out one leg, then the other, not bothering to pull my hem down when it rode up. 'You're suddenly chipper.'

'Leave your purse. You won't need it.'

'Even if I feel naked without it?' I asked, unable to resist teasing him.

'You're not a vacuous bimbo. You don't need props to get you through an hour with me.'

'I was thinking more along the lines of important phone calls I might miss.'

'It's almost eleven p.m. Who the hell is going to call you at this hour?' he demanded, even as he drew me away from the door. He slammed it shut after I tossed my clutch inside.

'We're busy professionals. It's not completely unheard of.'

He took hold of my arm and walked me towards the double doors of The Sylph. 'Well, whoever needs you urgently can leave a message. For the next hour, you're mine.'

In truth, I didn't mind not having the distraction of emails and texts for a while. For one thing I was enjoying his hand on me a little too much. In the suddenly restrictive confines of my bra, my nipples tightened, my skin felt flushed, and electric tingles pulsed in my clit.

Just like this afternoon, we went past a fully manned security desk.

'Back again, Mr Mortimer?' one of the guards said with a respectful nod.

'I am. Glad to see you awake, Bob.'

The guard reddened and grimaced. 'I'm never gonna live that down, am I, sir?'

Bryce's lips twisted. 'No, you're not.'

'What was that about?' I asked when we entered the lift.

'Nothing I wouldn't have left alone if I hadn't seen him checking you out this afternoon.'

My jaw threatened to drop.

'What?' he asked, eyebrows raised.

'Where is this Neanderthal side of you coming from?'

His smile was calculated, sending a skitter of something not quite unpleasant up my spine. 'You seem to think you know me so well.'

'I do know you,' I insisted, even though a voice inside me mocked me mercilessly.

He didn't say anything, just stared at me with those impenetrable eyes until the lift pinged to a stop.

'Aren't you going to say anything?' I blurted when he propelled me forward with a steady hand on my back.

'No. You're in the mood to argue a point just to prove you're right. You're not. Leave it alone.'

'And if I don't?'

He shook his head. 'You're not going to distract me by starting an argument, rosebud. Not tonight. And not here.'

We'd been walking through a glass-encased atrium at the very top of his building as he talked, and arrived in front of a wall of glass with the city spread out below us. The view was simply breathtaking. Across the bay, the city sparkled like precious gems tossed on an endless blanket of black velvet. Dazzling and magnificent.

'Wow.'

'It's something, isn't it? Takes my breath away every time,' he murmured, the last traces of tension gone from his body.

Even before I'd chosen the Singaporean investment vehicle to back my business, I'd fallen in love with the city. I didn't want to think that Bryce's presence here had anything to do with it, but I couldn't help but think it did. And to know he loved this place as much as I did...

'How can you bear to tear yourself away from this?'

I sensed more than saw his shrug. 'Like all great things, I enjoy it when I can and learn to do without when more important things hold my attention.'

My breath snagged somewhere between my lungs and my throat. I didn't want to look at him just in case he wasn't referring to me. Or just in case he was. God, he was turning me into a basket case.

Despite my warning to myself, I found my head turning, meeting his gaze, getting lost in the ferocious intent in his eyes.

'Bryce…'

He stepped behind me and caught my shoulders. For the longest time we basked in the view, his head aligned with mine as he pointed out landmarks.

But slowly heat and tension built, my heart racing with other sensory delights I wanted to fulfil. When I turned away from the view, he was waiting. With my back against the glass, I stared up at him.

'Truth,' I whispered.

He smiled wryly, as if he'd expected me to say that. 'Hmm?'

'I've wondered, once or twice, how you would taste,' I stated brazenly.

He exhaled choppily. 'Are you saying what I think you're saying, rosebud?'

I took his hands from my shoulders, placed them on the glass above my head. 'Are you prepared to find out?'

'Yes.' The sound was ejected from him.

With a smile, I slowly slid down the glass until I was perched on my heels, looked up at Bryce's stunned, gorgeous face. 'Stay right there and don't move.'

CHAPTER FIVE

Bryce

FOR THE FIRST time in a long time, I was…dumbfounded.

While sex had been on my mind ever since she'd confessed her fantasy, I truly hadn't brought her here to have sex. To get my hands on her luscious body every chance I got? *Yes*.

But this…?

My ability to think straight fractured when she reached for my belt and slid it out from the buckle. Her eyes stayed boldly on mine while her plump lips parted in anticipation.

Every step of the way since my absurd proposal at dinner, I'd expected her to laugh and tell me to stick my filthy desires where the sun didn't shine.

So far she hadn't. Hell, that glaze in her eyes said she was into this, just as much as I was.

I didn't know how to wrap my head around it. Was it even me she wanted or did all this stem from that stubborn need for her to prove something to us both? Frankly, I had no idea.

But was I going to stop her?

Hell, no. My scrambled brain was already turning to soup and she hadn't even lowered my zip yet. The sound of her doing just that ripped the breath from my lungs.

Pitching forward, I rested my forehead on the cool glass, hoping to gain a little control. No chance. My normally revered view of the botanic and hanging gardens by night paled in favour of the more enthralling view of Savvie tugging down my trousers and gasping softly as she took my dick in her hand.

She was rapt with her ministrations, but I was rapt with her. The way she looked as she stroked me guaranteed to turn me into a blathering fool in under a minute. But before that happened I had time to accommodate a few things. Firstly, that, despite my having seen her naked twice before, this was the first time she was getting intimate with my cock.

Secondly, *dear God*, where had she learned to do that?

That bite of jealousy from earlier resurged. I pushed it down in time to hear her sigh. To watch her swallow. To see her gorgeous eyes lift from my cock to meet mine. Her sultry arousal weakened my knees, forcing a groan up my chest.

'Bryce…'

God, the way she breathed my name. Was she even aware she sounded like that?

'What is it, rosebud?' I asked, my throat thick with lust.

Her gaze dropped for an instant but I felt the heat of her stare all the way to my scalp. 'You feel amazing.'

I squeezed my eyes shut just as she squeezed my tip, drawing out that bead of liquid before running her thumb lightly over it. 'Fuck, rosebud. You're going to make me come before you get that mouth on me, aren't you?'

My tortured question elicited a smug little smile I swore to pay back the second I got the chance. For now I was literally and figuratively in her hands. And I was going to disgrace myself if she didn't get on with it.

'Open that mouth, please. I want in.'

With a delicate little inhale, she settled back against the glass wall, pulled me close, and wrapped her glorious lips around me.

My groan burst free. The sensation of her surrounding me, suckling me, was like that first dive off a sheer cliff face, that moment of exhilaration when every nerve ending was doused in adrenaline. Every thought dissolved save for the sight, sound and touch of Savannah drawing me deeper into her mouth, her wicked talented tongue flicking and swirling, tasting and swallowing from the heady combination of her hands and mouth.

I wasn't going to last.

That firm certainty tumbled from my lips in raw admission. She withdrew her gorgeous lips long enough to breathe, 'I don't care. Just enjoy the view,' before redoubling her efforts to chop me off at the knees.

A laugh barked from me. 'Can I touch you?' I begged.

She didn't answer for a handful of seconds. When she eventually gave a, 'Hmm,' I tangled one hand in her glorious hair. Fisted a handful and thrust urgently a half-dozen times before a primitive growl announced my blinding explosion.

Time and the billion-dollar view outside ceased to exist as I drowned in delirium. But I was aware of her softening touches, the sexy little sounds she made as if I were the one pleasuring her, not the other way round.

I breathed deep, wondering if my months-long sexual drought was what was heightening this experience, only to dismiss it.

Our history was why this climax held an extra edginess. I'd not only experienced a mind-bending orgasm but had ticked off an essential box on some important document that held life's secrets.

Or you're going stark raving bonkers.

I pried my eyes open to find my hand still entangled in her hair, my forehead braced on the glass and my breathing as erratic as a leaf in a hurricane.

With another smug smile, she tucked me in, zipped me up and, still on her knees, rested her hands on my thighs. Bloody hell, that supplicant stance, while satisfyingly contrary to her true nature, threatened to get me hard all over again.

But even if she'd have allowed me, the plan wasn't to fuck her here tonight, no matter how much my eager libido was all for it.

We needed a few guidelines set in stone before that happened. What had happened here only proved that the chemistry was much stronger than anticipated. I needed a little time to regroup.

I redirected my gaze to her face, brushed her swollen lower lip with my thumb. 'That was incredible, rosebud,' I managed.

Her smile widened, a blush darkening her cheeks. 'Thank you.'

I took a step back and finished adjusting my clothes, a little gratified when I caught a flash of disappointment on her face. That little balancing of the control scales made me hold out my hand and help her to her feet. Unfortunately, it brought that sinful mouth far too close to mine, reminded me that there was still another heady box to be ticked in our destination-undetermined journey.

'What are your plans for tomorrow? I have a meeting with my architects in the morning but I can meet at some point for dinner?'

She grimaced. 'I can't.'

About to turn away, I froze, unsettled by the deep disappointment slashing me. 'Why not?'

'I'm about a day behind on the installation for the showroom so I'm working on it all day, then having dinner with my investors.'

'Don't you have people for that?'

She shook her head. 'Relying on others is the reason I'm in this position.'

I wanted to ask her whether she meant specifically or generally but, hell, my brain hadn't quite righted itself after that incredible blow job and, frankly, I wasn't in the headspace for another deep dive into the past or, heaven forbid, another probe into strained relationships with my family. My skin tightened in recollection of what she'd said about Graciela.

My sister was the only one who knew just how fucked up I'd been for a long time over our parents. She alone knew about the letters we'd written separately to our parents. She'd shared that knife-edge's experience of waiting for several empty months for a response. And then that final death blow when it'd arrived.

Graciela had never shown me the contents of her letter but the stark horror on her face, one I was sure reflected my own, had said it all.

We'd never spoken about it in the intervening two decades.

That she'd taken now to start probing that scab every time we were within talking distance was a situation I'd grown increasingly weary of.

And while I hated to admit it, that was the reason I avoided her like the plague.

'Bryce?'

Savvie was frowning at me. I pushed thoughts of my sister and buried wounds away. 'You're not planning on making those installations yourself, are you? Because I'm sure it contravenes a few leasing clauses.'

Her lips twisted impatiently. 'Of course not. But I still need to be on-site, check and double-check the inventory. Often the vision of a set-up changes once equipment is slotted into place. It's easier to make changes during set-up than when it's done. Less expensive too, which is better for my investors since I'm working on a budget.'

A peculiar little thread in her voice brought me up short. 'Everything okay with the investors?'

She blinked, then glanced away, but not before I caught a hint of worry in her eyes. 'It's fine.'

I caught her chin in my hands, directed her gaze to mine. 'Talk to me, Savvie.'

She held it for several seconds before she shrugged. 'Last quarter's sales weren't stellar. I haven't reached the everything-is-riding-on-this-launch stage yet, and I'd like to avoid getting there if possible.'

I bit my tongue against asking if that was why she chose The Sylph. Whatever her motive for reconnecting with me would reveal itself soon enough. As long as I kept messy emotions out of it, it didn't really matter. 'If I can't take you out tomorrow, can we meet on Sunday? You're not planning on working all weekend, are you?'

'Of course not. Sunday's fine.'

'Great. There are a few more things I want to discuss about this arrangement.'

One sleek eyebrow lifted. 'And you can't tell me now?'

'It can wait till Sunday. It's almost midnight and I have to call London before I crash.'

She got that stubborn light in her eyes, but then gave up after a beat. I didn't want to admit my relief as I walked her back into the lift and out to the car. As much as I loved Savvie's spunk it was a challenge to tussle with her when I wasn't firing on all cylinders. And everything that had happened since I'd answered her call today had sent me off-kilter.

And yes, a part of me wanted her waiting with bated breath for me.

'Where are you staying?' I asked when she belted in.

'I'm renting an apartment at Triona One. It's—'

'I know where it is.' The revelation that she was three short streets from my own apartment triggered another pulse-racing frenzy and visions of sleepless nights where I was plagued with her proximity.

Fucking hell.

'Why not a hotel?' There were several five-star hotels in and around Marina Bay, the world-famous Raffles Hotel a case in point.

'Hotels don't really do it for me. I like having my own space, cooking my own meals.'

'You cook?' I teased.

Her nod was a little wary. 'Yeah. I kinda had to learn.'

My mood plummeted. Fucking Dan again. '*Had* to?' I grated.

She avoided my gaze. 'To start off with. Then I found out I loved it so I took classes after…' She cleared her throat. 'After the divorce.'

My fingers tightened around the steering wheel, my foot sending the sports car flying towards the Central Business District and her apartment.

Silence pulsed in the car until she turned to me as I pulled up at the entrance to the boxy glass towers that housed her temporary apartment.

'You know we can't avoid this subject for ever, don't you?' she demanded huskily.

Since I'd arrived at the same conclusion ten seconds

ago, I couldn't very well deny it. 'Yeah. But it's not going to be tonight.'

In the reflected interior of the car, her eyes assessed me. Then she nodded. 'Fair enough. Goodnight, Bryce.'

I wanted to stop her from opening the door. From stepping out and leaving me with churning feelings. But to do that I'd have to resort to drastic measures. Like kissing her. Like sliding my hand under her skirt to find out for myself whether sucking me off had made her as wet as her soft gasps and decadent eyes had promised.

But I didn't want our first kiss to be a snatched event in full view of anyone who walked out of the building.

So I reeled myself in, managed a half-decent nod and even managed to step out and open her door for her.

She alighted, stepped close and attempted to scramble my brain all over again with her perfume.

'I'll expect your call tomorrow,' she murmured.

I nodded, leaned against the car and watched her walk inside.

She didn't look back. And I was grateful.

Because fuck if I wanted her to see me staring like a creepy, lust-addled fool.

Savvie

I stretched my back to relieve tension and blew a breath up my forehead.

Despite the air-conditioning, my exertions in the store for the last four hours had made me exhausted and sweaty. Not to mention a little cranky.

All morning I'd been plagued with flashbacks of last night. Lunch at Bryce's apartment had been tense and uncomfortable before nosediving into a sizzling sex appetiser that had left me gagging for more.

But last night…

My face heated up as I recalled what I'd dared Bryce into. I'd brazenly believed I could handle it until, alone in my bed, serious doubts had steadily crept in. The sexual angle aside, there was a huge emotional iceberg right in the path of my intentions to coolly handle this. One that had flashed its colossal silhouette in the dead of night and terrified the hell out of me. In that flash I'd seen my own deeper yearnings, skating dangerously close to Bryce's.

And in those early hours I'd been forced to admit to myself that there was nothing perfunctory about my actions. I wasn't cool about losing Bryce for ever.

Bryce Mortimer was the only person who'd caught a glimpse of the true depths of my bruised bewilderment about my family. He'd never quite touched the heart of the secret I kept closed off and locked deep inside, but he'd known enough to attempt to salve a wound despite our specific deficiencies.

But even then, he'd been at a loss to see why I was lonely in the face of familial affection.

What he hadn't known was that the affection and togetherness was all a carefully cultivated front. That away from shrewd eyes, the great Knight clan was far from lovingly familial behind closed doors.

That smiles hardened.

Eyes judged and teeth gritted long before I hit puberty and it became clear my interests didn't align with my family's. That no matter how hard I tried, I never fitted the mould.

That when I declared my intention to model at age twenty, my ethics professor father, after a shot of single malt, had pondered out loud why his daughter was interested in flaunting herself wearing nothing but several pieces of silk and satin stitched together instead of utilising the business degree he'd paid for.

The English professor mother who could barely meet her own daughter's eyes over the dinner table because of those same deplorable life choices.

And the stick-thin older sister, who taught disabled children and volunteered without fail at the homeless shelter every Sunday, never failed to voice her opinion about her younger sister's failings in life in general, while the whole ensemble unerringly plied her with their thoughts on her plus-size weight in particular.

Bryce had never witnessed any of it. While he'd heartily scoffed down my mother's shrimp jollof rice and charmed everyone with his sharp wit and Mortimer pedigree, I'd been busy biting my tongue against telling him that I'd felt like a stranger in my own family almost from the day I was born.

That hearing my mother scathingly berate my father for his insistence on a second child when she'd wanted to stop at one, thereby landing me in their illustrious midst, had broken something inside my twelve-year-old self I wasn't sure had ever healed properly.

And I'd been too ashamed to set Bryce straight on his misconceptions about my family. Perhaps that had been where I'd gone wrong. Did I secretly blame him for not seeing beneath the surface?

My lips twisted as I sipped my bottled water. Would he even have seen my attempts? When we'd crossed paths at the posh school my parents had enrolled me in after we'd relocated from Denmark to London for my dad's new posting, Bryce had been busy dividing his time between playing rugby and dating stick-thin girls who'd looked like replicas of my sister, Willow.

How he'd managed to extricate himself from the latest limpet-like groupie long enough to make conversation with me that day outside the school library remained one of life's great mysteries.

That flash of old jealousy and insecurity threatened to rise again.

I sighed, drained the last of my water before marching purposefully back to the centrepiece I'd been working on with my small crew all morning. The wide, revolving platform made of black granite would hold the crowning jewel of my new season's designs.

Without the chandelier in place I wouldn't see the full effect of the trellised metal mannequins, but that couldn't be helped until it was installed on Monday.

The matching hanging baskets from which a few of the models would be suspended from the ceiling before the runway show commenced were still to be put up.

My monumental to-do list seemed insurmountable but I'd risen to bigger challenges. After all, if I could withstand harsh, esteem-shredding barbs from my own family and ex-husband, then—

Nope. Not going there today.

Resolutely, I opened the first box bearing my company's logo.

Voluttuoso.

Voluptuous.

The name always drew a smile. The moment I heard the name drop from the Italian photographer coordinating pre-show clips for my third runway show in Milan, I knew that would be the name of my company.

It had been one more tiny step on the long journey to financial independence and emotional self-sufficiency after it'd become clear my family didn't want anything to do with me or my career choices. While it'd hurt, it'd made me more determined to turn my back on the trust fund my parents had attempted to use to keep me in line, each pay cheque I'd earned from modelling a much-needed salve to my pain and pride.

Both goals had faltered along the way thanks to Dan and his greedy demands during our divorce, but I was on my way to reclaiming the former.

As for the latter…

Determinedly, I grabbed the black-and-purple box holding my merchandise and headed for a quieter corner of the showroom.

My colour theme for the spring/summer season was deep purple with teases of bright and dark fuchsia. I opened the first box newly delivered from my manufacturer and felt a fierce bolt of pride as I pulled away the delicate decorative tissue paper and lifted out the first item. Pride steadily sustained me as I sorted through the pieces and jotted down where each item would be displayed for maximum exposure in the store, only stopping when my phone pinged an hour later.

My heart skipped three vital beats as I saw the name displayed: Bryce.

Done with my meeting. Fancy taking a break?

I had several more boxes to sort through but the urge to say yes immediately pummelled me. Would he think I was easy? That I'd drop everything for him the way I used to?

The loud growling in my stomach mocked me, reminding me that it was lunch time and I could do with the break. I hit reply.

I could be persuaded.

Think fast. I'm three minutes away.

The tingling in my body ramped up at the thought of seeing him again.

Fine. I'll take a break. But only if you bring lunch.

Already sorted.

I rolled my eyes, then hastily rearranged my goofy smile when I caught glances from my crew.

On the spur of the moment, I glanced at my watch, then I walked over to them. 'Once you're done with setting up the platform, we can call it a day.'

A chorus of cheers greeted me.

Smiling, I headed back to the boxes and was inspecting a purple dressing gown with a lace trim when the lift doors opened and Bryce walked in. Behind me silence fell, and I knew without turning around that most eyes would be on him. That the female ones would widen, then linger far longer than was necessary. And because I didn't want to confirm and fight another wily jealousy monster, I kept my eyes on him.

Watched him nod a greeting at the crew before fixing his eyes on me.

He was dressed casually in one of those deceptively simple polo shirts that cost hundreds of pounds and dark chinos. With his collar upturned and his hair windswept, he looked positively rakish. 'Hey, you.'

This time my heart skipped twice as many beats. And when he reached me and I caught a whiff of his aftershave, different parts of my body came to rude, vital life. It took an effort or three to drag my gaze from the twinkle in his dark hazel eyes to the large takeout bag he held in one hand.

'Hey, yourself. Give me a few minutes to sort through this lot and I'll be with you, okay?'

His gaze dropped to the silk-and-satin lingerie as he set the takeout bag down on a nearby shelf. 'Want some help with that?'

The thought of him holding my creations in his hands

did something to me. Something indecipherable that made me hesitate. We weren't on steady ground, Bryce and I, and after all this time I wasn't sure I wanted him this close to my most precious possessions.

Slowly, one sleek eyebrow spiked. 'You think I don't know my way around a woman's lingerie?'

The tingling abated and a tiny bubble burst inside me. 'I'm sure you do.' I shoved one box his way. 'Have at it.'

He frowned but I didn't want him probing my disgruntled emotions so I turned away and blindly grabbed a few empty boxes. 'I'll go and dispose of these. Back in a minute.'

I felt his intense gaze singe my back as I walked away. In the large storage room that held the rest of the deliveries, I tossed the boxes down, then lingered, attempted to get myself back under control.

What the hell was I doing dicing with the only man who'd been able to slip beneath my guard with ridiculous ease?

Because he's also the only man who's come closest to accepting you for who you are. The man you've secretly crushed on since you were a teenager.

Truth and truth.

And I'd dared myself to go farther, so cowering in the storage room was just pathetic.

With a deep breath, I marched back out. The box I'd left him with was halfway done, his sprawling handwriting jotted down next to my neat notes on the inventory sheet.

He flicked me a glance, minus the frown, when I arrived next to him. 'You okay?'

'I'm fine,' I answered a little sharply.

Despite my terse response, he didn't probe further.

Still unable to meet his gaze, I looked over his shoulder and saw the crew preparing to leave. A mixture of anticipation and apprehension assailed me. So far Bryce and I were two for two on getting down and dirty when we were alone. And if I was honest with myself, that had partly informed my decision to dismiss my crew.

Plus after my first addictive dare last night, I had a feeling things were headed for the hot and heavy way sooner rather than later.

The moment the lift doors closed behind the crew my breath strangled somewhere in my lungs.

But Bryce seemed to have other ideas.

With a lazy gait that drew far too much attention to his powerful shoulders and streamlined body, he inspected the half-finished showroom and stopped at the platform.

'Why the metal frames instead of traditional mannequins?'

'Every season I pick one outfit that highlights my theme for the season. On launch day there will be a live model under a spotlight wearing it. The runway winds around the centrepiece and once the show finishes there will be a few models positioned strategically around the showroom. Using traditional mannequins would take attention away from the model. This way only the lingerie is on display making it easier to imagine an item of clothing on yourself.'

He nodded, his eyes gleaming as he eyed the platform and the metal frame. 'Very effective. A stunning concept.'

I couldn't stop myself from beaming at the compliment. 'Thanks.'

He strolled back to where I stood and stared down at me for several seconds. 'So you want to explain that look on your face when I walked in?'

I didn't want to ruin the moment with thoughts of my myriad insecurities or, worse, my family. A little hypocritical considering I'd grilled him about his family last night, but, hey, I wasn't perfect. 'I'm more interested in what you brought in that bag with you.'

His speculative gaze didn't lessen but he gave me a pass. 'You can have it on one condition.'

My whole body tingled at the possibilities throbbing behind his huskily voiced statement. And the more we traded that charged, silent stare, the more intense that tingling grew. I knew my nipples had turned diamond-hard. That my breathing was erratic and my panties were damp.

'Name it,' I replied, my voice a husky mess.

He twirled an index finger around the room. 'You let me stay to help with whatever you're doing here after we eat.'

My lungs deflated. 'Oh. Sure, if you want.'

He nodded, thankfully turning away before I crumbled in disappointment. I watched him pick up the bag, look around for a flat surface.

'Here.' I pulled over a thick plastic cover sheet the

crew had been using and spread it out beneath the window. It was wide enough to seat both of us with space in between for our makeshift picnic.

Bryce smiled. 'Perfect.'

He fetched the takeout bag, folded his large frame into one corner and extracted heavenly smelling food boxes from the insulated bag. The smell of miso soup and duck spring rolls made me groan.

His smile turned into a chuckle. 'Sit down before you fall down with gratitude.'

I sat, folding my legs in a casual lotus pose that gave me closer access to the food.

Bryce glanced at my folded legs, then up at me. 'I always found it fascinating how easily you can do that.'

'Years spent as a yoga disciple will do that. You would be just as limber if you'd taken classes when I asked you to.'

He grimaced. 'You know how much grief I'd have caught if my rugby team knew I was doing yoga on the side?'

I couldn't help my own grin. 'Point taken but we both know you have a devil-given talent for talking people into anything. I bet they'd have all taken up yoga if you'd encouraged it.'

His grimace turned wry. 'You set too much store in my abilities. But you can feel free to strike the Downward-Facing Dog position for me when I have you naked.'

I was thankful I hadn't taken a bite of my spring roll because I was sure I'd have choked to death. 'Seriously, you need to give me a heads-up before you drop sex into our conversations.'

He looked at me as if I were certified. 'Where's the fun in that?'

'Watching me choke to death is your idea of fun?'

'I'm experienced in the Heimlich. Besides, some people find that sort of thing erotic.'

'I don't! Jesus. Bryce!'

This time he gave a full belly laugh, the sound and sight of him amused, even at my expense, so damned sexy I stopped breathing for a full ten seconds. Could our different path include this weirdly wonderful openness about sex where I'd desperately suppressed it before? My stomach flipped with excitement. As landscapes went, I wasn't displeased about it. At all.

'Calm down. I said *some* people, rosebud. I would very much prefer you present and conscious when we fuck. Miso soup?'

The hand I raised to accept the offering shook wildly. He saw it, smiled a little too smugly about it, and when his fingers lingered on mine, they told me he knew exactly what he was doing to me and was thoroughly enjoying ramping up my engine.

We ate the first course in silence, even while his gaze returned repeatedly to my folded legs.

'Don't get any ideas. I'm not doing a headstand during sex or anything that sends my blood rushing in the opposite direction of where it needs to be.'

Gleaming eyes captured mine. 'Don't worry, the rush will be exactly where it needs to be.'

I wanted to ask him to elaborate but I was a sucker for delayed gratification. An abysmal sex life where the act was over before I could count the minutes on one hand had a way of doing that to a girl.

So I spooned rice and spicy broccoli onto a plastic plate, separated my chopsticks and took a few mouthfuls. 'Since you're in a better mood, will you tell me more about this building?'

'Are you hoping to distract me into not talking about sex? Have you forgotten my multitasking skills?'

I hadn't forgotten a single thing about Bryce Mortimer, but I wasn't about to tell him that. 'The building, Bryce. Why mixed use and not a full hotel?'

He shrugged, letting me change the subject. 'Because regardless of our prime position and status, it'd be foolish to compete with six other five-star hotels within a quarter-mile radius. Instead of being labelled one thing, having a multipurpose function keeps it vibrant in the long term.'

I nodded. 'Like blood pumping through a central nervous system.'

He raised a brow. 'Are we back to talking about body parts and rushes, rosebud?'

Heat crept up my face. 'You're incorrigible.'

'And you hate that, I'm sure,' he mocked.

I didn't and he knew it. Every second I spent in Bryce's company reminded me of everything I'd missed about him. And right alongside it I was learning new things about him. Like the pride in his voice when he spoke about his building, one of the most innovative in the Northern Hemisphere. The way he paused for a considered millisecond before answering a question. Hell, the way his eyes darkened dramatically when he was turned on.

The intensity and angst surrounding our first sexual encounter had left me with little time to fully appreciate a sexually charged Bryce.

Now my heart thumped wildly with anticipation. All the same, I tried to remain on less risqué ground and knew I was failing even before I opened my mouth after another few mouthfuls of delicious rice. 'And why this particular design?'

His grin was a little strained. 'A nod to the female form? Gideon and I came up with the idea.'

I didn't hide my surprise. 'Gideon?'

He nodded tightly. 'We were supposed to build it together, even after he took the CEO job back in London. Damian, my cousin, was supposed to be involved too.'

'What happened?'

A muscle ticced in his jaw. 'What always happens. Family crap. Gideon went radio-silent and Damian relocated to New York. All I got was a memo stating that the project was now solely mine. So I made changes, starting with the name.'

The words were tossed out but I knew its effect ran deep. That the strain between brother and cousin had contributed to hardening Bryce even further.

'Anyway, architecturally it was challenging to combine form and functionality with beauty and one hundred per cent green sustainability. I'd like to think it turned out well. Sexy, even?' His grin was back, the shadow cast by his family temporarily thrown off.

I let that go. 'You achieved all four, hence all the awards you've been lapping up.'

He deftly tossed a cashew nut into his mouth with his chopsticks and chewed while his gaze rested on me. 'You've been keeping tabs on me.'

'You may have written me off but I didn't do the same to you.'

All signs of amusement evaporated from his face but before he turned sideways to grab the bottle of mineral water, I caught a different expression. One that made my insides flip.

'*Did* you keep tabs on me, Bryce?' I asked brazenly, because to hell with holding back with this man. He drove me crazy enough as it was. I wasn't going to add one more mystery to the equation.

He took his time to twist the cap off the bottle. To take a long drink with his gaze boldly on mine. I was twisting with desire by the time he lowered the bottle and wiped his mouth with the back of his hand. 'So what if I did? You setting the world on fire was kinda hard to miss. Kudos on that, by the way.'

I was torn between melting with pleasure at the second compliment in ten minutes and abject curiosity. The latter won out. 'Thanks. But why?'

'You know why,' he fired back with nary a raised voice. 'Isn't the one who got away supposed to be the most interesting?'

The melting slowed. 'Sex? You're reducing this to sex?'

He speared a piece of broccoli. 'Didn't we agree that it would be simpler that way?'

'No, we agreed on a *different* path, not a simpler, sex-based one.'

'And you agreed to my terms. Don't change your mind now. And don't act all hurt because I won't let you change the rules.'

'God, I really hate you sometimes, you know that?'

'No, because you don't. You want to pick yet another emotion to hide behind because you're afraid of this one.'

'Oh, fuck you, Bryce.'

He leaned forward into my space, his gorgeous lips curved in a sexy smile as his gaze raked my face. 'Finally, something we both agree on. I hope tomorrow still works for you because I've cleared my whole day for you, rosebud.'

I surged to my feet, my emotions too wild to contain. Stalking to the window, I stared blindly at the view, my thoughts scattered to the wind.

Behind me, I heard him rise, heard the crinkle of containers as he gathered the leftovers. His footsteps receded for a minute before they returned.

I didn't need to look to know he was directly behind me. Firm hands arrived on my waist, drawing me back into his body, and fool that I was, I went. 'You can scream if you want to, get it all out of your system,' he whispered in my ear.

I dropped my head and let out a long, frustrated growl. The movement of his chest told me he was laughing at me.

'Guess I should count myself lucky that you still don't believe in violence, huh?' he mused.

'Heads-up, I've been taking Krav Maga classes. Keep it up and I'll kick your arse into tomorrow.'

Laughter ceased abruptly.

He propelled me around to face him, and I looked up into his fevered scrutiny. 'Any particular reason why you needed self-defence classes?' he asked tightly.

I shook my head before the volcano in his eyes could erupt. 'It's nothing like that. Dan didn't…abuse me.'

The clench of his jaw said he begged to differ. And I couldn't argue with that. The dirty laundry of my divorce had been publicised for the world to see. Bryce probably knew to the penny how much Dan had screwed me over for. How fraught and acrimonious the whole sorry saga had been, starting with his bid to become majority shareholder.

Terse silence stretched between us until he dropped his hand and stepped back. 'Do you want to get the rest of this sorted?' He waved a hand at the rest of the boxes.

A little relieved that we'd stepped back from the edge, I nodded.

For the next hour we worked in relative peace, a silent moratorium placed on volatile subjects.

When we were done, he went to dispose of the boxes, then sauntered over to where I stood, staring at the platform.

'You good?' he asked gently.

I nodded, a little apprehensive of what happened next now we had no inventory to distract us. I jumped a little when he reached up and tucked a strand of hair behind my ear. His lingering touch sent a bolt of electricity through me. 'Thanks for giving me a hand.'

'My pleasure. Would you like a lift back to your place?'

I shook my head. 'I brought my car.'

'Okay, then I'm going to leave you alone now.'

Sharper disappointment lanced through me. The urge to tell him not to wait till tomorrow, that I'd happily see him when I was done with my dinner, rose to the tip of my tongue. He spoke before I could voice my desire.

'But I want you to do something for me.'

'Yes?' God, could I sound needier?

He stepped closer and replaced his fingers with his mouth, caught my earlobe gently between his teeth. 'I'm dying to see what you look like in these stunning pieces you've created. I want you to model them for me, privately. Starting tomorrow.'

I gave a little laugh through the delicious shivers coursing through my body.

'The Voluttuoso collection has over a hundred individual designs this season alone. No way will I have the time or the inclination to model each one for you in three weeks.'

'It's more like four weeks, but I get your point. Fine, show me the range and I'll choose.'

I grabbed my tablet, called up the right page and handed it to him. He slanted me a smug, sexy smile. 'Thanks.'

I waited on pins and needles as he scrolled through the entire collection at his leisure. After a few minutes, he whistled. 'Seriously, Savvie, these are fantastic.'

I wasn't sure which touched me more, his use of the shortened name my family never deigned to use despite my stated wish or his warm acknowledgement of my achievement. I chose both. 'Thank you, Bryce.'

His head snapped up. Our gazes collided. For a moment there was only deep pride and warm friendship in his gaze. Then his gaze dropped to my mouth, stayed, his hazel eyes growing darker as my tongue darted out, slowly licked before pulling my lower lip between my teeth.

I couldn't have stated more blatantly that I wanted him if I'd shouted it from the top of his building. His eyes flashed back to mine before dropping to the tablet. 'This one.' His voice was thick and so was the pressure behind his trousers when I desperately sought that final confirmation, making me swallow and yearn for another taste of what I'd experienced last night.

'If you want to make your dinner you need to stop looking at me like that and engage verbally with me so I can leave you alone.'

I dragged my gaze from his crotch and squinted at the tablet.

'There are twenty-seven outfits in that collection.'

'Perfect. Do you have express delivery?'

'Of course.'

'Excellent.'

The next three minutes were spent in charged silence as he filled his online cart with every item off the playsuits and bodysuits range. A few more clicks and he handed the tablet back with a thoroughly satisfied smirk.

Altogether the collection, which included a rose-and-platinum-gold chain playsuit with diamond-encrusted nipple studs that was worth eleven thousand pounds, came to over twenty-five thousand pounds.

I'd known for a long time that money was no object for the Mortimers but I'd never been the recipient of such cavalier generosity. I wasn't sure whether to be thrilled to pieces or wonder how often Bryce did this with other women.

'Ten o'clock in the morning work for you?'

My head moved in consent before my brain caught up. In the next moment, he was crowding me against the glass wall, his face a picture of harnessed arousal as he stared at me.

'I can't wait to have you, Savvie. Really, truly, have you. You have no idea how long I've waited. But you will. Soon you will.'

He walked away, leaving me weak-kneed and wondering if this desperate path I'd taken was worth putting my heart through such turmoil.

CHAPTER SIX

Savvie

I ARRIVED TEN minutes late the next morning, hating myself a little for needing to appear as if I weren't dying to be there.

Bryce was waiting in his doorway, just like last time. But this time his expression was less sexy-grumpy and more smouldering sexy. Not that it gave me any relief.

His gaze tied me up in knots for completely different reasons. Reasons that made it difficult to draw a full breath by the time I arrived at his door.

'Hi.' I was breathless and nervous like a damn teenager but, truly, even after having him go down on me twice, it wasn't every day a girl slept with the only person who'd earned 'best friend' status in her life. So I was going to give myself a pass.

'Morning, rosebud.' He leaned down, brushed his lips over my cheek, then trailed them to the curve of my neck. 'Hmm, you smell incredible. What's that perfume?'

A tingle of pleasure eased a layer of nerves. 'It's one of mine—Voluttuoso X by Savvie.'

'Right. That's the one with the ad where you were lying on a bed of pink roses wearing nothing but petals, right?'

Halfway into the living room, I turned in surprise. 'You know about my perfume range?'

He kicked the front door shut and grinned. 'You asked me yesterday whether I kept tabs on you too. Answer's yes. Besides, a giant kick-ass billboard in Times Square with you on it is kinda hard to miss.'

I wasn't sure whether to be upset that he'd been in New York the same time as me and never bothered to get in touch or elated that he'd followed my career. I didn't want to start today on a sour note so I chose the latter.

'As milestones go, that was pretty special.'

He approached, reached up and curled a strand of my hair around his fingers. 'I bet it was. I'm proud of you.'

For some absurd reason, a lump grew in my throat, the way it seemed to whenever Bryce complimented me.

For several seconds, he stared at me, then abruptly dropped his hand. 'Would you like brunch? My chef left a few dishes if you're hungry.'

I'd been too nervous to eat more than an energy bar after I was done with yoga. The butterflies going crazy in my belly didn't bode well for my digestive system. 'No, I already ate, thanks.'

He nodded. 'Then let me show you around. We didn't get around to it last time,' he said a little dryly, before tugging my clutch out of my hands and tossing it on the nearest sofa.

I followed him through to the kitchen that boasted every state-of-the-art appliance suited to his lifestyle.

A large study with two huge bookcases filled with psychological thrillers revealed that he hadn't stopped devouring his favourite genre. I slotted that information away for possible future reference.

The three guest bedrooms were lavishly decorated in neutral smoky greys and warm taupe. I didn't need to ask why a bachelor needed four bedrooms because Bryce had once told me that the Mortimer family dynamic was such that any member of the extended family could drop in on another family member and expect to be hosted.

Why that continued to be honoured considering they could barely tolerate each other was a mystery to me. But who was I to question how any family functioned?

My thoughts veered from the turbulent subject of family when Bryce's hand landed on my waist. Through the thin layer of my flowery knee-length chiffon dress, the heat from his touch seared me.

After a brief tour of his personal gym, we arrived at a set of double doors.

'And this…is my bedroom,' he rasped hotly in my ear as his free hand turned the handle and threw the door open. Twice as large as the others, the theme was grey and dark gold, with hints of platinum trimming the furniture and art pieces hanging on the wall.

But what caught and held my attention was the bed. For starters, the headboard was a breathtaking work of art comprised of vine-like intertwined wood and metal that soared all the way to the vaulted ceiling. The mattress was thick and high, the comforter invitingly luxurious.

Beneath my feet, dark gold carpeting muffled my footsteps and, opposite the bed, a large oil painting drew the eye to the jaw-dropping depiction.

'Is that a Wu Cheong?'

He smiled. 'You know his work?'

I nodded, bitten by a touch of envy. 'My investors and I begged him to design something for the launch. He declined.'

'Ah. Poor you,' Bryce teased. 'You should be nicer to people with artistic connections.'

'Like you, you mean?'

'Absolutely!'

I turned to berate him but the words dried in my throat when I spotted a familiar stack of black and purple boxes just inside what I assumed to be his dressing room.

'The stuff arrived?'

'They did,' he replied, his gaze intent on my face.

'And?'

'And we'll get to that in a minute. How did your dinner go with the investors?'

'Better than I'd hoped. I've been eager to add a brand of cosmetics to the perfume range. As of last night they were officially at the amber-light stage. If the launch and the season go well, they'll green-light my proposal for next season.'

Although I was happy to answer his questions about

my business, I couldn't pull my attention from the boxes. Had he looked? Did he have a favourite?

The hand on my waist trailed up and down my rib-cage, drawing my attention back to Bryce.

His gaze was riveted on my mouth, sparking that wild anticipation that finally, after all these years, the pleasure of kissing Bryce Mortimer for the first time hovered in the near horizon.

'Would you like a drink, Savvie?'

Despite my dry throat, I shook my head. 'No, thanks.' Now I was here, I wanted nothing to delay what was coming. 'Want me to help you open the boxes?' I asked.

'Oh, I want. Very much,' he replied gruffly.

There was something so infinitely hot about walk-ing into Bryce's manly dressing room it made my pussy clench with torrid excitement.

He left me at the large marble-topped centre island and fetched the first of the four oblong boxes. From a drawer he removed a penknife, handed it to me and I slit the edges open.

I smiled as he leaned forward in anticipation. To-gether we pulled aside the delicate dark purple wrappers and I let him lift the first item from the box.

It was a black playsuit, which consisted mostly of thin silk criss-crossed material held together by delicate purple netting. It was high on the waist and left very little to the imagination—just watching it in Bryce's hand made me hot all over.

'Gorgeous,' he murmured, before glancing back in-side the box. 'Next.'

I lifted a lace body from its wrapping. The colours were reversed on this one, with the purple more prominent. But still it was a frivolous and feminine creation that covered the front and totally revealed the back. Bryce swallowed as he eyed the outfit. Then, eyes a little wild, he returned to the box and with each unveiling his face grew tighter, his breathing a little more erratic.

Halfway through the last box, he looked up at me. 'You know how fucking hard I get imagining you wearing something you've created, just for me?'

I set aside the all-net, completely see-through bodysuit with purple and pink polka dots with shaking hands and tried to breathe through the lust fog engulfing us. If anyone had told me I'd be this turned on unboxing my own stuff, I'd have laughed. 'Probably not as hot as it makes me.'

He gave a low, husky laugh. 'We'll see.' He nodded at the box. 'One more and we'll have to take a break.'

The 'one more' was probably in the top three of naughty outfits in the range. The all-leather playsuit was held together by a central gold navel ring from which strips fanned out across the body, covering nothing at all in a blatant game of titillation.

'Bloody hell. The pictures online in no way do these justice. How is a man supposed to think straight after seeing that?'

'That's the point, Bryce,' I replied, tongue firmly in cheek.

He raked a hand through his hair, his fevered eyes

tracking over the outfits scattered across his dressing island. 'That one first.' He pointed to a net playsuit with faux-fur trim but his eyes darted to the leather suit.

I grinned. 'You sure?'

'Fuck no, I'm not sure,' he griped.

I took pity on him. 'How about you let me pick? Wait for me in the bedroom.'

He nodded eagerly. 'Great. Five minutes, okay?'

I raised an eyebrow. 'Is there a fire I'm not aware of?'

He skirted the island to where I stood and tugged me close. 'Damn right there's a fire. And it's been raging longer than you know.'

My pulse jumped but I managed to say evenly, 'Then you best let me get on with it.'

With another heated look, he walked out of the dressing room, leaving me with a sea of lingerie and a thousand questions. Slowly, I dragged my dress off, tugged off my underwear and set them neatly to one side. Deciding to leave the leather playsuit for another time, I chose the polka-dot body and carefully slipped it on. It came with a half-inch velvet choker Bryce hadn't seen and it gave me a little thrill to add that little accessory to the ensemble.

In the long mirror, I looked past the cellulite and chunky thighs to the impact of the outfit. I would never be a size six, but my heels made my legs look good enough, and with my hair caught up and choker in place, it drew the eye up from my full bust.

Momentary insecurity slammed into me, deflating the air from my lungs. Bryce might seem turned on by me right now, but how long would that last? How would he react when he got a better picture of just how many stretch marks were on my body?

Relax, he's seen you naked before.

Not fully. Not totally—

'Savvie, I *really* need you to come out here.'

I grinned at the tight need and impatience straining his voice even as it fired up my blood, burning away a layer of insecurity. But my heart still slammed into my ribs like a wild thing when I took a deep breath and headed for the bedroom.

In the doorway, I paused and cocked one hip, years of strutting down the runway kicking in despite the nerves eating me alive.

He was poised on the edge of the bed, minus his T-shirt, his hair even more dishevelled, as if he'd been running his fingers through it.

His gaze latched onto my face, then, almost immediately, dropped to my outfit. His breath hissed from between his lips and his hands bunched beside his thighs. Almost rabidly, he devoured every inch of my skin, lingering between my legs and on the nipples pearling in reaction to his blatantly aroused scrutiny.

I had to hand it to him. Bryce knew how to make a woman feel special. Who else had he made feel special in the time we'd been estranged?

Nope, not touching that.

Instead I revelled in the quick glide of his tongue over his lip as his gaze fixed on the velvet choker.

'Get over here, rosebud,' he commanded with a definite croak.

'Ask me nicely, Bryce,' I countered.

He squeezed his eyes shut for a split second. Then rose and padded on bare feet—at some point he'd discarded his shoes too—to where I stood. He stared at me for a tight little stretch. 'You seem hell-bent on driving me insane. But I'm not going to rush this. Do you know how long I've waited to kiss you, Savvie?'

The air left my lungs in a whoosh at the reminder that, despite all the filthy things we'd done to each other, Bryce and I had never kissed.

Heart racing faster, I shook my head.

Eyes locked squarely on mine, he lifted his hands and cupped my nape. Slowly his right thumb drifted over my lips, as if memorising their texture before he tasted them. 'Eleven fucking years, I've waited to do this,' he breathed, almost to himself. And the depth of feeling in his voice made my heart twist for a completely different reason.

Dangerous reasons.

'Bryce...'

'Shh, rosebud. No talking. Just...'

He lowered his head in torturously slow descent, drawing out the moment until his lips brushed, butterfly soft and fleeting, over mine.

A shiver cascaded through me, vibrating every cell in my body and sparking it to life. I gave the tiniest moan and Bryce lifted his head.

His eyes were hotter, his breathing a touch harsher as he stared at me.

Then, as if the feast was too much, he slanted his lips over mine.

Fever hot. Powerfully arousing. And oh, so brilliantly executed. I sagged against the doorframe for a moment before sheer hunger made me rise on my toes to meet Bryce halfway, fulfilling every last dream of what I had imagined kissing him would be like.

Within one instant and the next I needed more. Bracing my hands on his waist, I leaned higher into the kiss, fused my lips tighter, deeper, as intimately as I could taste him before I opened up, allowed his tongue to glide oh-so-sexily against mine.

We both groaned. Hunger ravaged us whole and eroded any attempt at finesse. Breathing hard, we strained towards each other, devouring each other in a bruising kiss that only fuelled the fire of lust.

Hot slickness between my legs made me grind myself against the thick erection swelling his jeans. My need was enough to propel him back a step, until Bryce was the one now leaning against the doorframe.

It was the perfect position to plaster myself against him, rub my aching nipples against the hot, hard landscape of his chest, while grinding my pelvis against his erection.

The fingers in my hair tightened, the sting a sweet pain that turned me on harder. Drew a thicker moan from me.

Breathing harshly, Bryce tugged me away, the separation of our lips a wet, decadent sound that sent a shudder through me.

'God. Nothing I imagined came this close, rosebud. Absolutely nothing,' he confessed thickly.

'For me neither.'

For some reason, that made him smile. A blinding display of pleasure that made my heart lurch alarmingly while filling me with equal parts of joy and trepidation.

'Again?' I asked.

His smile widened and his eyes dropped to my wet lips. 'God, yes. And again and again.' With a groan, he sealed his lips against mine.

Still kissing, I dragged him out of the doorway, then gasped when he swung me up into his arms.

Sweet Lord, but I loved it when he did that! I'd challenge any woman to deny they love being swept off their feet.

He laid me down on the bed and followed without breaking the kiss. Then he rolled us with expert ease, until I was draped over him, my thighs braced on either side of his hips.

In prime position to get closer to that hard, delicious prize, I didn't hesitate. Flicking my tongue brazenly against his, I widened my stance, arched my back and dragged my heated pussy against his engorged cock.

His groan was long and tortured. One hand clamped hard on my bottom, holding me firm and tight against him as he deepened the kiss even more.

Then abruptly he pulled away, his chest rising and

falling in harsh pants. 'Christ Almighty, Savvie, I'm going to lose my mind if I don't get inside you now.'

Despite the ragged confession, he didn't move, just continued to stare at my mouth as if it were the answer to world hunger. And since I loved kissing Bryce, I lowered my head and fused our lips once more while I raised my hips long enough to lower the zip of his jeans. He groaned into my mouth as I freed him, took his thick cock in my hand and drew down on his already hard dick.

He caught hold of my hand and flipped us over again. 'You won't do this to me, Savvie. You won't make me blow before I get inside that beautiful pussy,' he growled, even as he rubbed the underside of his cock against my cotton-covered clit.

The sensation was sweet hell, driving my nails into his back. 'You want to fuck me that badly, Bryce?'

He groaned. 'More than I want my next breath,' he replied.

'Then do it. Take this insane ache away.' My voice was a husky mess but I didn't care.

Slowly, going against the ravaging urgency consuming us both, he sat back on his heels. Eyes the colour of a dark forest dragged over my body, greedily devouring the pulse racing at my throat, the sinfully prominent points of my large breasts, the twitching of my wide hips.

'Fuck, you're so sexy, Savvie,' he growled.

Tears prickled behind my eyes, the knowledge that my numerous flaws didn't register with him lifting my spirits to unknown heights. Making my stupid heart fill with that dangerous hope that I needed to claw back to reason. But I couldn't.

Not with Bryce.

Never with Bryce.

He held more of me than he would ever know. But that beat of insecurity and rejection reared its head again, reminding me that, when it mattered most, I had never been enough for anyone. Not my family. Not Bryce, who'd let me in up to a point but never all the way. Not even my arsehole of an ex-husband, who'd taken pleasure in listing my faults on a daily basis before I'd found the strength to walk away. But out of sight didn't mean out of mind. And as much as I hated to admit it, some of the mud he'd thrown had stuck.

'Hey. What is it?' Bryce was frowning down at me.

I shook my head wildly, hating myself for tarnishing this moment. 'You're making me wait, Bryce. I hate waiting.'

He laughed, then, with a wicked gleam in his eyes, dipped his head and brashly caught one net-covered nipple between his teeth.

I cried out, the sensation almost too much to bear. Luckily, the intensity of my arousal pushed the fragile thoughts away. Arching my back, I chased after more and he responded, drawing my areola deeper into his mouth and flicking his tongue over the sensitive peak.

The dampness between my thighs intensified, leaving me slicker, hungrier.

'Bryce!'

Blindly, he reached towards the bedside table, and

returned with a condom between his fingers. After another minute torturing my nipple, he rose and shucked off his jeans.

The sight of Bryce tearing open the condom with his teeth was absurdly sexy. All I could do was pant and writhe in anticipation as he dragged the protection over his hard dick, grabbed my hips and jerked my body down the bed. Still on his knees, eyes pinned between my legs, he tugged the lingerie aside. 'You know this beautiful piece of nothing isn't going to make it, don't you?' he asked a little regretfully.

I shuddered.

He smiled. 'It turns you on, doesn't it? The thought of me ripping this thing off you?' His knuckles dropped between my legs, shamelessly rubbed my engorged clit.

'Bryce?'

'Yes, rosebud?'

'Shut up and do it,' I commanded, too turned on to play nice.

With unbelievably sexy ease, he caught the neckline of the body and ripped it right down the middle to my crotch. He fell on my breasts, moulding and licking and tasting and biting until I was out of my mind. Then before I'd gathered my next breath, Bryce yanked me lower still, and thrust hard inside me.

My scream ripped through the room, the sensation of being slick enough to accommodate his size and tight enough to feel every inch of him blazing delirium up and down my spine.

'Holy bloody fuck!'

He held himself deep, head thrown back, the muscles in his neck standing out in straining cords. 'God, Savvie, you feel so good,' he groaned.

Need ploughed through me, heightened by the pressure of his groin pressing against my swollen clit and my desperation to feel him *move*. 'Fuck me, Bryce.'

After another teeth-grinding moment, he pulled out and slammed back in. 'With pleasure!'

My eyes rolled, every inch of my body steeped in bliss as he fucked me with a mastery I'd never experienced before.

The last dregs of insecurity retreated. I knew it wasn't gone, that it would return to attack me, but for now I revelled in Bryce's every groan, every kick of my heart and every push towards that rarely attained peak of sexual fulfilment.

Even when Bryce's fingers dug into my hips a little too forcefully, when his thrusts grew frenzied, I welcomed the tinge of pain along with the pleasure because I knew my pleasure was his goal. He'd shown it twice before, selflessly denying himself where others had put their pleasure first.

That fact made me wrap my arms around him, kiss him deeper, throw my hips up to meet his thrust, giving and giving as much as he'd given me.

And yes, doubling our pleasure.

Sweat slicked our bodies from our exertions, the scent of sex wrapping around us in thicker and thicker waves until the decadence of it was unbearably erotic.

Until a familiar but altered sensation that whispered that I was nearing my peak startled me.

Usually, I needed more, much more stimulation to get me to this point. Specifically, subtle self-pleasure. The realisation that I didn't was a shocking but very welcome notion. One that made me gasp with pleasure.

Bryce dropped forward, pressing his hard body into mine, his fingers spiking into my hair. 'Are you close, Savvie?' he breathed against my lips.

The extraordinary sensation of an orgasm fuelled by penetrative sex was so unique, I didn't want to ruin it by talking. My nails dug into his shoulders and I silently urged him on, tightening my internal muscles to increase the pressure around his steel-hard cock.

Bryce's inhaled sharply. 'Jesus, how are you doing that?' he growled as I met his thrusts with faster pumps of my hips.

I secretly thanked the yoga gods for that extra pleasure delivery and was rewarded in spades when, with a series of fast thrusts, he fused his mouth to mine and pushed me that final inch to the peak.

I braced myself on the edge long enough to savour the incredible sensation. Then, unable to hold back, I screamed, wild bliss tearing through me.

Over the roar in my ears, I heard Bryce's hoarse shout, felt deep convulsions seize his body as he climaxed.

Minutes drifted by as we caught our breaths. Bryce left the bed to get rid of the condom. When he returned he pulled me back into his arms.

In the midst of my thrashing, I'd lost most of the pins

in my hair and, after he rolled us sideways, he removed the rest and trailed his fingers through my hair. His lips drifted over my damp shoulder to the shiver-making hollow beneath my ear, his other hand caressing my hip.

'Truth.'

My heart lurched and I froze because that word, in this space, reeked of nothing but off-limits subjects. 'I remember someone saying that's not how the game is played,' I replied.

He smiled. 'Taking a leaf out of your book.'

I forced myself to relax. 'Okay.'

'You seemed…surprised that you were about to come. Did you think you wouldn't?'

Heat filled my face and I was glad my skin was dark enough for it not to show. Not that it would've mattered.

Bryce saw my discomfort and, of course, compounded it by raising my chin to stare into my face. 'Tell me, Savvie. You obviously like sex so what am I missing?'

I expelled a breath. 'I do like sex. I just…usually need a little bit…more.'

He frowned. 'Explain.'

'Why? So you can gloat?'

'If there's gloating to be done, I will indulge. Right after I express the appropriate sensitive emotion.' Despite his joke, his eyes were serious, prompting the truth from me.

'I've never come with just penetration,' I blurted. 'Not until just now.'

Slowly, a smug smile spread across his face, once again filling my heart even as I rolled my eyes. 'While

I curse all the arseholes who've left you high and dry, I'm glad to be the one who did it for you.'

Before the moment could be ruined by dwelling on one particular arsehole, I rolled my eyes again. 'My turn.'

He kissed me short and hard before he drew back and nodded.

'What did you mean earlier when you said the fire's been raging longer than I know?'

He slanted me an assessing look. 'What do you think I meant?'

I took a breath, willing my thumping heart to slow even as I accepted there was no way to avoid the past. 'Are you referring to what happened three years ago?'

He gave a laugh that sounded eerily self-deprecating. 'For someone who's as clever as her illustrious parents, you're not very astute, are you, Savvie?'

My lips twisted. 'I think my parents will disagree with you on that score.'

He nudged me onto my back and raised himself on his elbows to look down at me with a fresh frown. 'What are you talking about? I know you had some issues with your family but your parents couldn't wait to flaunt your school report in my face every time I came to dinner.'

'Yeah, they were good at window dressing.'

His brows pleated. 'Window dressing? I saw some of those reports myself, Savvie. You were top of your class every year—'

'And they were good at singing my praises in public but behind closed doors was an entirely different story, Bryce!'

His eyes narrowed at my outburst and my stomach dropped, knowing he'd heard the anguish in my voice. 'How?'

'I don't really want to talk about it.' I tried to pull away. His fingers tightened.

'No, Savannah. Don't play that card with me. Yeah, I know it wasn't perfect, but if I've been totally hoodwinked I want to know why.'

'Trust you to make it all about you.'

'No, it's not about me. I can see the pain in your eyes and, yes, I want to know if I should be kicking myself for something I missed.'

The anger I'd been scrambling to cover my pain with melted away, and when he pulled me closer, I went. 'Don't blame yourself. They were experts at the game.'

His frown deepened but he didn't push for more. He simply waited me out.

After a minute of furious debate with myself, I sighed. 'I know you have your issues with your family so you'll probably know how it feels to wonder if you were born into the right family.'

He stared at me for a few heartbeats before he shook his head. 'Weird as it may sound, I think I was born exactly where I needed to be. There's no point wishing for things you can't change.'

'Well, in that case you have no clue what I'm talking about but the gist of it is that I've felt like a...like I don't belong for most of my life.'

A puzzled look replaced the frown. 'But…all the times you invited me home…things were that bad?'

'Behind closed doors, they didn't hesitate to point out my deficiencies. And it wasn't just an ugly-duckling-in-a-sea-of-swans situation. It was more like panda-in-a-tribe-of-gazelles.'

For the longest time he didn't speak. The look in his eyes was equal parts quiet fury and compassion. 'Was that why they never came to your show or your wedding?'

Pain lashed me hard. 'My father threatened to cut me off if I pursued the modelling, and he went through with it. I haven't spoken to them or Willow in…a while.'

'Savvie, why didn't you tell me?'

I shrugged and that little movement hurt more than the retelling warranted. Which said a lot about what I'd bottled up over all the years. 'You had your own issues going on. You couldn't get enough of the stories they regaled you with about my Ghanaian heritage, and I didn't want to spoil the illusion. Not at first. And when I tried to hint at it a few times you missed it. Then I kinda grew okay with it because I liked you being a little jealous of me, for a change.'

His brows spiked. 'For a change?'

I grimaced. Damn my runaway tongue. If this verbal tsunami was the side effect of sex with Bryce, I wasn't sure I was up for any more. But even that thought left a bruise. I was well on my way to being addicted to sex with Bryce and no amount of apprehension about baring my deep secrets would stop me experiencing more of him.

'You were the captain of a rugby team, you had girls falling all over you and you have the Queen listed somewhere on your family tree as a relative. Plus you could go without combing your hair for a month and still look like a damn *GQ* model. I hated you for a long time before I talked myself into tolerating you.'

He let loose a heart-stopping grin. 'And how long was this talk? Five…ten seconds?'

I slapped his arm. He gave a short laugh before his expression grew serious. 'You have a good idea how fucked my family situation is, Savvie. You had no need to be jealous. Not if you knew how hard I worked before you deigned to talk to me.'

It was my turn to frown. 'What?'

He shrugged. 'Since we're telling a few home truths… I didn't run into you by accident that day at the library. I'd been watching you, knew your routine off the top of my head.'

My mouth dropped open for a few unbecoming seconds. 'Why?'

'I said hi to you for a month straight and each time you looked right through me.'

'Because I thought…' I stopped, bit my lip, the memory of how off-balance he'd thrown me returning full force.

He nodded. 'I know what you thought. That because I hung out with meatheads that I was one myself?'

I grasped his lifeline. 'Something like that. And there was that dating stick-thin girls thing.'

'I had to pass the time somehow,' he said drolly.

'Seriously, what are you saying, Bryce?'

He shook his head. 'We're getting off the original subject. Why didn't you tell me how things were with your family? Besides the jealousy?'

'Because I was ashamed. Because it hurt. Because I was struggling to understand why they could be loving and respecting of each other but not me. It was like they had membership to a special club I couldn't join because I wasn't the right dress size and I despised tofu and politics.'

Mild shock flicked across his face. 'Savvie—'

I shook my head, on a roll now the dam had cracked. 'My parents I could understand, maybe. But I didn't get why Willow hated me so much. She was the most vicious of them.'

'Is it possible that Willow felt she had to take your parents' side or get the same treatment from them?'

I frowned, recalling that the very few times when my sister had been less bitchy towards me had been when we were alone. But it didn't make up for the times she'd piled on me in front of my parents. And the approval inherent in their silence.

'Either way, it's on them, not you. You know that, don't you?'

'I'm not sure that I do. If I did, I wouldn't have married Dan.'

His face tightened and I regretted bringing him up.

'Are we going to fight about him, too?'

Long fingers tunnelled into my hair, toyed with it for a minute before he sighed. 'No. I don't want to fight.'

'What do you want to do?'

He smiled. 'Totally up to you. I'm in your hands.'

'How about we head out for a while?'

He groaned and nuzzled closer, making me laugh. 'I'll sweeten the deal and promise to wear the leather playsuit when we get back.'

Immediately, his expression brightened. 'Deal. And I'll try not to rip it off when I put you on your knees and fuck you from behind.'

With a hard little kiss, he launched himself off the bed and held his hand out to me. I stood up, then stumbled when I went to take a step.

He laughed, the sound brimming with unabashed male satisfaction. 'That's it, rosebud, show me how tough it is for you to walk,' he leaned down to whisper in my ear.

I pushed against his ripped chest. 'Remember, pride goes before a fall, champ.'

'We'll see.' He stepped behind me and slapped my bottom. 'Now get yourself in the shower.'

I took a few more ginger steps, earned another smug laugh from him before his face grew solemn. 'Thanks for telling me the truth about what was really going on with you and your family.' He hesitated for a moment, then added, 'And I'm sorry if I was too self-absorbed for you to feel you couldn't tell me.'

I couldn't stop my heart from flipping over, from

running my fingers through his hair and tossing one small wish into the cosmos. That, if nothing else, I never lose his smile again. 'Maybe I couldn't have handled telling you then, anyway. But it feels right to tell you now. Does that make sense?'

After a moment, he nodded. 'You couldn't count on my reaction then but you're strong enough to handle it now?'

I smiled, my throat clogging with how perfectly he'd got it. 'Something like that.' God, I hoped there would be more moments like these, when I could just bask in the warmth of his friendship.

'What are you thinking about?' he asked. 'Besides how amazing I am, of course.'

Smothering my mushy feelings, I winked at him. 'That's for me to know and you to drive yourself crazy over.'

His gorgeous grin returned. 'No need. You're wishing I make it so you can't walk for another solid week.'

I opened my mouth to say *Keep dreaming*, but somehow the words twisted, tapping into the vein of need he'd brought to life.

'Kiss me again, Bryce. Make me stop thinking about all of the bad stuff.'

He continued to stare down at me for another half-minute, his fingers toying with my hair. Then his head swooped down and he caught my mouth in a searing kiss that did a fantastic job of wiping my brain clean.

CHAPTER SEVEN

Bryce

IT WAS A good idea to get out of the apartment. My head was spinning with sensory and information overload. The major one being how I'd missed the deeper undercurrents of what had been going on with Savvie and her family.

This time I couldn't escape the stinging arrow of guilt. But maybe she was right. Maybe I wouldn't have handled it then, on top of the crap going on with my own family.

But you can try now…

Could I, when I'd actively avoided the emotional for as long as I could remember? Did that fall under the purview of this *different path* we were taking?

Hell if I knew.

The sex, however…yeah, *that* was incredible. I loved sex in a healthy, non-obsessive way. But even before that first mind-blowing encounter I'd known I wanted to tie Savvie to my bed for an insanely long time that whiffed with notes of for ever. And call me primitive, but her confession that she'd never had a penetrative orgasm had made me want to roar and beat my chest like some bloody caveman and I wasn't remotely ashamed.

Yeah, that had stoked my Mortimer arrogance to an all-time high.

Sex like that could only get better. And with the promise of anal sex hovering deliciously in our future, it was a miracle I could leave the apartment in one piece, especially with Savvie wearing that just-thoroughly-fucked-out-of-my-mind look and her lips swollen from our first, second and countless other kisses.

I pulled her to my side in the lift, and when she rested her head on my shoulder, I secretly touched my own lips, that heavy throb of satisfaction inside me toying with the hunger for more.

But as the lift hurtled us to the ground floor, another emotion settled in.

Mild dread.

The reason for all of that was waiting to be dissected like an unwanted cadaver. And while I knew we couldn't avoid discussing the Dan issue, and even grudgingly got an inkling of what kind of family mind-fuckery had driven her into the bastard's arms, I wanted to spend what was left of the afternoon with Savvie without a crappy atmosphere between us. 'So, where to?' I asked, leaning down and kissing her soft mouth, my pulse jumping at how natural, how unbelievably sweet she tasted. 'We could hit the food first? You feel up to eating now?'

She nodded. 'God, yes, I'm starving.'

For a moment I wondered if she'd have been able to say this to anyone without judgement. Then felt glad she could say it to me.

I wrapped my fingers around several strands of corkscrew curls. 'We've done the Michelin-star thing. Feel like exploring the other end of the culinary spectrum?'

Her eyes widened. 'What do you have in mind?'

'Steamed clam and noodles at the hawkers' market in Marina Bay?'

She gave a pleasured groan. 'I'll have to do double my gym session in the morning but I can't resist a hawkers' market.'

'I can help you with the workout in some other way if you like?' I whispered in her ear. And earned myself a lusty little shiver and peaked nipples that assured me she was anticipating our next bedroom encounter as much as I was.

'Hmm, an idea worth merit. I'll think about it,' she said saucily as the lift doors opened at garage level.

Without my releasing her we walked towards my car and I held the door open for her. She didn't get in immediately. Instead, she slid her arms around my neck and pressed her lips to mine. The invitation was too tempting to resist. My pulse jumped, my hands finding her luscious arse and dragging her closer.

Right from the start, I'd been drawn to Savannah because of her inner strength. Finding out about the insecurities that had plagued her had been a mild shock because I'd been fooled by her outward confidence.

Call me sick, but those touches of vulnerability

made me want her more, but it was the unashamed desire to grab what she wanted—like a kiss in an underground garage—that attacked the walls I wanted to build around my more forbidden emotions. The ones that made me question the real reason behind staying away from her all these years. Had I been afraid of *this*? Where it could go? Whether I would fuck it up?

I shied away from the suspiciously affirmative answer.

But when she flicked her tongue against mine, when she whirled us about and pushed me against the car door and deepened the kiss, I called myself ten kinds of fool for waiting this long to take the risk.

Within a minute, I was hard as a rock. Desperately wishing we were somewhere more private. I wondered how she felt about front-seat sex.

Before I could drag my mouth away to ask, she was pushing off me, depriving me of her insanely gorgeous body.

I remained where I was, momentarily unsure whether my legs would carry my weight if I attempted to stand.

After a few tries, I stood. 'What was that for?'

Her hand dropped to my fly, caressed the eager bulge in my trousers. 'You're not the only one who's been waiting a long time for our first kiss, Bryce,' she replied huskily. 'Be warned that I might jump you every now and then until our little deadline is up.'

The reminder of our deadline soured my mood and sent my mind flying in many unwanted directions as I fired up the car's engine. Was the reminder some sort of warning?

A sideways glance at her didn't show the apprehension I felt but who the hell knew with Savvie?

I hated myself a little for that last thought. By all accounts while I'd been lamenting about my dysfunctional family, she'd been going through a hell of her own. Had my blindness contributed to our estrangement?

Chaotic thoughts chased through my mind all the way to Marina Bay.

A wave of heat hit us the moment we stepped out and I tossed my keys to the valet. I was used to the heat and humidity of Singapore, having lived here for a few years.

I glanced at Savvie as she fanned herself. Already a bead of sweat was forming on her upper lip. The sick sex freak in me wanted to lick it off. 'Are you good to walk? It's just through the Gardens.'

'Sure. Lead the way.'

She plucked a pair of stylish shades from her clutch and slid them on and immediately I wanted to object because I couldn't see her beautiful eyes.

God, I needed my head examined.

The walk took longer than planned because Savvie decided she wanted to wander through the Supertree Grove and take a tour of the Flower Dome. I curbed my impatience as she pulled out her phone and snapped several pictures of flowers she could use in her store for her launch.

The additional reminder that we were on a ticking

clock made me shove my hands into my pockets to stop from calling a stop to this grand decision to spend even a second with her outside the bedroom.

Nevertheless, I kept my mouth shut, pointed out places of interest along the way until we arrived at the street food market.

After getting our food, we found a bench close to the water. Savvie lifted her face to the sun and I couldn't help but stare at the smooth, dark bronze perfection of her skin. Like the sun, I wanted to worship the alluring expanse of her throat, unwrap the delicious globes of her breasts and feast on her nipples. Hell, I wanted to cover every perfect inch of her with reverent kisses—

'What's wrong? You've been brooding since we left the car.'

I skewered a piece of my chilli crab and held it to her lips. She took the offering but her eyes remained on me, awaiting an answer.

Since I wasn't going to make an arse of myself by confessing my rampant thoughts, I chose a safer subject.

'What's the agenda for the week?'

She shrugged. 'More of the same. Finish setting up and contacting the agencies I use to make sure my models are all booked. They arrive at the end of next week so it's imperative everything's completed so they can start rehearsals.'

'Can you carve out a few hours for me on Friday evening?'

'Why?'

'It's a surprise.'

She groaned, slid off her sunglasses to blast me with the full force of her glare. 'Why would you do that to me?'

I grinned. 'What?'

'I have to wait a whole *week* for a surprise?'

'It's five days. You'll just have to trust me this time that it'll be worth the wait.'

My statement was a little too pointed for her to ignore. And when her eyes shadowed, I knew I'd hit the nerve I'd vowed to avoid just so we could spend a few hours together without the past coming between us.

The water bottle clutched in her hand wobbled. She set it down next to her half-finished clam dish. 'Wow, I see we're going for the low blow.'

'Savvie—'

'It's fine.' She looked around before meeting my eyes. 'You want to do this here?'

'I don't want to do anything.'

'Tell that to your face. Tell that to your growly voice and white knuckles.'

I glanced down, noticed with an inner grimace that one hand was cupping the other so tight my knuckles *were* white. Consciously, I relaxed them, took several deep breaths.

'You're right. That was a shitty thing to say.'

'But you meant it, didn't you? To a degree?'

I couldn't deny it so I didn't. Not now I knew that arsehole hadn't even been able to give her all the orgasms she deserved. My mood took a deeper dive at the thought of *why* she'd given him the time of day in the first place.

Shit, I was going around in circles of my making, on the brink of spiralling out of control.

It was almost a relief when Savvie jumped to her feet and held out her hand. 'Come on, it's my turn to take charge of the afternoon.' Despite her bright smile, I caught the sheen of hurt in her eyes.

I felt a tightness around my sternum I attributed to everything else but the fact that I hated seeing that look in her eyes. To make up for it, I let her drag me towards the nearest street while she toyed with an app on her phone.

The taxi pulled up within seconds. 'Where are we going?'

'It's a surprise,' she lobbed back.

I sighed and leaned back against the headrest. I saw her watching me but I couldn't gather the energy to make idle conversation. And if there was one thing I could count on it was comfortable silence with Savvie.

Had everything really changed as irrevocably as I'd insisted or was I simply pushing that agenda so I wouldn't experience that stupid bewildered anger when she left again this time?

Bloody hell—enough!

I suppressed my frenzied thoughts as the cab pulled up to another street corner. Savvie jumped out, muted excitement in her eyes.

I looked around as I joined her on the kerb. 'Where are we?'

'You'll see, come on.'

I threw my arm around her waist to anchor myself to the present and let her lead the way. Two streets later, I realised where we were.

Kampong Glam.

Specifically the Sultan Arts Village. Home of street art.

'Have you been here before?' Savvie asked.

I shook my head. Surprisingly, I'd heard of this place but never visited.

She smiled as if gifting me with this place made her happy. I wanted to grab that happiness, bottle it exclusively for myself. But could I count on it?

I left that thought alone as the *click-click-click* of a spray-paint can being shaken hit my ears.

The village consisted of a few streets where graffiti was legally permitted. Wide, tall walls served as artists' canvas and about a dozen or so people were already hard at work creating their masterpieces on the walls.

'Wanna have a go?' Savvie asked.

I couldn't resist the twinkling in her eyes so, of course, I nodded. 'Sure.'

We headed to the shop for supplies, then walked until we found an unoccupied wall.

'Is it worth saying curb your competitive spirit and don't put me to shame?' she asked, tongue-in-cheek, her yellow spray can poised three inches from the wall.

With a light breeze ruffling her unbound hair and outlining her stunning body I could've stared at her all day. Resolutely, I redirected my gaze to my section of the wall. 'Nope.'

Although my major had been in architecture, I'd minored in art design, primarily so I could be in the same class as Savvie. I'd never told her that and I didn't intend to. She'd taken up enough of my angsty thoughts already.

Without hesitation, she plunged right into her mural, not one ounce of the insecurity she'd admitted to in bed showing as her arm swung back and forth in bold swipes.

She wore the front well. A little too well?

I frowned, my thoughts attempting to deepen once again without permission.

'Are you going to stare at that wall all day?'

My forefinger hit the nozzle, and, with a little relief, I let my subconscious run free.

Savvie didn't glance over at me once, her focus totally absorbed in her work. I was torn between admiration and irritation. None of the other women I'd dated before would've ignored me quite so totally. Hell, no other woman would be seen dead in this part of town frequented by poor artists, gap-year students and hippies.

The novelty of it finally seeped in. There was something wildly cathartic about spraying my frustrations on a wall and the hour passed in a blink.

When I eventually took a breath and stepped back, I wasn't altogether surprised at what I'd unleashed. But more than that, I was interested in what Savvie had drawn.

I glanced over. She was standing six feet away from the wall, her eyes riveted to what she'd painted, her head slightly tilted as she exhaled roughly. Catching my stare, she glanced at me and I caught the sheen of tears in her eyes.

'Are you all right?'

She gave a half-hearted shrug, then nodded. 'Yeah.'

Although it was a public space, I felt I was encroaching on a private moment.

'Am I allowed to see?'

She swallowed, then nodded.

Setting my can of black paint down, I joined her. Unable to resist, I kissed her temple, then I looked over at her section of the wall.

The scene was set on a beach, a solitary female figure sitting on a windblown dune, watching the sun rise through black clouds, frothy waves and a turbulent sea.

Despite the chaos, a beam of sun illuminated her face, its path unbroken by the darker elemental forces around it. The connection between the figure and the sun was almost sacred, a codependency so heartbreakingly beautiful, the grip on my sternum intensified.

On a stunned breath I realised the source of my turmoil.

I'd wanted to be that connection for her. I'd wanted that codependency even before I spoke to her for the first time outside the school library all those years ago.

But other forces had intervened, not least of all something inside me holding me back.

That force was still there. Unexplored but throbbing, fed by unresolved issues.

But yes, also by forces she'd let happen. Forces she'd let control our personal painting. We needed to talk about that but for the first time I hesitated. If we managed to get past that, then what? What would our new landscape look like? Would that beam of light illuminate my own failings?

The strong likelihood of that churned hard in my gut.

'You like it?' she asked huskily, dragging my attention from the mural and my own dark thoughts. That small but mighty ray of hope on the figure's face was reflected on Savvie's and it brought a weird lump to my throat.

'It's breathtaking,' I replied simply. 'Everything you do is breathtaking.'

A teary smile broke on her face and I wanted to kiss every drop away.

'Shame we have to leave it behind. But the rules are the rules, I guess,' she murmured.

I vaguely remembered that most of the paintings lasted anywhere from a few hours to a week before another artist painted over them. The thought of her work disappearing under a fresh coat of spray paint made my teeth ache.

I took out my phone, took a few more steps back and

took a picture. Even through a second-hand medium it was stunning.

'At least you'll have this.'

She nodded. 'Can I see yours?'

Feeling half defiant, half stalker, I led her to my section.

She gave a soft gasp. 'That…that's me… And that looks like…'

'Your favourite place at the top of the rugby stand, noise-cancelling headphones on, scowling into a book and at anyone who so much as glanced your way. That's how you looked the first time I saw you.'

Her mouth dropped softly open. 'You saw me?'

My head jerked in a nod. 'Every time.'

Her gaze returned to the painting, drifted over the school-issue dark green hoodie and darker clothes she used to favour, probably because she thought it made her unobtrusive.

'How?'

'You weren't as inconspicuous as you thought.' I trailed my fingers through the dark brown-and-gold hair. 'This, for starters. There's just so much of it, no matter how hard you tried to hide it under a hoodie.'

She elbowed me in the ribs. 'I meant how did you see me over the clamour and adoration of your rugby groupies and intense bro-loving?' she asked, tongue-in-cheek.

I didn't smile back. 'I always wondered why you didn't use the library in the afternoons like you did in the evenings.'

She grimaced. 'At that time of the day, it was tedious.

I couldn't sit five minutes without someone coming up to pick my brain about something. It was more disruptive than it was worth. That spot on the bleachers was much more peaceful once you lot left.'

I didn't tell her how distracting her presence had been. How I couldn't resist glancing up there every chance I got, only to find her scowling into her book. That, even visibly annoyed with everyone around her, she was the most beautiful thing I'd ever seen. 'Hmm, that's the price you pay for being a brainbox.'

She stepped closer to the wall, reaching out as if to stroke it. 'I wish I could touch it,' she said longingly. 'But I don't want to ruin it.' She stared at it for another minute before she turned to me. 'You think it'll be here tomorrow?' she asked, a sad note in her voice.

I shrugged. 'Maybe.'

She took out her phone and repeated my gesture, then we stood in semi-comfortable silence for another few minutes.

A light breeze blew through the alley. She reached up to brush her hair back and left a streak of faint yellow paint on her cheek. I glanced at my own hands, saw them covered in black, dark green and grey streaks.

'You ready to go?' I asked, suddenly wanting to get away from here and all the inner questions now amplified on a wall.

She put away her phone and gave a solemn nod.

'Wait, you have paint on your cheek.' She reached up before I could use the unblemished part of my hand to wipe it off, and left several more streaks. 'You've just made it worse, rosebud.'

Surprised, she looked down at her hands, then at mine. And laughed. 'How would you have made it better with those hands?'

A reluctant grin attacked my lips. 'Guess we'll never know. Let's go.'

The atmosphere was lighter as we left the artists' village and found a cab. The paint had dried on our fingers by the time we arrived at Marina Bay to pick up my car but we were still too messy to stop at any upmarket restaurants. By mutual agreement we decided to order takeout.

My phone rang as we entered the apartment. The name on the screen made my stomach drop.

Savvie eyed my ringing phone, one eyebrow lifted.

'It's Graciela,' I confessed reluctantly.

Her brow stayed up for another second, then she nodded. 'I'll go warm up the shower. Come join me when you're done,' she said graciously. I wanted to kiss her.

What I didn't want to do was talk to my sister. She'd either be in blame mode or in the other mode I hated even more.

Control freak mode.

My sister had developed that streak somewhere after her ninth birthday. Perhaps it was middle-child syndrome. But I suspect it had something to do with the letter she'd received from our parents.

My letter had broken something inside me. And overnight, something had snapped within her too.

Gideon, already a remote figure consumed by his own demons, had barely noticed the torment we were going through. But as the last born, I'd endured the brunt of Graciela's reaction.

Since then, she'd deluded herself into thinking she could control life just by wielding the reins of any situation she found herself in. More often than not all she did was drive people nuts and alienate those around her. The one and only time I'd tried to point that out to her, we'd had a monster of a row. One whose ghost still drifted through our interactions.

After the emotionally charged few hours I'd been through, she was the last person I felt like dealing with.

Reluctantly, I answered…just as she rang off. A little relieved, I sent a quick text.

Not a good time. I'll call you later.

Her reply arrived seconds later.

You're avoiding me because you think this is personal. It's not. Need a quote from you for the feature story for The Sylph, due in the next issue of Mortimer Quarterly. So get over your bloody self and answer your phone! G

I dismissed the bite of guilt after reading the text.

Our interactions might start off under some pretext of Mortimer business, but they inevitably veered towards the personal. Towards whys and wherefores and bitterness washed down by vodka shots when done in person.

I wasn't down for any of that tonight, even over the phone. Right now, I wanted nothing more than to bury myself in Savvie, inhale that incredible scent concentrated at that sweet juncture between neck and shoulder. And nothing short of the world burning down was going to stop me.

I typed one last, quick response.

Still not a great time. Let's talk tomorrow.

And then, because I knew she wouldn't stop until she'd stamped her control all over it by calling me at the stroke of midnight, I added:

Office hours. Ten a.m. Singapore time.

She replied with a middle finger emoji that surprisingly made my lips twitch. That twitch widened into a smile of anticipation when I walked into my bedroom and saw the trail of clothes leading to the bathroom.

Tossing the phone onto the bedside table, I swiftly disrobed, leaving my own trail beside hers as I snagged a condom and headed for the bathroom.

She was toying with the shower settings, the sound of the powerful jets masking my entrance. It gave me a chance to watch her unobserved.

The rich abundance of her curls.

Her beautiful dark skin.

The elegant grace of her neck and the way she held herself up no matter the circumstances.

The noble slant of her shoulders.

The strong line of her spine.

And perhaps my favourite part of Savvie—her flared hips and gorgeously plump arse.

It'd been a feature of many wet dreams and would probably fuel many more after I was done playing my part in fulfilling her fantasy.

After which she would leave.

I blocked out thoughts of her departure and joined her. Her soft gasp when I slid both arms around her waist made my cock harder, my balls heavier. Unable to resist, I slid my face into the crook of her neck and inhaled deeply.

'You smell fucking amazing.'

'I smell of spray paint and shrimp satay.'

'Like I said...amazing.'

She laughed, and just like that the tightness eased from my chest.

CHAPTER EIGHT

Bryce

BEFORE MY HANDS could glide up to cup her perfect breasts, she turned in my arms. 'Wonder what you smell like,' she mused, sliding her arms around my neck and rising on tiptoe to drag her nose over my throat.

I awaited her verdict with a half-smile.

'Smoky aftershave. A touch of spray paint. Angst. And horny. Definite whiff of horniness about you,' she finished with a teasing bite that made my dick throb.

'You don't need to smell me to know that. I've got the evidence right here.' I pressed my pelvis into her soft belly and was instantly rewarded with her tightening nipples.

'Hmm.' One hand slid between us to boldly grasp me while the other plucked the condom from my fingers. 'So you have.'

Her eyes square on mine, absorbing my every blink and breath, she pumped me slowly, torturously, and smiled when a deep shudder rolled through me.

'Enjoying yourself, rosebud?'

She laughed. 'Immensely. Are you?'

'Maybe. But I'll be happier inside you.'

Leaning forward, she boldly licked my lower lip while she continued to pump my ever-throbbing cock. 'I can make that happen.'

'Soon. Please,' I groaned when she twisted her wrist and sent stars dancing across my vision.

Wicked laughter broke from her throat as she ripped the condom open with her teeth and glided it on. 'I like hearing you beg, Bryce.'

I swallowed the fierce urge to tell her I would beg a thousand times more if she hurried. Because the condom was fully on and my need was echoed on her face.

Laughter ceased as I hooked one leg around my waist and penetrated her in a smooth, mind-bending thrust.

The sensation was beyond sublime. I was aware my head went back, a hiss flying from between my clenched teeth. I withdrew, and thrust again, the clench of her channel unfathomable. 'God, how do you feel so bloody good?'

'Yoga,' she gasped as I thrust back in, deep, wanting her to feel every needy inch of me.

Surprised, I paused, my eyes finding her lust-hazed ones. 'Seriously?'

She grinned and nodded.

My answering grin broke across my face. 'Promise me you'll never stop taking yoga.'

She didn't answer immediately, probably because that single-worded confession had made me harder still, so my return was a little more strained. Or it could've been because she was experiencing a little bit of the delirium coursing through me.

'Keep doing what you're doing and I promise I won't.' She gasped, then followed it with a moan laden with desire, weighted with other things I couldn't immediately decipher.

Her nails dug into my shoulders and held on as I thrust inside her.

Between her cries, the grip of her pussy and the wild desire in her eyes, I knew I was seconds away from exploding.

I forced myself to slow down, change angles even though the way our bodies were aligned was nothing short of perfection.

But I was a greedy bastard who wanted more. Who wanted…everything.

'You see that bar above your head?' I growled in her ear.

Her heavy lids lifted, clocked the wide bar that at first glance seemed like an innocent towel rack. Except it wasn't. I'd had the iron bar placed in the shower purely for moments like this and I wasn't one little bit sorry. Especially not when Savvie's eyes grew wilder and she licked her lips the longer they stayed on it.

Deep inside I felt her pussy ripple with excitement. Damn, she was going to kill me if I didn't get a move on.

Her eyes met mine. 'Yeah.'

I ground my pelvis into hers, and watched her mouth slacken. 'Can you hold onto it for me?'

Without question, she lifted her hands and gripped the solid iron bar. With her breasts high, her heavenly curves on display and unashamed arousal blazing in her eyes, I knew I had little time.

'Perfect. Savvie, you look perfect. Hold on tight.'

She lifted her other leg, wound it around my hips and gripped me hard. 'More, Bryce. Give me more!'

Lost, I began pounding her in earnest.

Electricity blazed through my pelvis and up my spine, robbing my lungs of oxygen. All I could do was grit my teeth and absorb the waves of pleasure rolling over me.

Much too soon, that blaze of pleasure exploded into an inferno, engulfing both of us in its evangelic fire. When she boldly sought my lips for a kiss, I dropped my head, greedy for another taste. Our tongues stroked and stoked our fires, our bodies growing jerkier with almost transcendent need.

When she dropped one arm to wrap my neck and draw me closer, I lifted mine to clamp over hers on the bar.

'Yes! Just like that. Oh, God, I'm coming!' The words were muffled against our fused lips but I felt every one of them resonate through me, pushing me closer to my limit.

I grunted as the intensity of her orgasm rippled all around my cock.

Christ, this was something else. Something I suspected I'd never get enough of.

With one last push into her glorious heat, I embraced

nirvana and emptied myself into Savvie. Her breath caught and I knew that the timing of my climax was prolonging hers. Which in turn prolonged mine for a few more blissful seconds.

The mind-bending effect left me weak-kneed.

When the hand around my neck crept into my hair and her lips rained soft kisses on my jaw I buried my face in her throat, wishing I could stay there for ever. But I couldn't.

For ever was a joke spun from fairy tales.

The reality was that this thing between us was finite, with a fast-approaching end date.

That thought haunted me, chasing me out of the shower with more haste than finesse.

'Where's the fire?' she half joked as I stepped out.

I arranged my features into something resembling the thoroughly well-fucked man I should've been and threw her a look over my shoulder. 'The fire's what will happen when I present you with cold Thai food.'

I didn't hang around to see whether she believed me or not. I tossed her a towel and hightailed it to my dressing room.

Thankfully, she didn't chase after me. Several breaths later, I'd managed to throw on some clothes and pull myself under control when she entered the bedroom.

But I wasn't fooled for one second that the status quo would hold for long. I was approaching a sheer cliff where Savvie was concerned. And I had a feeling I was going over one way or the other.

Savvie

'I like seeing your dress on my floor.'

Despite the apprehension prickling my skin, I couldn't help laughing at Bryce's unashamed leer. I wasn't fooled by his attempt to reduce this thing to its basest form, probably to stop from confronting the true depths of what we'd got ourselves into. And since I was a little terrified of examining just what today had done to me, I let him. 'That's such a gigolo thing to say.'

He shrugged, laughing as he picked it up and handed it to me. 'You got me. I'm shameless.' Walking past me, he slapped me lightly on the arse and I couldn't help the giddy little jump in my heart.

I examined my dress and grimaced. 'It's hopelessly wrinkled.'

'We both know you'll shine like a diamond whatever you wear.'

I dropped my gaze and shrugged, not feeling any of the pep I normally used to talk myself out of a funk. In two strides, Bryce was in front of me.

All sign of humour was wiped from his face and his fingers beneath my chin were firm as he redirected my gaze to his. 'Okay, that fell flatter than I expected. It's time to tackle a few things, yes?'

I raised my eyebrows. 'I thought we were going to avoid certain subjects for a while?'

His lips firmed. 'So did I. But I hate seeing that look on your face. And I hate that the bastard is some unspoken ghost between us.'

Whether I liked it or not, Dan was a wound we needed to excise. So I nodded. 'As long as you answer a few questions of mine too.'

His face grew wary for a few seconds, then he nodded. 'If you insist.'

'I insist.'

His hand dropped. 'Fine, bossyboots. Let's get this show on the road.'

Grimacing at my wrinkled dress, I tossed it on a nearby seat, strode into his dressing room and returned with a white V-necked T-shirt. 'Mind if I borrow this?'

He nodded. 'Go for it.'

I pulled it on, looked down and grimaced again. The thin material showed my nipples clearly, clung to my curves and barely covered my behind. 'I should've gone for a black one.'

Bryce swallowed hard. 'I disagree. Entirely.'

I hid a smile as I eyed his naked chest. 'Fair warning. You ogle me, I ogle you back.'

His smile widened. 'I can live with that.'

By mutual silent agreement we gravitated to the door. I didn't exactly want to discuss Dan where I'd fucked Bryce and I got the feeling he didn't want my ex's shadow lingering in his bedroom.

The intercom went as we entered the living room.

'Stay put, I'll grab the food.'

I settled on one end of the sofa and watched Bryce's broad back as he walked away. God, he was breathtaking. Years of rugby had honed him into a fine male specimen, one any woman would be thrilled to call her own.

I squeezed my thighs together as heat pooled between my legs, then further compounded my situation as my nipples peaked, eager to join in the sex-fantasy fun.

I dragged my gaze from the back that bore nail marks from earlier and crossed my arms as Bryce returned and set the food down on the coffee table.

'White wine okay?'

I nodded jerkily and he sent me a quizzical look before disappearing into his kitchen. Spotting a throw draped over the sofa, I hastily unfolded it and tossed it over my lower half.

Bryce returned, frowned when he saw me. 'Are you cold? I can adjust the temperature.'

I tucked the cashmere firmer around me. 'Nah, I'm fine.'

He expertly uncorked the bottle and poured me a glass, eyeing me the whole time. When I reached out to take it, his gaze shifted to my chest.

Expecting another smirk or a teasing comeback, I was surprised when he offered neither. Simply dished out the food and sat on the opposite end of the sofa.

In silence we ate a few mouthfuls, neither of us especially hungry. After my third bite, I set my plate aside and concentrated on the wine, the subject a monstrous anvil between us.

'This…thing between us didn't start with your ex. You know that, right?'

I nodded. He was right. If anything Dan had been the straw that broke us.

'Paris.'

He nodded. 'Yup.'

'My first catwalk. You hated it.'

'Wrong. I loved it. I just never got the chance to tell you.'

The hurt of that rejection still burned through my surprise. 'You had a funny way of showing it. You stood in one corner of the room, surrounded by models who hung onto your every word while you showed them the true meaning of smouldering hotness.'

He glared at me. 'I came to see you, after Gideon gave me hell for abandoning the project we were working on, I might add. You gave me one of those silly air-kisses and then spent the rest of the evening avoiding me.'

'Because you looked far from thrilled to be there and I didn't want us to fight.'

'Maybe I was tired of you paying attention to everyone else but me.'

'What are you talking about? That's ridiculous.' When he was around, there was no space for anyone else. He made it impossible to see anything or anyone else. Once upon a time I hated him for that, for shrinking my whole world to a six-foot-three aperture that looked exactly like Bryce Mortimer. But even that resentment had been trampled under the force of my secret crush, leaving behind heart-stopping excitement and pathetic gratitude that he chose to remain in my orbit.

'Is it?' he asked with a curiously bleak tone. 'Am I wrong? Wasn't there distance between us by Paris?'

I swallowed, accepting some guilt. 'Your responsibilities were pulling you in one direction and my parents were threatening to disown me if I did the show. I felt like I'd gone from having you and our little cocoon and even my family, broken as it was, to suddenly having only the modelling, and I was a little scared.'

If anything, Bryce looked even more bleak. 'And you couldn't tell me? You know how that makes me feel?'

I sighed. 'Okay, I accept Paris was on me. Forgive me?'

He stared at me for a long moment, lips compressed, but when he exhaled some of the tension left his body. 'Forgiven. But I disagree about that little cocoon you mentioned. Not after our second year at uni. Can you pinpoint a time when I didn't have to share you with someone else? Let's start with that guy—' he clicked his fingers '—Neville. Then it was your manager and your agent, then Dan.'

'Are you serious? *You* tell me when you didn't have some size-zero bimbo hanging off your arm, lapping up your every word, telling you how oh-so-brilliant you were? If I wasn't meant to feel like a third wheel, it was only because I was more like a bloody fourth wheel!' He started to frown. 'Don't you dare give me that look. You know exactly what I'm talking about. You had so many girls falling over themselves to get into your pants that you dated two at once, and discarded them just as quickly as they arrived on the scene!'

He set his barely touched plate and wine on the coffee table and raked his fingers through his hair. The look he speared me with both electrified and frightened me. It spoke to dark secrets and hanging on by a thread.

'And why the hell did you think that was, rosebud? Why did I discard them on such a regular basis?' he asked a little too quietly.

My fingers tightened around the glass and I wished I could down the wine. But I didn't want to choke on the volatile emotions swirling through the room. And I really wanted to keep a clear head for this. 'I hope you're not about to make out like it was my fault.'

He leaned forward, eyes narrowed. 'You think I've changed? You think you knew me then but don't know me now? Take a moment and really think about it. What was the common theme running through our little circus right up until you hightailed it to Paris?'

It was my turn to frown. To cast my mind back to those turbulent years between new adulthood and beyond. The boys I casually dated when I knew I would never have Bryce. The pressures of youthful libidos. The inevitable walls I threw up. The sometimes veiled and sometimes blatant accusations. One in particular had stayed with me for months afterwards and every now and then, when Bryce crossed my mind, echoed in my head. But those words weren't true. Whoever had said them… Colin Something-or-the-Other.

The way he hangs around you, you'd think he was hot for you or something...

Oh, God...he hadn't been right. Had he?

'You...'

'Yes?' he pushed. The mixture of anticipation and wariness on his face tripled my heartbeat. 'What did I do, rosebud?'

'You started dating when I did. And you broke things off almost immediately I did.'

'Give me a few examples, let's set the record straight properly.'

I swallowed, names coming alarmingly easily to me. 'You started dating Darcy when I started seeing Neville and broke up with her the day after I...'

He nodded. 'Who next?'

'Rachel. You dumped her after your second date, right after my third date with Humph,' I murmured.

He raised one eyebrow and waited.

'Naomi. You were about to go out with her when I said I wouldn't be seeing Zach again. You called and cancelled your date,' I recounted, more than a little stunned.

Bryce exhaled long and hard, his eyes fierce. 'And what does that tell you?'

My jaw dropped. 'No.'

'Yes,' he insisted. '*Yes*, rosebud. I won't allow you to deny it ever again.'

'But...you...why...?'

He laughed, a scraping, charred sound. 'You thought I was a vacuous arsehole who only cared about staying on the rugby team and dating groupies. And they weren't, by the way. Some of those girls were pretty special. The only problem was they weren't you. While *you* wouldn't even give me the time of day for six months after we first met.'

'So? You kinda…were.'

'Thanks for that. That does wonders for my manhood.'

'Don't change the subject. I found out later you weren't, obviously, but that doesn't explain why…' Again, I couldn't give voice to the words. Saying them out loud was dangerous. And awful. And heartbreaking. It meant I'd wasted…years…when I could…when we could… I swallowed and shook my head.

'You made it plain we couldn't be anything but friends. The possibility that I might want more never even occurred to you.'

My jaw dropped all the way to the floor and stayed there. For some reason, that annoyed him even more.

'Why? Why, even now, does the possibility of us fill you with horror?' he accused.

Horror?

I scrambled to find words to express my poleaxed thoughts. Then something else occurred to me. 'I never told you we couldn't be more than friends.'

'You barely tolerated me in the beginning. You couldn't speak to me without sneering and you rolled your eyes the first, second and *last* time I asked you out.'

Heat engulfed my face. 'It was self-preservation. I

thought you were messing with me. You tossed those invitations out like jokes. And remember, I was the girl who carried an extra fifty pounds on her arse alone and you were…you.'

He scrubbed a hand over his nape. 'So you slotted us into pigeonholes created in your head, sealed it up and threw away the key and, no matter what I did or said, you refused to even acknowledge that I might want something different.'

'So every time I broke up with someone…'

'I asked you out. And you said no.'

'Because I didn't want to be another notch on your belt,' I blurted. 'What did you do to prove I wouldn't be? Did you expect me to read between the lines and miraculously assume you would treat me different than every other girl?'

'Yes,' he said tightly.

'Bryce…'

He sighed. 'Yeah, I know how that sounds. But…you were my best friend. I needed you to see past my issues and give me a chance.'

'I can't really blame you for saying that because, guess what? I expected you to do the same for me.'

We stared at each other for an age. Then he shook his head. 'So you just moved on to the next guy who spouted off a ream of Latin or who could conjugate in fucking Spanish and then to Dan?' His hands dropped to his lap and clenched tight. 'Did I do that, rosebud? Did I drive you to him?' he rasped.

The fingers clutching the wine glass trembled. 'Dan

was an opportunist who exploited my weakness when I was at my lowest. That mistake is mine alone, Bryce.'

'I know he tried to take your company. But did he… hurt you in other ways?'

My stomach churned with bitterness and regret. 'Nothing physical. Just a few low blows in the months before I served him with divorce papers that made me feel like I was worthless—'

'You're not worthless,' he objected. 'Don't ever say that about yourself. *Ever.*'

Touched by his fierce outburst, I nodded, then took a deep breath. 'I won't recount everything that went on with Dan. I don't want to give it life. But for what it's worth, you were right. I knew I'd made a mistake very early. I think that's partly why I stayed away too.'

For the longest time he held his breath. Then he exhaled. 'This is the last I want to talk about him,' he grated.

I nodded. 'Me too.' My mind veered from my ex with relief. Back to the previous discussion. 'I still want to know why you didn't say anything about…wanting more…even in the days before my wedding.'

'And risk losing our friendship? Call me a glutton for punishment but I preferred to just be friends than nothing at all.'

God.

Everything inside me shook. Flesh and blood and bone. 'Glutton for punishment?'

He studied me for a moment, took in my shock. After a minute, his jaw clenched hard. 'I'm not confessing undying love if that's what that terrified look on your face is all about.'

Something fragile but vital ripped apart in my chest. 'Why? You were the most popular guy in our circle and even beyond. Why me?'

He shook his head, his expression resigned. 'You still don't get it, do you?'

'No, I guess I don't.'

'Someone only had to pick a subject for you to run rings around them in a debate. You were, and still are, one of the most intelligent people I know. Your brain was a turn-on. Your body followed very closely behind. Oh, don't curl your gorgeous mouth at me or I'll kiss you to within an inch of your life.'

Arousal shot through me but I rolled my eyes nevertheless. 'Promises, promises. Please, continue.'

'You were the only one who was hung up about your weight. You know how many times I dreamt of you parking that delicious rump in my lap, gripping it while you rode my cock?'

Heat throbbed in my pussy and surged through my bloodstream. Dumb, I shook my head.

'More times than we'll both be able to count. But more than your body, rosebud, you made me laugh. You made me think. You made me strive to be more than just another Mortimer going through the motions until it was time to cash in my trust fund and fritter away my life on the French Riviera. Hell, you even made going home bearable because I knew you would be at the end of the phone if and when I needed you. That was worth more to me than pushing our friendship further in case I was left with nothing.'

It was a huge struggle to pick my jaw up from the floor. 'God, Bryce.' My voice shook with the power of the emotion he'd evoked inside me. Pain tore through me. I opened my mouth to say something, maybe even did, but he was talking again, words I wasn't sure I wanted to hear spilling from him.

'If that's pity I hear in your voice, we're going to have a huge problem.' His voice was a dark rumble.

'It's not. It's…'

His eyes narrowed. 'What?'

'I just wish I'd known.'

He shrugged. 'Maybe it was better that way.'

'You speaking for both of us now?'

Hazel eyes slanted to me, daring me to contradict what he'd said. 'Am I wrong?'

'You've just laid a heavy load on me, Bryce. Do I get a minute to process it all?'

He stood abruptly, gathered the food we'd barely touched. 'Don't overthink it, rosebud. We're older. Wiser. Whatever. This agreement we've got going on works just fine for me.'

This time when he walked away, I was too busy blinking away stupid tears to admire his wide shoulders. I wanted to get angry, because how typical of Bryce to lay a feast before me with one hand and yank it away with the other.

Too agitated to remain seated, I flung away the throw and stalked to the window, not turning when I sensed his return. For a minute or two he remained next to the sofa, then, like last time, he sauntered over.

'Are you pissed off with me?'

'You bet your arse I am. You take great relish in pointing out how wrong I was about you and then draw a line in the sand and walk off? I don't get a chance to have a say?'

His eyes darkened. 'What's the point?'

'*What's the point?* Are you deliberately trying to be an arsehole?'

A muscle rippled in his jaw. 'I'm not the same person I was back then. We can't rewrite the past. And considering how blind it's turned out we were to each other's true issues, aren't we just wasting our time?'

His words sucker-punched me into agonising silence. The kind that made me wonder if I could take another breath. As I watched him, it was clear his mind was made up. That realisation struck an ever-expanding fear inside me.

'What if it's my time to waste?'

He startled, then stared at me for so long and so hard I feared he could see right to the bottom of my soul. Could see and was still searching for more because what he'd seen wasn't enough. He confirmed my fears by shaking his head.

'It's up to you what you want to do. Just remember our little deal and don't hightail it out of town before we're done. I've had enough of that to last me a lifetime, thanks.' The words were bitter but didn't hide the lifetime of bleak pain behind them.

I let the words settle, swallowed a mouthful of wine before tackling it. 'You're projecting, Bryce. I only left once. What's this really about? Your parents?'

His face tightened. 'You left more than once. And we're not talking about my parents.'

'Why not? We never do. You bottle everything up inside and wheel it out when it's convenient to push people away.'

He sent me a fierce scowl. 'Rosebud, leave it alone.'

'It's kind of hard to. You wear your family's dysfunction like it's some badge of honour. As if being hurt and let down and getting a little fucked up over it is an island you can retreat to when things don't go your way.'

'You don't know what you're talking about,' he bit out.

'Then tell me.'

His face closed up. For the longest time he just stared into the middle distance. My heart pounded harder with each passing second.

'Bryce, please,' I urged.

He blinked. 'You know my parents abandoned us when we were kids.'

It wasn't a question. Part of Bryce's way of forestalling questions about his parents had been to state openly that his parents weren't part of his life. But he'd never revealed the exact details and I'd learned not to ask.

I held my breath as he continued.

'There are two types of Mortimers—those who would give the last drop of their blood to make the last penny for the family firm. And those who think the family name is a curse and can't get far away from it fast enough. My father fell into the second category. He wasn't interested in building what my great-grandfather started. He just did what needed to be done to earn his place on the board. The rest of the time he explored the true meaning of decadence and debauchery. My mother kept her nose clean long enough to produce the offspring that would ensure they fulfilled the essential quota of my great-grandfather's family edict to access the family trust. Then they just…forgot about us.'

'Just like that?'

He shrugged. 'They didn't disown us like Damian's parents did. I think they were afraid total abandonment would earn them a black mark. My last true memory of my mother was the Christmas when I was six. She came home from a three-month bender in France and cleaned herself up in time for the family portrait. She stuck around long enough for us to open our presents before she left. That was the last time I spent any meaningful time with her.'

My heart twisted. 'But you saw her after?'

After several seconds, he nodded. 'She would drop in for a day out of the blue, then leave just as suddenly. It drove Gideon crazy to the point where he refused to see her.'

'But you did?'

'Graciela and I lived for those moments.' His jaw clenched tight. 'Until we didn't.'

'What happened?'

His eyes grew bleak a moment before he stalked towards the drinks bar, ignoring the wine that sat half-full on the coffee table.

'The periods between her visits grew longer the older we got. One year, Graciela convinced me it would be fun to write her a letter when she hadn't come home for about six months,' he said tonelessly while he poured a shot of cognac. 'She thought we could appeal to her sense of…whatever.'

A small clue fell into place about his puzzling relationship with his sister. 'Graciela suggested it?'

'She got the idea into her head and wouldn't let it go. She even managed to talk Gideon into it.'

'And?'

Time ticked by as he stared into his glass, his face a tableau of tightly held pain and anger, then he tossed the drink back. 'She replied three months later.'

I waited to see if he would tell me. When he didn't, I pushed. 'What did it say?'

'It said everything the child didn't want to hear and everything the adult deluded himself about for a while but eventually needed to accept about himself.'

My heart twisted with anguish for him. 'What does that mean, Bryce?'

He opened his mouth and I held my breath but when he shook his head after a tight stretch of silence, my spirits dropped. 'She just showed me who I was.'

'What did she say to Gideon and Graciela?'

His laugh was gritty with bitterness. 'Nothing good, I suspect. We never spoke about it but Graciela cried herself to sleep for a bloody month after.'

'And Gideon?'

Bryce shrugged but I saw the film of agony in his eyes. 'If he was closed off before, he turned into a damned black hole after. Damian was the only one he responded to.'

'That's why you and Gideon resent Graciela, isn't it?'

He froze where he stood. 'Excuse me?'

'We didn't just talk about you in New York. She told me about her…rough relationship with Gideon. Although his new wife seems to be helping them smooth things out.'

Bryce dragged his fingers through his hair. 'When did you two become so close?'

I shrugged. 'I've always liked her. So she talked you into it and it didn't work. I think a part of you holds her responsible for exposing you to whatever the outcome of that letter was.'

He glared at me. 'Don't shrink me, rosebud.'

'Tell me I'm wrong.'

'You're wrong,' he stressed through clenched teeth.

A mournful little sigh escaped before I could stop it. 'Are you going to tell me what the letter said?'

His eyes gleamed as they rested on me for a second before dropping to my breasts. 'No. I'd rather fuck you.'

God, I wanted that too. Badly. But I had to exercise a little control or he'd bulldoze right over me. 'I have a full day tomorrow. I should go.'

'It's barely eight. According to our little game, we have a few more hours before Sunday's out.'

A game. Was this all it was to him? I breathed

through the hurt tightening in my chest and tried to think rationally.

Did I blame him? It was what we'd agreed, after all, wasn't it? I could get up and leave and spend the rest of the night on my own, or I could seize the chance to show him…what?

That every minute that passed I cared more for him? Was he ready to hear it?

I stared back at him as I rose from the sofa but the shutters were well and truly down, at least where his emotions were concerned.

The only fire that blazed in his eyes was the sex-crazed kind. And while it kicked my pulse into gear, made my clit zing to life and my pussy throb, there was a bittersweetness wrapped around it that drained my smile as I approached him.

It also fired up a purpose in me, one that had me fine-tuning my walk so my hips swayed and my breasts bounced with pronounced emphasis. His eyes immediately grew hooded, a fine flush washing over his cheeks as he watched me.

When I reached him, I smoothly rose up on the balls of my feet and brushed my lips over his in a featherlight kiss. 'Hmm. I can be persuaded to stay. Even model another outfit for you like I promised. Would you like that, Bryce?'

He gave a jerky nod. 'Please.'

I allowed myself a smile at his gruff tone. I reached down and caressed the erection tenting his lounge pants for a sizzling few minutes. Until his jaw was clenched tight and his breathing was harsh. Then I nodded to the sleek leather recliner that faced the glass window overlooking the water. 'Make yourself comfortable there. I'll be right back.'

I walked away, aware his eyes were devouring my backside and legs.

In the dressing room, I threw off the T-shirt with a little pang, realising how much I loved wearing something of his next to my skin.

You're getting way too sentimental.

Impatient with my turbulent emotions, I grabbed the leather-strapped outfit and carefully stepped into it. I'd tried this outfit in its various forms of conception for critique purposes. Wearing it now, knowing it was for the sole purpose of sexual exploration and femininity sent a thrill through my body long before I stepped in front of the mirror and saw the effect.

The straps accentuated specific sections of my body. Shoulders. Breasts. Hips. Pussy. While the golden rings holding the straps together lifted the outfit from dark decadence to boldly sexy.

So far it'd held its place in the top three of my bestsellers and as I turned around and carefully adjusted the straps on the back, I felt another punch of pride.

Pride took a backseat to arousal as I settled the shiny black conical nipple shields in place and fluffed my hair. It was a little wild from the shower but I didn't care. It was going to get even messier before I was done with Bryce.

I stopped in the bedroom long enough to slip my

heels back on, grab a couple of condoms and slide one beneath each of the straps on my hips before heading out.

He was laid out on the recliner in a glorious vision of casual sexiness, one leg raised and one hand tucked behind his head, his other hand lightly caressing his stomach as he stared out of the window.

Seeing my slow, steady approach, his gaze flicked my way.

And he jackknifed upright. 'Jesus Christ,' he breathed hoarsely.

Hazel eyes burned everywhere they touched on my body. Combined with my own furnace-hot excitement, I was surprised I didn't spontaneously combust. 'Do you like your outfit, Bryce?' I asked, stopping six feet from him to pose, one hip cocked with a hand braced on my waist.

The hands dangling between his thighs bunched into tight fists. 'It's sensational. But only because it's wrapped around you. Can you come over here, rosebud? I want to see it up close.'

'Please,' I teased.

His face tightened further with arousal. *'Please.'*

I slowly closed the distance between us until I towered over him. His lips parted as his gaze dropped to stare at the single strap covering my sex.

After an age, his gaze shifted to linger on the condoms tucked into the hip straps. Slowly his fingers rose to caress the one on my left hip. 'Why is that so hot?'

I smiled. 'Might be something to do with the idea

that you might get lucky more than once before mid-night?'

His gaze rose to lock on my breasts. He swallowed. 'Or could be that I get to have you, at all, rosebud.'

The words held enough gravity to make my heart thud heavily before settling into a rhythm that raised my panic level.

'Bryce.'

He visibly shook off whatever was eating him up. His fingers stopped caressing and grabbed one hip to propel me to him, his lips reverently placing a kiss just beneath my navel.

I sucked in a breath, the sensation of his mouth on me still sizzling and overwhelming enough to weaken my knees. I allowed it for a minute before pulling out of his grasp.

'You've only seen the front. Care to see the back?'

When he blew out a breath and nodded, I stepped back and turned around, watching his expression over my shoulder.

His eyes were a smouldering collision of colour as they conducted a sizzling north to south scrutiny. 'Fuck, Savvie. You're so damned beautiful.'

The words, wrenched from the bottom of his soul, made my eyes prickle. Unable to fully take a breath, I turned. 'You make me feel beautiful, Bryce.'

His gaze caught mine and I saw a flash of something in there that wrecked me. It was a mixture of silent ad-monition and regret.

Before I could probe it further, it was gone and he

was back to devouring me with his eyes. 'I don't know where to look…where to touch you first.'

I placed a hand on his chest and pushed him back. When he was fully reclined, I swung one heeled foot over the other side of the recliner and stood over him. He shuddered as he stared up at me.

Leaning over, I ran a finger from his jaw, to his throat, to the centre of his chest, to the top of his lounge pants. 'That's okay because I'm calling the shots tonight. To start with… I'm going to kiss you everywhere…'

He squeezed his eyes shut for a second before they blazed on me again. 'Yes. *Please.*'

The plea was too strong to resist. I avoided his mouth mainly to save it for last, but trailed my lips where my finger had been, revelling in his erratic breathing when I flicked my tongue over one flat nipple and nipped the tight skin above his navel. Still dropping hot kisses on his skin, I dipped my fingers beneath his waistband and pushed his trousers down. Impatiently, he lifted himself free and kicked them off, leaving him gloriously naked.

And very, very aroused. The moment I straddled him, demanding hands grabbed. Bryce caressed me everywhere, his movements growing more urgent the more I played with him.

'Kiss me, Savvie. Please,' he begged gruffly when I bypassed his lips one too many times.

'Be patient,' I teased, tearing one condom open to sheathe his steely length, then drew my wet heat over him once, twice, then lifted myself long enough to fist his cock, caress him from root to tip.

His teeth gritted. 'You're driving me insane. Fuck me. God, just fuck me.' His nails dug into my hips and hot, imploring eyes met mine. 'Tell me you can do that without taking this off?'

'I can fuck you without taking this thing off,' I confirmed, reaching behind me to undo a little stud that held the strap between my thighs. At his satisfied grunt, I dragged the tip of his cock to my pussy, then, eyes locked on him, I sank down, impaling myself on him.

His hoarse shout was music to my ears. It turned my insides liquid, fuelled the exquisite roll of my hips as I set the pace, the conditioning I'd put my body through making my movements smooth and deep as I rode him. Listened to hot, sexy curses fall from his lips as bliss overwhelmed us both.

'Do you want me to kiss you now, Bryce?' I breathed against his lips.

'I'll die if you don't,' he pleaded.

And because I wanted to do exactly that, I gripped his face and kissed him deep and hard, not once losing my rhythm. We both groaned, the double pleasure of tongues stroking and his cock sliding in and out of me almost too magnificent to endure.

A keening sound rumbled from his chest and he tore his mouth from mine. 'Savvie, I can't hold on much longer,' he hissed, one hand leaving my hip to tug off the nipple pasties before he sucked one nipple into his mouth.

Teeth and tongue tortured the nub, dragging me to the same peak where he hovered. Our pelvises ground together. Coordination took a back seat and sweat filmed our bodies. My scream was right behind his loud shout as the bough broke and our bodies twisted and convulsed through a climax so intense, all I could do was collapse onto him in a boneless heap and attempt not to pass out.

Attempt not to think about what I would do without this. Without Bryce.

What my future would look like a month from now.

Because I had a wild feeling this breathlessness I was experiencing now would be ten times worse. And it would have nothing to do with sex and everything to do with the man I wanted more than I wanted my next breath.

CHAPTER NINE

Savvie

THE WEEK PASSED in a blur of setting up the store, meetings with stylists, photographers and event coordinators to fine-tune the schedule for the pre-launch, launch and after-party.

Then on Thursday came the part I liked the least—magazine and media interviews to generate buzz about the launch and collection. Even before the second one started, my hackles were well and truly ruffled. It was all I could do not to snap when the inevitable questions about Dan and my divorce came up. Instead I dug deep and delivered the usual rehearsed answers:

Yes, it was a difficult time but it's behind me now. My work is my only focus.

No, we don't keep in touch and he has no input on my collection.

No, there's no significant other in my life. Work is my only focus.

The pang that accompanied that last pat statement dug deeper with every delivery, the confirmation that this thing with Bryce was assuming a larger meaning in my life harder to dismiss.

Since Sunday, I'd seen him every day, although our interactions had been short. He had his own hands full getting The Sylph ready for the official opening. But he'd stopped by just as I was wrapping up last night. And things had got hot and heavy in the merchandising room. Although part of me was grateful for the distraction of work, the chasm opening up inside me warned the crash would be that much harder to bear.

A throat cleared and I realised the interviewer had asked another question.

Focus, Savvie.

Thankfully, she switched from personal to the subject I loved. My collection. Ending the interview on a high, I smiled when my phone buzzed with a text from Bryce.

How's your day going?

Now that I'm done with interviews…brilliantly. Hey, I have a question.

Shoot.

Is there a dress code for tomorrow night?

Pointless question. You'd look magnificent in a shroud. A special gift headed your way. You'll need to sign for it but I recommend opening it in private.

I couldn't help the grin that split my face.

Okay. But, seriously, I need a direction about tomorrow.

One of those flared dresses I can slide my hand under when no one's looking will work for me.

Aha, so we're going to be in company?

Yes. And that's all you're getting.

Bet I can make you give me more...

You can always get me to give you more, rosebud. Maybe that's my problem.

My bright mood plummeted and my fingers shook as I read his words. Something was happening here. He was wearing his hurt openly. Was this his version of personal therapy to rid himself of me or was it something else?

The disturbing question planted itself firmly in my brain, growing deeper, insidious roots over the next twenty-four hours.

By the time my driver dropped me off at the address Bryce had texted me in Keong Saik, an upcoming area bursting with diverse culture, I was swimming in an ocean of uncertainty, with dangerous riptides licking at my toes.

The interior of the building was long and large, rectangular, painted a blinding white, with a skylight that would fill the gallery with light during the day.

I spotted Bryce almost immediately. Easily the tallest man there, he was further illuminated under one of the three chandeliers hanging from the double-storeyed ceiling.

A glass of champagne in hand, he was in deep conversation with a man I vaguely recognised. I took my eyes off him long enough to accept a glass from a passing waiter, my nerves prickling as eyes swivelled my way.

Although I was used to it by now, the initial insanity that came with fame had never truly faded, especially in a world where people weren't ashamed to express their unsolicited views on your life. Despite my hardened skin, I tended to brace myself whenever I was in a gathering such as this.

I sipped my champagne, took a moment or two to ground myself just as Bryce's head swung towards me. His smile was easy but a little reserved, as it'd been all week. It triggered a domino effect of joy and trepidation inside me. To prevent him reading my face, I turned towards the first painting.

Recognition dawned just as Bryce arrived beside me. 'Is this place what I think it is?'

'If you think it's the venue hosting the private viewing for Wu Cheong's next collection, you would be right.'

'Oh, my God. How did you get an invite?'

He leaned down and kissed me before answering, 'I have my ways. Would you like to meet him?'

My eyes goggled. 'Yes!'

The man himself, dressed in a stylish burgundy

Singaporean collarless tunic and matching trousers, appeared as if by magic.

In his early thirties, he'd made a name for himself in the last five years and skyrocketed to international acclaim with a rabid following.

'Miss Knight, welcome to my show.' He bowed at the waist.

'Mr Cheong, it's such an honour to meet you. I'm a great admirer of your work.'

'Thank you. I understand we're going to be neighbours?'

I blinked. 'We are?'

He glanced at Bryce before his dark eyes returned to me. 'This place is growing too small for such events. My agent tells me turning down invitations ups my exclusivity but I'm not sure I believe him.'

'I talked him into taking the space in the floor above yours at The Sylph for his new gallery,' Bryce said.

'I'm not sure that's such a good idea for me. How on earth will I get any work done with such masterpieces to gaze at all day.'

'I think that statement can be applied to me too.' His steady regard deepened with male appreciation.

My face heated up and I plastered on a wider smile to hide my slight chagrin.

Beside me, I saw Bryce lose his, his eyes narrowing on my face.

'We'll let you mingle, Wu,' he rasped with a light clasp of the man's shoulder. 'Let's catch up later.'

With another bow, the painter melted into the crowd.

I glanced up at Bryce. His expression hadn't changed but his regard was a little fiercer, more contemplative than before. I wasn't exactly sure why a shiver lit down my spine.

'Your present arrived,' I said, more to dilute the tension than anything else.

His lids grew a touch heavy, a sign I was beginning to learn meant he was turned on. 'Did you bring it with you?'

The expensive-looking butt plug made of solid sterling silver wrapped in velvet cloth had arrived just as I was finishing up for the day. Just like everything to do with Bryce lately, there was the bittersweet mingled with the excitement of experiencing this fantasy. A signal of an end date I wasn't prepared for.

My fingers curled tighter around my box clutch. 'Maybe.'

A predatory little smile curved his lips.

'Don't get too cocky. Remember, I dictate where and when.'

'I haven't forgotten,' he said, then leaned closer so we wouldn't be overheard and slid one hand around my waist. 'It occurred to me that with how…tight you are, your arse would be even tighter, rosebud. This might be a rather enjoyable way to lead into the main event.'

I couldn't help myself. I moaned.

He gave a low, sexy laugh. 'Does that turn you on?'

'No more than you're turned on just by talking about it. I can feel your excitement.' I brushed the hardening bulge behind his fly with my belly.

This time his laugh was strained. 'Touché.' He stepped back with visible regret. 'Come on, let's go see your surprise.'

Our progress was slow. Several people stopped Bryce to congratulate him on his building while I signed a few autographs and posed for pictures with a few guests. Although Bryce remained amiable, his smile was a little tight around the edges.

'Everything okay?' I asked when the nearest guest strolled away.

His eyes grew a touch wary. 'Any reason why it shouldn't be?'

'You seem…tense. Is it the opening?'

His lips flattened for a moment. 'It just feels…off that I'm finishing what we started without Gideon and Damian.'

My heart lurched and I couldn't help the wild hope that blossomed inside me. 'You miss your family. You miss sharing your achievements with someone. It's natural, Bryce.'

A frown twitched across his face. 'Not sure those types of feelings are natural for me, rosebud.'

'Why not?' I challenged. 'You're not a robot, Bryce.'

He shrugged. 'Some would argue with that.'

'Who?'

He shook his head. 'Doesn't matter.' He strolled a short distance away and stopped before a large painting. It was the kind that needed its own place above a mantelpiece in a grand drawing room. In its own castle.

He pulled me close, dropped a kiss on my temple. 'Surprise,' he murmured in my ear.

Eyes widening, I glanced from him to the painting. At first glance it seemed simple—a crystalline drop of water suspended over a lily pad. But on closer examination, within the drop were a hundred tiny faces of men, women and children of diverse races, each wearing raw, naked expressions. It was breathtaking. 'What do you mean?'

He nodded at the painting. 'It's yours. My present to you for the launch.'

My jaw sagged for several seconds before I caught myself. 'I can't accept this, Bryce.'

He seemed genuinely puzzled. 'Why not?'

'It's too expensive.'

He frowned. 'So this is about money?'

I opened my mouth and closed it again, unsure how to object without giving myself away. 'I'll buy it from you.'

A muscle jerked in his jaw. 'No.'

'Then you can loan it to me. Just for the launch, then I'll return it.'

His eyes narrowed. 'What's going on here, rosebud?'

'"You can always get me to give you more"? And maybe that's your "problem"? What did you mean by that?' I asked.

His features tightened. 'My inability to say no around you speaks for itself.'

But not his ability to walk away without a backward glance. 'Then I'm saying no for you.'

'I didn't mean the painting, and you know it.'

We stared each other down, words arcing between us we weren't quite ready to voice. And perhaps I was a coward but I wanted to hang on for a little bit longer, not say or do anything that would trigger a faster ending to our dirty little agreement. 'I'll take it on loan. Final offer.' I would never be able to look at it afterwards and not yearn for him. And even without knowing the true depths of my feelings, I knew I wouldn't be able to stand that.

He glared bloody flames at me for a minute before he nodded curtly. 'Have it your way.'

A waiter walked by. Bryce snagged two glasses and handed me one. The clink of his glass against mine held a touch of cynicism. In silence we drank, toasting to God knew what. It was clear he was disgruntled.

For some absurd reason his unsettled state turned me on. Enough to spark a wicked little plan in my sexed-up brain when the crowd had thinned a little.

I took a sip for courage, took his glass from him and set both flutes down. He eyed me warily. 'What's going on in that head of yours, rosebud?'

I caught his hand in mine, led him down the short hallway to the unoccupied unisex bathroom. Flames ignited in his eyes as I turned the key and leaned against the door.

'You know we're twice as likely to be disturbed in here, don't you?'

Who was I turning into that the thought of discovery made me hotter? 'Do you care?'

His gaze raked over my jade-green multi-strapped dress, lingering feverishly on the exposed parts of my shoulders, arms and legs. Especially where my hemline ended above my knees. 'Fuck no,' he responded gruffly. 'What have you got in mind?'

'I want to try out your gift.'

He exhaled raggedly, his eyes squeezing shut as he gathered his composure. Yes…a ruffled Bryce definitely did wild and dirty things to me. Unwilling to give him time to regain himself, I swayed from the door to where he leaned against the vanity and brushed my lips over his, mimicking the butterfly kiss he'd given me earlier. 'Want to show me how this works?'

His Adam's apple bobbed when I dragged my lips along his jaw to nip his earlobe. He shuddered. Then he snatched the pouch from me, dropped it on the vanity before grabbing my waist. 'You're determined to make me lose my mind, aren't you, Savvie?'

I was determined to make him *find* himself. With me. But there were so many obstacles between us that I couldn't voice my deepest yearning. So I kissed him, channelling my feelings into the act that had him groaning in under a minute.

His fingers dug into my hips as I straddled one leg and shamelessly rubbed my pussy against him. With a thicker groan, he moulded my arse, his breathing turning harsher as he lifted the flared hem of my dress and encountered another one of my creations.

This one was a simple sheer black body with a thong design. 'Fuck, that's glorious,' he slurred, reversing our position before turning me to face the mirror. 'I can worship this beautiful arse all day, you know that, rosebud?'

My nipples tingled at the thick desire in his voice, at the hands that were several shades lighter than my light brown skin, caressing me. Turning sideways, I watched his hands mould my arse. 'Spank me.'

His eyes flew to mine, heat flaring across his hard cheekbones. 'Have you been spanked before?'

I shook my head. 'I've never wanted it.'

His hands tightened on my flesh. Then without warning he tugged the thong high, causing sweet friction between my legs. Shoving my dress up to bunch around my waist, he caught my gaze in the mirror and brought one palm down hard on my bottom.

I gasped at the sharp sting but pleasure flared simultaneously, dragging a moan free.

'Again.'

He granted my wish on the other globe. Pleasure. Pain. A heady combination I'd never been tempted to try with my ex or any other man before him.

I gripped the vanity tighter as Bryce delivered skilful intermittent smacks. With each slap, I felt myself getting wetter, needier.

His gaze crashed into mine in the mirror as his fingers delved between my thighs. 'Christ, you're soaking.' He dragged moisture from my pussy to my puckered hole, groaning as he gently pushed one finger in. I gasped at the different sensation that gripped me.

He caressed the tight muscles with the cool plug.

When it warmed against my flesh, when I couldn't distinguish between it and his fingers, he pressed it firmer against me. The alien sensation was wickedly, decadently pleasing. Tentatively I pushed back against it until it slid in.

A shudder shook Bryce's body, his breathing harsh. 'God, you're so fucking tight. So beautiful, Savvie.' His voice was heavy with arousal. 'I'm dying to fuck you.' He raised his head and stared at me. 'But you didn't bring me in here to have sex, did you?'

Getting hot and heavy was one thing, but full-on sex within hearing distance of others? Biting my lip, I shook my head.

He squeezed his eyes shut. Looking slightly relieved, he stepped back and arranged my clothes. 'Are you ready to go?'

'Yes.'

We left the gallery after saying our goodbyes. Bryce's hand gripped mine as I dismissed my driver and we slid into his car.

Riding in his sports car, my senses on fire, sex toy inside me, was one of the most decadent things I'd ever done. By the time he pulled up in front of my apartment building I was almost at the point of orgasm.

It was clear Bryce was caught in the same vortex. The hand that gripped the steering wheel was white with tension. 'I'm not going to come up.'

Disappointment pummelled me but I managed a nod. 'Okay. We do this after my launch party. We'll make it a private celebration. Does that work for you?'

Hot eyes met mine and a tingle shimmied over me. 'I'll count every damn second,' he said, his voice thick with relish.

He threw his door open and came around to open mine. I let him help me out and walk me inside to the lift, fighting the urge to invite him up, let him finish what he'd started. Instead, I fell into the goodnight kiss barely able to focus as he resolutely stepped back.

'Okay if I call you later?'

I nodded, then reluctantly stepped inside.

We stared at each other until the doors shut. And for the next few hours I existed on an electric plane, every movement reminding me of the toy inside me, keeping me on the edge of orgasm.

Bryce called just after midnight, then spent a decadent half hour in the sexiest version of phone sex that sent me right over the cliff.

With the fast-approaching launch, things kicked up to a frenetic pace over the weekend. Which probably helped with not descending into a pathetic heap when Bryce went AWOL on another project.

But it gave me time to compose how to break the news to him that Graciela had RSVP'd *yes* to my launch invitation and that, while I hadn't promised to keep her arrival a secret, she'd indicated she would prefer he didn't know beforehand in case he actively put her off.

Taking the coward's way out to break the news to him face-to-face wasn't helped when he texted on Monday to say he'd been further delayed and wouldn't be returning until Tuesday afternoon.

I was reading his text when he sent another.

Everything going okay?

No, I wanted to type. *I miss you. Desperately.*

Yup—usual last-minute headaches.

Anything I can do?

I toyed with taking one headache off the table by telling him about Graciela but chickened out.

Thanks for the offer but I'm fine.

For several minutes he didn't answer. Then...

Enjoying your toy?

I squirmed in my seat, my face flaming at the reminder of the sex toy currently in situ.

That's for me to know and you to find out.

Challenge accepted.

I ended our texting with a hollow feeling in my belly. Somehow that sexual fantasy had become a pivotal event with no clear indication where it would lead us eventually. If anywhere.

Putting out last-minute fires and calming nerves all

day Tuesday helped me keep my own inner hurricane at bay.

I plunged myself into every query, took the time to inspect every outfit and accessory. I fetched water and wiped nervous tears. All the while wondering if I'd have the nerve to confess my feelings to Bryce when the time came.

I was in love with him. Had been since the first time he sauntered up to me with a sexy smirk.

And if he planned on ending this thing between us with another disappearing act for another three years, I needed him to know.

He was convinced we were different people. Maybe he was right. But we weren't so different as to be totally incompatible.

My insides burned with fear and dread but I swallowed them down, reminded myself that nothing I'd wanted had ever come easy.

I'd launched and headed a successful brand where very few woman like me held their own for very long. I'd survived a difficult marriage and come through stronger.

I needed to know where I stood with him.

What if you stand nowhere?

My breath caught.

'Are you all right?'

Nellie, my assistant, stood next to me, concern etched on her face. She wore the headgear that connected her with each model's station, the photographer and stage manager. She was the heart of the operations

and my right-hand woman. We'd been together for four
years and she knew the ins and outs of most of my relationships.

But not Bryce. I shook my head. 'Last-minute nerves.'

Her eyebrow shot up. 'Really? You? The most *together* person I know?'

I let a wobbly smile slip. 'You're good for my ego,
Nellie.'

'Would it have anything to do with that piece of eye
candy prowling the back of the showroom?'

'What?'

'He's been wearing grooves in the floor for the last
fifteen minutes. I had one of the interns ask him if he
wanted a drink. He got glared at. But he came bearing
the most amazing painting so I let him stay...'

I was rushing for the short corridor that led to the
catwalk before Nellie was done forming her conclu-
sions.

One quick peek between the heavy black curtains
and I spotted him. I also spotted the reason for his
mood. Graciela Mortimer stood in front of him, her
arms windmilling as she made whatever point she was
intent on making.

Bryce's jaw clenched before he glanced sharply towards my hiding spot. His gaze announced his fury
and he left his sister mid-sentence and headed towards
me. The Wu Cheong painting was propped up against
a chair on the first row of the seating area with a care-
lessness that belied its quarter-million-dollar price tag.

'Hi, Bryce.'

His gaze raked me from head to toe before settling on my mouth. With almost impatient need, he pulled me close and planted a hard kiss on me before stepping back. 'You didn't think to give me the heads-up that Graciela was coming?'

I shrugged. 'You were going to find out sooner or later. Why make it sooner?'

'My sentiments exactly,' Graciela said, strolling up to join us.

Bryce took a deep breath. 'Can you give us some privacy, please?' he said between his teeth.

'Why? You've already kissed her in front of me so I know there's something going on between you two. Besides, we're not done talking.'

Bryce rounded on her. 'We're not doing this now,' he warned.

Graciela, a statuesque beauty with long, dark hair and signature Mortimer hazel eyes and as stunningly beautiful as her male relatives, folded her arms and glared at her brother. About to open her mouth, she froze when Nellie's voice boomed from behind the curtain.

'Thirty minutes to ignition, people!'

My pulse jumped into my throat as the frenzied rush intensified.

The soft drone of voices filtered in as the main doors were opened to welcome VIP guests. The event organisers were serving premium champagne and world-class canapés as the music seeped backstage.

I forced myself to take a breath. 'I have to go.'

Bryce stared at me for a moment before his features softened and he nodded. 'Everything looks amazing, rosebud. You've got this.'

A lump swelled in my throat, snatching the words from me.

It will be fine.

It will be a success.

I'd deal with business. Then I'd deal with whatever fate held in store for me and Bryce.

But the words, no matter how brave, couldn't stop fear knotting in my belly as I returned backstage and threw myself back into the fray.

It was still there, growing larger as the main lights dimmed and the thumping Afrobeat I'd picked for the event throbbed through the speakers. From my vantage point, I watched the gold-and-purple spotlights hit the four models suspended in wicker baskets above the catwalk. Legs slowly swinging back and forth, bodies seductively reclined, they looked like barely clad African goddesses, right down to the ethnic bangles on their wrists and forearms.

But the moment the cables lowered them on the four corners of the catwalk and they stepped onto the runway, the focus fell on the lingerie.

Bold and striking and proudly plus size, they strutted down the long purple carpet to the sound of gasps and applause.

My breath caught again, my heart flipping up to lodge in my throat for the solid hour the twelve models showcased the forty-eight outfits chosen for the show.

'Savvie?'

I turned at the soft whisper of my name. Nellie stood behind me, the garment bag draped reverently over her arms. 'It's time.'

Nodding, I stepped away from the curtains.

In my small dressing room, I changed into my outfit. The black-and-purple corset-and-garter ensemble was trimmed in predominately purple Ghanaian-made kente cloth, the matching black silk dressing gown also trimmed in the rich fabric. I pulled on glossy black lace-topped stockings, adjusted the garter belt, and fastened the bespoke headdress into place. My make-up artist had worked her magic earlier, so all I needed was a touch-up and the costume jewellery that completed the ensemble.

'Wow,' Nellie whispered when I stepped out.

Nerves held at bay by sheer willpower threatened to break out. I shook out my fingers and took three deep breaths. On the fourth, the curtains parted, leaving me framed in blinding light.

Shoulders back.

Chin up.

Smile.

For the longest time I'd faked confidence until it became second nature. But tonight felt…different. Maybe it was stunned gasps where there'd been electric buzzing for my models before as I stepped out in sky-high heels to begin my walk down the runway. Or the fact that *I* was different. That the concerns and hurts and uncertainty of my place in the world were suddenly reduced to a small, manageable kernel and in its place a wild acceptance that I was doing what I was born to do.

You've got this.

Bryce's words pulsed through me as I strutted down the catwalk. As the gasps turned into excited whispers and then outright shouts of admiration as I stood poised at the end of the long gangplank, hand on hip, letting the photographers have their fill before executing a neat pivot.

My gaze landed on Bryce. The raw intensity in his eyes made my heart stutter, then surge with wild hope.

You've got this...

I love you, I wanted to scream.

I bit my lip just in time. With my eyes on him, I slid off the robe, and while the audience basked in the full effect of the outfit, I basked in the look on Bryce's face and dared to believe that this wasn't just a risky little game we were playing.

That there *could* be more.

My robe trailing behind me, I completed the walk.

Each one of my twelve models stood ready for the last parade. Swivelling to face the audience once more, I led them down the catwalk to thunderous standing ovation.

But not everyone stood up.

Maybe his seated position was the reason my gaze flicked over to the figure on the second row. Whatever the reason, his portentous presence struck me harder than it should have.

Only years of training stopped me from stumbling

and making a total fool of myself. Only a strong force of habit kept the smile on my face.

But still, he saw me falter. And smirked.

And as much as I hated myself for reacting, I felt the slightest wobble in my chin as I stared at the spanner to end all spanners.

My ex-husband.

Bryce

My God, she was spectacular.

I couldn't take my eyes off her, and it had nothing to do with the magnificent outfit she wore or the perfection of her body.

From the start it'd been Savannah's spirit that had called to mine. A warm and compassionate place to land where I'd known only callous indifference and uncertainty.

Granted, I'd doubted the sustainability of those attributes for the longest time. Hell, I'd spent the last three days fighting the urge to test the true depths of the waters to see where I stood.

I still wasn't completely sure. But I knew one thing.

If I couldn't bear to be away from her for a measly three days, what the hell would the next weeks, months and years look like?

The only sure-fire way to find out is if you don't try.

The contents of the letter from my mother I'd unearthed in some hope of dissipating their power reeled through my head, a cold wash threatening to invade my system. It'd been happening with alarming frequency, as if my dear dead mother were trying to make her point from the grave. If you believed that sort of thing.

Enough!

My palms stung with the power of my applause, dragging me back to the present.

Back to Savvie.

A heavy dose of angst drained away as I watched her smile.

Someone shoved a hideously large bouquet of flowers in her hands, temporarily obscuring her face from me. Probably her investors, who must be ecstatic at how the collection had been received.

Or…the man her gaze slid to as she turned to leave the catwalk.

Even before I caught a full view of him, I knew.

Dan.

My leaden hands dropped to my sides.

Had she invited him here? Would she really do that?

'Jesus, Bryce. You look like you've seen Satan himself.'

The stark observation shattered my thoughts, reminded me of another situation I needed to deal with.

Graciela.

I swallowed the sour taste in my mouth and looked at my sister.

Wary eyes returned my stare. 'If you expect me to apologise for turning up unannounced, forget it.'

But beneath the bravado there was something else.

A yearning for a connection that resonated inside me.
'Gracie—'

'We don't need to talk if you don't want to. Just…let
me be here. Please?' The request was soft, vulnerable
in a way that made me feel like a heel.

My head jerked in a nod and the sensation of drift-
ing without a life jacket swelled larger.

I needed to talk to Savvie.

Needed to see her. Touch her. The growing suspicion that this…*thing* inside wouldn't fix itself without
her spiked hard.

'I need a drink,' Graciela announced.

About to tell her to entertain herself while I tracked
down Savvie, I froze, watching in disbelief as Dan
mounted the stage and disappeared behind the curtain.

The fury I expected to feel was shockingly absent.
Instead raw fear clawed at my insides, that paralysing
helplessness I'd felt watching her marry that bastard
returning full force.

I took a step, then froze again as Savvie emerged,
minus Dan, from behind the curtain.

She was a vision in gold. The cocktail dress she'd
changed into had a plunging neckline, displaying her
amazing cleavage and left her dark bronze shoulders
bare, ending just above her knee to showcase her spectacular legs. The headdress was gone and her mane was
free and a little wild, just the way I liked it.

God, everything about her was just the way I liked
her…but what right did I have to her? The need to find
out propelled me across the room to her. Perhaps some-

thing in my face alerted her to my mood. She stopped mid-conversation, excused herself and turned to me.

'Bryce—'

'What the hell is he doing here?'

That she knew who I meant further disgruntled. 'Ignore him. He's not important.'

'Are you sure?'

Her gaze sharpened, grew brighter with anger. And disappointment. As if I had something to be ashamed of. 'I didn't invite him here, Bryce. He's dating one of my models. He's her plus-one.'

Relief drained out of me but swiftly on its heels followed shame at how quickly I'd needed to hear that. Would it always be like this?

'That's our problem, isn't it?'

My stomach dropped when I realised the words hadn't come from my lips or even my psyche but from Savvie.

'What?'

'You're never going to trust me, are you, Bryce? Because of your parents? Because of that letter you still won't talk about?'

I opened my mouth to immediately deny that. But the appropriate words never emerged. 'We need to talk.'

Her eyes darkened to almost black, unmissable pain filling the depths. The churning vortex of dismay and uncertainty widened inside me as she shook her head. 'I… I can't. I'm busy. Anyway, I think it's pointless.'

'Excuse me?'

'This isn't about Dan and we both know it. It's about

you not trusting what's right in front of you because you think it's going to be snatched away at any moment. I can't change that for you, Bryce. You have to find your own way to change it.'

I wanted to rage at the harsh judgement but deep inside I tasted the truth of it. Wasn't Dan's presence here some sort of twisted sign that I was deluding myself into thinking this would work? When the only real things I'd made work for me were the towers I'd built?

The only meaningful relationship I'd thought I'd had had been with Savvie, and it turned out I'd been abysmal at it. She hadn't believed the foundations of our friendship were strong enough to sustain revelations of her issues. Truth was, I still didn't...

'Bryce?' I caught the faintest tremble in her voice and hated it because I knew it was my fault.

'Yeah?'

'Tell me what you're thinking?' Wary suspicion tinged the words. As if she knew my turmoil. Knew what was coming even before I did.

And that shaking inside? Yeah, my solid ground was gone, the foundation of belief that I could in any way be the person she needed eroded to nothing. I was a Mortimer. Fruitful in making money and bankrupt everywhere else.

Excerpts of my mother's letter flashed like neon ticker tape in my mind.

Bryce,
I was going to leave this until you were older

but...well, you'll just write me another letter, won't you? And, frankly, you need to know a few home truths.

You're a Mortimer. Mortimers are only good for one thing: making or spending money. Emotional entanglements are superfluous and will only lead to disappointment.

Cut it out of your life now, before you become a disappointment to the family name. Accept that in this you can't have it all.

I'm never coming back. Neither is your father. The family name will buy you all the regard you need. Don't bother looking for it some other way.

And for heaven's sake, don't offer emotional guarantees you can't deliver on. You only need to take a look at this family to see we're fruitful in one area only. Let that be your lesson.

We've done our duty. Stop dreaming and do yours.

Cold hard truth hit me. 'I can't do this.'

She exhaled shakily. 'Do what?'

'Go on this...path with you. I can't be another bastard who lets you down.'

'Then don't. It's pretty simple, Bryce.'

I laughed. 'For you maybe. I don't make guarantees without solid backup.'

Despite the suspicious glint of tears, her chin went up, her eyes challenging me. 'And you can't guarantee this so, what, you're going to run?'

Resentment welled. 'We agreed—'

'I don't give a crap what we agreed. Truth or dare,' she whispered.

Trust her to get it right for the first time in her life. The first time I didn't want to play. I remained silent.

'You always go for dare, right, Bryce? Well, I'm daring you, right here and now to pick us. To stay and give this a chance.'

As if her presence here were ordained by some cosmic entity, I caught Graciela from the corner of my eye. Another reminder of my emotional bankruptcy.

I shook my head. 'There's a project in Hong Kong Damian wants me to take over.' I'd thought Damian's email about a rare opportunity to secure prime land in Hong Kong for our next project couldn't have come at a worse time and I'd been sorely tempted to let it go before I'd remembered that nothing about what Savvie and I were doing was guaranteed to last.

She inhaled a stunned breath. 'So you're leaving me? Again?'

The soft, anguished accusation slashed me wide open. But it was better this way. Wasn't it? 'Yes.'

This time the tears rose. 'Then go.'

I watched her walk away while the earth beneath my feet shook.

CHAPTER TEN

Savvie

THE FUMES OF pride and sheer stubbornness kept me going through two hours of smiling, mingling with guests and talking to fashion bloggers about the new collection when all I wanted to do was curl into the foetal position and bawl my eyes out.

It also kept me from losing my shit every time Dan smirked at me from across the room. He'd managed to corner me for half a minute backstage and attempted to land a few mind-fucking blows but they'd bounced off me. And while the confirmation that he no longer had an emotional hold on me made me glad, he represented a long, deeply regrettable stretch of a life spent without Bryce.

The man I loved.

The man who'd walked away from me. Again.

I'd expected him to leave but he was still here, probably because he didn't want to be alone with his sister.

No longer my problem.

The thought hurt more than I anticipated, giving me

a glimpse of the hellish heartache facing me, especially when I caught his hazel eyes on me.

Eventually, the investors left, happy that the launch had been a success and initial orders for the collection were already surpassing expectations.

Every single thing had gone off without a hitch. The icing on the cake would've been Bryce.

Anguish raked through me, overwhelming me with a rush of tears.

I needed to get out of here.

About to do just that, I caught a glimpse of Graciela. As much as I wanted to put all things Mortimer behind me as quickly as possible, I couldn't leave without some acknowledgement of her presence. Heart lurching, I approached where she stood alone near the bar.

But she wasn't alone. At the last moment, I saw Bryce, half concealed by a stage prop.

Walk away...

'Tell me what was in your letter,' Graciela demanded. I froze.

'You go first,' Bryce responded.

Several expressions passed over Graciela's face before her lips set in a mutinous line and she looked away from him.

'Yeah, I thought so. What good will rehashing all of it do, Gracie?'

Bleakness turned her eyes dark. 'I don't know but I feel I have to...try.'

He said nothing. After a moment, she swallowed. 'Do you think we'll ever be able to get past it?'

I held my breath, realising the answer was as important to me as it was to Graciela.

'For like…half a second, I thought I would. Not any more.'

His sister's gaze probed his for several heartbeats. Then she sighed. 'You think you can ever forgive me… for my monumental stupidity?' Her voice was ravaged with pain.

He didn't answer for the longest time. Then he grabbed her and pulled her into a bear hug. For a moment she remained stiff and unyielding. Then, with a hoarse little sob, she wrapped her arms around his waist.

'It wasn't stupid but I would've preferred to have lived in blissful ignorance for a while longer. Or for ever, actually. Because, really, who the bloody hell wants to find out they don't have what it takes to sustain a relationship, never mind a family, no matter how accurate that assessment turns out to be?'

Graciela pulled away from him. 'You don't really believe that, do you? That we're *that* fucked up?' Despair wove through her voice.

Bryce stared down at her with hard sympathy. 'I think the evidence speaks for itself, don't you?'

'Then what are you doing here with Savvie?' she pressed.

Again my heart caught as I listened, knowing I needed to walk away.

'We had unfinished business.'

'*Had?* But I thought—'

His harsh laugh stopped her. 'Yeah, that's the thing with Savvie. She lures you into believing unrealistic fantasies. Which is decidedly the anti-Mortimer way, as we well know.'

'I think you're wrong, Bryce—'

'Enough, Gracie. It's over. Let it go.'

'Okay. Can you drive me to my hotel?' Graciela asked.

I waited till they were gone, then stumbled away, Bryce's words lacerating my heart into tiny, useless shreds.

Minutes later, I slipped away from the after-party knowing I had to get away before I disgraced myself by breaking down.

Within the hour, my bag was packed and I was heading for the airport. The store wasn't set to officially open to the public for another week. And since the day-to-day running of every Voluttuoso store was entrusted to an expert management team, I could take a week. Or a month.

But even as I hurried to the check-in desk and booked a first-class seat to Bali, I knew I would need much, much longer to even attempt to piece together my shattered heart.

One week.

The resort was perfect, the staff attentive without being intrusive.

The setting was paradise itself.

And yet I couldn't have been more miserable if I'd tried.

I told myself it was the abrupt standstill after going full throttle for months making time drag. But I was deluding myself. Each heartbeat sounded like a death knell, each forced meal a chore I would gladly have given up if I could.

The last time I'd felt like this was the first day of my honeymoon after I'd married the wrong man. Bora Bora had felt like hell, the look in Bryce's eyes as I'd walked down the aisle on the arm of another man a constant reminder that I'd taken the wrong turn.

But this time I hadn't. This time I knew what I wanted.

Bryce. Always.

I'd dared him to stay. And he'd gone.

Hadn't he warned me right from the start and then over and over again that we were different people?

I should've listened.

And what…? Not fallen in love with him? When I'd been in love with him since I was sixteen years old? When that love burned brighter despite the possibility that the only time I would come close to him again was through his business?

Harsh hot tears prickled my eyes, sent me off the lounger I'd plonked myself on in the hope that the sun would burn away some of my unhappiness.

My beachfront chalet was private enough to guarantee I wouldn't be disturbed and open enough to ensure I could stroll into the sea in two dozen lazy steps. The temptation to do just that, to keep swimming until I lost myself in the ocean, produced even more tears.

God, I was hopeless.

My feet crashed into the waves and with relief I dived into the crystal blue waters. I swam until exhaustion deadened my arms, then reluctantly returned to the chalet.

The first prickles of awareness tingled through me two minutes into my open-air shower on the front porch. I ignored it, wrapped my sarong over my naked body and returned to my lounger, determined to find a few minutes of peace in the pages of my novel.

He was standing in the gap between the hedge that formed the natural barrier between my chalet and the beach. His broad back to me, he stared at the waves crashing onto shore while I stared, slack-jawed, at him.

Every cell in my body had been dying to see Bryce again but now he was here…now he was a solid, breathing form in front of me, my brain scrambled to nothing.

He turned around.

We stared at each other in silence.

Then he prowled forward, lowered himself into the lounger next to mine and remained silent for the next five minutes. While my heart thundered as if it were preparing for a one-hundred-metre sprint.

Every inch of my body tingled and burned as if my frozen limbs were coming back to life.

After an eternity he fixed me with fierce hazel eyes. 'I think there should be a law against this extreme level of emotional devastation that haunts you when you walk away from someone you care about. Don't you think?'

My heart dropped into my stomach. 'I don't agree. The pain is there for a reason. What are you doing here, Bryce?' I blurted.

He swallowed. When he exhaled it wasn't quite steady. 'You owe me a dare.'

'That's why you're here? For sex? Forgive me if I'm wrong but aren't we in the past? As in "we *had* unfinished business"?'

He paled, then squeezed his eyes shut for a minute. 'Gracie? Or did you overhear?'

'Does it matter?'

'Yes. No!' He stopped, raked a hand down his face. 'Christ, I don't even know any more.' He stared down at the hands hanging loosely between his knees. 'You know why I used the past tense?' The question was ragged with pain.

Numbly, I shook my head.

'Because it was my way of bracing myself against exactly this…*helplessness* that I wouldn't be enough for you. I know you didn't invite your ex but I saw your reaction to his presence.'

Before I could ask what he meant, he continued, 'I may have been pissed when you chose to go to Paris but I loved how you took control of your life, loved watching you battle and grow out of your insecurities. Watching you take charge of your femininity, letting it empower you, was such a turn-on. And then I watched you hand all that incredibleness to that arsehole. And you know the worst thing? I know now that letting you get away was all my fault. I wanted to punch his lights out. He managed to win my best friend away from me because I believed I didn't have what it took. Because I wasn't emotionally equipped to give you what you needed.'

I swallowed the knot in my throat before I could speak. 'Because of my own shortcomings I talked myself into making the wrong choice. And when it was over, I guess…a part of me was ashamed for ruining our friendship. And the part of me that wanted…more was scared you'd see me as spoiled goods.'

His jaw rippled. 'Fucking hell, Savvie. I'd never think of you like that.'

The power behind his words sent more prickles to my eyes. Before I could snatch in a breath he gripped me tighter.

'Truth or dare?'

My heart lurched. 'Truth. Always.'

His throat worked. 'Am I still worth taking a different path with, Savvie?'

'Yes,' I answered with every ounce of love in my body.

Hazel eyes burned into mine. 'For how long?' he fired back.

'That's not how this works. It's my turn now.'

He took a deep breath. 'Truth,' he said for the first time.

Finally I dared to ask the question that had been burning inside me for longer than I could count. 'Why are you here? Truly, Bryce?'

'Because I went to Hong Kong for three days and I

nearly went insane without you. Because the thought of three hours let alone three years without you in my life scares the crap out of me. Because seeing you up there on that catwalk proved to me that, while I'm a damned Mortimer through and through, I also wanted to be a better version of myself.'

'Tell me about the letter,' I asked softly. 'What did you write to your mother?'

Anguish darkened his eyes. He took one deep breath. Then another. 'It was a typical come-back-home-and-be-my-mum letter, written by a desperate child with nothing to bargain with but offering everything anyway, kind of letter.'

I reached for his hand, my heart breaking for him. 'Oh, Bryce.'

He grasped my hand and kissed the back of it. 'It took her months to reply. And when she did…' his jaw tightened '…it was basically a list of all my short-comings specifically and every Mortimer shortcoming in general. I think, in some way, she thought she was preparing me for life as a Mortimer. Or she was projecting about her own relationship with my father. They had a peculiar relationship. According to Aunt Flo, they couldn't stand to be in the same room to-gether for more than a few minutes and yet they followed each other all over the world. Anyway, she told me Mortimer men weren't built for relationships and the sooner I accepted that I didn't have what it takes to sustain one, the better off I'd be.'

'God!'

'She urged me to be thankful for my birthright and concentrate on making money for the family coffers and forget about everything else.'

I leaned forward and cradled his jaw, redirecting his gaze to mine. 'She was wrong, Bryce. In every way. You know that, don't you?'

'I didn't. Not at first. Then I met you. God, you blew my fucking mind. I wanted to be with you more than I'd ever wanted anything else in my life. When I thought you saw me as nothing more than a friend, I was terrified she was right. And then when you married Dan...'

'You were convinced she was,' I finished.

He gave a grave nod. 'I didn't take it well. It was partly why I stayed in Singapore. Putting half a world between us seemed like a good idea.' He gave a twisted smile. 'Surprisingly, Graciela helped too. She's like a bulldog with a bone,' he mused with a new sort of fondness that lifted my heart.

'Things are better between you two?'

He shrugged. 'We're getting there. She grilled me about my letter but refused to tell me what was in hers,' he griped, but again in a lighter tone that gave me hope for at least one member of his family.

'I'm glad things are working out for you two. As for putting a world between us, it wasn't far enough. It never will be. Bryce, I promise, from now on, I'll always be there to remind you that you're worth everything to me.'

His eyes darkened and a breath shuddered out. 'God, rosebud. Please say that again,' he begged.

I repeated it, slowly, and watched belief seep into his eyes. Into his body.

He shuttled closer and gripped my thighs. My breath caught at the size and smell of him. God, this man made me feel things. He made me want. And I wanted more. So much more.

'Bryce—'

He yanked me close and fused his lips to mine. Soul soaring, I pushed him back on the lounger and went all in, deepening the kiss until we were breathless.

He caught my arms and edged me back, his gaze dropping to my thin sarong before rising again. 'There's a lot of shitty baggage to get through. But I'm not a saint. I need you too much. So you have two choices. Put some proper clothes on or we continue this in bed.'

My pulse jangled in response but this thing was too new, too fragile…

As if he heard my thoughts, his fingers tightened in my hair. 'I promise you, Savvie, I'm done staying away. Whether you want one weekend, one year or one lifetime, I'll be right here, taking whatever you give me. But be warned, I'm a Mortimer. I'll negotiate for the very maximum.'

This time my heart jangled along with my pulse. The thought that everything I'd dreamed of could be within grasp…

'Take me to bed.'

With satisfying urgency, he swept me off my feet and headed for the French doors that led to the bedroom.

Impatiently, he tugged off his clothes and kicked them away, then jerked his head at me. 'Your turn.'

My sarong came off with a simple tug, arresting Bryce in place. My skin had gone even darker in the sun, a fact he seemed to love going by his feverish scrutiny and his reverent caresses when he reached for me.

'God, Savvie. You're so beautiful.'

With a broken whimper, I fell into his arms. We tumbled into bed, our movements frenzied and breathlessly uncoordinated. He seemed determined to kiss me everywhere, especially my pussy. I returned the favour until he groaned and pulled me up.

'I need you,' he pleaded again.

'Where?' I asked boldly, a cheeky little dare, made what felt like for ever ago, teasing me with possibilities.

He caught my meaning and swallowed. 'Any bloody where you'll have me, love.'

My heart lurched at the new endearment and, rightly or wrongly, I let it inside me, let it lift my hopes. 'I want you to fuck me…there. Like you promised.'

Emotion and arousal shuddered through him. Renewed caresses flamed my body, his fingers wreaking havoc as he strummed my clit to fever point, making me soaking wet as his mouth devoured my lips. When he dragged my slickness to my puckered hole, I shivered in wild anticipation.

'Christ, you're so wet.'

He left me for a moment and returned with a condom and the pouch. Like before, he was gentle, taking his time to delight me with drugging, distracting kisses while I adjusted to his touch.

'Relax, rosebud. Trust me,' he crooned against my mouth.

'I do. I trust you, Bryce.' With my heart and soul.

His whole body shook in reaction to my words.

Slowing our kiss, his tongue lazily caressed mine as he intensified the pressure of his finger. Slowly, he eased inside and my breath strangled at the intense, weirdly wonderful sensation.

'God…'

'Look at me, Savvie,' he urged.

I met his gaze, burned in the blaze of it. 'How do you feel?'

'Good. Great…oh, God.' My nails dug into his shoulders as the peculiar sensation intensified with each deeper thrust of his finger.

Bryce's breathing grew choppy and he leaned his forehead against mine. 'Fuck, Savvie, I need to be inside you,' he growled.

The depth of his need fuelled mine. Shifting away, I repositioned myself on my hands and knees, my intent clear. 'Come here, Bryce.'

He didn't need a second bidding. He rolled on the condom, applied the lube and positioned himself behind me. One hand caressed my spine down to my bottom. The other held on tight to my waist. My pulse thundered, my breath emerging in pants as I felt the probe of his broad head.

At first the pressure was almost searing in its intensity.

'Breathe for me, love,' Bryce said gruffly, his hand reverently caressing my back, spine, bottom, anywhere he could reach, while pushing inside me.

Then he was past the tight ring of muscles. And I was gasping at the endless stream of electricity gripping my body. When he pulled out and pushed back in, I screamed, the intensity like nothing I'd ever felt before. 'Bryce!'

'God, Savvie. You feel so bloody good.' A wild shudder shook him and he stilled.

'Don't stop! God, don't stop.'

With another curse, he fell forward, braced himself over me. 'Never,' he breathed. 'Anything you want is yours.'

Again my heart soared, the hope that this would extend beyond this act filling my chest. 'I want you,' I said simply.

Words cut off after that, the only sound in the room our groans as I discovered a whole new plane of pleasure piled upon pleasure I'd never dreamed possible. And when I reached the threshold of orgasm all it took to send me over the edge was Bryce's fingers strumming my clit, the bite of his teeth on my shoulder and his hoarse pleading and I was soaring, stars exploding behind my eyelids.

He followed seconds later, his arms tightening around me as he shouted his release.

Afterwards, he laid us sideways again and gently

eased out of me. A quick trip to the bathroom and he was back, tugging me into his arms.

For several minutes, neither of us spoke.

In the falling light, his eyes glinted, and he swallowed hard.

'Ask me, Savvie. Ask me,' he implored, looking deep into my eyes.

I swallowed. 'Truth or dare?' I whispered.

His eyes darkened. 'Truth,' he said again.

I splayed a hand over his heart. 'Tell me who this belongs to.'

'You, my beloved rosebud. My heart belongs to you. It's been yours from the moment I saw you.'

'You've always been the beam of hope in my chaos, Bryce. Even when you weren't there. Even when I suspected I was making a mistake, I had the thought of you to see me through. To bring me back to myself, whatever that is.'

He placed his hand over mine, imprinting his heartbeat into my skin. 'That place is right here. For as long as I live, you will own my heart and my love.'

'I love you, Bryce.'

A slow smile spread across his face. 'About time. And I didn't even have to dare it out of you.'

Tear-soaked laughter spilled out. He kissed my tears away and sealed his mouth against mine. When he raised his head, the emotion that filled his face took my breath away.

'Truth or dare?' he whispered.

'Dare,' I responded.

'I dare you let me love and worship you, be your best friend, your husband and your lover, the father of your children, for as long as I have breath in my body.'

The tears fell harder. 'I accept. Every path I take will always lead back to you. So with my heart and soul, I accept.'

A slow, sexy smile spread across his face, and the hazel eyes that I adored filled with love. 'Game fucking *on*.'

* * * * *

MILLS & BOON
MODERN

Power and Passion

Prepare to be swept off your feet by sophisticated, sexy and seductive heroes, in some of the world's most glamourous and romantic locations, where power and passion collide.

LET'S TALK
Romance

For exclusive extracts, competitions
and special offers, find us online:

f facebook.com/millsandboon

🐦 @MillsandBoon

📷 @MillsandBoonUK

Get in touch on 01413 063232

For all the latest titles coming soon, visit
millsandboon.co.uk/nextmonth